Khrystmass

Holiday † Horror † Collection

K.A. Schultz

'Krampian' horror for you!

Oh, but when flurries strike with such fury
By their crystalline shards the scene is so beautifully lit
Its components snow-feathered, ice-fractiled
'tis by design, this wint'ry distraction!

Khrystmass

Holiday † Horror † Collection

K.A. Schultz

Dakeha Taunus LLC, publisher
Copyright 2024 by K.A. Schultz
ALL RIGHTS RESERVED

Inquiries may be addressed to butterflybroth@gmail.com

https://linktr.ee/K.A.Schultz
Amazon:

ISBN 979-8-9894856-2-8 paperback

Other Amazon IDs:
ISBN 979-8-9894856-3-5 hardback
ISBN 979-8-9894856-4-2 kindle
Ingram ID: ISBN 979-8-9938034-0-1

Library of Congress Control Number: 202491214

Also by K.A. Schultz

GÖTHIQUE – Ravenscraft Anthology of Horror III

NEITHERIUM – Prose & Poetry from the Neither

JACOB – A Denouement in One Act

RUGS ON PUDDLES COATS OVER OCEANS – Poems & Lyric Poetry

A LETTER FROM KRAMPUS

www.butterflybroth.com
www.jacobmarleystory.com
www.shewhowas.com

@kaschultz_writer
@butterflybroth
@lilahravenscraft

Cover art and back cover: Antique German postcard,
property of the author.
12/6 Santa Domnia re-edited.

Dedicated to the Creature and to the woman who created him, and to their co-joined legacy, which, alongside Charles Dickens and his Spirits, polished the orphic lens through which this writer views, well,

pretty much everything.

Graphic, possibly offensive & triggering content
Reader discretion is advised

For a comprehensive content guide
visit www.butterflybroth.com:
KHRYSTMASS CONTENT GUIDE

TABLE OF CONTENTS

Khrystmass

ka schultz

The Visit

Oh, to witness none other than Santa himself, here at our house on this Christmas Eve night!

I take the stairs two at a time, lest the sleighbells' melodic jingle fades completely away before I can rouse the kids from their sleep, carry them to the window, throw open the shutters, lift up the sash.

I rush into the nursery, hoping they too might catch a glimpse of the sleigh before it disappears, but come instead upon two empty, little beds, disheveled and littered with dismembered dolls and half-eaten sugarplums.

The moon on the breast of the new-fallen snow lends the stark luster of midday to the dead room below. And to me here, alone.

Santa Domnia 1

There was once a writer whose gifts for the lyrically imaginative fell unfailingly flat in the face of his ego-suffused, ambitious attempts. Beset with envy, he resolved to aspire to different heights – indeed, to their inversions – by way of a more morosely inspirational sort of Muse. He determined, he would call forth and conjure into his presence none other than the Queen Mother of all dark Christmas Spirits, *La Santa Domnia.*

All the candles in the house – every candelabra and chandelier, every brass chamberstick and glass votive – he changed out to black. Doorways and staircase banisters he festooned with black beribboned, poison-berried lengths of garland. The stately spruce in his parlour he trimmed with *Vanitas* invoking artifacts, decorations which reeked of mortality, decay, and degeneration. Even the crèche displayed upon the library mantlepiece evoked more a cold crypt than any warm, sheltering stable. It's possible, he may have felt a whisper of conscience when he painted the minuscule red slash marks across the infant doll's porcelain neck, but to summon *Her* up would require a blasphemous sincerity of effort. Nothing less than the deep-darkest, hell-firing welcome was required to usher *Her* in.

This moribund fellow did fervently come to believe that what he could summon from somewhere far below and then bear unholy witness to would place him right up there with the greatest of writers, nigh on par with the best of all his fellow, literarily bound ilk. With luck, it might even catapult him past the greats, past those brilliant upstarts, and straight – straight! – to the top. He'd show them all, by golly!

Santa Domnia, Santa Domnia! He would pray, would chant, would sing.

The writer, seated in his study night after interminable, solitary, and silent night in that button-tufted chair of his, would read from his prized possession, a dog-eared grimoire, reciting the stanzas over and over again until his voice grew hoarse and the room before him would begin to swim...

At long, long last, after countless sleepless nights spent with endless invocations and discordant incantations, it did so happen, that the clock on the mantle *did* begin to slow down, until *tick, tick...tick...*it *did* fall still and silent, all while the fire in the hearth did, in fact, chokingly begin to dwindle, and then to sputter, until it too flickered out and died...

The man stopped mid-verse. He held his breath to better listen through the heavy and quelling silence, which had begun to roar inside his ears, past his dizzied and befuddled sensibilities, from deep within the wilting remnants of his evermore fractured sentience and soul.

Has She. . .

Has She materialized?

The man listened.

It has to be. . .has to. . .

Yes! His Spirit approached!

Yes, indeed! There they were! Thick and heavy steps sounding in the entry below – plodding, plodding, steadfastly advancing over the tile floor of the vestibule, then over the oaken planks of the main hall. He heard the rhythmic shush of weighted fabric asway as it was swept over the plush, silken runner. He heard the rustling sounds of dry leaves and debris as it was scattered in the newcomer's wake. Presently, he heard the sound of metal scraping the floor, striking upon the stairs, a-clanging and a-thudding one tread, one plodding step, at a time. Up, up, closer, and closer. . .

She approached with the lumbering stealth of one freshly resurrected.

When at long last She appeared at the door of his study, the man sank to the floor, abjectly awestricken, utterly overwhelmed. Glory – such a beauteous horror was She! The apparition embodied it all: Ignorance and Want, misguided intent, all virtue gone vice, acts of spiteful, cold vengeance; violence and bloodlust, all murderous ambition, all hate-filled desire. . .

This was Mankind's underbelly, exquisitely flayed and draped, sublimely and fatally incarnate. Called up, come home, here, *for him. . .*

Santa Domnia, fair maiden, thorned ringlet, brow crested!
Your forehead and scalp pierced, your curls thickly matted.
Garnet rivulets flow 'pon a dainty lace collar, so painstakingly
knotted, so thoroughly spattered!

Santa Domnia, fair maiden, candle crowned!
Dripping, molten, hardening fast; ensconcing, encasing your thin,
pallid countenance.
Streams flowing unfettered with blood imbued wax!

Santa Domnia, sweet maiden, fair princess!
Snow-white was your dress, but with holly impaled, wet blooms
herald the gash from that stake in your breast!
Your heaving, your breathing, belabored and pained,
your moth-eaten bodice most thoroughly stained!

Santa Domnia, fair maiden, wings spread!
Not in flight but in fight, hardened feathers, sharp tines!
One hundred small daggers – they clink, cut the air, kill off
the last dregs of the peace in my lair!

Santa Domnia, your fragmented teeth mix with crumbs of black coal,
your small mouth cruelly stuffed until it is full.
Your leering smile bares gums, not of a soft rose, but grey-shaded,
the flesh curling off from the bone!

Santa Domnia. . .

Dear Santa, no, no!

Dear Santa, please stay right where you are now! Please let me worship
you from my spot here on the floor!

No, no, Santa Domnia – do not take my hands!

No, this I sought not – I plead, I implore!

No, please, not the spikes! No, not my left hand!

I beg you, dear Santa, leave my right hand alone!

No, no, blessèd Santa!

You were not called forth for to crucify me –

I foolishly thought you had simply come home!

Christmas Punch

"...We wish you a merry Christmas
We wish you a merry Christmas
We wish you a merry Christmas
And a Happy New Year!"

The suitable hours, as they were generally called, were long past by the time the carolers arrived at their destination, a stately brownstone whose shuttered windows and iron gated spate of uppercrust urban acreage promised the utmost in privacy and coziest of confinements. The cloud-filtered moonlight and falling snow had stilled the city in the way such weather generally always does, having rendered the streets, buildings and nearby park uniformly cast in a softly glimmering, velvet-blue sort of non-light. Even if a somewhat eerie sort of winter wonderland, it was lovely to behold, despite how discomforting or downright dangerous the nightscape might prove, were it enjoyed overmuch. This was not unlike the elegantly dressed, fur wrapped and top-hatted collective, which had just made its way across the glittering boulevard. And but for their muffled laughter and genteel conversation, the troupe moved in silence, with neither the first scraping sound of a boot, nor the first sniffle, nor any awkward shuffling of steps as the slick cobblestones were traversed. This debonaire group did, in fact, appear to be quite immune to the elements. They sailed smoothly, so smoothly, a single, flowing entity of willow-limbed humanity. The carolers, having now thoroughly serenaded the neighborhood, were quite done with their work.

'twas time to go inside. Time for *their* Christmas Eve party.

"My dears, my dears, enough of this arctic merriment!" the Hostess proclaimed as she turned the lock on the gate. With a wave of her arm, she swept her troupe up, up the stone steps and onto the broad veranda, and swinging wide the front door in a grand gesture of welcome, the lady of the house continued, "'tis time for our own merriment! We are accomplished of our good work of this particular night – and oh, what dulcet harmonies we have over the years perfected – and so I say to you all, it is *highest* time, that *we* now commence with our own, most festive celebration!"

In a few short decades, this Christmas Eve soiree had become a *most* eagerly anticipated annual event, a tradition, if you will. The evening of caroling permitted as cheery a scoping of the area homes and their occupants as one could ever hope to acquire. And the trust and good will sparked by the group's musical interludes, with their welcoming interactions during which warm glances and inviting gazes, nods of welcome and feelings of cozy inclusiveness were fomented and cemented, and then taken note of and stashed in their minds for let's call it future *socializing* was not to be topped. Why, an evening of caroling was tantamount to an evening of seduction for this collective, with nary an innocent but oh, so scrumptious neighbor wiser for the imprinting. Indeed, there was hardly any better or enjoyable method to secure one's invitation in for purposes of procuring, um, let's call it dinner. . .

The Hostess, with the even more highly anticipated *after* party about to ensue, was herself almost giddy with excitement. She, too, had counted the hours, then the minutes, in anticipation of the slaking of a most lascivious thirst, which had been roiling about in her core for days, if not months. This was for her too, all about the imbibing of a most most exotic holiday treat, a specialty of hers, for which she had come to be quite well known. And the hostess was *so* pleased; this year, everything – absolutely everything – was looking to be *just* right. The wintery weather had made for a veritable snow globe effect of the area – the lace-edged flakes had positively danced about the group as they had sashayed from one residence to the next. The weather would now further serve the Hostess and her guests, for it would keep the townsfolk off the streets and well at bay – indoors, in the warmth of their own homes, their cozy beds – so no matter the din, the screams, no matter the dervish, nor the fevered dancing which might possibly yet ensue, no one would be about to hear, or suspect, a thing.

Ah, the confectioner, the hostess mused as she stroked the sweets in their case, what an *artiste*, what an expert he had become. Franz had outdone himself this year, had filled her order to exquisite, lethal perfection. Every candy cane in the box met *precisely* with the details as she had requested them. Thick and sturdy as railroad spikes, the striped rods were each finely honed at one end to the most precise of weapon-like points, although unlike any wartime ancestor, these would taste positively *heavenly* to the tongue, them having been liberally infused with a bitter and most exotic blend of peppermint oil and myrrh. Crimson swirled, lovely and intimidating to behold, were these custom-crafted confections. The hostess could hardly wait to escort her companions downstairs, and to reveal to her group this year's largesse – and to then outfit each one of her compatriots with one of the sweet staffs.

†††

It took only moments for the jolly troupe to divest themselves of their coats, their cloaks, their hats, and their scarves, for all knew what delights were to come. Otherworldly senses keened towards the faintly wafting wellspring of delights which burbled up, up from far below, which spurred every one of them on to quickly make ready. Preternaturally astute senses could discern that most particular warmth, and the singular, faint odors, the pulsating presence of the banquet that awaited them, lured them, urged them on. . . The guests assembled in the foyer right as the hostess re-appeared to take charge, escort her friends to their final destination.

"Come along and follow me, my lovelies!" the Hostess called out as she led her flock first down one long hallway, and then another. There next came not one but two flights of steep, creaking stairs down which the eager participants practically flew. The hostess, with her own, bounding gait, deftly guided the group through the winding passageways, the torch in her uplifted hand lighting their path, a dancing beacon as fit for a ferryman of the underworld, as for a Spirit of some darker sort of Christmas Present. The flames shot about, bouncing off one gilded mirror to the next as the partiers made their way down the hall. The warren was riotously illuminated with a rapid-fire interplay of black and gold, gold and black, which only heightened the dramatic and celebration nature of the evening. The revelers and their mistress came soon enough to a hushed standstill. Before them, loomed a pair of monstrously enormous, carved doors, nigh two stories tall. The group had arrived at the grand doorway of a marbled, subterranean foyer, whose threshold was only ever breached this one time in the year.

Anticipation and delight kindled and sparked like torchlight in their own, dark, unblinking eyes. It sweetened their smiles, and energized their bodies, their arms, their clasped hands; it was as if a desirous surge of electricity had passed through the lot of them to interconnect them, and to turn their every bit of waking sentience towards what was behind those doors, so eager was this troupe to pass through into the next room, and to bear witness to the delights that lay within. The hostess turned the iron levers, which cried out as any such ancient devices ought. She pushed gently against the closed doors, which slowly gave way to splay themselves wide open, to permit the troupe inside. Audible gasps of delight burst forth at the sight which awaited them. Like a gaggle of genteelly raised but oh, so greedy children at the reveal of a gift-laden *Weihnachtsbaum*, this party of carolers was wholly enchanted and entranced. And oh, so ready to pounce.

The room before the group was, in fact, a vast and palatial underground ballroom. The cool, damp air of the space was more an atmosphere, for the distant corners receded into a foggy darkness, like that of a far-off and shadowed valley at twilight. But what captured all attention and fancy lay immediately before them, overriding any token proclamations as to architectural or art appreciation. The hostess's array that welcomed them in with the most seductive and alluring of promises, lay there, supine and languid, aglow in the brilliance of an army of chandeliers which hung high overhead. It was as if a thousand icy daggers hung over the banquet, suspended and at the ready, to fall and pierce the heads, shoulders, and bellies of the divine feast which lay, stretched out below them. Was it not, the Hostess gushed as she was wont to do, the most horribly opulent and disgustingly regal setting for a feast as had ever been created?

Awaiting the carolers was a circular composition of plush divans, which had been situated in circular fashion in the center of the ballroom. And upon these chaises there lay, draped in elegant repose but not much else, a carefully culled crop of scrumptiously robust and somnambulant human beings. These fine specimens, having been painstakingly procured, cleaned, and scantily dressed, had been then thoroughly mesmerized. They reclined upon their lounges in various stages of sleep. Many of them smiled. Perhaps they were dreaming of sugarplums, or of flowery fields, or puppies, or kittens, or some such other *nice* thing. Their contented faces were awash with the very essence of Peace on Earth.

The hostess could feel herself growing emotional, so moved was she by this beautiful sight. Desire practically oozed from her guests – a thick lust-imbued cloud soon filled the dank air, like a fog, a decrepit frozen breath.

†††

"So now, my dear, you hold it just like this," the Hostess said in a patient and motherly voice. She had chosen this handsome upstart for herself to instruct. It was always far more enjoyable when the kill was accomplished by an especially attractive novitiate, for even if things got messy – as it often did with newcomers – their bloodlust combined with their good looks always made for a rather erotic exposition of wet, crimson gluttonous consumption. The hostess *loved* to watch. Nevertheless, she aimed to instruct her student properly, to at least get him started on the right foot. So, she aimed her candy cane – the sharply honed, pointed end –

at the neck of the woman she had selected to share with her initiate. The healthy, young jugular on the woman's neck pulsated invitingly. It practically begged for a piercing by way of the tap-tap-tap it broadcast to the hovering pair, the teacher and her pet student.

The young man, taking in the curvaceous landscape of their quarry, listened carefully, quite entranced himself. Something faint played across his brain, an inkling of a memory. Yes, thought he; he could remember. Lust. Lust and . . . What that had felt like, how it had burned like a fire in his head, his loins. And what it had driven him to do, over and over again. So many victims. But oh, *this* was far more intense! So very much better! He tucked a stray lock of long hair behind his ear and leaned in, making ready to follow the lead of his mentor.

"Watch as I do it, and then you simply come in from your side," the hostess went on. "And remember; hit sure and hard. No hesitation."

The young man grinned, his garnet eyes glinting with this *most* overwhelming, new hunger. The Hostess smiled, recalling with sweet nostalgia her first time. . .

And then, with a practiced hand and preternatural force, the hostess pierced the vein of the slumbering human with her sweet staff and, quickly placing her mouth over the blunt end of the candy, she sucked. Hard. The hostess pulled, long and deep, and the candy delivered a warming mouthful of frothy human liquor, drawn up, up through its honeycombed fretwork. She drank her fill. What a deliciously flavored blood!

The hostess's young companion grinned lasciviously, and, following the Hostess' lead, he dove in for his first post-mortem Christmas punch.

Dance of the Sugarplums

'tis fascinating, how qualms, quirks and issues manifest as fashions, dialects, even units of measurement, is it not? Here is the story of one such event, that in the end, turned out to be as gruesome as it was innocently well-intended.

'twas but a simple mistake the Christmas Fairy did make, when she set out on her winter's nap rounds 'round Santa's Christmas Town, when, impulsively inspired, she upped the enchantment ante by bestowing upon every slumb'rous elf not one but a handful of their very own dancing sugarplums whilst they slept.

Problem is, the Fairy, enamored with that newly published ditty by a certain Mr. Moore, had spaced it quite completely on the precise wording of the text, forgetting that part of it having been "visions."

But what's to expect with a mighty flighty little sprite, who subsists on a liquid diet comprised solely of Christmas spirits? All that grog, all that glogg, that wassail, and that nog might taste awful nice, but leave much to be desired when it comes to interpretive skills-honing of the literary, literal kind....

Suffice it to say, on that very next day, on Christmas Eve morning, when the bells in the tower sounded the hour, calling their jolly minions back to the bench, not a single, solitary elf was roused from the biers that had served as their lil sleeping shelves.

Alas, a-snooze they were not. Instead, they lay dead on their hard, bookshelf beds, their pillows drenched in the goo of their pulverized brains, which had oozed from their pointed, elfin ears in minuscule rivers of troubling, bubbling crimson – a real nightmare come true.

For, 'twas not *visions* of sugarplums that had danced in their heads, but *real* sugarplums that had ricocheted like steel pinballs inside of their craniums – for hours! The sweets had come to macabre life, thanks to the Fairy's wayward hex, and did not enchant, as in Mr. Moore's text, but lob and bounce about within those small skulls until there was nothing, nothing left.

'twas about then, the grieving Clauses closed up shop, and took to ordering online instead.

A Killing Repose

Ice gathers visibly on the glass, crystalline rimes exploding, frosted dandelions gone to seed. The twins are fixated by the sparkling script as it charts its path across the window. The Grandmother peers beyond the distracting beauty, to the snowy vortexes spinning in the mead, just beyond the front stoop. A premature night is descending, lavender grays failing fast to an inky, opaque wash. Soon, but for the scattered peppering of the thick flakes as they spin about, it will be, as is said, black as midnight – and the clock has yet to chime the five o'clock hour.

Shaken by the harsh winds, the snowflakes tumble riotously. They will, like the waning day, give up, settle in, interlock, take hold, go dark. The Grandmother can tell, in no time will there be a blanket so thick, it will breach the window's ledge. The snow will then rise to block what remains of her view onto the fields. Never but when the arctic anomaly descends upon this portion of the world does the fracturing on the glass foretell a wintry cataclysm of this magnitude. The Grandmother has long wondered, not if but when it would occur, and when it did, where would it find her, or her daughter, or her daughter's family. Storms like this have scripted many a sorrowful tale. . .

The chalet holds fast to its foundations, but shudders as it is struck by winds that surge like frigid tides come ashore from distant, cold oceans. The small house backs up to the black-curtained brace of an *Uhrwald*, a sea of pines tall as clock towers, near as old as the hills they pierce. Their limbs are so densely linked, they force each snow-laden squall to topple over and back onto itself, against even the back walls of that poor, little structure, rendering it twice struck by the storm's gales, so exposed as it sits there, on the edge of the ancient forest.

Oh, the Grandmother knows what this storm is about. She has read of it in the dog-eared journals of her ancestors, been told of these storms since she was a little girl, by tradition and trepidation both, evidently, mandated. Hushed and reverential voices had relayed the stories for as long as she or her forebears could remember, the reasons behind this, the harshest of seasons.

How can she begin to explain to her grandchildren, who had grown up in the urban collectives her daughter had journeyed to, amidst the utter absences of anything borne of the historical, or the mythical, or metaphysical, which might help explain what was playing itself out tonight? How can the Grandmother broach the topic, or that of their own role, as circumstantial collateral for what Mankind has wrought?

The Grandmother turns her thoughts to the heavens, where the rent fibers of angels' feathers are making their way down through the skies, from what mystics might call the nethering realms, to journey far, so far, first into the uppermost reaches of mortal imagination, then into the stark realities of the present. And once entered into the planes of human existence, Grandmother knows, the silken petals eventually pass through what the more learned factions would call the troposphere, to dance amongst the nourishing vapors that fill and feed its living, breathing recipients, which hold a fortunate few of them aloft in their undulous arms.

The Grandmother wonders, how those precious, angelic remnants even made it this far, and how they could, when directed by the elements in such insidious fashion, coalesce into this, a winter's storm that will, by all predictions and ferocious display, like its predecessors become the stuff of both folklore and saddest irony.

The Grandmother and those who yet call the *Uhrwald* home had lost loved ones in the last, such storm. A taxed heart had given out as one tried to shovel a path to the well; a hunter, returning home with his catch, had instead become lost, then found the next day, mere meters distanced from his front door, buried in a drift at the base of a towering but unsheltering and indifferent tree. And the twins, a boy, and a girl who had been, it was whispered, lured outdoors to play in the snow by some childlike apparition, known to appear when the storms were at their worst, to entice the youngest and guilelessly unafraid away from the safe harbour of their homes. The children had disappeared without a trace, their footprints instantly erased by the blizzarding gales. . .

The Grandmother stands close behind her wards to make sure no apparition exists to catch the eyes of her little ones. Grateful for the preternaturally long night, she can soon draw the curtains on the children's curiosity, put them to bed. There is nothing else left to do.

No, the Grandmother thinks, safe as they seem to be, there is nothing left but to settle in to sleep.

The water in the bucket has frozen over; there will be no offering of a sip. The children, she ushers into bed fully dressed, then drapes every blanket she owns over the two, in hopes they can at the very least be granted the solace of sleep, perhaps with the parting gift of a sweet dream. The howling winds play the chimney like a flute, but with a melody so lonesome and discordant, it sings only of foreboding. A dirge: she knows its song. Even this grows muffled, the longer she listens.

The Grandmother also knows, the packed powder berm will only continue to build. By morning, it will reach above the roofline, drifting up and over the very peak of the chalet. In so doing, it will obliterate any visibility of the hovel. They are being buried alive. This, she will not tell the children.

As one accustomed to life off-grid, in which the modern world plays no part, the Grandmother knows well enough to keep goods stocked. Sustenance has always been attended to. But starvation is not at issue. Over the years, ever more distanced relatives had remembered less and less to circle back to her, relegating her to the peripheries of their own, hardscrabble lives. She has grown accustomed to living alone, with Grandfather having passed so many years ago, and her daughter and the young man she had partnered with having gone off to the big city, so sporadically heard from, her past having been set aside for a more modern-day present, presumed to be a better one. It has left the Grandmother feeling rather forsaken.

Tonight, it feels more like having been left behind. But now, with her beautiful daughter so tragically taken at such a young age – and that nice fellow of hers too – there is no one. The Grandmother's mournful isolation, after all those years on her own, has brought with it the inevitable – a regrettable forgettability. She, now with the grandchildren in her care, are all but forgotten. No one will even think to remember, let alone check in on the old woman, nor recall the fact that she had taken in the little ones after their mother and father had perished.

The storm holds entombment level potential. When the Grandmother arranges the last of the blankets around the three of them, she is mindful of how it will look come Spring, when perhaps their bodies will be discovered.

Tonight, she shall tell her grandchildren *the* story, if for no other reason than to not have let the storm's import be for naught. If unacknowledged, what is the point of the angels' sacrifice?

How else to honour what they have given up in the name of all the infant souls that will never possess wings, let alone fly with them, use them for their own accords, go somewhere, be somewhere, become a someone, forge the next links with which to connect to the next other?

†††

Time had come, for the angels to rejoin, silent and hands clasped, wings spread, and flexed.

Time had come for the angels to present themselves, to stand up alone, tall, and steadfast, still and stoic.

Time had come, for each angel to step up to the block, and to fall upon its knees, and for that angel to allow its wings to be lifted up and held aloft, be draped over the face of its brutally unyielding edge.

Time had come, for the Wielder of the Scythe, who unlike its brethren has not been cast down from the Heavens, but been permitted to subside there, in the shadows, in the periphery, in order to perform their one task, which is to raise up into the voids the razor-sharp arc of a mirror, and to cut with that blinding, bright and silvered blade into all doubt, all deception, all disorder.

Time had come, for that blade to strike with the force of ten-thousand brutes, all the strapping young men who knew no better.

Time had come, for the blade to strike with the force of fifty-thousand harpies, all the young women who knew no better.

Time had come, for that blade to sever from the angels' shoulders their wings, for which they had loved, had lived; for which they had fought, won, lost, had rendered from themselves the best they could muster.

Time had come, for the blood of those angels to spill onto the heavenly plains, to spatter in remembrance of the corporeal manifestation of a One who, despite all misguided circumstance, had been granted life, so to walk and exist, as potentially perfect and ultimately flawed as anyone before Him had ever been, would ever be, might never be.

Time had come, for the wailing of the angels to descend as howling winds, and for their cries to bind with the raging flurries, to carve by way of destructive intent their memorials, so that bit by bit, piece by piece, house by home, man and woman could be made whole again by their penance – all upon the back of one innocent child, one innocent child. . .

Time had come, for the whispering fronds that could span oceans, touch suns, warm even the smallest of hummingbirds' nests, to fall, and fall. . .

And as they fall, and crack in the cold as they do, they will crystalize, as even the most brilliant ideas of Man are wont to do, so they take with them on their journey every beautiful thought, and deed, and every last damn brickle of love that might ever have been felt. This is why, within their structures they hold the Eternal Unique, just as any soul might have held it, had it ever been given that chance. . .

For the few snowflakes that make it as far as the hearth, drawn in by the waning heat of the embers, they return to their original state. As the feathers strike the coals, they spark momentarily, then curl up, and turn to ash. As the three in their bed drift off, the Grandmother, eyes closed, fancies she can smell the faint odor of burning hair.

The dying fire in the hearth is soon wholly extinguished, and the small clock on the mantel winds down before it can herald the next hour. The chimney stones, even the benches begin to sparkle with frost. Skeletal fingers of ice creep in from under the threshold, make their way up the door. Glittering threads trail off, marking their stealthy paths along the planks of the floor. The candle flame begins to flicker haphazardly and grows smaller, smaller. . .

The Grandmother now sleeps, as do the children, whilst the obliterating snow continues to fall into its own quiet and killing repose. All those fragmented wings, with no longer any iota of feeling left in them, they bury the little house at the edge of the Uhrwald long before the midnight hour is never tolled.

As they would say, my little ones, Whenever a bell rings. . .

    . . . an angel gets its wings? The two chime in, hopeful, eager to please, their words hovering within the tiny frozen clouds formed by their warm puffs of breath.

    No, no, my dears, she softly admonishes, a sadness in her voice, *. . . an angel SHEDS its wings. . .*

Santa Domnia II: *Hellscape Wrought*

Santa Domnia – no, no!
Santa, stay where you are!
Let me worship you from my spot on the floor!
No, no, Santa Domnia – do not take my limbs!
This I sought not – I must plead, I implore!
No, please, not the spikes!
No, not my left hand!
I beg you, dear Santa, leave my right hand alone!
Inglorious Santa,
You were not called forth to crucify ME –
I had foolishly thought you had simply come home!

And thus, our passionate upstart cuts short his mortal sojourn on this, our beautiful earth, in his misguided quest, to resurrect the darkest deity among saints, la Santa Domnia.

Granted re-entry from the eternal twilight, to rejoin the plains of the living, She shall once more roam freely about and feed as She desires, much as any lividly famished, freshly re-animated entity must. La Santa Domnia has finally returned to reclaim Her rightful place amongst Man and Monster, on the very same terral plains across which all are swept, whether finely strung like marionettes or lashed together as beasts of burden. She walks among us, so together we will be made to slog through the pain in which *all* must partake. Agonies were wrought for Eve on our behalf, so that god or ruffian, we may be delivered to Mankind by way of our universal suffering, which still defines us as the starkest of Truths.

Abandoning Her hapless gatekeeper, pinned to the walls of his study a desperately skittering, insectuous specimen performing his last and dying dance on a barren stage of his own, meticulous making, La Santa lumbers off. The *rigor mortis* of Her cryptic tenure as yet renders Her memory rather spotty, Her mottled limbs less agile than might be desired for one of such hallowed and exquisitely base origins. Verily, with every footfall, our Santa limbers up, gains incrementally a purposefulness in Her stride. Trust me when I tell you this: She grows surer with each step taken. She knows just where to go.

Into the wintry night la Domnia vanishes, taking rapid leave of the writer in his study, his house, his corner of the city. Swallowed whole in the misting flurries of a December storm, oblivious to the cold, the night, the hour, our Santa commences on a junket most purposeful. Dust-laden memories hatch like flies' eggs in the curdled slurry that stirs, quickens, seeks to function as Her brain. A ravenous hunger is sparked; demand for sustenance pierces Her consciousness. First up, is to fill Her cavernous belly; after that, Her bottomless soul.

La Santa has carelessly left wide open Her conjurer's door. It yawls in submissive welcome to the avenue and elements, for practical tasks like this are beneath Her stunted consideration. Listen! The alley dogs bay offsides, having smelt the tang of the dying writer's panic, and his malodorous excretions, which stripe his garments wet and dark, grow the steaming puddle on the floor. No sooner does our immortal One turn down the allée, as do the hounds rush up the front steps, working their jowls and snapping at each other, in pursuit of their putrescent quarry, who calls to them with fetid promise, hangs in waiting for them in his posh, little chamber at the top of the stairs.

Do you, my sweets, dare believe a one like this desires to be so roused from so heavy a slumber?

How is one to know? How, children, how? Very well, then, I shall now tell you the Tale of la Santa Domnia!

Here we have a Being as profane as may ever have been by the constellations rendered, whose resurrection was accomplished upon such a nexus of nightmares, the sleepless themselves would nigh pride themselves of their insomnia. This is One birthed to heed desperation's every call, for whom prayers were never anything but limpid nursery songs and hymns the weakest of lullabies. Even if at the bedside of innocents, when whispered or dared sung bare above a furtive hush, unwitting postulants might try and keep one such as She at bay. But no. Rather, they invite la Santa in!

Not every child seeks to dream of sweetmeats and confections, longs to hear of princesses and cheerful, "happy" endings. Do you?

And so, She makes Her way down the street. Oh, yes, my dears. She will come!

Our everted deity of the underworld hears everything. If wrung from that residual nook wherein honest fear dwells, neither momentarily shaken off nor ever fully vanquished, She exists as a fear-filled call's requisite response, within the tickling nape of a neck brushed by an uncanny cold. She is in that spine feathering, cautionary flicker of unfortunate realization, the gut grown queasy with some nameless recognition. Santa Domnia resides within the infinitesimal falters of a tremblant whisper, the reluctantly uttered word as it falls off short, right there, at mid-gasp.

These are but the coarse vespers as delivered by la Santa's postulates, lauding Her, luring Her. These are the missives penned by Her iniquitous minstrels, who play to Her swollen, black heart, much as the poet once wrote of Isafrel, his angel, whose heartstrings were like a lute. Hers, we all know, are far darker, more wicked.

Who then, among us, seated upon the shoulders of wingèd beings, seeks to be carried aloft in this manner?
If that, my dears, be you, look not to the saccharin clouds above.
If that, my dears, be you, look into the shadowed corners below.

There is no need to reach for the soft, the benign, the forgettable if you seek the embrace of la Santa Domnia. Lean instead into obscurities, deep into the hubris of Man, where soot and flesh co-mingle and degenerate into the decrepit soup from whence all are born – and some re-born. There is indeed an incorruptible persistence amidst decay re-animated, and la Santa is your proof.

Come at last is She who has slumbered in a static suspension we humans euphemize as the deepest of sleeps. From that cold place, She has been made to rise. Slow, woefully stiff as the brittle linens which enwrap criminals and Saviors alike, la Santa presses ahead, against the hardened cloth that could stifle every harrowing cry until it too is drawn down to silence. There is nothing in Her hollows but a liquid, echoing quiescence. She remains oblivious to Her agonies. Any residual whimper here would be laid to waste, no matter which mouth might ever dare utter it. Nothing is heard when no one listens. Nothing ever changes. And no one will hear tonight. On Her singular foray, la Santa has no time to pay that sort of attention.

And oh, the misery She personifies! With Her own, small mouth so stuffed, any chance of a fighting fresh breath is brutally quaffed! Wretchedly gagged, slack jawed in suspended shock, Her countenance is hideously displaced. Coal ash spills from Her withered lips, brickles from the small ledge of a bone-jutted chin. Coarse gravel is a solvent offal ground to grains, an obsidian salt crystalized between two rows of ambered teeth worn down to their quicks, invoking the fundamental demise of the prehistoric doomed. Rotted remnants curl up in a tenuous grimace, but any semblance of a smile was long ago erased. For She has been fed from the ashes of the very same beams that were cast down on the square, to encircle the righteously, falsely accused, to immolate them as they stood guard against their accusers. La Santa can nigh taste the burning martyrs, who roasted like fatted beasts, gruesomely exonerated by way of their incineration, whose virtuous sisters and brethren observed in smug silence, stoking their apocalyptic passions by way of their nemeses' annihilation. They too will rise from the beds of their own ashes to serve as kindred cutthroats, in deference to our Santa – but only when the time is right.

Fascinating is it not, the ones who created and let be fed the Beast, all partake in its insatiable lust for destruction?

Oh, children, children, have you any imaginings of what pain truly can be?

Such a sweet and brutal agony as what our la Santa endures opens wide the subterranean doors, from which caskets She was extracted. Her mind is but the fleshy cradle wherein rests Evil's wizened eye, deep seated, unblinking. That eye, it cannot see as we simple humans do, but yet imagines the worst. And so, it sees *everything.*

Past, present, yet to come. . .

Every sin, every vile deed and rank wish, all base desires. . .

. . . each trifling cry of some lost babe, or the bellows of an enraged father; or the silence of a stone-hearted mother, false friend, or turncoat partner. La Santa is there at the ready and has partaken of them all – and they reside in Her.

The lacteous all-seeing eye lolls about in its cavity. Ignited by forces of all that drives our Santa, it gathers in and broadcasts back to its host: *Think! Do! Act!*

React! Destroy, destroy! Blink and something might be missed. It knows this. Torn open, gawking, frozen, it shall remain on dreadful, constant watch.

All the better to see you, my dears!

And once within the husk of yon hollowed skull, whence the incantations have been re-commenced and recited upon the strikes of midnight, how quickly that skull of Hers fills itself anew! Vermin gathers in a bizarre dance, creeping, and clinging, growing, and grabbing, branching off each orifice, tail to head in a beastly chain, orally affixed coral twining and taking root as do creeping fungi spawn in their beds of sludge. Waxen matter encrusted, melding to fill the void, reaching first one eye socket and then the other, then breaching the sinuses, the mass crawls and slithers towards the mouth, wherein fanged teeth have long lain embedded, petrified within the gums. All takes root, tears at the mandible, until, agape, Her grin is laid open in an expression of wonderment, the nightmare having manifested itself as a terrified awakening. When, from this macabre hive, the collective skittering calls to Her, tickles Her hollow belly, She is at last roused in full from the stasis of Her oblivion.

Time, time, Santa Domnia, to enter into the odiousness of Man once more!

Come, Santa Domnia, come!

And the children recite:

Santa Domnia, fair maiden, thorned ringlet, brow crested!
Your forehead and scalp pierced, your curls thickly matted.
Garnet rivulets flow 'pon a dainty lace collar, so painstakingly knotted, so thoroughly spattered!

Laborious endeavor is required indeed to bring Her forth. Everything, everything must be in place. Everything must be just so. There can be nothing of kindness, nor hope. Not one iota of wisdom. Only fools and misanthropes are granted their say in Her domain, wherein the bleakest of magic can flourish. How else to knit back together the rotted parts and dried bits that will have lain fallow for eons upon folds of stained rouching and mold-imbued lace which line the sunless berth that has served as Her cradling sarcophagus? These are but the ill-made beds for sleeping harpies. From that place – where no scream, nor cricket's lament nor cry of a dying cicada could wrest its way past walls cemented with mortar made of blood scraped from the flayed backs of its victim builders, She will make Her way through the soil to announce, to beg of all wayward souls.

Here I am! Here I am! Save me!

If you could see with your own eyes the resurrection, bear witness to la Santa when next brought forth from Her burial chamber, there would be nothing at first but a layer of black silt, a few stubborn nubs, a swath of matted hair, an empty ribcage as delicate as a coop for a songbird. Ancient of days come and gone, Her reconstitution is a time to re-craft what once was undone.

With spittle and secretions, the vermin toils and spins and combs. Pinchers plying and splintered, tiny legs fabricate from the remnants a mottled ball of cranium and skeletal bone. Liquified skin seeps over the housing and hardens like wax. Cobwebbed masses writhe lividly, grow as do tendrilled hatchling snakes. They intertwine, pull long and lank their primeval forms, until proud as Medusa, la Santa can toss Her hair with the impudence of a rabid filly.

Dissolved by the very acids her dying struggles fermented – Such fear! Such panic! What a delirium! – la Santa lies awash in a bath that once boiled the very skin from Her flesh, curled it, and curdled it into a stench-imbued slop. It is now the bath in which Her corpse is stewed. Dull bone to rancid flesh, to one transparent and pallid human beast. There, at last, She is.

If you must, know this: La Santa crafts Her own piercing requiem. Her laments ascend in pitch to a dirge of screeching metal, only to resolve in a string of guttural, spit-slurried pleas. When the air has been duly tainted and the spirits of Hades sufficiently riled, they creep in to impart in Her a first, whistling breath. It is then when She can ascend from the infernal depths to answer, clawing Her way through fissures carved by the very knives sharpened by all those of whispering shivers. She will fight Her way from the depths to invade our homes – *your* home. If you do not take care, She will breach your floorboards, pass through them and then through you. She will catch hold of the underside of your scalp with Her nimble hook and like a bit of crocheted lace, She will then pull you out through your belly, turning you inside out. And then, She will grab you and roll you up like wet fabric, and then She will take you back to Her realm!

Santa Domnia, fair maiden, candle crowned!
Dripping, molten, hardening fast; ensconcing, encasing your pallid, pained countenance. Streams flowing unfettered with blood imbued wax!

Aye, it must have been a stubborn and stolid chap, to call la Santa from Her depths. His remains bear witness to all he managed, the words he spoke, the blasphemes he invoked. Hear him, She did. Heed him, She did. Visit him, She did. Haunt his home, She did. Crucify him, She did. Leave him nailed to the very wall of his study, pine branches spiked through his outstretched hands, his feet, through his breast, She did. Left his mouth stuffed with the glowering coals from his very own fire, much as Her own mouth had been packed so long ago, She did. With twin sprigs of holly threaded through each of his eyelids to pin that panicked gaze of his wide open, She left him, there to reap the rewards of his impudent conjurings. She walks off to the cadence of his weakening sobs, leaving Her suitor for dead. She has forgotten him by the time She has crossed the avenue.

> Santa Domnia, sweet maiden, fair princess!
> Snow-white was your dress, now with holly impaled blooms darker, red-pocked from that gash in your breast!
> Your heaving, your breathing, belabored and pained, your moth-eaten bodice most thoroughly stained!

Now, listen, my dears! Cast your sound seeking ears to the shutters I say, for 'tis none other than La Santa Domnia now coming our way!

Listen for that most peculiar of footfalls, that stumbling trip. . .

She will soon be near, and starved for the sweetmeats of you, children, here!

La Santa has set off to wander the emptied city streets. Midnight just passed, deathly cold fills the night. 'twould be no living soul about but a spectral entity such as She!

Listen for Her lumbering stealth, as yet an awkward gait. What would one expect as much of an ancient corpse, so freshly resurrected? Heavy of foot, la Santa carves a rickety path through the snow, leaves a scattered trail of detritus in Her wake, so packed are the layers of Her skirts with graveyard matter. Droplets of cold, thickened blood drip from Her fingertips, proof of endeavors of a few minutes' past, and what was made of Her host. Left him nailed to his own walls, She did, him not being to Her taste, such a soured old soul was he. Quite unfit for our queen. Santa seeks something far more delectable!

Crowned 'pon a mass of tangled webbing is now a brambling wreath of thorns, thick and wicked as a black-needled sea urchin. Spikes point to the sky, skewer drifting flakes of snow, and are turned inwards as well, breaching the calcified depths of Her patchy skull. Stigmatic perversion renders sound the mockery of an agonized crowning, as the good books of yore still tell. But la Santa seeks no salvation, oh no. Inverted, Her glories lie not in prophetic resolution. Ink-black liqueur slides like machinist's oil over temple and sallow cheek, dripping onto Her collar, Her bosom. No bridal purity exists to preserve the sanctity of Her sordid radiance. La Santa is flower bedecked by the very brushstrokes of Her own bloodied seepage as it gathers and spreads crimson blooms and black streaks. What was once a grand burial gown is repugnantly spoilt.

Let us recall those wondrous wings with which She was blessed: Broad, leathered expanses, wilted and folded, inset at each peaked, little shoulder, each mummified appendage pleated tightly onto itself, tapering horrifically, gracefully, in both line and form. Accordioned arrays, a means of flight, clad in serrated, metallic tines. Next to the brackish muck that marks the ground with each step She takes, if you look, you will see the snow raked into tight lines, bitten by teeth, pointed like knives.

Our Santa comes now 'round to the town square, spies the wan colors of the chapel windows, its portals alit. The vicar has hung out his shingle. At least, *He* is in. Yon feeble beacon calls to all sinners, admonishing them to gather:

Midnight mass, children; save yourselves.

Santa's brain endeavors to frame a rounded, sentient thought:

Big stone house. Human, fresh. Food. For me. Inside. Go.

The pipe organ's caterwaul stops short in the frigid rush of wind and snow as the doors fling open in spirited compliance with Her desire, which is to cross the hallowed threshold, breech the sanctified air of the Lord's chapel lair. Last notes linger sadly; their echo weakens and falls to silence, the sort of audible absence Mankind like his gods has long recognized as the harbinger of tragic denouements for those who have come – they presume – to worship, who in that moment fall still as mice as the barn cat approaches. Supplicants and sinners, reduced to one and the same, equally subject in their frailty, remain stock still, eyes locked into a distance devoid of neither seraph nor redeemer.

In this space, la Santa Domnia need not plod about. Here, where magic is christened a miracle, where incantations are re-titled as canticles, She sails down the long center aisle, a Mephistophelian vestal, held aloft by all the unanswered prayers which yet languish in this hall, in supplication to the One designated as having dominion, the penultimate recipient for all the countless pleas, wishes, and invocations intended for a far finer ether than the frosty dirge She has just allowed in. Futility hovers suspended and weighted, atop the stone floors, a slurry as thick as the bogs. Here exists a wallowing swamp of stifled entreaties, wholly deflated in the face of Her uninvited imposition. La Santa by Her arrival alone has quashed each confession 'neath the soles of Her mud-encrusted, satin slippers. Upon the loft of every heaven-shunned missive, She positively floats.

Lest we forget, tales of monsters and saints are both born of Mankind. All reactions and results are of His feats, His deeds, His sins, and misdeeds. Where the universal is refracted and shot back to earth, much like the snowfall is sent when winter deepens and the year is killed off, the sublimely horrific transmogrifies and is spiced – sweetened – to become the stuff of bedtime stories, which is where the malleable mindset can still be shaped. Perhaps a few dare question or challenge; most will conform. By design. Still, all delight in the resonance of a tall tale, well told. And so, our Santa gains in stature with each word written, every recitation uttered. Dreams of la Santa are reliant on the questionable bridges built, one fallen soul, one compromised generation, at a time. In our wake, endless room for evolution is left. Story upon story, over and over again.

Santa Domnia exists, my children, because WE do.

. . .and mind, you, as She makes Her way towards the apse, our Santa reaps a transformation most magical! Bigger and bigger She grows, children, until Her thorn-crowned head reaches nigh to the arches, brushes 'gainst the carved ribs of the vault. See there, bloodied smears She has left high up there! Santa must soon crouch to fit, so quickly She seats Herself 'gainst the altar from where She can better gaze down, 'pon the cowering parishioners below.

No, no Santa, not me! the simple fools plea.

Those who can, fall hard to their knees.

Little do they know, 'tis not their sweat-salted carcasses She desires for Her feast.

No, no! La famished Santa casts a hungering eye towards the plump cherubs lined up the choir; there seated like pigeons, a passel of plump, savory boys!

With a long-armed sweep of Her outstretched hands, la Santa spans the distance with a motion so quick, 'tis but a blur to those stagnating at Her feet.

And with a One! and a Two! Before the first folds of a choir robe are stirred, before a blood-curdling cry is expelled from a single Cupid's bow, Santa tears Her jowls open wide and then swallows them whole!

One choir child! And then two, and then three, and then four!

Chomp, chomp, and a belch, and She eats them all whole!

With a gobble and a crunch, yon souls be swiftly wrested as their bodies squeeze down – down to the gullet they go, one, two, three, more. Such unfortunate children, so to meet with their doom.

Which you too, my dear ones, ought remember when done, whether crumpets or children our Santa devours, She will cast all others aside with Her shoe, leave them piled like refuse; for want, nothing more.

Thus, our Santa departs the hellscape just wrought, and now I will bet She is coming for you!

So, rush, rush to your coffins, you little minxes, you two!

Enough of tall tales for the morning now looms.

You must now quick a-bed, lest the sun strike your heads, bake you both like fresh bread, leave me with no choice but to eat you instead!

Jacob – A Denouement in One Act:

Introduction

(SCENE: The curtain rises on the closing scene of Charles Dickens' A Christmas Carol. Surrounded by celebrating Cratchit family members, a jubilant Ebenezer Scrooge takes Tiny Tim up, into his arms. Carolers wander about to depict old London city street activities, reciting the closing lines of the Dickens story, as taken from the original text)

CAST
(Alternating)
Scrooge was better than his word . . .

He did it all, and infinitely more; and to Tiny Tim, who did NOT die, he was a second father . . . He became as good a friend, as good a master, and as good a man, as the good old city knew . . .

Some people laughed to see the alteration in him, but he let them laugh, and little heeded them; for he was wise enough to know that nothing ever happened on this globe, for good, at which some people did not have their fill of laughter in the outset . . .

His own heart laughed; and that was quite enough for him . . .

. . . and it was always said of him, that he knew how to keep Christmas well . . .

. . . and so, as Tiny Tim, observed, God bless us, Everyone!

(Lights fade to black. As the curtain lowers, one cast member, elegantly dressed and poised, extracts himself from the chorus and approaches the audience. He is, as yet unknown to the audience, the adult Tim Cratchit)

TIM:
. . . better than his word . . . you know the story.

You, dear participants, are here to listen and revisit, as the Spirits did back then and will doubtless do again—when least expected, but most needed—to this great tale.

You are here to honor and invite back into your own hearts a story so known and loved it has woven itself into the very fabric of our lives. What illuminates today, as it did back then, the darkest slice of a midnight hour, is no doubt what also brought you here, before me now.

When night outweighs the day and Time's passages are steeped in cold, Man yearns for that which invokes warmth and light. And love.

What we seek comes in many forms, be it a liberating truth, a restful solitude, or some small instance in which the giving supersedes the taking. Indeed, good want places me here, before you, as well, to introduce a small aside, a denouement if you will, of something intended to shed light upon what I warrant not a few of you have at some point asked:

What about poor, old Jacob Marley?

(As Tim recedes and is swallowed in shadow, he concludes)

Let once more the whispering shivers and ghostly specters haunt us onto a better path! As we aspire to what is best in all of us, let us employ, for a second time, the dark to illustrate the light.

(Lights come up to illuminate a room)

There. Look upon Jacob Marley, who yes, indeed, was, is dead. Dead as a doornail.

(Tim exits)

Jacob – A Denouement in One Act:

Stave 1

(SCENE: A compact room, both a bedchamber and an office. Monochromatic, in shades of blue and gray, the space is dimly and mysteriously lit to evoke a never-ending night, a standstill of time. The only light comes from a lamp situated upon a desk. Coins are stacked upon the desk. There is a fireplace, but no fire. There is a daybed, rendered so as to appear comfortless and unsleepable. Tattered curtains hang at the window. There is an ornate and massive wardrobe with double doors at center stage. Rubbish is strewn upon the floor. The room's entry door is at stage right. Behind the stage left wall, there is a void, cloaked in darkness.

The door opens, slowly, smoothly, and without any sound. A vastly tall apparition dressed all in black, with a hood covering the head, and face shrouded, slowly, smoothly enters, as if afloat. It carries a scythe. This is the Ghost of Christmas Yet to Come. The Ghost reaches the center of the room. Suddenly, the ghost's regal, stiff, and stealthy posture collapses into one of slumped-over weariness. As the hood falls, we see a rudimentary scaffold, like the prop of a puppeteer. As the robe is shrugged off, we see an old man, pale, with long hair, dressed in yet another costume, featuring a garishly cheerful dress shirt and vest of crimson and deep green. A sprig of holly appears to be pinned to the vest; perhaps, it is not a boutonnière, but instead, a stake of holly, pierced through his chest, its topmost leaves and berries splayed over the lapel. This is the costume of the Ghost of Christmas Present.

The old man was, is, dressed up as both ghosts; that he still wears most of the second ensemble suggests he had no time to change completely out of the red and green costume for his next role. A matching, luxurious coat of green velvet is heaped upon the floor, as if tossed aside in a hurry; it is part of the costume of the Ghost of Christmas Present.

The old man lifts the black robe, now puddled about him, and walks wearily to the wardrobe, dragging it behind him. He gathers the velvet coat into his arms as well. As he nears the closet, the doors slowly swing open in unison on their own, further suggesting otherworldly powers. Artful illumination lights the interior of the wardrobe. Another costume hangs within the wardrobe. It is a white gown, luminous, but as if lit from within. A pair of wings hangs next to the gown, as does a tattered, white wig. An unlit torch is propped up to one side. This is the costume of the Ghost of Christmas Past.

The old man hangs the Christmas Yet to Come robe upon a hook in the wardrobe; he lays the green coat onto the floor of the closet, and stashes additional items—black boots, a black face cloth, the scythe.

The man next shrugs off the rest of the Christmas Present costume, which reveals yet one more ensemble, having been worn underneath the previous layer: It is a decrepit, faded, and molded suit, now recognizable in the context of the previous Spirit reveals, as that worn by Jacob Marley when he paid his lamentation visit to Ebenezer Scrooge.

The old man steps into a pair of weathered shoes, next removing a tattered and dirty, white folded kerchief from another hook in the closet. Looping the fabric under his chin, the man secures it at the top of his head, resituating a horrifically slackened, but rigid, creaking jaw.

He takes a pair of shackles from the closet floor and fastens one around each ankle. The old man next lumbers to a large travel trunk, the ankle bracelets clanking. From the trunk, he removes a length of chain from which padlocks hang, like charms on a bracelet. The last links of the chain are never fully removed from the trunk, suggesting infinite length stored within. The man threads and hooks the chain to his shackles, grimacing, his hands at his lower back as he straightens up. A section of chain he loops up and clips to his belt. He is now tethered at numerous points. Henceforward, the old man makes a great show of struggling with these chains with every move.

The man is Jacob Marley. It was he alone who, in magically rendered costume, enacted every ghostly apparition who visited Ebenezer Scrooge on that fateful Christmas Eve. This set of performances was Jacob's task upon his visit to Earth: For one night only, he was to try and save his friend, spare Scrooge from a fate similar to his own.

Having completed his four visitations, Jacob has now returned, exhausted, to the dismal room that is his solitary purgatory, there to resume his penance, which is to count his coins, over and over again)

JACOB:
(Inhales deeply, overcome, and begins to cry—wailingly, broken heartedly—and then to speak, as he commences with his activities)

"How now?" How now, indeed!

My task is done!

Or is it?

A lifetime in one night—a lifetime in three hours! What light and life I gazed back upon in the smallest of slivers granted me, and how dark the black now beckons in contrast! Oh, the agony! Oh, the void!

Dreariness and silence, my only companions, they tug at my wretched soul. And this splinter that pierces what in life was once my heart, it is now nothing more than a pinion that marks a most lonesome infinity. What, I must ask, have I crafted?

This room is my prison, a torture chamber, reserved for only the most selfish of architects.

Oh, I demanded, loud and clear, and the Fates, those baleful sisters, they listened and granted as much—an isolation that makes mockery of solitude and solace!
They gave me what I wanted, what I in my life's course so charted. But, to suffer it forever and in this fashion? (Jacob trails off, wailing, crying) Aye, three hours, three crumbs stolen from the manna served at Mankind's banquet! Three hours in which I was made witness to all from

which my lone friend might one day be deprived, as I myself have hungered . . .

(Wailing)

Friend! 'twas but a name for like-minded scoundrels in communion with each other! What lone title bestowed upon two cantankerous men, co-joined? And what did I know of "friend"? Could I have imagined, the only links I would forge would be these damnable iron ties? They slink like vipers at my ankles and waist, binding me to this space . . . . . . aye, wisdom's bitterest apple is to know the taste of all Might Have Been's and Should Have Been's, a dour zest, indeed! And a chance of redemptive course? Ha! I cast that aside as I plotted. I sailed as I assailed . . .

And now, I am left with this wrenching echo, which would twist my gut, had I yet a gut to twist. Still, it somehow manages to gnaw ceaselessly in the depths of this hollow carcass, and goodness, it leaves me famished. . . .

(Jacob pats his belly)

But the absence of knowing—what did I accomplish? It is but a penance upon penance! Did the grand task of my visitations upon old Eb do their work? In life, the Fates held wide the drapes of opportunity and allowed me to pass through, unfettered in my ambitions. They watched, dispassionate, as I, the deprived dreamer, became instead the most ruthless of lenders.

The sisters were seated in silence long before that, as my father, in ignorance, presumed prosperity would alleviate the thespian predilections and eccentric inclinations of a son he would never understand.

Not the first of men to err as paternal guide, the father trained his son to wield wealth like the sharpest of swords. A stage was built, but from which neither sonnet nor story were to be delivered. 'twas a perch from which percentages and penalties were promulgated with the bombast of an enterprising divo! Not rich was I, though possessor indeed of vast legal tender . . .

Funds I finagled to deprive others of their inconsequential security, not only to build my accounts but to finance the eventual takeover of my very own mentor . . . And where did it land me? I am left poorer than any debtor in prison. I have Want for companionship and Ignorance as my advisor . . . wicked urchins; they claw at my shirttails even now . . .

(Looking behind and around him, as if these beings lurk close by)
I understand and see too well. I know not only what I wrought in life but more so what I left in its wake. So, in this pathetic place I must remain, blind to the transformative effects of my endeavors of one night. Aye, my former cohort cried with fear and writhed with remorse, most divinely demonstrated; but do I not know as an actor the risk of suspicious exuberance? To have seen passionate demonstration, promises, and contrition is as likely to have seen a co-conspirator at his Shakespearean best! (Bitterly, paraphrasing Shakespeare, from *As You Like It*) All the world's a stage . . .

And this apparition in his time did indeed play many parts. Ha! The question lies in what follows, when the curtains are drawn and no audience is nigh, when no applause exists to foster the doling out of generous good will. What is said or left unsaid when the onlookers are gone home? What is achieved when exchanges of gratitude or adulation are not at hand?

What is Man—and what is Ebenezer—capable of, if reward is not placed on some near shelf, there to shine and magnify . . . and further tempt him?

(Lamenting, to the universe)

Man, how great, yet how paltry and selfish a servant you are. Gods and monarchs, crooks and rakes, our commonality as drying human husks reduces us until at last we are equal in dust with each other. Back, back into the soil we go! When moved no more by invisible puppet strings of Fate, Free Will, and Destiny, when no more tied to the very crossed beams that housed both a Savior and a thief; pray tell, what are we?

(Jacob pauses to consider his words, shaking his head in sadness)

Ignorance, you are the victor and as such shall remain my master. Another stretch of chain, one more padlock hooked to my weary wrists . . . . . . so heavy . . . nowhere to go, nowhere to fly, nowhere else to be . . . Alone but for the one night granted me, to sail amongst the earth-bound poltergeists, and find my way through the alleys of a city, to the wasted chambers of one familiar to me above all others . . .

(Jacob cries out in agony)

Scrooge! The name, it pains my bones to speak it! (Jacob shuffles over to his desk. The wardrobe doors close themselves) And so, I am left, bereft. This is my nether-worldly space; my one assigned task. My gold . . .

My old, cold coins of gold . . .

Damned bits and pieces, unfeeling tokens . . . indeed, I reaped for which in life I toiled. . . and now I pay eternal price, alone, oh so, alone . . .

My God, I pray Eb listened. Hades, I pray he learned. Sisters, I pray he fights against your ropes and hides well your intrepid shears. Cut him not off too quickly. May he yet un-build what in life I never did, what now chains me to this hell of my own making . . . Oh, Jacob Marley, you fool . . . back to work you go . . .

(Jacob seats himself, arranges his chains, and takes up his one task. He begins to count his coins)

One thousand one, one thousand two
Better for me than low-born you.
One thousand three, one thousand four . . .
If the pithy monk can do this,
Every hour in obeisance bent,
Then any man can do it and any man so should.
And when he does, and done is did,
And as a doornail is fulfilled,
He can yet find rank
Amongst scoundrels, cads, and kings . . .
. . . one thousand five, one thousand six . . .

When nothing's broken, what's to fix? . . .
One thousand seven, one thousand eight . . .
Oh Midas, sir, I replicate . . .
One thousand nine, one thousand ten . . .
Oh, foolish, merry gentlemen!

. . . one thousand eleven . . .
Out of sight is out of mind . . .
One thousand twelve . . .
The smallest coin, the miser tithes . . .
Thirteen, fourteen . . .
With blinders on . . .
Fifteen and then sixteen . . .
To lock myself within these walls . . .
Avowed to keep prosperity
For only, only, only me! . . .
Seventeen and eighteen . . .
As I played so I must pray; my penance paid, full price . . .
Nineteen, now is twenty . . .

(Jacob will have at this point stacked the coins, or placed them on a scale or some such device; but then, he dumps the coins back into a heap on his desk and begins stacking them again, reciting the poem once more, from the beginning)

One thousand one, one thousand two . . .
Better for me . . . (etcetera)

(The light fades. Jacob's voice trails off as he recites and counts)

continued

www.jacobmarleystory.com

K.A. Schultz

3:00am Christmas Morn'

Jingle balls, smell 'em all, jangling in your face...

Isn't my version better?

I'm an asshole prankster and proud of it. Damn proud. So proud, I can hardly keep from telling tall tales of my misdeeds to any willing set o' ears I might meet up with when I'm traveling on business and hanging out at some bar to pass the evening; which is to say, having dinner and drinks on the company's – or some client's – dime; never my own. You see, I'm a salesman who works damn hard at his job. It pays me enough to keep me around, which would be two decades plus now, soon going on three. That's loyalty, right? Work takes me on a long-term rotation of many cities where we do business, a slew of accounts I have managed for ages. I am a total professional, but catch me with a few drinks in my system, and chances are, I will regale you with play-by-plays of some of the clever mischief I have cooked up. One's gotta keep their high functioning smarts honed, and a devil-may-care spirit must keep in top shape. And, so far, my antics have left me with an unbroken chain of under-the-radar chaos, pretty much untraceable, in my quickly smoothed wake.

Now, I won't launch into my stories until we have first chatted a bit and I have determined 1) that we are indeed truly total strangers, *and* 2) that we will remain as such. You know how it can be, that small world coincidence thing, which way too often has you disclosing way too much to some random person, with whom you wind up crossing paths with in some other, far less random context. I do *not* want to be interacting with you in any workaday situation come next morning, or next week, or in some other location anytime soon. . .

I prefer that you remain one of those types I like to call human space fillers. So, if with no paths to cross, nor intentions to fake, we are good to go. Trust me, I need nary a knowing wink nor congratulatory nod from anyone ever, for all the crap I have doled out to unwitting morons along the way; I am not necessarily looking for *your* praise. But for the momentary misery I put upon others – not unlike you, to be *perfectly honest* here – since I do consider you to be a safe set of ears at this juncture, I will continue. We have nothing to lose by it.

Fact is, my easy-going intellect combined with my predilection for fun at others' expense is such that I have been able to fuck with pretty much everyone I have ever known. Siblings, friends (well, former friends), bosses, colleagues, amicable strangers not unlike you, have all had the distinct privilege of having been duped by me. We schmoes, all of us, we *all* go about making our living and doing the best we can to make our short time on this earth something of "value." Well, my trickery has great value *to me*. If some lofty and holier-than-thou worthiness is not the goal, then let there at least be something of *fun* conjured up, to spice my road, make the insufferable boredoms of an ordinary existence a bit less stifling.

Therefore, I will tell you about one of my favorite games. This happened on my last trip to the Big Apple, where I was staying at this prissy boutique hotel. Never been there before. Fat and ostentatious crystal chandeliers hanging all over the place, so thick and dense, it was like walking under a fucking grape arbor of cut glass. I kept thinking I needed to duck. And the whole hotel was done up in this nasty, neon cherry- red. You'd think I'd have booked a room in a gold rush era hooker's roadhouse. Well, those walls there happen to be thin as paper, the result of a major renovation they had advertised bigtime, where however – of course – they had cut corners in all the wrong places. This, of course, they *did not* advertise. The walls there are, to put it philosophically, about as thin as the patience of the uppity-ups who think hotels like that actually reflect who they *believe themselves to be* – belief being the operative word. Walls so thin, that when a guest sneezes or coughs, it can be heard over the entire floor, and even on the ones above and below. What a perfect venue this hotel was going to be for my favorite, an alarm clock trick. I immediately landed on that ruse once settled in my room, having listened to some old fogie a few doors down hacking his lungs out as if he was gonna die. This hotel had, like most hotels, outfitted its rooms with clock-radios on their bedside tables, the old school kind with those red-lit digital numbers and toggle switches so one could set it to have either a radio station or an alarm to go off at a given wakeup time. And those alarms on those clocks – those beat-the-clock-with-a-fist kind of shitty alarms with their ear-piercing, repetitive *beep beep beep* – sure as heck would cut through every wall, ceiling, and floor, in every damn direction in one of that hotel.

Well, here is my trickster's secret sauce. Being on the company dime – that being practically endless, given how expenses can be cleverly structured and submitted – I would often book my room for one additional night following my actual departure, leaving it effectively unoccupied for the next night. The hotels, of course, never noticing or asking me the first thing about my comings or goings, never checking in on me so long as that 'do not disturb' tag was hung on the doorknob, made all this way too easy. I mean, they just want my money – well, my company's money. They don't give a shit. And so, before actually skipping out on that last booked night, I would set the room's clock-radio alarm to three am sharp, and then I would set it to the beep tone, and from there on in, fantasize in idle moments as to the results of what would then transpire the following night, once I, unbeknownst to anyone, was long gone.

We all know full well how that drill play out, right? The alarm would kick in and sound off for some indeterminate length of time, until some random, irate hotel guest would have taken it upon themselves to call the front desk to bitch and demand that some kind of action be taken, which of course the hired plebes on the overnight shift would have to address, something I know for a fact they always dread. If hotel staff take their sweet time getting around to doing room checks for other, obviously far worse reasons, this kind of call ranks right up there with dread potential. Who's to know what anyone might find in a room with an alarm going off like that?

I love to imagine how filled with trepidation those staffers would be. Who might they encounter? Someone naked and passed out, splayed across the coverlet of a still-made bed? Someone unconscious on the floor, drunk to a stupor, asleep, or unconscious, or – heaven forbid! – dead? How many times has any hotel staffer walked in on a stripped-bare naked and piss- or blood-covered carcass in one of their hotel's rooms? What a picture that paints. . .

Remember, all the while, that alarm would be going off. *Beep, beep, beep; beep, beep, beep,* to the chagrin of *everyone* in that wing, including above and below that floor. In an instant, with only the click of a button, the flick of a tiny little switch, I will have royally fucked up a night, and the sleep – hopefully fitful and restless to begin with – of *at least* a dozen stupid hotel guests. To imagine their anger over their night, ruined, gives me pure joy. Might anyone have the wherewithal to consider, this may have been done with intention? And how much angrier would *that* make them were they to realize this? Ah, it makes me sigh with pleasure even now. With luck, I will have screwed up not only that night's sleep, but their following day as well. Heck, I oughta be on retainer with Sternbock's Coffee Shops. Their businesses will have no doubt benefited from all the elevated need I will have generated in every city in which I have done business, for that dark-roast silt they dare call coffee. All those groggy, sleep-deprived losers who will have as their only recourse multiple purchases of Executive Pours. . . Now, that is influence. Of course, pigs that they all are, compensatory donuts would be likewise required, to go with their XL-sized coffees. Nothing like sugar-coated trans fats to keep the guts roiling. And therein lie even later repercussions. . .

And then to think, all the while, I will have slept like a baby as all this was manifesting, a place *where I no longer am myself*; left only to contentedly anticipate what all I will have wrought with so many humans about whom I don't give the first shit. Fuck them. Fuck them all.

Three am, kids! Time to rise n shine! Time to rise n whine!

†††

I am always a bit taken aback when I don't get the laughs at the intervals I would expect when I am telling my stories to my carefully culled barfly audiences. Once, there was this one fellow who actually scowled at my antics, said something like that had happened to him, not all that long ago, in Houston. My show of innocent shock hopefully parlayed how much of a coincidence my story was to him – and that my narrative had *nothing* to do with him. For good measure, I told him I had actually heard the original story from some stranger myself, and that I had only re-phrased as a first-person narrative for pure shits n giggles, for effect. But I could not help thinking, again, what a damn small world it was.

I *had* spent time in Houston.

So, I simply assured and re-assured the fellow I had never been there. Well, at least not in recent years. No matter what role I may have played, whether about the commotion at the hotel on that night or related to the car wreck he then went on to tell me about, how he had gotten himself into a pretty bad one the very next day, because, as he had said, between jet lag and the sleepless night, the crash had been almost inevitable. . . Well, shit does happen. But stupid moves will always be *the most* direct fault of the idiots involved in any given situation. And we were strangers, just having a random conversation at a random bar. Innocent ships passing, blah, blah, blah.

That asshole better watch out, crashing cars like that.

Resentment for human stupidity, which that particular stranger had exemplified, only amplified the thrill I felt as I set my hotel room alarm for this last, most recent time.

And, here it was, Christmas Eve day of all days. So, before catching my flight home for the holidays, I set the lil motherfucker once more to go off at three am, on the dot. Radio music set to play? Nope. Beeper alarm? Yes. And the toggle on the back switched to full volume for good measure. Oh yes, this particular contraption had a setting for alarm volume!

I was checked out well before noon; auto checked out, that is. No need to proof the bill for errant charges, being that it never comes out of my pocket anyway. But having fun on others' dimes, that is my bonus to myself. I am a cunning son of a gun.

Time to head for home. Have a good evening, *friends.*

Over the river and through the woods, to the bitch's old house I go. . .

†††

Though the string of lights on the lantern post are still on when I arrive at the house, it is otherwise dark inside. Good. I bet *she's* still at her Mom's for the weekend. *Mama's*, as she always says it. I could vomit. That southern drawl sounded quaint at some early point in our relationship; it now rings stupid and twangy to my ears. Always to Mama's she runs. *Mama, Mama, Mama.* So, what if Mama's cancer has come back? Serves her right, the way that old woman would always go on with her tanning and her eternal, fake dieting. Brought it on herself, she did. But at least an ill *Mama* gets my wife out of the house, even keeping her away overnights, evidently; like tonight.

When I enter through the garage door into the kitchen, there is no sign of life, no one to greet me. Even the fake Christmas tree looks dead, so dark and colorless it is in its corner. And not a single, fucking thing under it, either. Barren carpet where there should be at least a few wrapped packages. Like, am I supposed to be some kind of Santa and be running around shopping with *my* kind of work schedule? Oh well. I do have the house all to myself tonight. Home alone. Yay.

Again. I could get used to this. Hell, I *am* used to this. And I do like it this way. Come to think of it, I *prefer* it this way.

I begin to ruminate on this realization as I unpack, throw my dirty laundry onto the floor of the closet, shower, change into my pajamas. The ideations tripping about in my shrewd noggin are as tantalizing as a gingerbread house doused in rum and set afire. They dance in my head and lead me down a path which, I quickly realize, might just work. . .

How little *additional* cleverness it would require, to fashion some sort of circumstance in which I could create for myself a scenario that would leave me this sturdy, mid-century ranch all to myself, *permanently*. All to my little old, hard-working, traveling self. A quiet enclave of rooms through which I could pass unencumbered by the presence of someone I suppose I once loved, who has become over the years someone I can hardly bear to look at, let alone touch. To split up officially at this point in our lives would be costly. I would no doubt lose out on the house for sure, being that I was not its purchaser in the first place. *Mama Mama Mama* had literally *given it* to my wife – and thereby, more or less, to me too, if you ask me – when she had *finally* decided to down-size to an apartment at the retirement home. Well, the last thing a hard-working Joe like me needs, is to be kicked to the curb after so many years of dedicated service to the institution of a marriage he had committed to, for better and, boy oh boy, for so much worse. I realize as well, that I believe in my heart of hearts that I have *earned* this place, considering how much I have had to put up with. I conclude, my wife effectively *owes* the damn house to me.

There's *got* to be some way I can wrangle a fall, a slip on the basement steps, the front stoop, some innocuous wiring snafu. . .

But those will be brilliant musings for another day. I am home sweet home, and as anybody knows, good ole Santa is surely on his way. I better be nice, so he doesn't leave me with just a lump of coal in my shoes. I do think, however, I will in the meantime gift myself a little something in our – no, *my* – bedroom on this hallowed eve. Pour me a nice, tall whiskey – the good stuff – grab my laptop (the one she doesn't know I own), watch a little action, see what's up in the chat rooms. Been a while since I dialed in. . .

I have, after all, earned my down time, my proverbial winter's nap. How nice to have all that, and this house, all to myself.

†††

(2:55 am)

I awaken with a start, look at the clock alarm – yes, *my* clock alarm – on the table by my bed. The winds must have picked up. I did hear on the radio in the car on the way home from the airport, that a storm front would be moving in during the overnight hours. Possibly up to three inches of snow, too. That damn tap-tap-tapping at the window just roused me out of an especially kinky dream. Fucking branch. It sounds just like Mama's ugly, long, painted fingernails, striking over and over the kitchen countertop in the way she does it just to irritate me. I remember, some time ago, I had thought to trim back that tree. Idiot landscapers planted it way too close to the house. Why couldn't *Mama* have called someone to take care of that ages ago? Why does it always have to be me? Hell, I'm gone all the damn time! Some of us have to work!

Tap, tap, tap. . .

I flip over to my other side, punch the pillow, scrunch it up under my head to create a bit of a rise to baffle the sound.

(2:58 am)

When a car alarm goes off – must be close by – its *hoop, hoop, hoop* startles me. Awake again, damn it. We have very little crime in this neighborhood, for all its dense development. Moreover, we have even fewer residents who dare venture out after the sun goes down. Our populace is the kind that fills the restaurants before the happy hours are even over with, with all those cheapskates done and paid up and back home by six or seven at the very latest. With so much interminable content to watch these days, this is what our clutch of demographics does to pass the rest of the evening hours. Basically, nothing.

And there it goes again! And again. *Hoop, hoop, hoop.*

Hoop, hoop, hoop. . . Alternating with that infernal tapping on my window.

Tap, tap, tap. . . Hoop, hoop, hoop. . .

I prop myself up on my elbow, glance again at the clock. I did not set the alarm. The cherry red digits read 2:59.

Well, how about that? I imagine for a moment, the alarm going off in just a minute or so at that "nice" hotel in the city. I picture the guests in the immediate vicinity of my former room, waking up and cursing. I imagine the proactive, pissed-off one calling down to the desk to complain. And then I wonder – and I smile at this – how long it will take for the overnight staffer to send someone up to the sixteenth floor to investigate. And I know (from personal experience) that, even if they are able to locate the source of the disruption, it will take quite a while for security to then also haul their asses up there, to stand by as the door is unlocked (but only after a series of loud and equally disruptive knocks, plus a set of requisite *Please, open up*! or *Hello-hello*!s are shouted out to no one in particular, to further bug the bejeezus out of anyone in earshot. My fantasies warm me, calm me down by way of the silent joy of an asshole's job, well done. Despite the cacophony here where I am now, I fall back onto the bed, exhaling long and loud into the empty room, assured of an imminent onset of wonderful, rewarding slumber. . .

    (3:00 am)

    The radio on my clock alarm springs to life. There is that quick, static click, followed immediately by the strains of – what else – *Silent Night, Holy Night,* this rendition a dated, mid-century milquetoast recording dominated by a screeching, high-pitched gaggle of violins. Silent night, my ass. . .

    I sit up. Something else is calling my attention. I am quite sure I am awake and not dreaming. However, this is starting to have the residual qualities of a nightmare, and it's getting worse by the minute. My phone; it has sprung to life. It's the Frontporch Sentry app which is lighting it up. The phone buzzes three quick bursts, and then again, alerting me to activity at the front door. The phone is in its charger near the clock alarm. I don't know why I do this, but I count the moments of quiet before the next set of three beeps go off, which likewise cause my phone to vibrate in the most irritating way: *One. . .two. . .three. . . zzz. . . zzz. . .zzz. . .*

    I grab my phone before the next trio of beeps and buzzes strike. I don't want to hear anything anymore. I am furious despite my feeling so intensely groggy.

    I have no idea why, but I am unable to power down my phone. So, I wedge the damn thing between my mattress and box spring. Unfortunately, I can still hear the low hum of the phone, which is now both muffled *and* amplified by the bedding, that stupidly expensive coil construction which was to give me the best sleep of my life. It is now resulting in a low frequency *mmm, mmm, mmm*, which resonates straight up from below, as were it some kind of tectonic wave rising up through the earth's crust and through my mattress and then me, and set to repeat.

    Mmm, mmm, mmm. . . Mmm, mmm, mmm. . .

Tap, tap, tap. . . Hoop, hoop, hoop. . .

Mmm, mmm, mmm. . . Mmm, mmm, mmm. . .

Tap, tap, tap. . . Hoop, hoop, hoop. . .

All while the violins keep wailing.

Shit. Merry fucking Christmas to me.

I suppose I best take a look outside and confirm there is nothing – no one – at the front door. It's got to be the wind. I am irritable but not afraid. Fear is not my thing. Assholes coast through most of life by way of their special brand of bravery.

I shuffle down the hall, flick on the exterior porch light. I open the front door but leave the storm door locked. It's all glass, with only a half panel of scrollwork at the bottom, so my view onto the sidewalk, the front lawn, is unobstructed. There is, as I expected it, no one, nothing, out there. A sparkling whorl spins across the driveway, which does indeed indicate a new, light snow has begun to fall. Apropos the weather, the sky is clouded. There is no moonlight to facilitate my view. The whole world appears to be asleep; there is not even one window lit across the street in either direction. Silent Night, yes, indeed. I convince myself I am satisfied. I feel my way back to the bedroom and over to my bed and I lie down. The computer, I had left lying open on the bed when I fell asleep. I guess, it was still on my lap when I had dozed off. It must have slid to the edge of the bed, for as I pull up the covers, the laptop slides off the bed and falls to the floor. The lid snaps and breaks off. *Damn it.* I can't very well take that evidence-bearing device to some computer shop for repair. . .

Old man Claus is gonna have to give me a new one.

I shove both the computer and lid an arm's length under the bed. No need to fool with it; there is nothing I can do with it now.

I determine to make myself drift off again. I am jet-lagged and want to reap the benefits of a solid night of sleep so that I can rightly enjoy what may well turn out to be a solitary Christmas morning at home. I have some very important, very clandestine planning to do – some *real* thinking, as it were – and I want to be able to enjoy even that process. Assholes would wish to relish the laying out of murderous strategies, just as any enterprising killer wannabe would.

(3:00 am) (Still)

This time, when I awaken, I jump. I literally jolt upwards what feels like it could be a full couple of inches off my mattress. A slight outbreak of perspiration dampens my face, my armpits, the small of my back.

I heard that. I know what I heard.

It was the latch of the front door. I heard it click. It is the only such latch in the house; a heavy, decorative unit, and as such, it is the only thing to make that distinct metal on metal double-click.

Someone has opened the front door.

My phone, still buried between my mattress and box spring, has resumed its muffled alert.

Mmm, mmm, mmm. . . Mmm, mmm, mmm. . .

The branch at the bedroom window is still tapping.

I swear, that damn car alarm has been set off again as well.

Tap, tap, tap. . . Hoop, hoop, hoop. . .

Mmm, mmm, mmm. . . Mmm, mmm, mmm. . .

Tap, tap, tap. . . Hoop, hoop, hoop. . .

The infernal cacophony of the repetitious familiar was one thing. This new, unexpected sound has now caused adrenaline to shoot throughout my system. My heartbeat has joined the chaos. It beats wildly, almost painfully in my chest.

That skeletal branch at the window has seen fit to keep up its thing. Like it's trying to catch my attention. It feels as if the tapping is coming from a spot right above the top of my skull. No. *I can feel* the tap-tap-tap *between my ears.*

But I do not sit up. Like a panic-stricken child, I remain prone. I draw the comforter up to just under my nose. I feel the need to lie still, very still, and to keep listening, as if somehow my motionlessness can render me a tad more invisible, regardless of the enormous, lumpish mass I also know I make as I lie here.

If someone just now opened the front door (but wait, wasn't the storm door also locked?), well then, they will have to first make their way down the hall. It is the only path that can be taken, being that this house is as simply laid as ranch homes generally are. My ears are now keening towards the possibility of this newest sound of some kind of approach, which would then be coming from *inside* the house.

And there, finally, it is. The unmistakable creak of the floor in the entry. The very same spot I know to avoid when coming home late at night, or early in the morning.

Impulsively, I venture a call into the void. My voice is squeamishly childish.

Honey? Is that you?

And then, and why I say this, I do not know:

Santa? Is that you?

Since I do *not* keep a gun in the house, I have no real weapon. Certainly, no training, either. I might be an asshole, but I am *all* for gun control. But it is times like this, when I start to think I maybe should have not been so, um, *stern* with that little rug-pissing flea bag of my wife's. A dog could be of some real use in this moment. . .

Well, what's done is done. The mongrel had it coming. . .

†††

(3:00 am) (Still)

Tap, tap, tap. . . Hoop, hoop, hoop. . .

Mmm, mmm, mmm. . . Mmm, mmm, mmm. . .

Tap, tap, tap. . . Hoop, hoop, hoop. . .

. . .and there it is!

Again!

No question, that was a footfall. A heavy one. A step taken with a contemplative, unhurried pacing. There is not one spark of light inside or outside to aid my inquiring sensibilities. No working night light, no moonglow at the window, no stars out; plus, all the curtains *and* sheers have been drawn. There is only darkness and this crazy mix of sound.

The branch tapping, the car alarm sounding, the irritating Christmas music that would not stop until I yanked the clock alarm's cord from the wall. . .

The dark is so thick I cannot see my own hand in front of my face.

Tap, tap, tap. . . Hoop, hoop, hoop. . .

Mmm, mmm, mmm. . . Mmm, mmm, mmm. . .

Tap, tap, tap. . . Hoop, hoop, hoop. . .

Mmm, mmm, mmm. . . Mmm, mmm, mmm. . .

Thud of a footstep. Then another. And then another, and another.

Someone, something, is walking down the hall, towards the bedroom. Towards me.

I may be an asshole, but I have no recourse. My quick wit has abandoned me. I may as well be three-year-old me, in my little race car bed, with my guard rails, and the plastic sheeting, my bedroom door locked *from the outside*. . .

There is nothing I can think of, that I can grab to wield as some kind of makeshift weapon against whoever – whatever – is coming my way. Should I reach for my laptop lid? Use it as a shield?

The footsteps are entirely too heavy sounding to be those of my wife's. No; there is no way it could be her. Unless she is carrying something; something very heavy, which is adding weight to her already ungainly physique, something which could be slowing her down, slower than she has already become in her middling years. Is she carrying an enormous, wrapped present for me? What would she be giving to me to make a package *this* heavy? A new stereo? I have been ogling them online and dropping plenty of hints. . .

Assholes are quickly distracted when it comes to imagining largesse for themselves.

Mmm, mmm, mmm. . . Mmm, mmm, mmm. . .

Tap, tap, tap. . . Hoop, hoop, hoop. . .

Should I call out again? To whom?

Thoughts of gifts having quickly vanished, I am so nervous that I am shaking now. Quaking. I might be an asshole, but I have never been in a fight; at least, not a physical one. Sure, I have started plenty, pushed all sorts of buttons, triggered more dumb dorks than I can count; and, while to date I enjoy a one hundred percent success rate in stirring pots to the point of boiling over – and with fabulously dastardly results – I have so far caused only trouble for *others*. It's never been *me* on the receiving end. Having grown up cute and short and a cunning motherfucker all at the same time has, up until now at least, made for an asshole's trifecta.

Tonight; well, tonight is starting to look like it might be a big, new, next step for me, as a potential participant in an actual confrontation. No slimy, offsides act of aggression, this looming event could very possibly be some kind of physical invasion that will warrant my being forced to defer and give myself up to whomever – whatever – is making its way down the hall, towards my bedroom door, and no doubt, towards my bed.

If I go along for a while, surely something will occur to me. . .

Mmm, mmm, mmm. . . Mmm, mmm, mmm. . .

Tap, tap, tap. . . Hoop, hoop, hoop. . .

I decide to call out my wife's name. I know; I will make it sound as if I am expecting her! As if her arrival is imminent and logical, which it really sort of is. No, I do *not* miss the bitch, but I will sure as heck make it sound like I am glad she's home. Damn glad. Yep, it's *got* to be her.

I take a deep breath and make like a bellows. I will make myself sound like a *big* man. . .

Mmm, mmm, mmm. . . Mmm, mmm, mmm. . .

Tap, tap, tap. . . Hoop, hoop, hoop. . .

But nothing comes out. Nothing but a croak. No; it is worse than a croak. It is nothing but a wet crackle caught in my voice box, a bare sputtering. I can hardly breath through the glitch and would cough, if I but dared. Instead, I try to suppress the cough by holding my breath, my face buried into my folded arms. I then feel my pajama bottoms grow hot with the reactive seepage of a bladder that has just collapsed in a tell-tale gesture of defeat. Defeat of a spirit that was never anything more than some puny field of negative energy, hidden behind a massive front of rage-fed bravado. All that bullshit I have been doling out for, well, decades now.

I am a fucking coward, lying in my own piss.

Lord, how I *wish* it were my wife walking towards the bedroom door.

I feel like I am going to throw up.

Then, there it is again! That infernal static *pop* a couple feet away from me. It is my clock alarm being switched to on. And it is my alarm kicking in, and it is louder than I have ever heard it before. But it is not the digital drone of a *beep-beep-beep* as I have known and loathed it all these years.

And then I realize, the clock alarm's cord is still clenched in my right hand.

No. There is no *beep, beep, beep.* Nor is it some other lame Christmas carol that starts to play. Instead, it is the shriek of a dog that is being broadcast. Repeatedly. It is the repeated, high-pitched, anguished shriek of a dog. A small dog *screaming.*

Eeeaaarp, eeeaaarp, eeeaaarp!

And then again.

Eeeaaarp, eeeaaarp, eeeaaarp!

Over and over, again and again.

If I could scream too, I would. But I cannot make a sound. My throat has completely constricted, and my mouth has gone so dry, I cannot pull my tongue down from the roof of my mouth. All I can do is try to cough, try to breathe through this feeling of strangulation. . . I drop the cord and press both of my hands to my ears, to try and block the blood-curdling screams of, screams of. . .

(3:00 am) (Still)

A pair of massive, gloved hands grab mine, yank them away from the sides of my head. They pin my own two hands onto the mattress to either side of my head, pushing me hard into the warm, wet bedsheet. All the while, the screeching wails of my wife's dead dog continue. It is a cadenced blaring of shrieking squeals, howls in sets of three, sets of three, sets of three, over and over again. . .

A new sound has been added to this symphony of insanity. The gloves worn by the invader must be either fastened with or trimmed in – what else? – jingle bells. Fucking bells. Their infernal tinkle is erratic and sharp. They keep time as I am violently, repeatedly shaken as I just lie there, the spineless hand puppet that I am. The bells' tintinnabulation, a bright *ching, ching, ching,* rides high above that of the branch's metronome tapping, my phone's buzzing, the car alarm's honking, the piercing howls emanating from the radio. I wonder in an oddly calm aside: in the next-door neighbors' houses, are the kids all nestled and snug in their beds? And are they by chance dreaming of a sleigh and eight tiny reindeer? I would bet a nickel, they are thinking they might be hearing bells. Bells, bells, bells. . .

And then, all of a sudden, for lack of any better option, my cold, black heart decides it's had enough. I may be a highly motivated asshole and a coward, but I am also a middle-aged, clot-ridden desk jockey with enough anger, stress, and cholesterol to strip any stalwart bastard of life and limb at a moment's notice. I pass out. And pass on. Into a dark oblivion I slide, devoid of all petty rewards, all blame gaming, all falsely gained superficial regard, all self-loathing. My clock alarm, stuck forevermore at 3:00 am, keeps on and on and on. . .

†††

It will have been three business days before someone happens to stop by to deliver some useless thing my wife must have ordered, and given the stench and strange, persistent sounds from within, for these odd and unpleasant goings on to then have motivated this delivery person to call the "front desk" (the cops) for a wellness check.

By then, my once rather piquant, pointy-chinned face will have swelled up and taken on a color more commensurate with the shit-sourced soup that flowed through my veins all these years. And the neighbors, they will have found a way to add an official by-the-way to the police report, something to the effect that *Yes, he was definitely an asshole,* but that they *couldn't rightly think of anyone who would have actually wanted him dead. . .*

And that stupid widow bitch of mine? She will have already gotten herself another damn dog.

In honor of Edgar Allan Poe and in special recognition of the pulsating musicality of his "The Tell-Tale Heart."

Krampuss
A Khrystmass Splatterphukk Tale

Gather 'round, you mischievous imps, for the small gift of a tale I will tell you, in gratitude for your keeping company with me on this cold winter's evening. It is not often I am alone here at home when a blizzard such as this bears down with such vengeance. You, my dears, will help pass the hours until my husband – yes, your Papa, I suppose – returns.

When, indeed, is the best time to share a dark Khrystmass-time tale? Why, that would be now, whilst the arctic winds howl and the bestial wolves prowl; whilst the coals roil with heat sparked with as much fancy as lust. If it stirs the loins as you draw in to listen, then come a bit closer, have some fun, nestle in. For here, as you know, it is quite permitted, to slip a hand beneath an unlaced bodice; for a finger to prod some unseen, wet place; for a burgeoning bulge to push into the small of a gently arched back. Anticipate my words as coming from one such as yourselves, for I make no pretext as to what I am, nor to whom it is that I am attached. Together, in our merriment, we will keep the bitter bite of this long, dark, winter's night far from this most coziest of places.

So. You there, stoke the fire! And you there, fill my goblet! Now, lend me your ears for this bit I'll now share.

†††

There once was a wicked and slovenly *Hausfrau*, who never lifted a finger but to shake it when she berated all she compelled to bear witness to her slanderous untruths and hateful reproaches. Now, the one household task she deigned undertake was in the morn' to sling her feather-filled bed out the window to air, as was the custom back then, in those parts out there.

Upon the bedding thusly situated, the *Hausfrau* would lean, her pendulous breasts equally on display. And, oh, I might add, how the town's folk would stare! From this voyeur's perch did this piece of work undertake the one trade she dared claim as her own, which was to eavesdrop on the discourse of all who passed by below.

Come afternoon, the Frau, primped and dressed to the nines, would commence on her rounds, their purpose being neither of virtue nor need, but the dissemination all the prattle she would have deceptively gathered, to whomever the telling could best serve a willfully inflicted spate of injurious pain. Should any account have been partially captured, this never did pose the first care or concern, for what the *Hausfrau* possessed with a singular pride, were the devious talents of a colossal liar. It was but too simple to flesh out every partially heard missive, so to then force upon whichever unwitting ears the *Hausfrau* saw fit, her own snidely sown add-ons, her corrosive intent.

You ask how that went? Oh dear. I have heard that her blather ruined fine families, sent good men to prison, caused some heartbroken patsies to jump to their deaths! The *Hausfrau* was feared so much more than revered for all the damage she wrought, all the goodwill she fought.

As for her husband, at end of each day would he be found trudging resignedly home, slogging through the snow with the gait of a lackey led yet again to the trenches, knowing full well what would greet him once he passed through the door, which would all be then as it had been before. Breakfast and suppertime scraps on the table, mangy cats lapping the leavings and yowling and scrounging; jam-painted, crack-edged plates, and stained cups stacked way to the heights; dust-ridden, warped tables, dirt-streaked pillows and cushions, cobweb-laced doorways and stairwells and windows; floorboards grossly peppered with pestilent matter; sills paved end to end with bug hulls and bird droppings.

Once passed through the small foyer, he would sigh long and loud, hang his hat, tuck his cane in its corner. No fire to be seen crackling in the sooted, tiled stove, no welcoming candle left lit, a creeping chill seeping through the chinked walls like the silt. The air in there, it hung thick like a damp, frozen fog; and while things had always there smelled of decay, these days, the befouling cloud cover was far more decidedly so. . .

Why, is that, do you ask? Hold on; I shall tell you.

The *Hausfrau*, waylaying her return by all she dispensed, would only come home long after her man. Evening supper was never more than a starved laborer's futile afterthought, and when at last laid out, served without fanfare. The offerings never more than stale breadcrumbs and crusts, set out with soured tubes of some nondescript sausage. The soup in the kettle, yes, still had potential, although it too sported a bloom with its own sort of pestilent and blotchy green matter. In due course, the Frau might deign to the compost to toss it, but on that night, the muck was once again to be skimmed off (at least for the husband) and warmed up once more. For good measure, into his bowl did she surreptitiously spit, leaving the husband to wonder on the tang in the dish. The *Hausfrau*, by contrast, would slurp from her cup of some odd, watery tea, to be sure with some noxious liquor laced most heavily, something she insisted was but a digestive. What a fetid brew like this might not do for a bilious tummy, it sure did make up with its addled benumbing.

†††

But on this night of all nights, I will tell you here now, things would prove to be most decidedly different! Different, indeed! All would soon take a most horrible turn!

For this night, my dear imps, was none other than *Krampusnacht*. It was, as we all know, yet another December fifth in a long, long line of nights just like this. On this evening, the benevolent but stern old Saint Nicholas would descend once again upon the good folk of the town, to bestow upon the children a glimpse of his stately visage. He would bless one and all with the grace of small gifts; and perchance, if he saw fit, with a marzipan pig or fat pickle or two. For those deserving of the good Saint's visitations, this was a night of great, virtuous celebration.

It was as well – as you well know too – the very same night when the grim envoy himself would ascend from his iniquitous circle of Krampian hell, so to make his way amongst the homesteads out there, to strike ice-cold fear in those who deserved it, who, having wasted their year in destruction and lies, would now have to pay in the most horrid of ways. This envoy was of course, none other than our very own Herr Krampus!

Krampus has always heeded his calling, which was to push past the good, and to mete out to fools the stinging, harsh thrashes of his thorn-laden switches. Once laid 'cross transgressors, Krampus' lessons doth quickly impart the rewards not of gifts but of swift, painful punishment. Little, however, do all those unsuspecting sinners know, how much more our Herr Krampus is capable of, provided their sentence has been duly earned. . .

For you see, Krampus can sense honest, true evil ahead. And on this particular evening, corruption's stench had laid out for him but the clearest of paths. Its odor slithered towards him like a snake lying in wait, slinking into the valley from where else but the *Hausfrau* and husband's old, run-down chalet.

Its rancid emissions were to Krampus a call to harsh action!

And thus, did Herr Krampus, with now the gravest of depravities clearly identified, have none other than the *Hausfrau's* own home in his perilous sights!

The chalet nigh emanates a great malintent in a perverted kind of welcome, as were the whole chalet slathered thick like a cake with a visible excrement, the kind that could attract a vast legion of fiends, and with a fanfare as did some devilish sentry standing out front by the door, with him hollering loud into the dark, winter night, *Oh Krampus, Oh Krampus, do come, Sir, right here!*

††††

With a spin of his hooves and a swish of his staff, Krampus makes his way up the chalet's steep path. Though up past his boots lies the thick winter snow, his pace only grows quicker, it never does slow. It belies his great hunger, his clear malintent. The fallen snows drift apart where he steps, for the fires of perdition obey as he wishes. And with but a glance, Krampus does melt every icicle affixed to each eave on his route. The icicles dash to the ground like a volley of glass daggers.

Krampus anticipates tonight's visit with a particular glee. His licks his cracked lips, now curled wide with intent. His serpentine tongue whips about as it tests of the air, for Herr Krampus can taste of the pain in that lair. A lecherous wave awakens his sweat-dampened phallus, which until now has remained coiled within and at low hanging rest. Ah, that member of his is one sex-seeking python! 'tis an old blood-filled wurst with a life all its own! That Krampian pecker comes to as it twitches and thickens, and poking out its fat head, it inquires as to what on this night might soon transpire. Upwards it eyes its parental grand bastard, for whom it more often than not serves as true master.

Krampus commands it to wait, and he shoves it back in and resumes his fast gait. To be sure, Herr Krampus knows that Sir Phallus will be soon availed of his prurient purpose. Krampus himself is assured, on this night, his gift will be given to one most good and ripe. Ripe for fucking, for plowing, for bursting tonight!

The village below has been cast all a-glow by the candlelit windows, their small patches of gold. But up by the chalet, 'tis quite the opposite; the darkness now fallen comes from within. Up in there, alongside those two decrepit, old souls, Krampus senses something far more wretched, if the truth must be told. And that, my friends, is what 'stinks' to the heavens, an otherworldly missive likewise delivered, for which nothing but his best work is demanded. . .

The acids, the bile, the semen, are all set to churning; the Krampian wants seeking equal appeasement; a deluge is coming! With an unearthly appetite now bawdily kindled, it will be not just one who will serve as Krampus' victim.

Offsides the husband observes as the horned shadow approaches. The latch of the door, he's thrown wide in his welcome. The *Hausfrau*, now drunk on her spirit-laced brew, reclines lank in her chair, she feels not the chill air. But he, upon seeing the unholy Krampus breech their front stoop, with his knife does he carve a wet, second red smile at the base of his throat. 'tis his plan to watch his wife pillaged as he bleeds 'til he's gone. The floor is soon soaked in his iron-laced foam. But, may he hold on just long enough to watch Krampus rip off the wife's loathsome head whole. The husband as he fades stares wide-eyed from his chair, with what hate-filled glee anticipates he this last, brutal show.

Krampus doth recognize the miasma; he is now amongst peers.

There lays his quarry, collapsed in her chair. She snores at full volume, has piddled her quaffings. With her sonorous rattlings and blubbering cheeks, her splitting corset, her encrusted bare feet, with her legs splayed so wide, like two fence posts askew, here lies a most loathsome specimen, a womanly beast!

What a rare thing indeed, to meet with an Odalisque this perverted! And though Krampus is incapable of love in that sense, his phallic wurst knows what it must now do: it shall locate for its own the foulest of orifices. And so, Krampus homes in, his cock at attention. It springs outward and up from the demon's furred belly, its wrinkled red cap drawn and peckishly ready. Krampus grabs that flesh monster with both of his fists and notes his cock's eye is curled up in a smirk.

The Krampian prick will now guide as commander!

Krampus, the crazed bull, extends that third arm, guides that throbbing prick in. And lo, there it is, the Frau's cavern a-drip! What a feminine sap does it leak of its own, as sour as lye to the immortal nose. The Frau's well-worn cunt indeed has a stench all its own.

And what would one expect, when how many vegetables were first plunged in as playthings for this lust-ridden wench? Aye, my friends, there was many a meal basted with the *Hausfrau*'s own juices! For our Lord Krampus, this sodden, old strumpet will serve well to slake his lust. She bucks like a fresh corpse as the demon impales her. It takes hearty shaking to rouse her from her stupor, but before too much time passes, the *Hausfrau* is stoked by the Krampus invasion. And when, moments later, blood and fuck water spurt hard from her larder, the Krampus, now heaving, will push even harder.

The *Hausfrau*, but mortal, soon screams bloody murder. The chalet walls, begin to shake; at first, just a little. But when Krampus drills in with that pecker of his, the *Hausfrau* with shock feels it push past her throat! The Krampus has brutally mined his own flesh and blood tunnel!

That not being enough for this horny hellion, Krampus next reaches over, rips off the half-severed noggin of the near-dying husband. And as the head of the Krampian cock pops out of the Frau's wide-torn mouth, Krampus twice corks his meat with a next, gaping mouth! This stopper he pumps with every bit of his might, the *Hausfrau* plus husband make for one fucking fright!

†††

It has long been known that Herr Krampus comes but once a year. But, when he does, and this I surely would know, 'tis enough any town square fountain to fill up, overflow!

Krampus' viscous fuel erupts forth, hot, full, and unfettered, uncaring to whom by its girth it is tethered. And when Krampus' semen is thusly done spurted, it spills onto the floor, where it mixes and curdles the dead husband's own still-warm gore.

But then – and here comes the fun – from the bubbling mixture, there arise on the floor, a whole host of small spider-limbed goblins, all fresh and newborn!

This famished, new brood sets upon the dead husband and reduces his form to a heap of red mush. While the satisfied Krampus wipes the last slime from his cock, the hobgoblins make quick work of the 'man of the house'. It will be next up for the goons to turn onto the Frau, who though ravished still wheezes from her kitchen corner. The goblins descend upon her as a carnivorous flock, to partake in their first meal of a *Krampuss*, fresh-fucked.

. . .and yes, my imps; this is the murderous mess from which you were born!

One by one dive the sprites into their bosomy bog, into her fat belly, into her loose twat. They eat up her carcass – and do imagine this – not from the outside in as one might expect, but instead, the *Hausfrau* is devoured from her innards on out. When at last, one by one, their pointed heads do burst forth, their Father Krampus plucks them plum out, like grinning berries, the lot. He then tosses his ghouls into his sack of hard coal, on the chance there are others who need Krampus thinning.

But before Herr Krampus can take final leave, there is still one more thing it is he must seek. He searches the nooks, and 'neath the dead tree, its once verdant branches gone dark, sharp as needles. And there, sad to say, does he find what he sought, something that stood out with its singular sweetness. It is what is left of an innocent girl, who some weeks ago from the village went missing. What remains of the poor thing is little more than a rag puppet. Her small limbs now all fractured, her skin charred and blood-spattered. A breath, this tiny being has not taken since some weeks ago, when her life by the Frau and the man was forsaken. Her small hands still tied fast in their straps, her slender neck in twine still enwrapped, her two little feet both irreparably broken.

All the better, my dear, the *Hausfrau* had sneered, *to keep you from running back home.*

Krampus gathers the small relic, wraps it well in his coat. This innocent *Kind* he will transport to the great forest's edge, to consign his wee ward to the benevolence of the eternal. For, none other than the Christkind awaits in the glen wherein long ago was built a small shrine in His holy name. Calmy, reverently, and in silence will the Holy One keep steadfast vigil until this next, little angel is at long last delivered.

Upon handover, the tiny girl's eyes flutter feebly and open, her wounds dissipate. Her spindling, small arms she lifts into the snow-filled, cold air. As the waif, grown translucent, is taken into love's eternal embrace, she lights up, like a flame, awash in newfound and peace-filled, sweet grace. Nevermore shall she suffer. Nevermore those hurt-filled cries will she be forced to utter. Everlasting life, and with laughter besprinkled, will be hers, will be hers, forever, amen.

So, now you see, my precious imps, how the *Hausfrau* and husband more than earned every bit of their final rumpus. They've been sent to their hell on a path they did pave. All what is left to do now is for Herr Krampus to set fire to the chalet's dry, old timbers. And before the sunrise arrives, those two in their house are both burnt to mere cinders.

With that, my pets, I have now come too, to the end of my tale, delivered to you. You must now take to your rooms and be quick – off you go! I hear even now the locks turn on the door. My husband returns from this year's brutish tour! Even you surely hear the *clomp-clomp* of his hooves!

†††

Ah, Krampus, my dear! Pray tell, how did everything go for you *this* year?

Imagine It

Imagine, your favorite Christmas carols are playing on a radio.

And that this is taking place back when radio stations switched over to Christmas music programming for only one brief twenty-four-hour stint, usually at sundown on Christmas Eve, in a time before terrestrial stations and web-based sites launched Christmas feeds running from Thanksgiving Day weekend up until New Year's; before the Hallmark Channel's saccharin epics streamed 365 days a year, and back when Christmas decor "only" showed up in stores the day after Halloween, not a quarter year beforehand, at the tail end of summer.

Imagine those songs are playing, and now think of your favorites. Which ones are they?

First, it might be one sung by, say, Dean Martin, something to set the overall mood; and then, following right on the heels of that song, there'd be another classic, this one belted out in signature fashion by Ella Fitzgerald. Two of your favorites, played in a row, just as if you had requested them! What a miraculous sort of serendipity is this?

And then, wonder of wonders, a *third* holiday favorite of yours starts up, right on the heels of song number two. Who sings this one? Mel Tormé?

Long before we could build our own playlists and be quite literally plugged into them, one could only hope. . .

But here they are now – or rather back then- one beloved Christmas song followed by another to mark the season, set the tone.

I love Christmas music as a genre, all onto itself. Don't you?

Ah, those early Christmas pop-classics, with their mid-century vibes, their glamorous band leaders, and celebrity crooners. Mellifluous voices, arrangements, reminiscences that will someday cross easily over into the holiday tuneage of the next millennium. Songs for the ages. They inspire, instill cheer, and spark childhood nostalgia much in the same way that crescent-shaped almond cookies, glittered gift tags, and hand-knit mittens all do. . .

This Christmas music happens to be emanating from a radio in a living room. It could be from the one set atop the bookshelf, an early, space-age device cast in yellowing Bakelite – but it's not. The songs are coming from a console placed opposite a davenport. The console is a massive piece of furniture, with fabric-covered speakers that flank a carved center panel. It houses both a turntable and an AM/FM receiver. The console is made of finely grained walnut, and because it is a pretty and a hefty thing, it has been placed dead center against the long wall of the living room. Atop the console resides an oddly shaped ceramic object d'art, a-drip with a coagulated slurry of avocado green and pumpkin orange glazes. This is situated atop a crocheted doily. It happens to be a lamp, which casts a fragmented illumination by way of a small light bulb tucked deep into its recesses. This TV lamp would have been switched to "on" hours ago, being that it has been dark as night outside for some time; dark and silent, with the sun having long since set, and the birds all having gone to sleep. The evening does come, after all, on the heels of the year's shortest day – or longest night, depending on how you look at it. The hour could be going on, oh, about seven, maybe eight o'clock. It is not early, but nor is it terribly late.

The cheery holiday music fills the silence in what is an otherwise unoccupied room. It is presently devoid of human inhabitants, as they are just down the hall. The living room's décor is dated, but from some unidentifiable decade gone by, for it is outmoded in an organically, cozy way. The ceiling is low, and textured, a troweled floral design. The front door opens directly into this room, which boasts two additional doorways on opposite walls. One opens into the dining room, and the other, into the bedroom hallway. A picture window faces streetward, disproportionately large for the space, as most picture windows all tend to be. Barkcloth drapes with another a layer of sheers are all drawn closed to obliterate any view in or out. The window is outfitted in a heavy frame painted the palest of toothpaste greens. This complements the deeper colors of the plush carpeting, a looped and cut field of sherbert-colored yarns. The carpet effuses a forced effeminate; it is clean but heavily tracked.

The melodies and voices carried by the soundwaves pouring forth from the console wrap themselves around every object in this room, making for a boxed domestic practicality enhanced with a hefty dollop of store-bought holiday festivity. It could be a shadow box display, or a diorama created to showcase a mid-century dollhouse product line.

The Christmas tree, a bit irregular in shape, looks real. It appears to be a scotch pine. This tree was, in fact, a one-off found amongst a stack of unchosen, lopsided balsam firs, severed from their tree farm roots for what will soon prove to be a foray into abject purposelessness, for most good folk who prefer live trees had by the time this one was sourced, already purchased theirs. The lonesome evergreens and their unadorned demises, we can mourn for a quick moment.

Alright.

This lucky tree, chosen from all the others, has needles almost as textured and furred as is the plush carpeting. The tree is conveniently also of a complementary, blueish-green hue, though many shades darker than the wood trim, and a few shades darker than the carpet. It is mounted and skirted, ready in all its glory for the day to come. The tree is centered to the picture window and trimmed – all the way around, mind you – with a collection of thoughtfully placed satin and glass ornaments. Red, white, and blue balls are evenly spaced and alternate in color. The tree also boasts that kind of angel hair tinsel, *lametta*, which hallmarks the aesthetic of the time, toxicity and laborious application being not much of an issue at all. The *lametta* has been applied with great care, strand after strand after meticulously draped strand, over pretty much every single one of the branches. The whole thing is a veritable Christmas bouquet a-drip in silver, whisperingly shimmering any time anyone walks by, or whenever a door is opened and closed, or anytime the furnace kicks on. No cat resides here, nor dog. In a household such as this, where angel hair tinsel is this abundantly employed, that would not be possible. Nor are there any human children – or worse yet, toddlers – with their propensity to stick everything into their omnivorous cherub's maws. The tree is enjoying its brief reign radiant and undisturbed.

And packages, presents? No, there is not a single box underneath any one of those glistening boughs.

Yes, it is December twenty-fourth, but no one is expected until morning. "Santa" this year will be represented by way of the arrival of a very special guest, one who has not paid a visit to this particular house in many years. Many long years. Many long and quiet and uneventful years. Many thankfully uneventful years.

The fireplace mantel flanking the window wall boasts an arrangement of scented votive candles placed just so, to appear randomly, casually situated. The candles are several years old but have yet to know the melting warmth of a flaming wick. They, like candles in so many homes, will never be lit, having been rather oddly elevated to knickknack status for who knows what reason. I dare say, these will remain unlit and are destined for First Lutheran's charity resale shop in the not-so-distant future.

The fire in the hearth has nearly burned itself out despite the rather early hour. It could by most inclinations burn cheerily for another couple of hours, but that would require stoking it with a few, fresh pieces of wood. Small flames snake about the charred logs, coals keeping stoically their liquid dance of deep orange and gaseous blue, right at that lovely confluence where heat and luminescence do their elegant exchange of the elements. It is a hypnotic intertwining amidst an otherwise motionless setting.

This all makes for a perfectly lovely scenario, on a night which per the calendar in the kitchen rests benignly up against a day when all manner of celebration and commotion, feasting, gifting, imbibing, chatting, and arguing can and do take place, a holiday where as much dutiful obligation as pure, spontaneous joy is purchased, endeavored, partaken of, remembered.

Tonight, however, still a point in time where one could make ready for family and guests.

Over the toll roads, through the turnpikes, to grandmothers' houses they go. They all go; some in groups, families, some by themselves, in solitude.

All that said, whilst momentarily confined to this cheery, albeit quiet enclosure, there is much here that is not (yet) seen. Here is what *you don't see*:

Grandmother is already in her bed. Or, rather, on it. And she is fully dressed.

As is Grandfather, who happens to still be dressed for work. His cardigan, his trousers, and woolen socks, along with his pajamas, are still all to be found on his valet chair. Wicker backed, arms like small shoulders, always at the ready, the silent valet has no comment, although it is always at the ready.

It is nothing out of the ordinary to see two elderly individuals reclining upon their beds at this somewhat early hour. They are stretched long upon their mattresses in somewhat formal fashion, their legs extending straight out, their respective pairs of feet close together, shod toes pointing upwards. The Grandparents sleep on neighboring twin beds, Desi and Lucy style, which are identically made up: chenille bedspreads with each bed sporting a folded comforter and not one but two hotel-quality feather pillows, stacked at the head, enveloped in two sets of matching shams. Stripes on the top, florals below.

The closet doors stand wide open, as do all the dresser drawers.

The door to the bedroom is closed.

Lying there, neither Grandmother nor Grandfather can hear the holiday music wafting from the living room.

Assorted articles of clothing, formerly folded, lie strewn about. Socks hang over one drawer front, boxer shorts lie in a small heap on the floor. Pantyhose and thermal long johns also hang limply out of half-opened drawers. Grandmother would not like this. Not at all.

But Grandmother will not have an opportunity to rectify this little situation.

Nor will Grandfather, for that matter, even though he was never much troubled with a little disorder, most especially of unmentionables, which he ironically persisted in calling them.

Imagine now, that outside of this bedroom, outside of the living room, as well as the rest of the rooms, the snow has picked up. What had started out as a benign smattering has now become a proper snowfall. And prior to the onset of these fatter, wetter flakes, the wind had, not unlike that old furnace in the cellar, kicked in, and with a similar *whoosh*.

In this very moment, gusts howl like distant, baying hounds. And though Grandmother and Grandfather cannot hear the off-tune whistle coming from the living room chimney flue, they should easily be able to discern the wind cutting around the tall evergreen just outside the bedroom window, whose branches brush repeatedly against the siding, the tree having been planted far too close to the house back when it was built.

The snow is gathering, quickly, filling crevices on the windowsills, the corners of the mullions – it is that heavy, that viscid.

A more robust squall strikes the west wall of the house, causing a shiver-soft tremor to pass through the bedroom, down the hall, past the guest room and bath, and on through of the cheery living room with its tree, its bedecked mantle, the faintly glowing hearth. The *lametta* shifts in unison – barely, barely – a one-two *whoosh*.

Could Grandmother and Grandfather sense the squall, feel its gentle push against the house, they would comment on the power of Mother Nature; they would commend the weatherman for his accurate forecast. They might make for their afghans, perhaps also a shawl or a thicker cardigan, and they would give silent thanks for their comforts, and their safety, and for the fact that they had managed to live in peace for another year, almost to another Christmas, another anniversary.

And this year, twenty by one count and ten by another, it would be for them to finally and at long last have an opportunity to see their estranged grandson, who was due to arrive on Christmas morning.

Ten years gone by, without the Grandparents having heard the first peep from their only grandson, born also of an only child, a son who they had lost ten years before that.

What the Grandparents feel is complicated. What one feels is also vastly different from the other. What each person *really and truly* feels, the other knows nothing about, although it is safe to say, one of them has been decidedly more presumptuous in their assumptions than the other. Arrogance, fear, and a stoically maintained decorum formulated on principles of both courtesy and cold avoidance are the glue that holds these two together.

And you know how that generally plays out.

Ten years are a long time, and twenty can be an eternity. An eternity, if by way of alternating moments of pain and numbness are the increments tallied. To then at last cautiously pop open the final window on *their* particular advent calendar would be to have counted down a series of difficult days until this one. Number twenty-four is about to open.

For, as if by some miracle, the Grandparents *did* hear from him.

And so, he is expected. Was expected.

Although neither one of them knows, knew what to expect.

Although they each had their own notions as to how all this might play out.

Over which, like everything else, not a word was spoken.

Better to carry on, keep on as is, decorate the house again, await the season with all the trimmings and trappings in place. As if everything has been, is, okay. Hence the sparkling tree. Hence the decorated fireplace mantle. Hence the fresh bedding in the guest room, the stocked fridge, the clean towels on the racks, the pine-scented guest soaps by the sink.

Grandmother and Grandfather have, in fact, not really celebrated Christmas in ten years. To them, it became a dispensable holiday ever since. . .

No, they can still not bring themselves to put into words what any one of them allegedly, or actually, had done.

Or to whom.

Never uttered, often thought about, sometimes dreamt about. Memories, nightmares – no difference. A constant source of stress-inducing, fight *and* flight triggering chemical commands which had rendered the Grandmother's heart feeble and irregular, the Grandfather's quickened and tensed.

Why, look at me, he would think to himself, *look how strong It has made me*! Made a man of him. A real man. Like his father, like his father's brothers. Asshole uncles, all of them. The trick always having been, to rise with a mindset leaning towards vengeance, to recast *It* as a form of empowerment. Or, as it were, a martyr's cleansing by fire, by way of adding log after log after log.

Now, that these two elders had had *It* coming at some point, that none of *It* could have been helped in the end, would have made sense to them both, had they been able to discuss any of this before today.

Well, how about counseling? Where things might be brought up? And possibly recorded and notated into caustic light of day? No, the Grandmother did not go there. Grandfather would have raged, had he even gotten wind of Grandmother's having ventured that one, trial visit. Nothing will be spoken of out loud, therefore nothing will be deciphered, nor be given any chance to heal. Sweep *It* all under that rug. Sweep *It* up like everything else gets swept up and off that plush carpeting!

They, the Grandparents, barely manifesting this to their consciousness, actually hate themselves. They also hate each other. They hate themselves in unknown unison for the relief they felt back then when their son was shot dead almost twenty years ago, and again when, ten years later, similarly carried out murders had occurred, and how they had felt relief when their grandson had so suddenly left town after that, granting them a few slivers of presupposition, he may not have done it, even though. . .

They have considered the alternatives, secretly and with shame: had his father not been shot dead, might he have lived to do *It* again? And then, what about. . .?

Is this sort of thing *contagious*? Inherited? Passed down? Passed forward?

The Grandparents hate themselves because they ask these questions, secretly.

Had bad seeds resulted in too much incidental and chemical connection? Was, all this an inevitability? Too much silent bonding and binding – tethering, as it were – over the course of too many generations. Chains forged and worn.

But without anyone ever addressing any single iota of *It,* no one will ever know, especially after tonight.

The songs, the three favorites as you may have imagined them, have finished.

An odd hush hangs pensively in the living room air, for the radio has gone silent. Never a good sign.

Is the power on? How to tell, in this house? The light from an array of battery-powered candles on the coffee table, plus the waning glow of the embers in the hearth, are the only source of illumination. The security light on the utility pole next to the garage does its due diligence from the backside, casting blinds and sheers in the faintest of blue glows. There is no light per se, but the pale walls reflect the gloom, as does the pale carpeting. Even the faded upholstery pays it forward, this weird, wan visibility, this ice-cave sort of radiation. Grandfather had often chided his wife about all the pastels with which they lived, said it belied who actually ran things. . .

If only.

A fourth song to break this silent night? No. Instead, the hoarse voice of a broadcaster cuts in. It is the station manager, interrupting his holly jolly soundscape. The announcer's voice betrays a haggardness. He is being made to relay information he would give anything to not have to share. But he cannot opt-out, cannot avoid resurrecting *It.* A teen when he had last heard of *It,* the station manager had never thought this would factor in his adulthood. He had heard the rumors as a child, leaned in on the hushed conversations amongst adults, remembered the conjecture, the points made connecting what to many seemed obvious disconnects. . . And then again, years later. . .

The city, per the hand-written note he is reading (the consonants sticking to the roof of his mouth), is as of this moment "officially' under lockdown. Which means, everyone is to stay put – home, if at all possible. As if anyone would voluntarily venture out in this weather.

The station manager hopes the weather will help keep everyone home, easily in keeping with the customary holiday hominess that would normally be the case anyway on this night. The announcer prays his family will be safe without him, him now being stuck at the station, which is under lockdown itself, doors already bolted, alarm set. He cannot help that constricting ache at the base of his throat. It literally pains him to repeat the declaration.

Could the Grandparents awaiting their grandson hear this announcement, were they still seated in their living room and not in the bedroom, they would have likewise turned the locks, front and back. They would also have picked up the receiver on the phone, made sure there was still a dial tone. Retrieved the shotgun from its locked closet in the cellar.

Would they have been able to do all that. But *had* they checked their phone, they would have already heard no dial tone. The line would have been dead. Cut. Silence would have greeted their expectant ears, shot cold dread through them. Both fear and recognition would have turned their stomachs, squeezed tight their hearts in a moment of instant, agonized realization. And uncertainty – no details or how's or why's – would have come flooding back. A deluge so sad, so horrible. . .

Twenty years is a long time to live in pain *and* fear, to live with *It*.

Hence, no real Christmases, for all the tangible markers in the living room.

For, *It* had come to be embodied in that young man, that grandson, who still danced unbidden in their old heads. A skeleton in their mutual closet not unlike the two actual skeletons which still lay undiscovered, buried deep under where the compost bin stood, behind the garage. Two bodies, which, ten years ago had been folded up tight as folding rulers and buried like vermin behind the garage, in similar fashion to those who had been killed some ten years before that.

Turns out, the grandson, the Christmas day guest, has indeed already come and gone, and *he* has taken care of *It*. He did not find the watch he had hoped to find, nor the coins, which Grandfather had, incidentally, pawned years ago; but then, he had not set out specifically for those items, so their absence was incidental.

The grandson had come to see his Grandparents. One day early. To set *It* straight.

So, let us look once more in upon the Grandmother and the Grandfather. Their stolid, recumbent poses, feet together, toes pointed at the ceiling. This is due to the fact that each Grandparent has had their ankles bound with duct tape.

And their eyelids, they are open; they are not closed. But they are sightless, empty cavities, for their eyes have been removed. Gouged out, in fact.

And that weak heart of the Grandmother's, it is gone as well. That one barely quivered upon being yanked from its wet cavity.

The much sturdier and robust ticker of the Grandfather's is likewise extracted.

Now, this being a time of miracles, the Grandfather's heart had inexplicably kept beating after being pulled from its ribcage. With his eyes still intact, and wide open in abject terror, the Grandfather witnessed what he had always seen coming. He actually witnessed his own murder. And the grandson, who had held that heart aloft, and seeing that his Gran'pop could somehow still see, had decided on a whim to take a bite of the pulsating muscle for good measure, which he had spat back into the face of its donor. The two had watched, each from their respective spots, their respective realms of love and hate, as almost a dozen waning beats struck their final moments. The two had looked at that bloodied apple, then at each other, then back again to the mass in the grandson's hand, awestruck. Both of them.

A wordless, nearly soundless execution, there in the bedroom. The extractions had taken place quite in silence, being that each one of the Grandparents' mouths had been stuffed with a thick sock selected from that neatly folded array in the dresser drawer. This, to stuff his grandparents' mouths, had been the grandson's first task, once his Grandparents had lain themselves prone on their beds, as he had commanded them to do it.

That trifold mirror over the dresser had even captured the grandson's stoney glance as he had selected the socks, a pair of nearly new woolen ones. The grandson also grabbed a pair for himself. The only pair he owned, the pair he is still wearing, has holes in them.

Funny thing is, there had been nothing of a forced break-in, but an open-armed welcoming in of this guest who had, in fact, arrived a day early. The Grandparents had willingly, almost happily let him in, despite their intuitively knowing what he had done, what he had likely gotten away with. And where from his deeds in all likelihood had been paid forward. The Grandparents had let their Christmas visitor in and then even locked the door behind him, even making sure all the curtains were tightly drawn, to ensure an uninterrupted and unmonitored visit between the three of them.

No, the Grandparents had not expected precisely *this*, although they had both known in their now-absent hearts, they had had *It* coming to them. For a long time.

Gruesome, though, to dismember a couple of old coots like this, even if they did have *It* coming, and most especially unfortunate on a Christmas Eve, of all nights.

Nasty, and oh, so messy, to saturate a pair of nice, clean mattresses, and bedding, with so very much blood.

Funny, though, how despite all that blood, none of it had even made it to the floor. Lucky for the house, I guess, that nowhere were there any tell-tale tracks but for the damp imprint of the boots, going both one way and the other, in the plush carpeting.

Fascinating, too, how all it had taken was for their grandson to utter the command, to follow him to the bedroom, and for the Grandparents to place themselves on their beds, fully clothed, shoes on, and to complacently permit themselves to the strapped down, and for them to *Hold the fuck still* as first a crochet hook and then a switchblade were retrieved from pants pockets, and then as their chests were sliced open and their brittle sternums were punched clean through, first the Grandmother and then the Grandfather, and for a pair of erratically palpitating hearts to be yanked out, one after the other, from their housings. Fascinating, then, how their eyes had been likewise brutally extracted. Neither received any ersatz eyes either – no marbles or glass stoppers – for that was not in the repertoire of the grandson's methods.

It's possible the sock-stuffed mouths had dulled the Grandparents' senses somewhat, deprived them of oxygen, numbed them of some small percentage of their pain. Their adrenaline had to have been, however, kicked into highest gear, so it remains possible they experienced this visitation with heightened senses, that eerie slowing of time, where every pang, every spasm, every bit of panic, was that much more agonizingly registered.

It remains quite likely that the Grandfather could at least still hear and comprehend what the grandson had said to him, when he had leaned over and rapped his knuckles on that bald, freckled head as were he checking to see if anyone was still at home, and as he hissed something along the lines of, . . .*and this, Pops, is for my Father. Damn you to hell, you sick, old fuck. This is for what you did to him, and for what he then did to me. This is the kind of legacy sick mother fuckers like you leave. So, this is me now, giving It aaaall back to you. Merry fucking Christmas, you sick piece of shit!*

In truth, the grandson had no idea, what all had really happened. He had no idea what all had been done to his father, what all his father had endured. But he had known enough, had inherited enough by way of his father's not having been able to set aside what he had experienced. Whatever *It* all was, it was a lethal enough legacy to have spurred this final outcome.

This is why neither the Grandmother nor the Grandfather fought their grandson. Why neither of them resisted, not even one iota. He for his deeds, her for her compliance. Thousands of silent skeletons. How sad for the others, the real ones, four of them back then, and counting, including those two out back, about whom no one will ever know. . .

A psychic had once warned the Grandmother what was still in store for them. This had occurred in an odd moment's altercation, polite enough, at the local library, about five years ago. Turns out, that became the last time the Grandmother ever went to the library. It was, in fact, the last time she went to town. All what was left for the Grandmother to do was to cook and clean and bake.

It happened to be the Grandfather who taken the phone call that came late one night, soon after Thanksgiving. It was he who had spoken words of welcome to the caller who was, yes, checking in to see if these two were still among the living, still at the same house on the edge of town.

So, here they lie. Nothing as poetic as a stake of holly through their hearts. Only wet, blackened holes where once eyes had been, where hearts had beaten. Only a few torn garments; a blouse, a red velvet coat, the buttons off of a shirt. Only two mattresses and bedding drenched in blood, wet and acrid. Only a bathroom sink stained pink, and a pine-scented soap coated in sticky, red froth. While the grandson had been as deft as a battlefield surgeon in the bedroom, he had not been interested in masking fingerprints, nor his tracks. This was someone on a death wish path. The demons, Satan – whatever you want to call *them,* were close by, lifting the wings of the grandson's soul. They would not leave empty-handed.

And being that this pair of Grandparents had now faced their retribution, and that the devil had got his due, there is nothing left but for the house but to continue to exist in its passive status quo.

Grandmother's last words to her visitor had been a whispered plea to *please, dear, close the doors* on his way out.

And so, this is why the bedroom door is closed, as are all the doors to the house. It is why the tinsel hangs undisturbed, and why the embers are unstirred, nearly extinguished. This is why the living room, with its tree, its cards, its virgin candles, subsists so quaintly and festively innocent, so pensively in-waiting for the official start of a holiday which will now never be celebrated, but for a homecoming that did come one day early.

Turns out, this long-awaited guest, who had come back to pay back what he had been dealt, is now himself gone.

Turns out, there had occurred more than plenty of giving and sharing between the three of them.

Turns out, two sets of eyeballs and two dripping, vein-dangling hearts had already been left behind in town, in a single, steaming heap, right there in the manger at First Lutheran. Laid right up alongside the Baby Jesus, a doll the pastor's wife had outfitted some years ago with a white flannel swaddling cloth and wire halo stuck into its rubber temples.

Turns out, First Lutheran was of all places right next door to the police station. It is their gruesome discovery which triggered the town-wide alert, which at this point in time can only be disseminated via the local radio station. Just before going on air, the station manager had inquired of the sheriff, *Couldn't y'all just sound the tornado sirens?* The sheriff, thinking of the traffic issue potentials, and then about that cold six pack in the fridge, had guffawed and said the townsfolk would either ignore the sirens or be crazed and confused by them, and that it would only make things worse.

Turns out, when the manager did break in to announce the alert, he knew of the gory details, had instantly recognized the gruesome signature of the killer from his teenage years. But that killer had been presumed dead, out of commission. A body had been found, which had matched the vague descriptions of the suspect enough to satisfy both the do-nothing sheriff and his inept prosecutor. Tonight, however, with a fresh set of body parts discovered in the manger at First Lutheran, which details the announcer was not permitted to disclose, everything was back on the table. The station manager hoped, prayed, that at least a few astute citizens were listening, and heeding his warning.

The killer, way back then, he had done *It* in pairs. Four victims, killed in two sets of two. Eyes and hearts.

And about ten years after that, some other fiend had done it in the just same way, to the same number of people. Two sets of two. Eyes and hearts. The difference being, only the first perpetrator had been caught, shot point blank in the head in his parents' driveway, the story always having been, he'd been on his way to take his son back by force – kidnap the kid, as it were. That son, a gangly boy the station manager could still remember from confirmation class, had started coming to church with his

Grandparents a few years before the shooting. Those Grandparents, they lived a few miles outside of town. And that grandfather – he didn't like that one. That was one weird, old fuck who had, of all things, played Santa at Segel's Department Store for as long as he could remember.

Who will be next?

Turns out, Grandmother and Grandfather *are* the next ones. The second set of two. As yet undiscovered, as it will remain for weeks, being that the weather is about to take a major downturn. This snowstorm which will go down in the books as the big one of the decade, and the Grandparents will remain undiscovered nearly until spring.

Turns out, the first set of two on this Christmas Eve, to whom the body parts in the manger belonged, were a couple of students who had themselves traveled back home for the holidays. Their bodies had been found behind the dumpster in the alley behind First Lutheran, by the church custodian. These victims had been made quick work of, for their killer had had more important plans. He was expected somewhere else.

Back to that house now, where everything remains quiet, almost dormant.

It must now be added, off to the side, behind the wiry honeysuckle on his own makeshift bed lies the Christmas Eve visitor himself. The grandson's bloodied switchblade and mottled crochet hook have both sunk into the fresh snow, having slipped out of his pockets and weighted themselves into their resting places, where they will also reside for some weeks before being discovered. The grandson lies face-down. He never made it to his car, which is still parked offsides in the brush at the end of the driveway.

For you see, before the grandson had exited the house, he had helped himself to the plate of cookies Grandmother had left out especially for Grandfather to commemorate his last stint of the season at Segel's. This particular batch of cookies possessed the customary almond flavoring Grandmother was known to use in her baking, but these had an odd edge to their sweetness. The grandson had idly noticed this as he had scarfed down the entire plateful. They had tasted good, though. So good. Chronically malnourished, the grandson, still lanky, almost gaunt, he was always hungry. Grandmother, in typical and proper fashion, had set the cookies out on a hand-painted cake plate. How pretty, how sweet, and of all things, *for that motherfucker,* the grandson had idly mused as he finished off the last of them

The cookies, Grandmother had planned on baking – and "spicing" – for her husband for some time now. This plan, she had finally, actively implemented, setting for herself a deadline she had intended to set for years, which this upcoming surprise visit by their grandson would *not* deter. Some things were meant to be, and whatever the outcome, she was ready to work with it. Grandmother had even dared fancy a sort of fairytale ending, wherein she could leave with her grandson, disappear in a sense, start life somewhere else as some old single, anonymous lady, a widow or a spinster.

But fairytales are not real, nor can happy endings be cherry-picked by violent perpetrators or their good etiquette keeping henchmen.

These almond-flavored cookies, Grandmother had baked during her final day at home alone, while Grandfather had been busy at work on his last day at the store. Seated there on his throne, he had eagerly foisted one, bony, waifish ass after another onto his despicably receptive lap, always angling, re-arranging the brats, pressing for more, more, more, hugging and squeezing and kissing those little shits until they cried real tears, which the parents always, oddly, thought was so fucking cute, which had always warmed Santa to his. . .to his. . .let's call it his core. . .

Grandfather's red velvet Santa hat had kept his bald head nicely covered for the duration of many a December at the store, so much so, he had often kept it on at night once home, while he lounged in his easy chair and listened to the radio. He had always thought the tasseled cap stood him handsomely well; that is, up until the moment the grandson had yanked it from his head and placed it atop his own head, over his greasy, long hair. The red velvet cap now lies on the snow-covered ground, right above the grandson's head. Bloody vomit can be seen to either side of the grandson's half-buried face. Death came quickly to the grandson, but agonizingly so. He expired knowing only pain and hurt, in addition to that perpetual hunger of his. As for Grandmother, she had managed her final foray in baking to perfection; and although her own escape plan had fallen quite flat, it had only partially backfired. Perhaps a few more sets of two will have been spared. Eyes and hearts.

The birds in the branches overhead, oblivious to *It* all, begin to twitter. They serenade by pure happenstance the corpse below them. The birdsong urges on the reluctant, winter sun, assuring it to hold on for just another minute, until the earth has turned enough on its axis enough to permit her this first glance over the eastern edge of this much bigger shadowbox display. Their tittering ushers in this year's Christmas Day – for happy, groggy families with their greedy offspring squealing like piglets; for the far less happy, heartbroken souls who will face this day alone; for anyone or anything at all participating in this next revolution of our beautiful but indifferent Earth. The birds, they can detect the benevolent, life-gifting light before any of us humans can ever hope to. And so, the birds will keep adding their *cheep cheep* programming to the Christmas carols now playing on radios everywhere, including those emanating from that console in the living room, where there is no one left to turn it off. I am certain this next song, the one playing right now, is an old favorite of yours, too.

This story is a Goffmanesque Frame Analysis inspired narrative dedicated to:
~ My husband, who introduced me to this sociologist's illustrative, picture-in-picture methodology
~ The cleverly accessible narrative stylings of Chuck Palahniuk
~ Laird Koenig and his 1974 THE LITTLE GIRL WHO LIVES DOWN THE LANE. I don't know how many times I read this book. And the almond-flavored cookies, they are a nod to the methods therein.

The Khrystmass Elf

My eyes pop open, wide. Unblinkingly, I peer up into the familiar, velvet-black opaqueness. I never did need bedside candles or lamps to feel "safe." But something – some jarring disturbance – has registered in my subconscious, hurled me into wakefulness.

Did I. .?

Yes! I did!

I lie perfectly still, not closing my eyes even for a moment, even though I cannot see a thing. On highest alert, I feel compelled to *listen* with every sense I possess.

And there! There it is again!

I know what I heard!

But I dare not awaken Mother or Father. I am small, I am quick. I can and, yes, I will seek out whatever it is I just heard, meet up with it – whatever it may be – as one who is both brave and daring, one who will be able to render herself nigh invisible by way of all the wily and sneaky small-child skills she can muster. I can do this; I know I can! My curiosity overrides the latent onset of fear I might want to indulge in, so it is my primary drive I will heed, and appease. I cannot help it, having been wired the way that I was, the way that I am.

I rise slowly, lifting myself into a seated position, easing my knob-kneed legs up under me. I roll back the coverlet, and as I extract myself, I tuck my doll back underneath the quilted satin, for she must remain safely ensconced in our bed whilst *I* venture out, the fledgling huntress, the urchin sleuth. If *this* little girl is to be pursued by thieves, stealing their way into her house at some ungodly hour like this, she must hurry! Dolly will understand. Dolly will wait. It could be, it is a monster in our house – perhaps a whole herd of them – snuck indoors to wreak havoc on us all! There is no doubt in my mind, that whatever I do encounter, it, or they, will be positively *fiendish*.

I am already quite fully dressed, having slept in my knit stockings, which are so pretty, so lacey. My ruffle-edged shawl is securely fastened around my shoulders. I wear a sleeping gown which, suitable for this time of year, is a heavy one, and quite ornate at that – ribbons, satin rosettes, tiny pearl buttons. My mother is partial to this sort of fashion. But the gown's fabric is perfect. It is of the softest wool and will generate no tell-tale rustle whatsoever. This dress will serve me wonderfully well tonight as I navigate the dark chambers and passageways, make my way towards the booming sound I *know* I did not imagine. I must take care, however, to remain wholly out of sight. Now, *were* the interloper to catch sight of me, I would no doubt appear to them like some small, luminous spectre, afloat in a white cloud of a dress, possibly quite innocuous, perhaps a little bit spooky. The notion thrills me but is of no use to me, and so I cast that fanciful thought aside. I must be as secretive and clever as a jewel thief on the prowl.

I know the house well, know every clandestine path, every shielding turn, every physical visual obstacle behind which I can tuck my petite self as I make my way through the labyrinthian brownstone I and my family have called home for I don't know how long. It will be easy to navigate to whichever room it is, where my quarry happens to be lurking. And I will accomplish this with virtually no fear of being detected. I am *that* confident.

I do feel a tickling inkling of fear, but I am cognizant how this curl of anticipation twists in my belly, and how that *energizes* me. I have long wanted to prove myself to my parents – they are so loving, so terribly, suffocatingly loving and protective of me, it has been a somewhat stifling thing to be their daughter. Tonight can perhaps turn out to be the perfect night to show them what I can do. Mama and Papa even treat me at times – which is far too often – as were I still some sort of *baby*, and I am not an infant at all! They have no idea what all I do know. I think they make it a point to not even *try* to fathom what I am capable of. It leaves me cast as the darling girl-child, which of course I do oblige. It is a sort of game, isn't it? Nevertheless, I want to prove myself to them. Surprise them. Make them nod their heads in agreement, that they may have underestimated their little sweetie pie. It is possible, my parents might become angry with me, especially Papa, but I can persevere against this sort of reaction and ultimately override any initial anger or dismay. I *will* do this. It is, after all, that time of year, which means, time to get going.

I take leave of my baby doll, my snug nook. I slink through the first rooms, almost slithering in my trepidation-inspired stealth mode. I cannot, can absolutely not, awaken my parents.

I make no sound. I am as furtive as a feral kitten, as determined as the tiniest spider – all eyes, all seeing. Wary and small, I am able to make myself disappear in the blink of an eye. Behind a partition, a swath of curtain, a fringed tablecloth draped nearly to the floor. I feel quite brave, toy with notions of an imaginary invisibility; of invincibility too, as I invoke fairy tale methods and folkloric powers of the ancients so to prepare myself for the worst – or the best, as it were. I climb first these stairs, then those, and then turn countless corners as I make my way down the long hallways which eventually bring me to the head of the broad, central passage which will lead me to the grand salon and its glassed-in vestibule, where I can investigate as I clandestinely stand my ground. I must first actually see who – or what – it is that made that terrible sound, and where. I believe it was a rapping against heavy wooden planking, likely against one of the shutters in one of the street level rooms. And that it may have come from a window being tested for its accessibility. I must assess the infiltration, calculate the risk, and formulate a plan.

Father has always chided me on my great and silly wish, which is to meet up with a real monster, face-to-face. He tells me, my imagination ought to try and keep up with the rest of me. Yes, well, I am precocious. And terribly adorable, but I am as well-read as I am anything else. I can safely say, I have learned through both research and trial and error how to employ girlish wiles, how to get what I want, get things done my way. I really do get my way most the time, come to think of it. This has been going on for what seems like forever. But my antics contribute nicely to a happy family dynamic most inclusive of fun, of laughter too, where *all* roles are played to the hilt. And so, we all let it be. Being that there are no siblings to compete with, our small family remains a rather solitary trio, and our hierarchy a simple one. We live quite autonomously, as well our ancestors did – still do, some of them, in far-off lands where my parents, refugees in a sense, refuse to return to. Tragic bygones, they call them, although they have yet to share with me what all really happened. Still, Mama and Papa convey, when they do share kernels of their pasts with me, a wistful longing in their looks, their tones of voice, which even I in my relative immaturity can pick up on, even though my experiences have yet to include any kind of the tragic stuff which might make one's gaze linger like that, one's voice trail off with sadness. . .

In this moment, however, it is accurate to say, I have other quite important eggs in my basket; and with both Mother and Father still asleep for the time being, this is my time.

Oh, it is dark up here in the hall. Not a single glimmer of illumination. No lamp, no hearth fire. No staff. No signs of life at all. The curtains, massive lengths of velvet, are tightly drawn, as are the shutters behind them, carved panels taller even than my father. Everything is latched tight against the elements, against meddlesome passersby, neighbors we prefer to keep at arm's length. Not even the second-hand reflections of bouncing, shifting moonlight can worm its way into the rooms to dispel the darkness. Here and there however, hairline splits between the windows' panels and drapes permit the smallest, striated slivers of white to splay across the hall floor, as had snipped ends of a silken floss been laid out to demarcate any given window's centerline. As I kneel behind a brass planter, I reach out to touch one such thread – just barely – with my fingertip. I make believe I can feel a vestigial warmth; such is my acumen when paired with my ever-present flights of fancy. *So many talents, my precious*, Mother always says with an indulgent smile. I do love to learn; I do love to play.

Quiet! Freeze!

I am a like my dolly. No breath, no hint of movement.

Hold on. No. . . Yes.

I *did* hear something. And now, I can see something! The smallest suggestion of a foreign light source has crept onto the hall runner, out from under the door at the end of the corridor.

The monsters are here. And they are turning the doorknob slowly. . . slowly. . .

The beastly intruder – how many are there? – is trying to be as surreptitious as I am. But it's not working. My advantages, including their ignorance of my presence, will serve me far better than anything they think they have going.

I can see now what the source of the light is. It is a lantern, held just back behind the door's front edge. I can discern its small form by way of the hard, black corner of its frame, starkly outlined in shadow. A hairy wrist, bony and deformed as one broken at least once or twice before, is attached to even bonier, hair-knuckled tentacles, which hold fast to the lantern's handgrip. Serrated claws black with filth protrude grotesquely from each tentacle; they are the cracked and diseased hooks from which a fever-inducing infection is but a slashing grab away.

Atop the lantern, I spy a lurid, yellow eye slithering out from behind the door. It is bloodshot and brimming with a thick, oozing mucous. I can feel my stomach roiling at the sight of that repulsive organ. The orb rolls and ogles, attempting to override its weak and compromised capabilities in order to peer further into the darkness, discern some sense of depth, gain an inkling of place, detect anyone in here on guard, awaiting it, them.

There is no second eye. Nothing emerges after the first yucky eyeball, to follow the warty beak that has next presented itself. Instead, there is only an empty cavity, ripe with a deforming decay, eating away at its ragged edges. I practically retch upon realizing, what a monstrously ugly death's mask it is I am forced to behold.

Oh, the hideousness of this beast, which has come prowling into my home, my family's home, to do. . . to do. . . what? What does it want from us?

I smile a mean, little smile, for that affords me no betraying reveal of cover.

I think I know what has brought the monster here.

Whatever else I think I might know, I also know that nothing will change the dire fact that I must remain on highest, highest guard. I must be ready to flee in the flap of a bat's wing. I suppose I must be ready to fight as well, even if my actions might amount to little more than the crazed flailings of a manhandled rat, which I do admit is a stretch, given that I can already tell from the height at which that goggling eye is seated, this creature is a big one. A sunken and scarred cheek has now been likewise exposed, stretched taut between the jagged ledge of a cheekbone and its corresponding, Neanderthalic jowl. The leather-clad skull of a giant! A gargantuan, hideous giant. Yes, that is what this beastly, ghastly thing is. A positively monstrous monster!

Imagine the surge of dread which overcomes me when I *then* see a second gruesome countenance press forward, immediately beneath the hoary, worm-ridden chin of that first monster. A second set – this time a set of two – waxen eyeballs push their way into the space just beyond the door. The pale, dead orbs roll about, jittery, faultily playing about on their wiring, trying to take in what lies beyond the cover of the open door. Trying to see into this vast and elegant and pristine space which is my beloved home – my mother's and my father's, and mine. Our lovely and beautiful and untarnished domestic universe.

How dare they mark this place, infest the very air they are displacing with their base presence, their utter decrepitness!

I can smell them. They reek of rot. Rot and mold. I can all but discern the maggots that no doubt creep up their sallow and crinkled visages, and the half-digested flesh that is left in their tracks. The monsters emanate decay – it seeps visibly – I can see that much from this far away. From every orifice, every oily pore, from every slimy trail of fat and muscle which maps their nightmarish faces, flow the very energies of two creatures not even hell itself would welcome.

The bilious cloud they exude makes me want to retch. Again, and again. But I do not. I remain stone still. I am a statue. I am a doll. Whilst on guard, I will endure the poison that hovers over them, drifts beyond them, like some acid green cloud within which only monsters like that could possibly exist. They emanate a fetid beastliness with every exhalation. The air of the Underworld, indeed, is what inflates their lungs – or whatever fleshy pockets are held within their cavernous breasts – and gets siphoned back out into *my* atmosphere, tainting it, befouling it.

In keeping with their slug-like progression into my home, the monsters continue to push their bulbous masses further past the door, farther in and into the sacred space that is my world. I make the rash decision to dash from my hiding place. I will head with intent into the butler's pantry, whose twin doorways lead one way into the library and the other into the dining room. I let myself become that small ghost as I run. The skirt of my dress catches the breeze of my flight, and as a small blur of shadowed white I flit across the hall, catching the monstrous duo's eyes as planned. I disappear again behind the door.

I know the monsters will follow.

No two seconds pass before I hear the *clomp clomp clomp* of their hooves; their beastly, meaty feet, whatever they may be. The monstrous duo possesses the feathered tread of elephants, for creatures like this have neither the build nor intellectual capacity to move quietly or clandestinely. They must, like dim-witted dragons or pea-brained dinosaurs, rely solely on their heft for impact and advancement. Therein lie all advantages with such a one like me – quick as a flicker, bright as a spark, crafty as a wizard's elfin spawn.

In two winks I have re-established myself behind the cover of an iron-banded wine barrel set into one corner of the pantry. I await the inevitable. And from there, once again, I will track the monsters' repeated offensive, undertaken at their same, slug-worthy pace, which is to first sketch a path by way of that small lantern's light, after which, one after the other, the monsters will proceed to slowly push in, guided by their ogling, clouded eyes, until they then imbue this space as well with their ever-present fog of putrefaction.

But I am caught off-guard, for the monsters have grown bolder. They, with their deformed skulls with their mottled patches of skin barely covering the jutting precipices and crevices of their disgusting features in some horrific mockery of humanoid affectation, thrust themselves all at once into the small room. What happens next is truly the stuff of nightmares: they both tear open their rubbery maws and begin to howl in unison. They have spotted me, and they are either roaring at me in some form of animal speak, or they simply wish to frighten me. But while they think they have found me; it is in fact *I* who have lured them here.

The one monster, the tall one, flexes its blubbery, stained lips so to expose what looks like a crooked row of charred beeswax candles stuck into a fleshy length of blackened gums. Spittle sprays as it chokes and sputters and proceeds to vomit the following words, full force and so bellicose that it causes my delicate eardrums to pop:

"WHA' 'AVE YOU DONE WI' OUR FOOKING KID?"

I slap my hands over my ears, the pain nearly unbearable. I have never experienced this kind of assault, this audial boxing of the ears which is so profound, it causes my entire head to buzz. Even my chest hurts, as if the wave of sound was such that it had the capacity to strike me a solid blow. If this is what monsters can do to me by merely opening their mouths and bellowing at me, there is no telling what they might do, were they to have the opportunity to lay their stinking paws on me, sink their claws into my skin. . .

So, what else is there for me to do?

I scream in reply.

I scream that scream only little girls can scream. It is a shriek worthy of a rabid banshee. A furiously raving, screeching fury. I have heard of decibels; Papa talked of them once, not terribly long ago. Had, in fact, once told me of a late-night conversation he had with a Mr. Bell, a man who is evidently crafting some conceptual language by which to measure volume. Well, if the scream I scream could be measured, I would say it would have to measure gobs and gobs of decibels. Oodles of them!

I scream loud enough for my parents to hear. That is with intention at this point. My scream is like that of a siren – both kinds – the wail blasts unchecked through the house. It shoots through every keyhole, plays the banisters like xylophones, it reverberates through every wall and down every hall, ringing and echoing all the way up, all the way down, this way and that and further still, and then down, down, into the network of catacombs below the second cellar. I could raise anyone from the dead with my scream, Mama has said. Oh, how my parents do love their sleep, but seeing not who but *what* has infiltrated our home, this matter has become something my parents can far better contend with than just little old me, as I must confess, I rather suspected from the get-go, might ultimately be the case.

The ghastly creatures start to advance on me. They are encumbered in myriad ways, these lumbering imbeciles; every laborious step is now even more slowed down due to the fact that they have intertwined their hairy, scar-lined arms, as if in some desire to co-join their forms into one larger, more ominous beast in the way other, primitive creatures – like small fish, or ants – do it. As one hideous mass do they proceed towards me, one lopsided step after another, to a point where they will very soon have me cornered.

But the monsters are so bumbling, that before a third step is taken, before they are even half-way across the room in line towards where I am crouching like a frightened ladybug behind a massive, old barrel Papa had set there ages ago, my parents quite literally materialize in the doorway opposite them. One moment, the empty doorway was a pitch-black cavity leading into the rest of the house. But in the next moment, it is a frame, at which center, there they stand. Regal, and with a sort of calm that is *quite* menacing. My parents' presentation of self comes in starkest contrast to the fetid hominid coagulation that must now bear witness to them.

My parents are, like I am, still dressed in their sleep attire, but that is to say, they are dressed in elegant, heavy garments. It is simply the way we spend our sojourns whilst in our slumbering phases. But I have never seen them so drained of color. My parents' perfectly expressionless faces are like those of ancient, classical statues – so beautiful, they look unreal. Their dark eyes are fathomless, yet hard as obsidian, utterly impenetrable. I recognize their mood. It exists as a single, quantifiable aura of explosive energy, held momentarily in check – absolutely still, calm as a toxic cave pool, wholly devoid of any sign of life.

The monsters appear to be in some kind of shock. What did they expect? They too stand stock still, but their expressions are of abject fear, coupled with a primitive rage in the face of a turn of circumstances their imbecilic sensibilities may not be able to register for some long seconds yet to come. I do believe they have quite forgotten to breathe.

"Darling," Papa addresses me as he eyes the monstrous interlopers, "who are these, these *people*," he sneers the pejorative, "and do you have anything to do with their being here, tonight?"

"Papa, I can. . ." I start in, my voice intoning a lilt which I have learned can help me deliver a confession with minimal consequences.

My mother sighs, rolls her eyes. "Sweetheart. . ." she too begins.

But before anyone of us can finish a single sentence – and mind you this takes place in seconds – the co-joined beast lurches forward. It clearly has the intention to come after me.

Again, the taller one of the two roars, gutturally spitting every consonant, wet acids weeping rivulets down both sides of its pock-marked chin.

"WHA' 'AVE YOU DONE WI' OUR FOOCKING KID, YOU FOOKING. . ."

All four paws are now reaching for me. Two sets of ten fungus-ridden, cracked claws are grasping at the air and getting closer, closer to me as I. . .

And with that, my mother glides forward, crosses the small distance with the swift smoothness of an arrow shot by Diana herself. She takes one ragged sleeved, diseased forearm of each beast into her own hands. Her long nails pierce each hairy arm, effectively embedding her fingertips in their rotting flesh, her piercing grip like that of an iron maiden. Bruises explode and blossom beneath the beasts' hides, dark purple shadows growing visibly and spreading like stains beneath the canvas covering their veiny and mottled limbs. Blood pools around my mother's entrenched fingertips and begins to drip in time to what are, evidently, heartbeats. Glistening crimson threads trail to the floor, forming bloody puddles that spread and even give off steam, for it is exceedingly cold in this room, as it is in every room of the house. It is that time of year.

Both monsters howl in pain. I realize, they are little more than a pair of sick and mangy trapped creatures, more animal than any far nobler, mythical monster would ever be.

The smaller of the two somehow yet manages to regurgitate a few more primitive syllables as the spittle flies from its flapping jowls.

"GIVE US BACK OUR BAIRN! IT DI'N'T NOT DO NOTTIN' TO YE!"

"Oh, shut up," is all my mother says, again rolling her eyes. With a sweep of her arm, she flings the taller of the two in Father's direction. Father, with barely any visible motion, with nary a hair nor cravat nor silken sash moved out of place, immediately wraps one arm around the monster. His elegant, long fingers sink into the depths of the creature's thick neck until it begins to moan again, then to wail, whilst the blood, still leaking from its punctured arm, grows yet another messy, rug-staining puddle on the floor.

"I suspected as much, dear," Papa says to my mother.

"Yes, love, you did warn me of this stage; I just didn't think it would come quite this fast. . ." Mama glances my way, shaking her head.

"It is what it is, darling," Papa rationalizes in my defense.

To me, my father's tone of voice resonates with an authority that is insurmountable, even to me. Papa looks lovingly at me as he holds fast to the wriggling mass of whatever it is.

"Sweetheart, *what* have you done?" he demands, a stern emphasis placed on the *what,* as any astute parent would do it.

"Papa," I begin, but then I also start to cry, knowing I can let my infantile guard down now that I am safe again, for certain, now that my parents have detained these two disgusting creatures. I also know that tears will always help the cause.

"But, but, I just wanted to surprise you. . ."

I sniffle for effect and continue.

"It's Khrystmass Eve and I wanted to surprise you! I loooove you and Mama and. . ."

"Oh, dear," my mother says, touched – I think – a little. She has by this time wrapped one of her arms around the smaller creature's neck, her long, satin-smooth tines splayed across its hideous face to muffle it. I do not know how she can bring herself into this close of contact with something this dirty and pestilence ridden.

"Love, what *have* you done?" my mother persists. "What have you done for Mummy and Daddy that has brought these, these *people* to our home and into our midst? You know full well that. . ."

"Mama, Mama" I shed a few more tears, "I found an elf for you for Khrystmass! I found a pretty and fat and plump, soft Khrystmass elf for you! And I was going to give it to you upon waking this evening – as a gift! For Khrystmass! It is my present to you both!"

The beasts, one whose mouth is still covered my mother's hand, the other still in the vice-grip of my father's, both start up again with their bellowing, their bulbous limbs flailing. They even try to kick their hind legs but achieve nothing more than a reptilian sort of wriggling, which just irritates my parents even more, makes them tighten their already steel-hard grips. Wet globs of oily liquid leak from the corners of the monsters' bloodshot eyes. The smaller one is positively blubbering; it is quite incoherent, the cacophony being worse than a disordered melee on some barnyard butchering day: beasts bleating, children weeping, fathers yelling, axes flinging, mothers screeching as they whip their dishcloths and wooden cooking spoons at both the children and headless livestock, all running amok in circles around them. What a mess, all this ugly sound, all this commotion.

But I keep on with my drama-laced entreaties, to help underscore the depth of my good intention, despite the way my love-founded ruse has almost come to backfire on all three of us.

It was, is, all for the sake of a gift of love for my parents.

Father's attention has been piqued. I do know, he is bound to be hungry. Famished, in fact. It has been not one but two days since he has had anything. Same for mother. It is that sleep thing of theirs, how they love to remain curled up together, and to hibernate through not one but two days at a time sometimes, especially when the nights are this long, this cold. This time of year, there is ample time to glean our harvests, with more than enough time after that to while away quiet, studious hours within the peace-filled realm that is our world.

My parents happen to be hungry now, and they are curious. Never to dilly dally, they make quick work of things.

Father deftly encircles the taller monster's neck both hands and twists them, one this way and one that, until the ugly mug of the creature is peering sightlessly backwards over Father's shoulder. The *snap snap snap* of ripping cartilage and crushing vertebrae is as staccato a grating as were it the gears of a big clock being forced forward by several hours. It reminds me also of the rats parading down our subterranean passageways, with their minuscule claws going *click click click* upon the floors of the catacombs where our beds are situated, which gives me the creeps something awful.

Mother is the more creative one of the adults in our little family. She, instead of imitating Father's quick dispensation with the taller creature, with her grip still firmly around the shorter one's neck, forces a slender hand deep into the beast's gullet, and amidst a horrific chorus of gaggling chortles spewing from that one's yap, pulls out the entire length of its tongue. This Mama does as she closes her other hand into a fist, thereby squeezing the beast's pliant, newly emptied larynx into a tight wad of lumpish sausage casing. The wet crunching of ligaments is less pronounced, given that all is muffled by the protruding flapper. The beast's gurgling soon wanes, its cries tapering off to a quivering litany of spasms. It finally goes limp, slides to the ground, and expires.

Father tosses the twist-headed carcass on top of the fleshy heap of its companion.

My parents wipe their hands on linen towels my mother has retrieved from a cupboard next to the wine barrel. The blood- and spittle-drenched, yellow-skinned, limbs on the floor have folded in on themselves. What was a pair of gruesome monsters has been immediately reduced to a stinking heap of humanoid offal. No doubt Father will incinerate these two just as soon as possible. They will go into the furnace fire intact; in other words, untapped. No one in our family would dare partake of creatures this *base*. One could catch something, something truly bad. Monsters of this vile composition, in death, they are merely dreck, not even fit for a wicked witch's garden compost heap.

Mama faces me. I have ceased my crying, have dispensed with the emotionality that, while I know it is still more or less expected of me, does have its limits. My mother is not a chatty woman, never has been. Most of the words I have ever heard coming from her have come in the form of the stories she has read to me. That is our cherished connection. Although I am an avid and expert reader myself, my mother has held onto this one predilection of hers with me, with which I have gladly played along, always will. With her dulcet voice, Mama reads to me, and I listen, listen, and listen to her. As if I could not otherwise do so myself. I meekly await her verdict in the face of the situation I inadvertently created, and the bit of drama I subsequently managed to deliver.

Turns out, she has something for me.

"Darling girl," my mother starts in, "we do have something for you, too. But in return, you must confess to us what oh what on Earth you have done. What have you come up with? You must show us now, so that we may understand if your gift might cause us to be confronted with more of these, these, *people*." Mother's voice falls to a whisper when she speaks that vile word. "But, as it is, I have a gift for you too. A book, darling. A lovely, lovely book I shall read to you this very evening. It is about a ghost – and not just one ghost but several. Four, in fact. And I had the lovely man who wrote it sign it. That was some years ago. I have kept it a secret from you, a surprise, until now, for I wanted to save it for a just-right moment to give it to you. So come now, let your Mother push you to a quick resolution with this elf situation you speak of, and you shall receive your gift from me."

"From us," Papa adds with a smile as he drops his blood-soaked hand towel onto the pile of dead monsters.

Very well. I will be a good girl and quickly reveal what I have in store for my parents, for I do understand now, how it could present us with more issues, were there more monsters to come in pursuit of my elf, or even the dead ones over there. It is, after all, that time of year; we have awakened into that most special and happiest of Khrystmass Eve nights. A time indeed when families would be driven to seek each other out, including and most especially for festivities, and for celebrating. It is a time for gratitude, which at least the three of us share in droves.

I escort my parents out of the butler's pantry and through the dining room, and then down a small flight of stone steps which lead to a subterranean root cellar, where once upon a time apples, potatoes, things like that, filled its deep shelves. I guide my mother and father to a large box on one shelf, whose lid is affixed with a series of decorative latches. The box is of a carved shale, far too heavy to move; it has sat here for ages, for as long as I can remember. The box is long, and black, and decorated with cuneiform swirls which I know are some sort of ancient lettering.

My elf is here, inside this box.

My elf is in this box, because no matter how long or hard it may have cried or screamed or wailed, this box's stone sides will have contained and stifled the horrible noisemaking of my gift wonderfully well, and kept that fun element of happy astonishment – of a happy, merry Khrystmass surprise – intact. And my ruse of attainting a mouth-watering elfin vessel for my parents' Khrystmass dinner – and well, mine, too, for just a sip does it – will have been a wonderous and delightful success.

You see, I am as ruthless as I am precocious and cute.

Papa lifts the lid, claps his hands with delight.

To my relief, my elf is still alive. It kicks up a fuss. All the better to spike all that fresh, untainted blood with a skosh of primordial panic. My father has always claimed, there is nothing else like the taste of sweet fear.

"Well, Merry Khrystmass, indeed, to our darling girl! Well done, you!" Papa exclaims as he extracts the wriggling thing from its makeshift bed and holds it out towards Mother, for her, for all of us to see.

"Darling dear," Father says to his wife with gallant aplomb, "after you."

†††

Mother reads to me whilst I follow the words, albeit surreptitiously. She is pretending I cannot read, as am I.

Father reads from his own volume, a history of some long-forgotten city. This book, he tells me, he discovered at a monastery, in a secret library the monks would access by way of a hidden staircase built into the walls of a crypt. Papa has promised to take me with him, someday, when he goes back to get some more books. He loves to pretend I am as yet too young and small to venture out into such places. I love to pretend these places might still frighten me.

Mama continues:

"...he looked the phantom through and through, and saw it standing before him; though he felt the chilling influence of its death-cold eyes; and marked the very texture of the folded kerchief bound about its head and chin, which wrapper he had not observed before; he was still incredulous, and fought against his senses."

And presently comes to:

"But how much greater was his horror, when the phantom taking off the bandage round its head, as if it were too warm to wear indoors, its lower jaw dropped down upon its breast!

Scrooge fell upon his knees, and clasped his hands before his face.

'Mercy!" he said. "Dreadful apparition, why do you trouble me?'

'Man of the worldly mind!" replied the Ghost, "do you believe in me or not?'

'I do," said Scrooge. "I must. But why do spirits walk the earth, and why do they come to me?'

Whereupon my mother gently closes the book, signaling that our story time is ended. I whinny impishly but only briefly, for she knows that I know, when it is time for bed, it is time for bed.

I glance towards the east-facing window, as does my mother, both of us noting the horizon, as we have for decades. The faintest brushstrokes of a deep azure push against the pitch-black edge of the night sky, signaling the close of our "day." This suggestion of light – all we can afford our eyes – plays against the countless buildings of the city, now also outlined by snow that has fallen overnight. It has glazed the rooflines, a gentle, fairy-land dusting of a cityscape none of us ever tire of.

Khrystmass Day is about to dawn. So many plump and juicy tots will soon be waking up to. . .

Father has already returned his book to the small stack that lives upon his side table, there with his spectacles, his never-used snuff boxes. My parents turn down the flames of the two lamps which have illuminated our cozy library, leaving the room now in a far more restful, fully darkened state. Already I can feel myself grow sleepy. We have our cues, we sink deliciously, too.

"Give us a kiss, my love," Mother brushes her lips against the crown of my head.

"And now, off you go," she says. "We must be at it. Oh my, how I can use this sleep. I am full to the brim! Nothing like indulging from time to time, though, all thanks to our darling daughter."

Papa winks as Mama speaks.

"We were only obliging our daughter's generosity," he chides, contented as can be.

Mother no sooner chuckles in return, as does she belch into her lace handkerchief, causing us all to laugh. Well, a tinkling tittering is more like it. Bellowing and guffawing was never for us. Even for Father. We are nowhere near that primitive.

I realize suddenly, these two might be perfectly happy to lie dormant yet another two days straight. They do that when particularly well-sated. I take girlish pride in knowing tonight, this is thanks to me. Me and my gift. The appearance of the elf's parents, which is what Father later explained to me, was but an incidental and temporary issue, easily solved. Those two *people* (I cringe to use that word, but Papa insists I should at least grant them that designation), took rather little time to incinerate, for, surprisingly, there wasn't much to them once their many layers of rags were peeled off of their lumpish, natted bodies. Those rags, we tossed into the furnace to stoke it before Papa heave-ho'd their carasses in. But, oh my, the stench they made as they burned. That will stay with me a while. My nose crinkles even to think on it.

Nonetheless, while my parents quite seem to look forward to the partaking of their unconsciousness, I am still much newer to this whole game and eager to be up and about, to learn and to do more, more, more. I am already looking forward to sneaking out tomorrow evening, just as soon as the night has fully dawned. And I shan't make the tiniest bit of sound. I am adding to my skills. I will skitter through the rooms, the halls, and steal out of the house like the smallest, cutest field mouse, and I will find myself another elf.

Hand in hand, we take the stairs and descend the ladders, never once touching the rungs. It is more of a floating downward alongside the devices, for when no one is watching, it is quite fun, to shirk all mortal fakery. We soon reach the caves and then presently, the third catacomb, a clean-swept chamber devoid of any animal corpses or their droppings, with not a single mottled, old skull or scabby bone in sight. Our beds await us. The lids are lifted, at the ready. I surreptitiously pat my left pocket to make sure the key to the kitchen door is still there and draw my angelic face skyward to the marble-smooth sun and moon that are my parents' loving countenances, to receive from each of them a last kiss goodnight.

Turn the Lights to Party

"Alexa: turn the lights to party."

I learned how to do this silly little thing from Alexa – my real, human, living breathing girl, my daughter, my darling Alexa – who has been dead now for almost one full year. To the day. It's Christmas Eve and I am sitting in the living room, alone, on what is now also to be called, I suppose, the anniversary of her death, if one must go by these things. It has been one massive stretch of a long and painful, bogged down and sluggish year, through which I have slogged. My own special kind of forever. I feel like I have aged ten of them.

Christmas Eve, and it is just me here alone, quietly observing the softly pulsating glow of Alexa's tri-colored party lights. They wink benignly and predictably into an otherwise undecorated, utilitarian living room.

She didn't have to make it a surprise arrival! She could have just called us, just said "Be there for the eight o'clock arrival from Boston," and we could have planned our entire evening around the pick-up, spent the entire day preparing the house, joyfully anticipating that moment of utter relief when we would see our child standing there, where we would have taken her into our arms with no intention of letting go until we were forced, as had for so long been customary, to concede our embrace to our enthusiastically oblivious high-action girl, who had always been ready to gently break free far sooner than we, her not ever having been as reliant on our hanging on as we had been of her. Our hanging on. . .

If only she had not had the stupid idea to make this a SURPRISE. . .

Her card – that accursed card with *all* of the relevant information on it – arrived on Valentine's Day. *On Valentine's Day,* of all days, almost two months after it had been supposed to arrive. Two months after Alexa in her sweet, error-ridden way had intended it. The envelope's corners shredded, the stamp all but peeled off, the dirty print of a shoe's toe, even, defacing its reverse side (*whose* shoe?), the beastly delivery arriving so horrifically belated – but hermetically sealed inside a clear Zipclose bag, as if to keep the precious missive in its defiled state forevermore, after who knows what kind of an odyssey it had been on.

Having read its contents – more times than I can count – I have since then driven out to the bus station, where we were to have picked her up, nearly every single day. No; *every* single day. There is no need to downplay the obsession. The bus station – *that* station – is the smaller of the two, the one on the far side of town. Who knows why Alexa had picked that one to arrive at. I have always assumed it was a default destination based on whatever was available when she selected her ticket. And as she paid for the ticket herself, we saw no transaction on any of our credit cards to clue us in on the purchase. I take the quiet of the drive time to the station for all it is worth, considering the condition I am in now. It is not cathartic, but it gives me time to conjure up a certain fortitude that I need afresh each time I arrive there, to look upon the place where my daughter last stood, last walked, the spot where we saw the last and final image of her on the security camera's video recording from that fateful night – the building, the parking lot, the three small shelters. I scan the area, making what I believe are practical assessments, just in case there is something, some little thing, I may have missed when I last scoured the place. It is a completely innocuous bus stop in an inconsequential part of town, neither here nor there in terms of being more or less safe for any single passenger, let alone a young adult woman. I see kids hanging around there every time I drive by. I scan their faces, keep imagining one of them could somehow transform into the blessed countenance I hold in my heart, what resides in every nook and cranny of my brain – her face, her sweet face, her sweet and precious face.

I admit, I also imagine that every time I am on my way to the station, I am on my way to pick her up. And so, each time I cruise the parking lot, crawling slowly, slowly past the terminal, I also then experienced anew that physical plunge of the gut, when reality hits me broadside with such pain, such pain, when I realize all over again that she is not there, nor will she somehow magically emerge, as if she could emerge from a humanoid chrysalis that is in reality just another random stranger standing out there, still alive unlike my daughter, who is just out there, at the station, taking up some small sliver of space in this living world that should have been hers.

. . .where instead she was picked by a someone else. Taken. Taken from us. Abducted? Seduced by sheer friendliness? A ride happily accepted? No one has any idea who it was, who she rode off with. And to think, they were calling it a cold case before her body was even released to us! Zero clues, no traces of anything. Crumbs too small. The faintest glimpse on video, greyscale and so heavily pixelated, choppy for the interference of that damned snowfall. A small car, older, no plate visible, no model or year could be made out. And Alexa quickly striding over to it and jumping in as if she knew the driver, her just having set out – possibly – to cross the street to walk over to that small roadside plaza where either the diner or the drugstore might have been her destination. To call us? We will never know what her plan or her problem was, with her phone gone missing too. We will never know the reason for her not having contacted us. We will always be forced to wonder, if in some stubborn and silly spate of holiday cheer, she was still, even then, wishing to surprise us.

I am past crying as I exit the station parking lot, past navigating back to the house through a veil of tears. But each drive home, I feel a little more dulled, a little more dead inside. As I see it, the only way to survive this is by subjecting myself to a punishment I mete out upon myself, like a self-flagellation. Every time I make the futile trip to the bus station, it is with a ridiculous hopefulness, that I might see her *this* time – or just see something, anything, different, which might hint of her presence, past or present. As if she could still be hanging around there after all. It serves in a bizarre way to re-animate my festering spirit, helps me trudge through yet another day, and through subsequent, solitary evenings, until I can finally lay my body down to bed, to pass on into another night of fitful, dream-littered sleep.

There was no reason, no reason at all for her to have made this trip home without us knowing she was on her way. We could have tracked her! We would've been just as happy to anticipate the arrival! And then she never would have had to accept that ride! She would have never gotten into that car!

My husband, who had gone to the coroner's to identify *the remains* – as the too properly worded voice mail had indicated – had also become angry with me when he soon after found out, I was still making daily trips to the bus station. He called me a glutton for punishment, told me I should not intentionally set out to do something like that to myself. He was actually mad *at me*. On top of all the pain I bore, that barbell I had affixed to the back of my skull, my husband had had the audacity to conjure up anger directed specifically at me. Just another wedge driven into whatever remained, of what I had shared with him. He himself had taken to walking around like a zombie, hardly speaking to me – or anyone else for that matter – since the day he had been summoned downtown to identify our daughter's body.

Something had changed in him when he went there to identify the remnants of what I will steadfastly think only of as our daughter Alexa *as she was in life*.

Everyone and everything, killed off in ice cold blood, a hoar-frosted reality affecting us all.

Alexa's father eventually insisted I quit driving over to the station altogether. He threatened to take the car keys to work with him. Told me to find a full-time job (I had worked part time from home for some years now), that my responsibilities – or lack thereof – were leaving me with too much free time, which the devil in my head was using to find ways to kill me off, too. Of course, he euphemized the necrosis of my spirit, called it "the negative affect on my denying the grieving process." As if schooled words could help the perspective.

I know we were each handling our grief in diametrically opposing ways, and that it would, inevitably, pull us apart. Miles apart. I still don't know what precisely he saw at the coroner's that had affected him so, taken him down this other path of mourning. All how he put it to me was that what had awaited him there was not "our Alexa." I do not know what exactly he meant by that, but I have never asked him to elaborate on it. He spoke absently that night, after coming back home, to me, to the deadened room, to the shadows, of a Christmas Eve double murder some fifty years ago, in our city no less, where one of the victims had also been a young woman fresh home from college, who had been found dumped in an alley behind First Lutheran. The notorious and disastrous city-wide lockdown which had resulted from that Christmas Eve discovery had coincided with one of the biggest snowfalls in recent history. People had been stranded everywhere, including at church, where they had been attending Christmas Eve services. Turns out, additional victims, discovered much later, had included family members of the killer, and the killer himself, who had remained buried under a snowdrift for weeks.

Would people someday talk of our Alexa in the way that girl was still brought up? By strangers who didn't much care either way about her demise? By other victims' parents who were perhaps trying to make heads or tails of the hells visited upon them? By all the left-behind loved ones who slowly, incrementally perish after the fact?

My Alexa as I knew her, saw her, loved her, *love* her still, will remain for me the real and true Alexa. Alexa had also – just like *that* girl – moved away for school. And she had then stayed on for work, had until the very last texted me her odd strings of emojis at the most random times, which I was supposed to decipher, who had then seen fit in a moment of odd, old fashioned pre-tech fun to try and surprise her parents with a Christmas Eve homecoming, who never called once while en route, who had never texted us either, never done what would have been the logically safe thing to do. . .

So much futile anger. So many questions.

These days, when some young person is on the road, it is so much better that loved ones are informed and able to track them! And waiting to pick them up! There was no need for her to have tried to do it this way!

For Alexa's father to force me to bear additional guilt on top of the grief that was already crippling me proved to be too much. Our world, by way of some colossal mitosis, finally cleaved itself in two. When my husband packed his things and moved out, I actually felt relief. It would be easier to walk this treacherously narrow, cliffside path alone.

††††

It is also easier to pretend Alexa is alive in an otherwise empty house. An empty house is a far better stage for the shucking of reality, for the partaking of the intoxicating effects of an imagination so strong, one can start to hear movement in random parts of the house whenever a stretch of absolute, fertile stillness permits. And when that occurs, it's always on some other, opposite side of wherever it is I happen to be. There will be a distant door latch clicking, the tread of a stair creaking, the soft hiss of water filling a line, the sound of a cell phone or a book being plunked down on a bedside table in that casual, careless way a young person might do it. . .

I swear, I have heard Alexa's voice a time or two. And I have welcomed it. There is no fear, but a hope of sorts. A willingness to reach into some otherwise off-limits realm where maybe just maybe some aspect of her still lurks, still wanders, somehow resides. . .

I ruminate on the card, her Christmas surprise card which she had mailed to our house a few days before leaving her apartment, before embarking on that fateful trip home. I wonder on the hate-filled, wicked powers out there that had set that card off its course, let it subsist in a netherworld of undelivered communications – messages in bottles, futile screams in the night, lost radio signals wandering the cosmos – to wander about like Spirits of Christmases past, to only turn up two long months after she had accepted that other, fateful ride, two months after she had not been heard from by anyone, two months after her body had been found and the police had first called and then shown up in person at our front door at 9:00 pm on the dot on a Tuesday evening, December the twenty-eighth, right about when the snowstorm that had started on Christmas Eve was finally letting up. I cannot help but think about that other girl, too. And her mother.

And then I ruminate some more. I think enormous questions, for they fill the voids of my solitude, all this silence. No Christmas carols, no Yule log are streaming on the television. Not a single decoration is set out. That would be blasphemous.

Why had no one noticed that envelope lying on the ground or some floor, wherever it may have fallen, and seen fit to correct its course? Who the hell had stepped on it and not turned it over to see that it had a real and rock-solid address on it, a destination? A purpose? And I will, always, wonder why Alexa had simply not seen fit to just call or text us with a heads up, a happy heads up, rather than try to communicate with us with only a stupid card, gone lost. Fun as her idea had been, it had come at direct and dire cost. To her. To all of us. Had we only known she was due to arrive that night. Had we only known. . .

Had I only known! Had I only known! I would have been right there to pick you up, Alexa! Call me, text me! Alexa!

When Alexa *was* home, when my darling daughter was home, she loved to command our voice-activated assistant, Alexa – fake Alexa as we had dubbed her – to "turn the lights to party." When Alexa was home, when our living breathing human daughter Alexa was home, she would turn on our living room lamps with this directive every evening, the moment dusk would begin to settle over the house. The retrofitted vintage fixtures would then "party" for her and slowly flash the evening away in their innocuously festive array of a warm amber followed by a rousing fuchsia, which would then morph to a pleasant and cool teal blue. Over and over, all night long, the lights would blink to mark the gentle passage of the evening hours, even long past our bedtime, being that our daughter, a night owl, would stay up way late into the night, long after we had gone up to sleep.

Suffice it to say, to kiss the real Alexa on her forehead, to wish her a good night, and to then head upstairs with those party lights flashing like little dockside beacons as we exited the living room – blue, gold, pink, blue, gold, pink – became a symbolically enriched send-off in its own right. There is nothing like going to bed knowing that your child, your baby, is right there at home with you, under your roof, safe and sound, doing their own quiet thing, contented to just be there. Just as you are too, the only difference being, that you as parent are *downright and positively, ecstatically joyous and relieved* that they are there. But you don't bare that much of your soul – as parent, you will have learned some time ago to keep demonstrations of both deep fear and joy in check, so to grant these new humans the space they need to start to become *themselves*. So, you simply place a little kiss on their forehead, and you gently but quickly touch their chin as your eyes meet for a fleeting, wonderful second, and then you go upstairs like it is no big deal, no small miracle, no priceless, little memory forging itself. . .

Now, that colorful light play has come to represent Alexa herself.

For, my real, living Alexa is gone.

My daughter's ashes are contained in that ceramic urn over there, which resides upon the credenza right in front of me, which is flanked by the two lamps that she – Alexa, the real-life Alexa – always would set "to party."

Alexa's remains were cremated. Her body, the lifeless body that had been Alexa, had lain too long, exposed to the harsh winter elements for too many destructive hours, for her to have been able to serve as a donor, as would have been her wish, as had been noted on her driver's license – which had also disappeared. And so, her ashes fill that urn. To the brim. I have opened it, looked at the silken, sifted matter inside the container. Her father, he is alive as I am, yes, but with his life wholly separated from mine, cut off from whatever it was we had shared – he may as well be dead, too.

I suppose I wish him well.

I do not know what I wish for myself. No; I do. I am just afraid to admit it.

These days, the first hint of dusk descends nice and early. It helps bring about the prompt waning of the afternoon. And as soon as I sense that end-of-day shift in light, I set aside my work-at-home folders, I put my laptop to sleep, and I resume my place on the sofa in the living room, directly opposite the credenza. I am already dressed for bed, never having changed out of my pajamas in the first place.

I then tell fake Alexa to "set the lights to party." I sit and watch, I sit and watch. Imprisoned within walls built of memories and this painful present tense. I remember and ruminate on this very same spot, where, just a few lifetimes ago, it had also provided the real, living Alexa the simple, happy sheltering space that was her *home*. Therefore, to sit with the lights set to "party,", as my real Alexa would have those lamps do it, seems to be the only thing left for me to do, to pass the evening until I can put myself to bed.

†††

Alexa: turn the lights to party.

I sit in the dark – the gloom, the perpetual night, the state of my heart. I quietly observe as the soft-colored lights play out from under the lampshades, which stand like sentinels to either side of her urn. They go from gold to pink to blue and then back again. . .

Gold, pink, blue. . . gold, pink, blue. . . gold, pink, blue. . .

Alexa!

Gold, pink, blue. . . gold, pink, blue. . . gold, pink, blue. . . gold, gold, blue. . . gold, gold, blue. . .gold, gold, blue. . .

Alexa, honey, are you there?

. . .gold, gold, gold. . . gold, gold, gold. . . gold, gold, gold. . .

Alexa, my sweet girl, are you there? Show me something, anything. Give me a sign. . .

. . . gold, gold, gold. . . gold, gold, gold. . .

Alexa, turn the lights to. . . Alexa, turn the lights. . . Alexa, honey. . .

. . .gold, gold, green. . . gold, gold, green. . .

Alexa? Alexa?

. . . gold, green, red. . . gold, green, red. . .

Alexa? Is that you?

Green, red. . . green, red. . . green, red. . .

Alexa has turned the lights *to Christmas.*

And then I hear it, and I realize this is what I have been waiting for.

It is why I sit here, in the full fallen dark, with only those little lights *speaking* to me. I sit here with all the love I still hold for my daughter, which doesn't have anywhere to go; it neither dissipates nor diminishes. And that love thrives despite all the pain, despite all the stale confusion, those unanswered questions, all that horrible apathy others seemed to hold about her case, which they called "cold" way, way too soon.

There is this feeling of a world that has been thrown off its axis. It spins about me like some crazy carousel while I hover offsides, not included. I am mired in grief, and it leaves me feeling as were I treading thick, gelatinous water. I am not getting *anywhere,* while the rest of existence seems to be spinning ever faster, with that carousel transforming itself into some kind of space station about to take off, which will head towards some galaxy to which I have not been invited. I have only this. My empty house. This is my world.

Green, red. . . green, red. . . green, red. . .

But now, I am hearing something. Noises. A disruption of some kind.

Green, red. . . green, red. . . green, red. . .

It occurs to me, it could be Alexa's father stopping by. Perhaps he forgot something. Perhaps he thinks he owes me some kind of holiday visit. A wellness check? Nah. Nothing occurs to me, that it might be him "coming back home" to me. Alexa's father may as well be the ghost in this picture.

Green, red. . . green, red. . . green, red. . .

But then another thought occurs to me. It could be Alexa's killer. The contents of her backpack were all gone, discarded or stolen. Her backpack was empty and filthy, as had it been stepped on, repeatedly, by the time it was found alongside her body. Aside from her wallet and other, customary personal items, the contents of her backpack had included, as she had once confided to me, a small stack of the birthday cards I had mailed to her while she was away at college, which she always kept with her, double rubber-banded, so to be able to look at and re-read them whenever she was missing us, home, me. . .

Green, red. . . green, red. . . green, red. . .

Could it have been, those cream, pink, and lavender envelopes with our return address on them were opened, read, and their return address noted by whomever had emptied Alexa's backpack?

But I don't care. All I care about, all I care about in this universe, is the possibility – the *distinct* possibility, which is as real as anything I could ever wish for, is that it is *Alexa* who is somehow coming home. Home to me. That my darling girl is coming home, as she had planned it all along.

Green, red. . . green, red. . . green, red. . .

I still have so much love for my child, so much to give to her. It is all still here. My un-given love is piled up so high in my heart, it is filled to bursting. It exists big as thunderclouds, stagnant and pregnant in the heaviest skies imaginable, ripe with tens of millions of unshed tears, a flood waiting to hit.

It's all still there.

Green, red. . . green, red. . . green, red. . .

And I have nowhere to go with it, for the self-loathing that fills me to overflowing leaves no room for me as just me, by myself. All I am in this moment is a vessel for something-anything as sublime as would be the smallest glimmer of hope, that my daughter might yet rise like a phoenix from those ashes over there, from what this subsistence has become for me.

Green, red. . . green, red. . . green, red. . .

My daughter, my girl, this angelic, little creature who would look up at me, so small, who two minutes later had transformed into the fantastical makings of a young woman I could only be in awe of. . .

Oh, Lord, dear God! I would give it all up, if only. . .if only. . .

Green, red. . . green, red. . . green, red. . .

And then, whether it's prayers answered or a final descent into madness, I hear something else. Something definitive. Whether any of this is borne of Christmas miracles or the most fiendish of deceptions demons might visit upon the most decrepit leftovers of humanity, souls truly lost and wholly available and ready for the hijacking. . .

. . .I hear the clunky latch of the screen door at the back entry into the kitchen being depressed. It is a distinctive, metallic one-two which echoes like a gunshot through the house. I hear the weathered hinges of the screen door screech in protest as the door is yanked open.

Green, red. . . green, red. . . green, red. . .

Alexa? Alexa?

Then I hear the signature knock I know all too well, all too well. Quick, hard-knuckle raps, it is a series tapped in two sets of three, right on the glass panel of the kitchen door, where it will make the biggest impact, the most noise:

Tap tap tap! Tap tap tap!

Green, red. . . green, red. . . green, red. . .

Tap tap tap! Tap tap tap!

Alexa?

And immediately following that – for I have left all doors to the house unlocked – I hear the unmistakable sound of the doorknob being turned, its grinding *clank clank* preceding the much softer and longer creak of the hinges, resisting as those old things ought, as the kitchen door is swung open.

Green, red. . . green, red. . . green, red. . .

And then I hear,

Mom? Mom?

Perhaps a rather macabre nosegay – amber, fuchsia, teal – but a bouquet, a tribute, nevertheless, to my beloved daughter, who, whenever she is home from college, loves to turn the lights to party.

Mermaid's Tale

Not one, but two sets of vertebrae; flawless, gently undulating lengths of
interconnected jig-sawed pieces
Interlocking and sculpted beads of bone, cartilage lined, freshly injected with as
much of the pliant stuff as each interval can hold it
Brilliant man, I am, this scientist craftsman who has toiled in his laboratory until
the recipe was just right. . .

Infused and cooled, formed and fitted, the breathable, bendable spaces between
each calcified talisman receive my ministrations, every one of them a milestone, a
crumb on a path, designed to lead not only me but her as well, deeper into the
enchantments of my meticulously engineered forest, from which there will be,
gladly and willingly forsaken, no return
One to the next
To then the other
Look how they move in gentle unison!
I bend the masses as were they ropes of a pastry dough, freshly kneaded, now
direly needed
To which her feet, with fantail extensions partially replaced, will be attached
Slender whalebone tines, each one as fine as a quill
As elegantly tapered as a dressmaker's pin
Their glint, I have whispered to my sleeping beauty, may well shimmer through
the translucence of the grafted skin

Just think, to embody the prism of a radiant Koi on its slumb'rous sojourns
'round and 'round 'neath the mirrored plain of a still and pellucid, saltwater pond
Kneecaps, tossed aside; there is no need for them
Tendons, muscles, threaded and sewn, weft to warp and back again
Yet the Achilles heels, intact, mythologically eulogized, may remain there still,
less for the legend as for the better kick they will facilitate
For quicker action, once my poppet is laid afresh in her everlasting bath
Yes, she will have to re-learn to swim, to acclimate herself, as anyone thusly
transformed ought
What a liquid and lyrical dance, a most beauteous undulation to witness, to track!
Oh, I can feel desire, such a desire
That weighted heat, right *there*, in anticipation of what will soon come, despite my
scientist's mandate, that – for now – she must remain perfectly, perfectly still
Untouched, kept sterile – all the better, my dear, for to heal. . .
Ah, there she lies, outstretched on her bridge, the surgical bed I built just for her
Affixed like a martyr is she, to a network of tubing, which for now is keeping her
alive, but just barely
Eyes closed, hardly breathing, her pure heart pensively beating. . .

My love, who by the iron wheels of the ice-thrown, wayward carriage was ripped
asunder
Who lay there, split and pouring of her poor, torn self upon the cruel and sleet-
spattered pavers
(What crimson effusion to explode in such stark contrast to the new-fallen snow!)
To gather her up – what a nightmarish task! – with entrails caught in the folds of
her gown
And velvet ribbons from her bonnet, ripped off and wound 'round the small, wet
parts which would otherwise have slipped from my frenzied and desperate grip
And fallen to boot-trodden and offal-strewn ground
. . .*anything* to keep my love from touching all that filth. . .
(May never there roost any rot, nor blossom any pestilence once I have been able
to stitch the pieces of my love back together!)

Diligence wed to a manic devotion will now rule every single step:
I will bathe every shredded scrap, each limb, and, every bit of this fine and fresh-
harvested dolphin skin, so my Ophelia can be rejoined from the self-same pureness
which will have birthed no less than an Aphrodite herself

I shall then take her, my adored one, and all the pieces by Fate duly rendered,

Down to the secreted chambers of my basement lair, wherein so long has waited
my subterranean, oceanic holding tank
Within this water-bound boudoir shall she be by calming waters received
As has been meticulously planned, for which I have oh, so long prepared
This singular space, more a tropic's warm bath, this watery respite, which now by
dark fate has been recalibrated
Into a direly needed imperative!
Our new, small universe – submerged; a new home, effectively inverted
For these elements shall now herald the delivery of a brand-new sort of sea maiden
Who, when awakened by true love's electrified and hard-wired kiss,
Will open her eyes, resurrected. . .

A virginal naiad borne on the intentional crests of both legend and lust
A feminine wellspring for all manner of a decadent seafarer's saltiest lore
She'll be thusly cradled in the arms of Poseidon's most faithful brethren
And ruthlessly schooled as a vestal siren apprentice

So, in time, my Undine – mine! – will offer herself like the pelican is known to
offer up her very own, blood-feathered breast
To welcome *me* in
Only me
Her predacious lover and devoted Creator
Just me, with my oh, so exceedingly exotic predilection

K.A. Schultz

Xmas Letter

Hey Sam

Am forwarding the letter I told you about, from the computer that was found in the living room of the Bates' place. Bo Bates, the son, has confirmed, it was his mother's laptop. She was a bit of a writer, a polemic you could say – you might recall her many letters to the editor over at The Herald. This, what I'm calling a stream of consciousness outpouring, is imo anything but an annual Christmas letter. I am hoping, you can provide some insight as to her true state of mind, aside from what appears to be the obvious. Was this a letter really intended for distribution amongst her friends and family? Could it be a plant – narrative crafting, if you will – or is it indeed an exposé of a criminally triggered mind? And here is an odd question that occurred to me: did Sue Bates even write this? Whatever this "letter" is, it's a weird read, but given what was all found at the crime scene, I cannot help but think, it needs more interpretation than what I or my guys here at the precinct are qualified to do. If you need access to the crime scene, just let me know. We are keeping the entire property taped up and under wraps, the garage too, per Forensics' request. Too many inconsistencies to even start to draw conclusions. Let me just warn you, though, if you do want to tour the house, don't do it on a full stomach. Hell, maybe empty is worse? Btw the hard drive has been removed from the laptop. It's under lock and key. I can arrange for you to view its contents, but that has to be done officially and would take some time to approve, which is the problem, and why I am reaching out to you now and via this email, friend to friend. The laptop itself is sealed up and in a freezer at the lab.

So – below is the full text, which, while it seems like a nearly completed work, was only auto-saved, still on the desktop as a WIP. Thank goodness for that function. Let me stress, DO NOT SHARE it with anyone – consider this a sneak preview, which in due course we can disclose more officially, as needed. If and when you have some insights as to any of these ramblings, just give me a call. No texting. Staff here is firmly split down the middle on this case, as to who did what to whom. I'll owe you big for this. How does a nice, fat ribeye at Rubi's sound for compensation?

M.

Well, if it isn't that time of year – deck the halls and trim the tree with silver bells and cockle shells and what all else do they say about that with all of us centering our days, our nights, our paychecks, and what's left of anyone's sanity ;) towards the manifestation of the season's mandates as decreed by all those damn Spirits of Christmas Now Now Now and On Sale! Sale! Sale! as we celebrate another year gone by and welcome another Holly Jolly you-call-it come around once again at this most wonderful time of the year and so on and so on etc etc

It is now year twelve that this fine lady dancing is penning her missive to you, one of holy-day cheers prost and skol please pour me another one yes to the brim with updates as well on her Lord a-leaping and their two turtle doves whose rumpled heads are now as before chock full of Joojoo chews and candy canes as they are wont to be this time of year with about as much positive net effect as what all gets ingested and fills their bellies always just making them sick to their stomachs remember how all that pink puke would stain everything so badly and later on how it would stick to their braces when they got older you'd think they'd outgrow their penchant for that crap but whatever they will never learn so why the hell not let me tell you what is REALLY up I say it's time to check in a bit differently this year first yes to wish you and yours all the best although for myself I can't rightly say BEST

Best of what?
Who knows?
Who are we kidding?
Who am I kidding, least of all ME?

I've got updates for you yes fuck it all I've got some pretty damn juicy updates for you so strap yourselves in pour yourself tall cold one I already have and settle back with me for a while okay now as many of you know Lord a-leapin' and I were high school sweethearts you know we grew up together age fifteen on I gave it up for the bastard so what back in the day that sort of thing actually sealed deal so to speak and so when we spoke our vows it was like yeah sure I know for better or worse it's always the same it's always something who can ever to know what kind of roller coaster one signs up for oh shit the job changes and the moves yes indeedy we stuck it out he hung in there climbing climbing who knows what kind of ladder I guess for a while it was working and well I played along too but what is a wife and a mom to do who doesn't even really know herself one gets lost in all kinds of processes but yeah sure we hung in there and then eventually so did the kids because they came along almost by default as kids generally do and that itinerant life we led one has got to wonder don't you wonder too I mean where the hell does one go from wherever it is one is if they don't even really know where the hell they were in the first place oh lordy this just makes me feel that much more weary to think that forever one is pulling up shallow roots it's really more like perpetual weeding you know what I mean by any means any way one thinks it can go and that what they are doing is right what is right who is to know and you know what they say about assumptions just some kind of foundation upon which to build anything at all let alone maintain what one has or built or whatever is so damn hard especially when what they thought they had or what they thought they were building separately or together as founding members of that time-honored was never really attained and you just find yourself mired in dysfunction for that my friends is what it is to be normal any more whatever it means anymore to be FAMILY

sheesh fuck that but anyway let me get to the year itself for things went south pretty much a month after the new year had begun in February after me having endured Bob's ever later and later nights at work my god those were lonely nights for me I mean there I'd sit there alone on long winter evenings that felt like they went on forever with my wine or my snacks usually both oh Kristos yes I did put on some stress weight from just sitting there like a lump staring blankly into the TV watching one massively boring and endless train of CONTENT you know how it is now one mediocre series after another but where the hell was I to go it's not like you can have both parents running around night after night and when he would finally drag his arse home sometimes in the early morning hours I mean who the fuck was he thinking he was fooling and on top of that there was this cold cold fog of a void when he was around me anyway with his near zero attentiveness and we both suffered along with that basic drying up of any semblance of regard it can get so palpable what did I have left to say to that son of a bitch well forget about conversation as if there were anything left to talk about when two people like us no longer do anything together whatsoever I mean we had nothing in common anymore and so when we ceased to speak altogether but for the most absolutely necessary exchanges which pained me both to speak and to hear you know that tightness in the voice when someone simply can't stand you anymore you can hear it too well so of course serendipity brought me all the evidence that I needed to see quite accidentally what needed to be seen I swear I never went looking for anything I mean heck I knew too much already it was just so scary to be confronted with the stark reality of the situation and all it would foretell for us both and God help us the kids and lo and behold my husband of almost twenty years I realized feeling sick to my stomach I thought I was going to throw up all over the living room floor when I found that stuff yes it confirmed ye olde Lord a-leaping was seeing someone else and had been in this relationship for from what I could tell well over a year one singularly miserable and lonesome and dying set of months which in retrospect I cannot even fathom why I held out that long to finally let myself see the obvious and confront the bastard over the inevitable why oh why did he have to go that route I mean if he wasn't happy or whatever he could have been HONEST about it I could have taken well heck just about anything but still what could have possibly driven him to hook up with that piece of work who shall forever remain nameless outside of "Snake-in-the-Grass" that is about all the name any sleazy sneaky slut deserves but oh well they deserved each other to be honest even though I know irony of ironies that things have already pretty much already gone bust between the two of them but that's karma for ya oh yes shit yep it does hit the fan and sometimes it doesn't take that long for that to happen but what else is to be expected when someone goes scavenging for attention in the lowest places well I'll tell you one's instincts don't lie and so the weeks before the discovery I could tell something was wrong and I would try and try lordy it was pathetic I mean I was practically begging the more I asked the more I pushed the more closed off he would become it was like talking to a wall more like like the cliffside of some glacier it was that cold between the two of us us and well so I kept asking repeatedly what was up what can I do can we talk about it can we talk about it PLEASE come on you owe me that much you you son of a bitch and you know what my non-stop persistent questions he called me a fucking nag they were met with increasing hostility from him and get this of all things and this is where shit really hits the fan is that he would start to get mad at me for asking for some kind of well what do you call it? Sharing? Disclosure? Admissions? But when the perpetrator of the hurt starts holding it against the recipient of their hurtful actions when they don't fucking get what is going on then of course the next thing to start up are the accusations coming from THEM those nastily delivered jabs intended to cause a blow-up since evidently that becomes the only way some of these things get thrown out into the open well meantime my sanity was being chiseled away he held everything against ME like I was some nut case while it was HE who was driving ME fucking nuts and in the end what I was discerning was absolutely correct and the truth which he was too fucking CHICKEN to be honest about you know when I think way back I remember my mother once told me Dick was going to be trouble but then I was no picnic either hell I didn't know anything sometimes I still feel I don't know anything especially these days but be that as it may I had learned to listen to my gut I was feeling that thing that thing you know what I am talking about and for that I was accused by that son of a bitch he accused me of having gone crazy of having issues of needing help needing meds well fuck that I was maybe never saner in my life as I was pushing my way out through a web of deceit that had gotten too damn thick how selfish was that of him it is only those who have gone through this who can possibly start to understand what a slow crawl across the desert it is when one is forced to keep slogging through life as they have only known it up until THAT day when everything every fucking thing is put on the line and about to collapse and you've got to somehow get to the ledge on the other side of the chasm before the bridge falls it is truly truly ironic that the person who can drive someone to insanity can then accuse them of the very thing that they will have done themselves needless to say after that horrible eruption it became what I think back on now as my new day #1 those terrible arguments that ensued oh we both said bridge burning hurtful things and we fought for days we fought at night too because he then had the audacity to stick around for a time after that can you imagine how awkward that was how I would lay there in the bed alone and ruminate and fume and bet he was doing the same in the guest room downstairs and then one day when I came back from a long-scheduled appointment you know how that is these days it's like third world get in line hope you don't die before you can actually see the damn doctor before you fucking die so after that appointment I came home to an empty house you could feel the emptiness in the very air itself the silence was so oppressive I felt pressure in my ears which felt to me just like I was underwater well HE had packed up and moved out took his things from the bathroom and most of his clothes I suppose he just threw his SHIT into his car because the suitcases they were all still there in the closet and how else could he have accomplished this in the space of a couple hours I was only gone a short while to that doctor's it being the only thing I had to do that day and no it was not for anything psychological nothing like that I think I am pretty sure he just hauled ass and got his SHIT over to that piece of work's place a shitty little duplex is where she lived yes I sure as hell knew where her place was and he just moved in with her that woman with that piece of work Snake-in-the-Grass low-life homewrecker not to say I don't just blame him but me yes I blame myself too every single day including wondering why I ever stuck with him in the first place hilarious I remember back in college coming thiiiiis close to breaking up with him and I probably should have and it's not like I am wishing away the kids but I sure as hell don't bank on any kind of meant to be hell there are a fuck ton of FISH out there for anyone isn't love just all really quire random that at least is what I think now had I been more secure with myself back then when I was young I bet I would have said bye bye see ya later and never ever ever looked back but given the time we did have it leaves me now in a place where I can't even begin to describe what a nightmare it is to try to get a handle on my own personal will to survive I mean the pain is fucking palpable I was literally sick for days after he moved out and then oh boy to have to figure out how to present some kind of picture to the kids that was going to be emotionally survivable to them as for sure I was not going to want to burden them also with my own collapse you know it can be the pure anger one can felt it is so destructive among all the other things I did feel as anyone would I was disgusted by the abandonment that I had been forced to absorb and that the kids were going to be burdened that much more by a loss they were never meant to endure oh sure I would have to hang on indefinitely because the role of parent you can't ever completely set aside but if I could have only seen it coming I would definitely have taken steps to at least better prepare myself for the handling of all those basics that never stop coming at you there never was any choice really but to turn that corner catapult myself onto a different path and forge ahead come hell or high water yeah for better or worse the end is just as profound a start as any beginning

Well suffice it to say in the months following the separation Bo who had been struggling at his new school you remember we had to transfer him two years ago the bullying was just never handled right by the administrators and he was afraid just to be there and we were afraid especially as it felt like we had no backup nor recourse whatsoever anyway but that is water under the bridge Bo was failing in all of his classes and then unbeknownst to me he dropped out of soccer and of course what did he do but he took up with this group of kids who I had neither seen nor met nor even heard about before and all of a sudden not only am I sitting alone so fucking alone at night at the house but my kids were disappearing right out from under me as well and it seemed like I could do nothing about it my God was that an oppressive to be home alone it felt like I had no friends in the world well but of course here you all are my friends but you are all so far away hence these goddamn letters every fucking year you know people just don't stay in touch anymore do they but it's all good I don't blame any one of you out there I mean what's a person to do but anyway those horribly quiet evenings quickly degenerated even lower into worrisome nights and I mean late nights late late nights when I had no idea what the hell Bo was up to or where or with whom he was and good grief there were entire weekends when I would not see him at all either I know he was escaping the pain I know he was having problems I know he already had issues before that he was contending with and I damn well know why but there seemed to be NOTHING I could do about it but he was in with the wrong kids and it was at a particularly susceptible time for him and oh wow so much more dangerous you know a parent can hardly keep up with this kind of stuff and all the trends and the drugs out there my God the names of the stuff that is available on the streets what the kids are taking and yes you bet he as experimenting with everything that crossed his path and sure enough not only did he wind up in jail but by the time April came around he'd also been in the hospital he wrecked the damn car and do you think it was totaled no so I could get it replaced hell no I am now left driving a broken down barely street legal piece of crap contraption that insurance won't replace and they are giving me shit over the work that does need to be done and Bo he broke his leg snapped his tibia clean in two thank heaven kids heal fast but the real damage has nothing to do with bones or fenders so soon after that he was put into a treatment program the hope being it would keep him from serving time but no why should we benefit from any sort of logical path to any semblance of wellness no let's all take the low road the hard road yes indeed let's just suffer our way through life well so Bo saw things about that way and so what do you think he did he got it into his head to run away from rehab not once but twice well it wasn't really running away per se he always arranged to have one of his new-found weirdo buddies there to fetch him yes always those new friends who would come and get him and to this day I have no idea how to reach them or Bo I assume he's still amongst that circle of friends and yes here I must confess that I have not spoken with or seen Bo since Halloween it's been almost two months and it is killing me I am so damn afraid I am going to wind up being ONE OF THOSE MOMS called downtown to identify a body

After the second time Bo left he got caught breaking into a pawn shop on the south side of town Bo was put into a different rehab facility where even I had no access to him it was a lockdown type psych ward situation as good as having been put back into prison I suppose maybe hopefully safer but I don't know I just don't know Nik well she glommed onto this boyfriend of hers that she had been dating off and on since about Valentine's Day she wound up packing her shit up as well she was always so like her father too much like her father so much just kept reminding me of the bastard like a curse a fucking curse it got harder and harder to interact with her I must be honest here it was like having a vestigial representative some kind of minion consigned by her father to remain here at the house with me to torment me after he had left and Su's attitude and oh God even her facial expressions so much disdain so sour a nature in one so young so pretty but oh yes that was her dad too well she moved in with her boyfriend and get this this is straight out of a fucking movie she moved in with him and his parents into a double-wide in this trailer park over in Hawthorne along with as I heard it a sister a single gal and her three kids oh my now that sounds like a nightmare I can't honestly say I miss the girl especially being the way she was to me in those weeks after Dick left but it's been weeks precisely six weeks and four days and let's see ten hours and a thirty minutes since I last heard from her she actually told me to go to hell we had this argument on her last day at the house and as we were yelling at each other and she starts throwing her clothes into a box and with me in my condition I panic and I really let loose on her I actually TOLD her she was just-like-her-father but of course words like that will only push anyone away let alone a volatile teenage girl who thinks she is in love and totally on the fence about BOTH parents and so now all I get as proof that she is alive are the doctor's bills the damn bills which of course are still coming to me so on top of all what I do not know and what all I worry about where she is concerned I now know she's got some kind of health issue and it is scaring the shit out of me I even tried calling the doctor's office made some story up but oh no HIPAA rules and all that they cut me off her own damn mother they cut me off and had I not hung up on them they would have no doubt hung up on me it was the most bizarre call they were so hostile it got me to wondering if Nik was there at her appointments bitching about ME and getting treatment for ills which she might be claiming I of all people had brought on in her my God I have only been trying to keep to some semblance of sanity myself but do you think a selfish teen is going to fathom any of that like the world doesn't revolve around them and it sure as hell includes hurt and pain being meted out yes the kids hurt I know this and even that pains me but I hurt too and I HAVE NO WHERE TO GO WITH THE PAIN so anyway with her still being on my insurance I am paying her bills but I do not know what the fuck am I paying for dear God I wish someone would let me know what is going on with my kids so then to really top things off Spot ran off on this beautiful morning back in June we were both standing outside just standing there on the back porch looking out over the field and off he goes like a bullet after something a sound maybe something he saw or heard I will never know but he's old and his sight is not so great but what is really heartbreaking is that I DID NOT deserve this I have never seen Spot since that day I know he is gone I worry that he is dead I can only pray that maybe he found some happier home and is sprawled on a rug in some other kitchen where there would be some LIVING breathing humans who now can claim him as their own and love him since I can't I suppose the negativity and anger poured so thick from me it had to be hard for that poor little fella to just be around me oh I do miss him when I think of Spot it is the closest I have come to crying no I have yet to shed a tear and that is the one thing that has worried the shit out of me something really truly died inside of me

Well par for the course in September I lost my job got squeezed out by new associates with these truly bizarre job titles that I swear the firm them made up to entice the little fucks they hired the bosses the powers that be those assholes told me they were having budgetary issues so my position was being downsized out of existence yes it is a kind of forced extinction and that my tasks were going to be absorbed into the other new positions effectively pushing me out of the company but I know it is because of my age and seniority it was all simply costing them way too much and damned if they were going to actually pay me my pension how's that for loyalty I was competing in the end against hirelings willing to work from home for fewer hours with less benefits and naturally that led to me me depending on unemployment payments to help me get by while all this other crap was going on yes I am still looking for a job but it is stupidly difficult to even get an interview at this age even though I don't disclose it they can do the math and I think these days I am looking positively ancient this year has aged me something awful and so of course I have waaaay too much free time AT HOME which is the last place I want to be but I have NOWHERE to go that's my conundrum in a nutshell also having been the single child of older parents I am as a technical matter quite on my own

I am worn out

I am a miserable shadow of who I guess I only thought I was

So the really weird thing is as I write this letter to you it is with a peculiar sense of calm for I am feeling there's a certain resolution that is working its way up through my subconscious and it's messaging to me all will be well when I think back now on all of the Christmases for which I worked like a slave spent way too much time and energy trying to conjure up shows of festivity and joy to the world and all of that other bullshit I've come to realize that you have been able to take a break from all that and this year being due to the hardships which have been tossed my way one after another I wouldn't wish anything on anyone at this point

Fuck every last so-called TRADITION

I'm just sitting here in the dark drinking my wine It's a Wonderful Life is playing on a loop on some streaming service I'm starting to understand that I am just a shadow period I don't really exist and that maybe I probably never did and that Dick and Bo and Nik exist in some different dimension altogether maybe you all do too maybe we are all like satellites afloat in an empty infinite universe that doesn't give a shit

Well while I don't feel any happiness in this moment I certainly don't feel any pain either I am as that lovely little song said comfortably numb

Dick called me this very afternoon he's due here in about an hour the really weird thing about this is that I'm absolutely dreading seeing him I think back on when I was a little girl and I was afraid on Christmas Eve that Santa might be lurking in a dark hall or a closet somewhere I remember I cried and my parents got mad at me why did they get mad at me I was just like three or four or

Fast forward to tonight and Dick may as well be some demon expected to rise up from the depths of hell some Black Christmas Santa-dressed killer or maybe that sad sad guy remember him those of you from around here do I bet you still do that guy his own father was a serial killer and then years later he murdered his own damn grandparents on Christmas Eve I mean it's the stuff of urban legends so awful body parts found in mangers and the killer he was found early spring under a snowbank my mom used to talk about that yes the worst kind of horror is what happens in real life because of the very fact that it is REAL you know like WAR it's amazing how we all take THAT in stride again and again and and so far no one has learned a damn thing

It says it all doesn't it but I digress horror doesn't always come with dumped body parts and bloody sacrifices there exists horror that comes in the guise of normalcy cloaked in the everyday awash in shows acceptance and apathy and the boring commonplace that is the kind of hellscape I am wallowing in for nothing looks different on the outside the house is just the house this town is the same place it always was and so are all its indifferent inhabitants just as dull and ordinary as they ever were likewise me here I am look at me you wouldn't notice a thing well but I have dropped more than the few pounds I gained and isn't that ironic I had wanted to shed that weight for years I just never knew it'd happen by way of having my guts spilled all over the carpet along with my heart for me to scoop up and somehow figure out how to squash them back up inside of me so they could continue to function on my behalf at least in the fundamental physical self my heart it is in fact dead dead DEAD that is what true horror is horror is when love has died and that pile of shit is left to decompose inside of you it's practically indigestible horror it is a mind devoid of color and music or nice little fleeting thoughts or memories god how all my memories are now tainted and clouded so many many years are lost so much was invested it was all so layered and now everything EVERYTHING from these last few decades has been rendered moot I may as well have skipped from eighteen to forty-two what was my life is no more no horror is NOT haunted shit like dusty old houses or monsters or immortals with bad intent horror is when all you have is all of a sudden not what it was and when even that ceases to be and it all feels like some kind of personal end times that is coming only for you you still see and hear a world out there but you are standing offsides and you are the only lonesome lonely one alive in your circle and all around you everything else seems to go on for everyone else and you're the one who had to get off the merry go round and it leaves you looking in from a short distance away so close you can almost reach out and touch it but you can't you feel you can't and you don't even feel like you're alive but rather you're in some kind of standstill just a dead weighted mass of human nothingness just watching ogling and staring but unable to participate with the rest of all existence which is turning turning right in front of you like a fucking happy carnival ride I gotta wonder is this already like being DEAD?

And is dreading the arrival of someone who with so little fucking effort with so little consideration for anyone but himself was able to turn everything inside out and upside down and the just leave you hanging from your own chain in the doorway normal well it has to be because that is all I am feeling in this moment but I have never seen with this much clarity the answer is right there too now and so then I ask is it HATE or is it HURT?

It comes upon a midnight clear

When the bastard moved out, he left behind his pistol mainly because I had some weeks prior hidden the key to the gun safe you know when things were starting to feel weird and any semblance of trust was going down the toilet and that safe thank goodness he had bolted it into the wall ironic in a sense otherwise he would've likely taken the whole damn thing with him too but no way did he have any chance to uninstall the cabinet when he was simply throwing his shit into his car so he could hightail it out of here before I showed up well that cabinet and its contents became my property you could say and so I've got it out it's in my hands and I KNOW HOW TO USE IT and YES it is loaded and if I point I will shoot that's what they teach you and I am a pretty good shot truth be told and three guesses who trained me yep he said it would empower me make me feel safer in my own home isn't that ironic and so yeah I am thinking of using it the question being on WHOM so let's wrap up this little greeting and annual update wow that's some update huh let me then wish you and I do mean it I am wishing you all truly truly a very merry Christmas and all the best to you and to whomever you THINK is yours do NOT EVER make assumptions on that note for trust as I see it now is reliant on a very special kind of arrogance do you get it that no one ever really really knows who is there for them and who ever knows what is real or what is not or what is to come or never will be as for myself I am already neatly seated in my first-level hell so whatever the outcome may be I am GOOD TO GO so I will sign off I just want to sit a spell in the dark and enjoy the silence this calm before the storm it is about the closest thing to PEACE I have felt in a long long time and I think you know what I

This was written also as a nod to Selby Hurbert's "Last Exit to Brooklyn," published first as a series of short stories in the late 1950s and early '60s, and then as a single work in 1964.

Here is a clue as to this story's flow: read it out loud. Fast.

Degenerate Crèche

I had this dream.

I dreamt, I was stuck in it, like a bug in a drop of pinesap.

Not dead. Alive, I think. No, I want to believe I am alive as there is no way in hell this can be a forever situation. I will wake up soon, I hope. I am fully aware, I guess, but neither as a living nor deceased participant; rather, as observer forced into passivity – a prop – with me, of all things, at its central point. Its grotesque apex.

And I am still here now.

I want to believe that I am just asleep, that I am indeed still dreaming, and that I can rouse from this, this something I am in – just not into what I am quite sure I left behind but a few minutes – hours? – ago. I know I am way past *some* critical point; the question is, what point? Of time? Of state of mind? Of place, perhaps? But, where or how to go back to what? And then, what to try and face going forward? If I could go back, how far back would I need to go to make any difference in whatever this all is? And what the hell do I call this?

I know there is a chance, that when I wake up from this place, this moment, I will be either back home, or perhaps still at the church, sprawled out on the floor. Heaven, at this point, would have me resituated farther back still, maybe seated on the edge of Bea's bed, reading a book to her. With her at peace and feeling safe. And I would have an honest and open talk with her, something to break the wicked spell that was brewing, the undercurrent which was sweeping us all along. No; perhaps I need to go back even before that. If nothing else, I would want to go somewhere, anywhere, that was back far enough to spare at least her.

Is there anyone out there? Here? Anyone to lift me up and out of this rabbit hole, to take me back to a point where I could have done something, anything about *everything*?

But that possibility does not seem to exist. Thoughts idle even as they pass through my brain. My isolation is more than complete. It threatens to close what portals remain cracked open, to the rest of my consciousness.

There is nothing of faith in any of this imagery, the setting, the cast of characters in which I do find myself. Underlying everything, there is some kind of perversion, an inversion to a flip side, wherein a repulsiveness exists as its very basis. Truth stripped and flayed; unadulterated wisdom. That apple bitten, then swallowed. Whatever repertoire was conjured up here, it has to have come from the fragmented childhood impressions I still held in my passive recall, when I like any kid – like Bea – I was confronted with ancient and universal archetypes and lore I had no way of understanding. Lurid images and narratives decidedly *not* intended for little ones, however Christ-like the passages and adages may have posited: *Let the children come onto Me.* This nightmare has to have come from all the piecemeal impressions I gathered up, tried to assimilate in my adult years in order to fake my way into some delusion of self-actualization and leadership role playing as husband, parent, and pastor. Shit.

But neither does anything I *feel* have to do with faith, this believing I am wherever I may be, in this weirdly suspended moment. It feels more like I have been sentenced to something. I readily admit, I did onto others as I *felt* had been done to me – constantly. The Golden Rule, personalized and then inverted, just like this place is inverted. There is something decidedly Boschian going on here, but I have a sense, it is all borne of my own mind, my puny, perverted rationalizations. My image, re-cast into my very own incubus.

To be sure, I have been forced to witness things I would never wish or dream to behold. And I cannot undo nor unsee anything in this here and now, for I am being made to play along in a way that makes it feel as were I being subjected to a wrenching of my very soul. My spirit, and everything I have ever believed, or believed in, is being raped, plundered, and thrown into the hollows. I am being wrung out like a wet rag; I am being hung to dry. It's like the vile stuff in that unseen container over there – whatever the hell that thing is, for I cannot see much of anything – and what its made of. Whatever else it may not be, it is in large part *of me*. My very own circular subsistence.

This could be a fate worse than death, this hell of my own making. But I just can't convince myself that I am dead. Nothing points to it. I cannot rightly say either which way, having nothing to compare this present tense with outside of any other insanity bender in which I might find myself stuck. Stuck in time, stuck in between existences, perhaps dimensions. Stuck in a nightmare. I once read about this other intra-dimensional place; they called it the "Neither." Makes me wonder if I could at least get there, even if it did mean losing the last dregs of my sentience along the way.

For now, I will stick with this: the facts appearing to be as they are, I have no choice. I am trapped. Being punished, perhaps. Perhaps not. Maybe I *want* this.

There is in this moment only a bizarre, immediate present, which is as horrific as it is insanely ridiculous.

†††

Who was I to think that the twelve-foot fake evergreen would support my weight?

And no, it wasn't enough to stay on that night, lock up the church in a pretext of putting the place to bed on an advent Sunday, sending the custodian home without him having finished up for the night. It wasn't enough to close the always-open Bible on its stand on the altar, even to lay a spare cloth over it, as if needing to block its view (as if it had eyes) of the very man who had read from it only a few hours prior, who was back again, but this time not to preach but to perpetrate a heist. Yes, he shalt steal. Yes, he sure as hell did covet. And it wasn't enough to take the donated gifts from under the tree – toys and clothes for a trio of "lucky" families; well, unfortunate lucky families who would enjoy the spoils of an entire congregation's largesse. This year, almost one hundred – the most ever – gifts had been gift-wrapped and placed under our 'Giving Tree,' to be handed out to an iffy passel of needy recipients when it was, in fact and in all irony, an actual hardship for many of us to buy those items, to then donate them to perfect strangers right out from under our own kids' noses.

Well, *my* kids would this year pretty much have to go without altogether, and so I had made the executive decision to reap the harvest of my congregation's Christian generosity on behalf of my own three. The kids could sort out what would go to whom (I had no idea what was in those boxes), the main point being there would be a nice batch of wrapped gifts under *their* tree this year. The biggest batch ever. The last couple of cash-strapped Christmases had already resulted in horribly meager pickings for my three children, and now with another year of age behind them, they would notice, and feel, even more acutely what was all missing in their lives, and in their parents' ability to provide. And not only that, they would have to perceive this in the face of being forced to watch the ribbon-tied boxes accumulate over these last two Advent Sundays, under that twelve-foot fake fir, there in the chancel, decked out with its beaded and lace-trimmed Christian monstrosities − Chrismons, as my wife more properly called them. Shit tons of presents for others. For perfect strangers.

Meg had, in fact, headed up the adult Bible-class committee which had painstakingly fabricated those hideous ornaments over the course of the summer and autumn months. Our littlest, she had begged and begged for her Mama to let her hold the crown she was working on, had begged Meg to let her put it on her curly-topped head for just a moment. But, oh no, Meg had acted as if Bea had uttered a blasphemy. Had told her daughter the crown was symbolic for the Prince of Peace, and that only a Baby Jesus could wear it, not any 'regular little kid' like her. Bea had thought her mother had called him the Prince of Please, and so her own pleas had escalated, rising to a tear-choked, "Please, Mama, pleeeease?" to which Meg had inappropriately responded (she was under so much damn stress, with her position imploding at the office due to the downturns for which no one took responsibility) with a harsh right-left-right slap upon Bea's little apple cheeks, which had turned them a dreadful shade of pink, especially when contrasted to the ashen color of the rest of her face, which soon went flush again, once she overcame her shock. Bea burst into tears and ran out of the room.

My daughter had been inconsolable that night. She went so far as to re-open the bedroom door she had initially slammed shut before creeping back into bed to recommence with her wailing, just to make sure we would hear it. Not that I blamed her. I was myself shocked with my wife's reaction. Bea's belabored sobbing went on way past bedtime. We were exhausted; it was physically painful to hear her cry like that. Meg eventually went to bed, drained of emotion, run dry in so many ways. I stayed up to listen for Bea to quiet down. She eventually did. And when she did, I went up to her room, took her a cup of water. I never said a word; I just held her. I was afraid, were I to have opened my mouth, I would have either damned myself for trying to excuse her mother's behavior or damned myself for having cursed the woman who bore this child, who as yet existed at the center of this little girl's universe.

Well, damn that crown ornament too, which had per chance been decreed by Cesarian equivalent of the church's august decorating committee (chaired by a woman Meg couldn't stand) to serve as the tree's crowning glory. They had precariously suspended it from the topmost leader branch of the fake tree. It hovered at the tip-top by way of a cleverly devised fretwork of fishing line, which held the crown seemingly in mid-air. Well, it was going to be that accursed crown that was going to go home with me as well, and it was going to find itself placed by yours truly upon Bea's own nightstand, so that when she'd wake up on Christmas morning, that fucking crown would be right there, glinting and sparkling right at her, ready for Bea to place it upon her head where it belonged, where I would make damn sure it would stay. I would tell my little girl, that baby Jesus had delivered it himself, right after Santa had finished up with his work, and I would warn Meg ahead of time, to keep her mouth shut, or else.

I also had the jist of a story fabricated, to utilize at whatever point in the coming week someone would have had any reason at all to enter the sanctuary, whereupon they would discover the gifts (and that damn crown) missing, and then in a panic come crying to me with the terrible news, that everything – including any fucking crumb too small for a goddamn mouse – had been taken.

I was, and remain, sick and tired of both me and Meg working our fucking asses off and never getting anywhere, never getting ahead, and especially for never ever getting any single fucking break. We work, and we work, and we work, and it doesn't ever change a thing. The bills still keep adding up ahead of our ability to pay them, even though it sure as hell would seem as if our good intentions – honest, honorable roads taken; all that damn loyalty – ought to pay off. But no, no, no! Stay jobless, stay single, have more kids so you can take, take, take, take! Because, what does that get you? More, more, more! Like shit tons of free, gift-wrapped, brand-new (they can't be used!) toys, toys, toys, and more clothes handed to you than any one of my kids has ever had in their entire closet – that actually fit – at any single given point in time.

Nope! All that crap was coming home with me tonight, and so was that damn crown. Like Napolean, I was going to self-anoint, proclaim myself King of Kings, and upon the merits of that coronation, I would bestow the glories of that sequined and beaded contraption over which my messed-up wife had labored long hours over the summer, over which she had repeatedly smacked our daughter over something so trivial, so fundamentally inappropriate in response to the crime committed, so to burn a toxic memory within the curly-headed noggin of my youngest child.

I was still raging, quietly, wordlessly, over the fact that Meg had yet to apologize to either our daughter or me for what she had done. Neither one of us had ever hit our kid before, and both of us having come from families where the rod and the hand *were not* spared, we had always been keenly, silently, and painfully aware that we each stood on the cusp of parental cross-over behavioral patterns which we had long ago agreed upon, we could never ever step over, because it would only lead to subsequent lashes, more striking out, and more anger projected onto the innocent collateral of our union. A part of me *hated* Meg for what she had let herself do – as if this had been some wicked indulgence that she had permitted herself, like taking an illegal drug, or drinking way too much, or parking in a handicap spot. But worse. Way worse. A part of me hated Meg because she had forced an introduction upon Bea to a sordid reality, Meg and I both knew of, intimately. Bea – no more than any child ever did – did not deserve to know what it felt like, to be hit in the face by an out-of-control parent. But it was already too late for that. I knew myself, from experience, that sort of thing is something you put into your back pocket and set aside. You grow up and out of it, but you always have it with you. And it changes you. It changes forever how you regard that parent. Possibly how you regard all humans. As such, I knew Bea had also already been forced to take a bite of that forbidden apple. She had crossed over, now held in her young soul a heart-rending slice of wisdom all humans possess, who have known corporal punishment, especially of the wholly unwarranted kind.

That night Bea had also not said a word when I went to her room with that cup of water. Her wet lashes, and the look which emanated from between those lashes had said everything.

So, Bea was getting that damn crown. And tonight, I was going to plunder it.

I don't think the ladder I had grabbed was very stable to begin with, it being about as old as the church itself, them both having been built around the turn of the century. And I should have known better, but I was tired – so tired – and eager to get home, and woozy from the long day at work combined with the absence of any food in my belly, lunch having been some seven hours prior, and not much at that (I packed sandwiches these days, mostly peanut butter).

All it took was for me to reach out that one inch too far, my arm outstretched to the max, my center of gravity skewed farther away from the ladder than was safe, about as far as anyone in my state of mind – filled with rage, love, and everything-in-between – would attempt, which was way too far. And I am not a giant; I am barely six feet tall myself and not particularly long-limbed. I somehow fancied I could lengthen my arm. I just kept reaching and reaching, further and further. And right about when my fingertips came into contact with that crown, and just about when I realized the fishing line support inside the crown was going to hold on way too effectively, and that I would not only have to be able to grab hold of the crown itself but also find some way to lift it up and off the tippy-top of that lead branch, that was about when the ladder gave way and began its slow arc of descent in the opposite direction from where I had been directing my weight – my entire weight – leaving me to grab at the sharp and bristling tree with my outstretched hand, but not catching hold of anything at all. And so then, as the tree began its own, slow arc down, down, in the opposite direction, I, being the rather solid and skinny deadweight that I am as an adult male, I plummeted straight down. Down, down, as hard and fast as a rock or an anvil or some such thing I fell, though I somehow managed a half-turn of my torso, so that, by the time I landed – hard – on the stone pavers of the sanctuary floor, half of me wound up on the landing, with the other half of me splayed into the aisle, my spine having met up with the knife-edge of that single, uncarpeted step. I landed with such force, I shattered my vertebrae, severed my spinal cord, and knocked the wind out of me to the extent that even my heart – my not terribly old or bad heart – was made to go into a pulsating shock, from which it may or may not have recovered. . .

As I blacked out, there in pieces on the church floor, I did so seeing the broad, lower branches with their glittering Chrismons coming right at me, falling down to crash over me like a wicked, spike-studded blanket.

Funny, immediately in front the altar, and now also my face, stood the figures of the nativity, a ghastly papier mâché set sourced at auction some years ago. As the bristling branches with their gold and white ornaments came to rest over me, and as my vision went dark, I do remember this one last bit of imagery: A flash of light shot through the nave like a bolt, perhaps from one of the windows nearby – I don't know – and struck the gold-painted halos of the fake Holy Family, splashing them garishly bright, as if electrified. Atop the lumpy, pinkish-beige painted faces of the trio, with their thin, crimson lips and black-rimmed almond eyes, those halos shone like crescent moons at midnight.

And then all that light somehow centered itself on the focal point of this menagerie, the child-figure Jesus, who was gazing innocently from His faux-bois manger. *He was looking right at me.*

As everything went dark, it was those three crescent-shaped haloes which seemed to burn through my eyelids; for, just as quickly as my world seemed to collapse, so did those haloes grow larger and larger, until their luminous masses filled my entire field of awareness, and the entire space in my consciousness was blindingly lit. It was against this glare that I began to blink again, slow and hard to shield my eyes, my hands having lost all feeling, my legs seemingly having gone numb too. It was during this brief series of blinks, this coming to, that a new scene came into focus. . .

†††

Back to this now, to my whatever.

What I see now before me, with not one noticeable moment of closure of one realm, nor of any riff having been opened into another, is this:

I lie here, a fifty-two-year-old man, a husband and a father of three, and although it is through the eyes of my mind that I peer, from what I can tell, my consciousness has somehow come to be housed in some sort of soft-tissued, long-limbed infantile form, bare and hairless. Smooth-as-butter arms flail involuntarily right in front of my face. I can feel them moving as I watch, passively. I can barely make them obey the commands of my thoughts, my muscle memory. Now and again, I manage to close those (my?) hands into fists, but just as soon as my consciousness discerns this and I send a flash of awareness to *keep them closed tight*, the fingers splay themselves again and begin to wriggle and jerk involuntarily some more. I cannot see the rest of me. This frightens me more than anything I have ever known as fear. My torso and legs seem to be compacted, wrapped, as if I were swaddled tight in a coarse, ever so slightly pliant sleeping bag, made of some kind of woven fabric. I can feel my legs crossed, hard and tight, at the ankles, so snug have I been wrapped into this thing. My toes tingle with numbness, my ankle bones dig into each other. It hurts. I am stretched out flat, like a cocooned worm, a human in a casing, and I lie upon a pungent bed of some prickly, straw-like material. I am nestled deep within the stuff, inside the trench of what appears to be a massive, wooden trough. Its sides are so high, I can only see up, but not over and past its edges. My field of vision is constricted, almost exclusively vertical. It is as if I had been placed in a fresh-built sarcophagus. I am looking up from a deep, smooth-sided abyss I cannot breach.

Over me hover two gilded crescent shapes. Those halos. Two brilliantly shimmering arcs, big as billboards. They come into focus. The crescents, I can now see, are at rest upon the headdresses of two enormous – at least to me and the scale at which I am perceiving all this – characters, two manifestations of what all my childhood iconography would tell me, *might* be a Mary and a Joseph. One appears right at the side of my primitive bed, hands – or rather, hooves – braced in prayerful stillness. But where I would have expected to see the face of a young woman, there glowers an elongated, fleshy snout similar to that of nearly hairless sheep. Long ears, flaccid and folded over, lie at rest upon its shoulders. Just above me, for this long face is centered above me in a show of attentiveness, I see rows of square, caramel-colored teeth which slowly grind away at some unseen mouthful of something. Rectangular pupils – huge, shiny, black – are set square upon me, studying me but with a blankness that speaks nothing to me. Nothing at all. The breath that emanates from this creature's maw – so close, too close over me – reeks of decomposition, of offal. The Mary bleats, sends spittle flying into my eyes. A whiff of barnyard halitosis descends over my face like a heavy cloud, causing me to cough and sneeze violently in a purely reactionary attempt to repel it.

The Joseph is even more bizarre, more hideous. The Joseph appears for all intents and purposes like some like of lizard. It peers over the first animalistic mothering creature's shoulder, benignly, casually, and curiously as any lizard might ever convey any iota of attentiveness, its rubbery neck bending this way and that, thin folds of skin pleating and spreading themselves like the bellows of an accordion as it observes us. A pale pink whip-sliver of a tongue protrudes from its lipless mouth, flies in and out, testing the air, flicking up and down and slapping itself back into the split of its receding jowls. The Joseph's eyes jerk about, separately from one another, scoping the perimeter in repeated, circular increments. They dart back to me from time to time, as if seeking to re-consider what the hell it is that I am, to assess me a little more thoroughly, for who knows what purpose, before the unblinking orbs resume their compulsive roundabout scanning.

The slight rattle of the Mary's laborious breathing and the whip-slurp of the Joseph's lizard tongue create a sort of cadence. I in turn observe it, him, and fixate on its tongue, which repeats its unfurling, then the left-right slapabout, and the quick suck-back into its, his, mouth. This is all I can hear in what is otherwise a heavy, rather liquid silence. Well, that, and the rustling hush of what must be crisp, dry straw beneath me, which my flailing arms strike at occasionally.

I am, we are, in a vacuum of sorts. But then, all of a sudden, this quiet and dark, wall-less space is disrupted, given further form and dimension when from high above us, an ear-splitting crackle and grinding commence, as if a set of ancient, rusted gears had been suddenly forced into action. Their mechanical protestations wail down upon us, even reverberate through the trough, or whatever it is I am lying in. I can feel the grinding. Does this onset make my bizarre initial impression more real? So, am I to understand that I am in some much bigger space, a lofted room of some kind? I am now starting to really wonder what could be beyond this box I am lying in; what might be behind those two hideous, enormous creatures which fill my view.

I can see past their ugly mugs easily enough now, and their crescent billboard halos of gold, for a burst of light has forced its way through the crack in the ceiling, to expose what now looks to be some sort raftered, pitched roofline, quite far away and ever so high above all our heads. The fissure broadens incrementally, in jerking movements, as the gear grinding continues.

It is a trap door opening high above us, just past a fretwork of heavy, timbered rafters, which are now easily discernable, thanks to the light being let in. An enormous, square hatch has been opened far enough to expose what is most definitely a sky. Beyond the ceiling, framed picturesquely, is an indigo blue-black heaven, peppered with glittering stars and the salted swath of a constellation. Is it the Milky Way? At midpoint, at the very center mark of this square opening, sits proud and pulsating, front-facing us below, a brilliant blue-white pentagram clearly intended to represent the Christmas Star, which has come to rest in its framed field of inky blue. It looks just like one of those detestable Chrismons. I am reminded of my Sunday school lessons – all those Bible picture books, all that cultural vernacular, and I know what all this is – or at least what the Joseph and the Mary and I are *supposed* to be. It is as if a laser pointer were targeting the heavens, messaging to a universe of simple-minded youngsters, or perhaps to Pharoahs, wizards, and faraway kings of the desert lands – anyone at all out there who just might be curious in the least, little way, that our little Nativity is here. *We are here! We are here! We are heeeere!*

But being anything but real – this must be a dream, for what else can it be? – or anything remotely close to *normal*, I have no idea what or who will show up next.

I wish to yell at these creatures, command them to heel, to go sit, move away from their hovering stances over me, but I am unable to formulate a single word. I open my mouth with the intention to speak. . .

. . .but what comes out merely sounds like the loose-lipped babbling of a baby plaintively bleating *Baa Baa Ba Baaaaa*!

I want to scream, display some modicum of indignation. I want to attempt some aspect of assertiveness, reset my vocals to sound off for the Me who resides within this beached human being, but that too is emitted and sounds like nothing more than a mewling wail, *Waaaaaaaaaaaa.*

Rage and frustration surge through me. The anger is such a physical sensation, so heated and solid, I can feel my swaddling cloth grow tight. It is almost as if the elements were pushing back against my protests, as if I had been slipped into one of those woven Chinese finger trap toys. The harder I resist, the tighter it gets. I can hardly draw a breath, refill my lungs, which feel now so compressed by the constricting cloth that a surge of anxiety is triggered. In a moment, I will not be able to breathe. I *know* I must set aside the panic that is about to strike. But I have nowhere to go with anything. So, having no choice, I tap my most mature and rational inner self and will the rest of whatever I am to a quieter place. What a perverse meditation. I hold my breath for just a moment. I wait, counting some abstract tally of nothing in particular, until the swaddling cloth responds, seems to relax its python's grip on me. I will simply *believe* I can feel it loosening. Sure enough, I can soon once again inflate my lungs with a full breath of air, albeit as malodorous as it was before. My stomach heaves, but being empty, nothing comes up.

The Mary has mistaken my angry reaction for hunger. Clumsily, for she has no hands but those cloven hooves, she lifts a sopping rag from some sort of vessel situated right next to her and brings it to my face. Awkwardly, she drops the dripping cloth onto my face and proceeds to push the wet fabric into my mouth, covering my nose as well so that I have no choice but to open my mouth and take in a wad of fabric in order to free my nostrils so I can try to breathe, again. I retch, imagining the mucky, viscous liquid could be something freshly expressed from her udder. Whatever it is, the fluid trickles into my nostrils, causing me to cough violently all while still being forced to hold that sopping rag in my mouth. I hack between pain-filled, forced swallows. Mouthful after mouthful, the cloven hands keep pressing at the fabric, forcing more of whatever it is into me. I cough, I retch, I swallow. I repeat the tortured ingestion. My stomach tries to repel the acrid soup, my eyes fill with reactive tears which slide down my cheeks and drip into my ears, causing me even more discomfort and stoking my pitiful, helpless rage. And no sooner do I seem to have finished, as does the Mary cease to squeeze more of the stuff into my mouth, as half of it comes lurching back up my esophagus, going up into my nose as well, spewing out my mouth and dripping down my cheeks and trickling into my ears, even into my eyes as I sneeze to expel the liquid from my nose. It is a sticky, and stinking wetness and I am helpless against the vileness in which I am bathed. This is a retch-inducing baptism spurs me ever closer to wishing

I *were* dead. I long for a full-on loss of sentience. Dead and unconscious; dead and done. I try desperately to bring my arms to my face to shield it, but the Mary has meantime managed to lift the broad end of the swaddling cloth up and over my upper body, thereby trapping my arms beneath the fabric as well. They are now pinned to my sides. I am now wholly inside the python. Swallowed whole in my nightmare.

The Mary begins to bleat. My immediate atmosphere becomes inundated with hot breath, spittle, and an ear-ringing chaos. At best, I can only turn my head, push my face into the straw so that the noise boxes only one of my ears, so that the heat and spray land on only side of my neck, against that jawline. I press my eyes closed, wincing to try and block the deluge striking at me from above. I feel violated. My face is drenched in a runny glue; I feel filthy.

The grinding sound resumes. My attention and that of the Mary's and the Joseph's are immediately jerked skyward once more. All eyes reach as far as they can into the depths – to the dark ceiling, the trap door portal, to the sky beyond that, and to that artificially shaped, pulsating star, still seated plumb center in the opening. The star lurches slightly, as if it were being dislodged from a fixture. It begins to creep forward, grows in slight but smooth increments, bigger and bigger. Somehow, I have managed to not yet feel much of any actual fear in the face of these beastly, gigantic beings. It reminds me of the way Alice in her Wonderland so casually journeyed through one extreme and into the next one. But I still feel trapped, and I am still livid, and I am feeling horrifically violated. For reasons I cannot explain, this fake star, this glimmering pentagram, as it grows and makes its geometry more clearly defined to me where I lay, *this* thing manages to strike fear in me. Deep seated, it causes my heart to palpitate, my suffering belly to lurch afresh. Again, I suspect, these are deeply ingrained responses being set off in me, for which I have no name, no active memory of imprinting, or understanding. There has to be some sort of primal fear that was singed into my psyche before I even knew the language by which to categorize the impression. Perhaps the instinct preceded me. Maybe this all is borne of a fear knit into one's DNA, something I, we, have intuitively known to dread as a matter of fundamental survivalist instinct. That star up there is not a benevolent image or icon or fucking Chrismon made of beads and glue and sequins. This star, *I know*, is representative of a falsehood.

Is the perversion borne in its geometry? Does it lie somewhere between the very notes of that insipid little ditty Mozart himself is credited with, which has shifted the trajectory of all childhood perception for centuries now? Celestial bodies rejiggered as benign diamonds in the sky, which are in actuality vaporous bastions of super-heated toxicity? Annihilation gift-wrapped by way of a cult-like adherence to the sheer possibility of lame and stupid wishes coming true? Happy endings? Yes, that has to be it. This star-thing is somehow illustrative of everything any fool has ever been made to believe, it being in the end just another digit, another co-opted symbol in a zero-sum game. Always and only futile extensions of a good-for-nothing Humankind, which nevertheless persistently pretends to be in some possession of supernatural capabilities, somehow worthy of an indifferent universe's incidental consideration.

How I wonder what you are in actuality points to us never knowing about ourselves.

And so, Meg's raging on our daughter was nothing.

And Bea's heartbroken state after that was meaningless.

And my lust for the damn crap piled beneath that fake Christmas tree was a trifling folly, as was my act of stealing a passel of gifts intended for those even more misfortuned than I, than any one of my kids, than our entire, borderline dysfunctional family which, in its abject craziness, was just how it was always supposed to be.

And my falling from that ladder and the fracturing my spine was a joke. Nothing more than the snapping of some random twig in two. And my heart giving out was nothing more than a piece of fruit bypassing its expiration date, tossed into a bucket for the farmhand to dump into a trough for the barnyard animals to feed on.

And there she is, the she-goat, the Mary, and her slippery rubber-faced Joseph, watching over me, not comprehending much of anything.

And here I am, slithering over my own precipice towards *extreme* knowledge, being made to realize that nothing means everything. Anything whatsoever, in life, or in whatever this sick Garden of Delights is. I bet Stephen Hawking, the more he figured out, the more fancied himself at about the level of an ant, or less. As for me, I may as well be a maggot. I know I sure look like one, wrapped up, cylindrical, compressed and useless, sentient but unable to formulate a single fucking word.

And I am trying to ignore the derelict and overwhelming feeling, that I am about to take a dump within these constricting bandages, this baby Jesus paradigm in his swaddling cloth in His with a capital H gravesite manger for a shithole bed. God help me, I have already wet myself and there is nothing I can do about that. My practical ken kicks in and I realize the horrible potential for the onset of an irritation, consider the potential for infection I might be subjecting myself to, which is in and of itself an infantile perversion for any adult. I am blaspheming my conscious self with involuntary bodily functions which will defile me from the inside out, and I will be made to wallow in my own waste – lesser than a barnyard animal, leagues beneath the lowly Mary and even the limpid Joseph who both still hover over me, their uncomprehending gazes still ogling that evil, shimmering entity which glowers down upon us, grows bigger and closer by the moment.

It long ago oozed through the trap door, is now in the hallowed stable's atmosphere, right above our heads.

The center point of that vile star makes itself known to me, to us, by way of a black spot, an indentation, or a hole of some kind, at dead center of its mass. The hole seems to fluctuate; it pulses of its own accord as the entity continues to emanate light. The hole begins to grow, pulling and stretching against itself as were its dough-like orifice being manhandled from within by an invasive, invisible hand. Before long, the hole has become so misshapen, it writhes in an erratic, globular fashion, closing a little only to open again, bigger each time, as if it were drawing in air and then expelling it, and growing larger with each exhalation. A memory flashes, and I connect this stationary writhing to Meg in the hospital, in the labor room, three times, giving birth. I realize, something is going to emerge from this void. Be born, right over our heads.

As if my realization were some cue, the orifice is suddenly tainted at its wobbling rim with bright red, viscous matter. A liquid. Blood? Giving birth in a literal sense? Are we staring into the depths of a cosmic vagina in its last stages of labor, for Christ's sake?

The red – yes, it looks like blood – begins to drip, drip, drip, down upon us.

The droplets, thick and elastic globular emissions, are heavy. They pull long from the puckering hole before breaking free and jellying their way down to us. They make audible, plishing sounds when they strike the Mary, and then the Joseph, who seem non-plussed, though they are fascinated and fixated, even more dumbstruck than earlier. They lick clean the droplets which land near their mouths. The thick splats strike me as well. I can feel them landing along the length of my swaddled form, *tap, tap, tap*. A droplet strikes the crown of my head. Strikes my left cheek. Mixes with the damp tracks of my tears and that vile mystery milk, runs like everything else has so far, into the curvature of my ear, for which I would give an eyetooth – a literal eyetooth could be yanked from my gums this very second –

to have a free hand to be able to wipe that miserable trickle out of my ear, and to rub it clean, ease that nasty, nagging itch which has become such a torturously persistent annoyance.

We all watch, me wincing whenever a bloody drop randomly strikes me. The Mary shifts her attention ever so often to me in my bed, wiping clumsily the red muck out of my eyes as best as her hooved "hand" permits. I cannot understand why I lie here, so still, so perfectly still, in other words, so compliantly. But I also know, there is nothing I can do. I am bodily trapped. I may as well be strapped onto a gurney. I am also in some alternate reality I cannot figure out, hostage to my awareness, this nightmarish place and condition. It is equivalent, I realize, to night terrors, those paralyzing states of mind where all one can do is *watch*, unable to even fully close one's eyes to shut "it" out.

A bare foot emerges from the seeping pucker. It is pale and fine, the peach-crème alabaster foot of a renaissance nude. The toes flex. A second foot emerges as the first foot pushes onward and down, exposing a slender but curvaceous calf, then a knee. Soon both legs are exposed, dangling like twin appendages from this fatty, birthing pentagram. Blood continues to drip but is now minimized due to the fact that the orifice is filled, stretched tight, with body parts. The legs and feet are smeared with blood.

Fabric, damp and heavy, slithers out from the lips of the birthing maw. It appears to be layers of a thin, silk-fine fabric which slide out alongside the rest of the legs. The orifice stretches even wider – the Mary groans involuntarily, as if in empathetic understanding of the ordeal – as what must be the base of a torso is exposed. It wriggles and forces itself out from within, the widest section of the hips being quickly and suddenly pushed out. From there, the slender waist and upper body emerge quickly. Bloody droplets, livery gelatinous particles rain down upon us all. The Mary and Joseph appear to me as would two ogres, had they intentionally taken crimson showers. But they remain non-plussed, are transfixed by this birthing apparition they are witnessing.

We – the Mary, the Joseph, and I – all startle when, all of a sudden, in the way that births often do, the remainder of this emerging entity falls free from the writhing hole – which seems almost to spit the rest of it out – and plops wetly, noisily, and heavily to the ground, just a short distance from us. The Joseph, with his quick, reptilian reflexes, jolts himself over to the other side of the trough, to side-step the spot where the heavily draped and dripping wet, red-stained being lands. It is, at least as I had suspected it, a human, or at least a humanoid creature, which has just been – born? But the newcomer is an adult figure, lankily proportioned, at least as tall as the Mary and the Joseph both are. These beings, these creatures all loom inordinately enormous to my eyes for I still *feel* my full adult height, and my heft as I have always sensed it. It is as if I and my entire universe may have existed on some different and much smaller scale than this one. It occurs to me, I have perhaps landed in some cloud-seated realm of giants, on the gargantuan flip side of Alice's wonderland. Their heads would, I bet, strike the ceiling of my home, or my church's nave, were they to appear in my world. Could hell consist very simply of full-on absurdity?

I cannot see where exactly the being is now, cannot see them where they are lying – or perhaps by now seated – on the ground, or floor, or whatever constitutes the surface below my bed.

But what I do see almost right away, are the tips of white feathered appendages, lifting themselves up, high enough to breech my field of vision. These things move back and forth, slowly, rhythmically. They are drying themselves, spreading visibly. Huge, rounded contours rise up. I can now tell, these are wings. Wings as articulated as those of an enormous bird of prey, a snow-white owl, or an eagle.

The newly birthed being – these wings belong, clearly, to them. The being is now itself rising up, its entire form stabilizing alongside the wings, as anyone newly hatched would come to, as it were, from a particularly vulgar and uterine-like chrysalis.

That star, by the way, having given birth, has folded in on itself, reduced in form to the extent that it is now a far smaller, globular pentagram. Its buttoned up, black orifice looks now like nothing more than a dried current on a hot cross bun. I am instantly revolted by my casual comparison of an edible morsel as it relates that grotesque thing up there. The extensions of its five arms are re-compacted, and relatively stable. As such, the entire birthing star – a bizarre and primitive cousin untold light years behind, say, a cloud nimbus – appears to me almost like a pre-baked Christmas cookie. Doughy, soft at the edges, but recognizable as is. It pulsates only the slightest bit, with a regular pacing, as were it catching its breath. I wouldn't mind having a bite of something sweet. I am disgusted with myself.

At least the infernal drippage has stopped.

I look back at the winged newcomer, who is now standing upright, undertaking a reconnaissance of its surroundings. Blank-faced, with little comprehension, it is scanning the Mary and the Joseph, up and down, up and down;

it is looking me up and down as well. I can feel its eyes run along the length of my white fabric casing. There is actual *heat* where the being's gaze strikes the fabric. The sky-blue eyes come to rest momentarily and without the first hint of recognition on my face. I am feeling the sun on a spring day, and it is bathing my features. It makes me feel like the most repulsive, low-born slug that has ever existed. I have never been beheld by something in such stark contrast to what I have ever considered myself to be. I may as well be a bacterial growth on the rotted hull of a nutshell ten feet underground with the eyes of God deigning to gift me with the grace of this split-second glance. That is how sublime this being appears to me.

I am stunned by its beauty. It is, for all I can tell, and based on everything I have ever seen or learned or been taught with rapturous intention, an angel. And not just any angel, but an archangel; a regal and beauteous seraph on par with any renaissance era manifestation. With Gabriel himself; a Christianized Psyche, a pure and guileless Venus. It – he? she? – gazes about, takes everything in with an air so intense yet so full of child-like absorption, it is nearly awe-inspiring, to witness this pure intake of *the now*. It is as if the dawn itself has for the very first time breached the horizon of a brand-new Mother Earth, to look down upon an Eden, and for the first time is able to acquaint its perfect and gorgeous self with the base playgrounds of fools, to which it has been oh, so generously consigned.

The liquid sapphire angel eyes only glow more luminously the more they take in. A literal enlightening, this newly born immortal sentience is as brilliantly vibrant as the minute constellations which have come home to roost in its depths. I am deathly afraid of the magnitude of the being which stands so close to us, but cannot categorize the fear, for I am likewise deeply and instantly in love. It is a love I have never felt for anyone in my life, so powerful a surge, it twists my gut something awful. Such is the power of a heavenly aspect. The Mary? The Joseph? They are what I perceive to be equally smitten, but in their far more limited capacities. They just stand there, thunderstruck. I myself, I want to cry, I feel this moved. But I dare not shed a tear, nor even allow my eyes to glimmer with emotion. I am terrified, absolutely terrified, the Mary will take notice and immediately set about to stuff my gullet with more of that rag soaked in whatever it is that fills the container I cannot see, but which I know is set right at her feet. And there was no way I could stomach that lactosey swamp water again. There is also no way I could bear to let anything hinder my ability to gaze upon this sublime creature, even for a millisecond.

My eyes, my mind are stymied. I am utterly and completely addicted to this pansexual, angelic transfixion, unbound. A part of me wants to be taken and forced to her breast, to suckle from her cherry blossom teat; a part of me wants to break my bindings and jump astride her, fuck her, or be straddled and fucked in some way myself. I am aghast yet enthralled by this bizarre mix of adoration, and I hate myself for how quickly and completely I have displaced my very own wife, and for how every concept I have ever embraced of attachment, commitment, sacrifice, and human connection has been negated. I know now beyond any shadow of a doubt, it all – all of it – meant nothing. Nothing, when compared to this intense, kaleidoscopic awareness, to where instinct borne of this inversion of reality has instantaneously re-wired me. Everything I ever learned, or thought I knew, prior to this, was meaningless. Waste.

But in the way any perception of perfection – adoration – is dashed, in the way the most loyal and obeisant regard can be inverted and turned inside out in the blink of an eye, so is my adulation destroyed in the space of a few moments.

My angel, which wasn't *mine* to even call mine to begin with (such perfection cannot be owned by anyone or anything) seemingly rouses, comes to. She, he, it shakes herself, much as a dog would when come in from the rain. It is a full-body shudder that runs through the entire being's form, involuntary and vigorous. Like a rippling wave, or a breeze through a wooded glen, I see a series of vibrations work their way down its entire length, beginning at the tips of its wings, which convulse with a powerful whirring sound. The quaking makes its way across the outstretched span of the seraph's intricately laid, feathered armaments, and disperses at the tips with the softest of shivers. And then he, she, it shakes their head, tossing masses of golden-brown ringleted curls back and forth. Then, there go those slender shoulders, the wet-draped curves of its Galateaian form* – piquant breasts, slope-waisted torso, hips cut in an elegant spread, all further delineated by the damp, silken robe which has yet to completely dry off. Perfection, visually cut with the precise delineation of the most finely carved marble that was ever permitted to step off of any pedestal. What exists below my limited view, I cannot see, but hardly care. I know, of course, still recall – having seen it, him, her being born from below – those long legs, the delicate feet as they emerged from the nimbal birth canal. I know that underneath the clinging, flowing robe, exist whisper-thin legs which hold this being aloft with the grace of a blown-glass ballerina. Perfect and pristine from head to toe, and so far beyond all of that.

My angel, he, she, it, steps forward, abstractedly scanning the scene as I and my parental figures present it. The Mary and the Joseph do not appear to hold its attention much at all. I can see the constellation eyes flitting past the two without much pause at all. It is as if the two creature-like ogres are too insignificant to notice much, hence, almost invisible. Even I can construe how the angel's gaze, traveling right through them, is a form of disregard, but that it is quite involuntary. And me of all things, me as a participant in this crazy ménage à quatre, the bound slug, the hideous, beige-faced humanoid caterpillar wrapped in its fabric cocoon, I lie here like a white turd. But I am, by contrast, the only figure the angel seems to care about, seeks to study a bit to learn more about it – er – me. Moreover, I am the only one with enough intellect to discern the disconnects in this wordless conversation. I can see the emptiness in the Mary and Joseph's joint dulled states; their dumb anticipation of, well, nothing, really. They cannot help but exist in their versions of their present, in each moment as it marches on mechanically, with or without them.

Which is why, when the angel without warning takes the Joseph's staff from his webbed hand, I am startled. And when I notice that the head of the staff is nothing short of a three-pronged trident, with a trio of massive and sharp points made of what appears to be iron, I am surprised. And when the angel hurls that trident point blank into the Joseph's bulbous chest with such force it is instantly embedded in the Joseph's breast to the depth of almost one-fourth the staff's length – I can actually see the black tines protruding out through the back of Joseph's tunic, sending a fresh spray of blood into the air with them – I am shocked. And when the angel takes hold of the staff with the Joseph skewered point blank upon it and turns the trident skyward, taking the Joseph up with it like the gigged frog he now is, and when the angel hurls that trident towards the doughy nimbus which still hovers over our heads, and the nimbus spreads its vagina-maw wide, wide, wide to engulf the gigged Joseph, who meantime has begun to hiss and flail about in both panic and in pain, and as I see the Joseph swallowed whole, little by little in that way a python ingests any animal far bigger that it is, the last thing to be engulfed being the Joseph's noiseless crying maw, agape and frozen in abject terror, with more blood seeping out of the sides of that star's obscene birthing orifice-cum-jaws as it consumes this scene's Father figure, I realize that I am *just like* that Joseph up there. I am about to disappear entirely, into the face of a horror so unexpected, so seemingly random, and done so matter-of-factly, that it hurls my worshipful regard into the deepest of all abysses, leaving me physically sickened. I am sickened by what I am seeing *and* by what I am feeling – and what all I have ceased to be able to feel.

What did I as a motionless slug just participate in? Is the Mary next? And worse yet, for it seems more imaginable than anything: am *I* next? The way the angel – demon? – dispatched of the Joseph, it reminded me of the frogs I hunted with my own father when I was a boy, in the swamps by our house, way late at night. My father in the space of one night taught me how to kill off the song of the midnight swamps, the songs of the countless, dumb, and innocent frogs that lived in the woods and waters of my home, the lands I had wandered as a child.

And when at one point I made one little comment that night, over the distress the twitching frogs may have been feeling, all skewered and smashed together on the cord my father had latched to his belt, it was then that my childish empathy for lowly edibles had earned me one of the most painful right-left-rights my father had ever let loose upon me. I can still hear the zinging echo in my brain, the resounding buzz which lingered in my boxed ears, along with the smell of the swamp water, the decay, the salt of my involuntary tears, which I tried so hard, so hard to hold back, for I knew my tears might trigger another round of beatings.

Yes. I remembered and recognized the whole thing. That was the night my love for my father died. And when, the next evening, he forced me to sit at the table until my plate of pan-fried frog legs was completely eaten up, down to the last crunchy membrane of frog foot that I still think my father put on my plate on purpose, that was the day I came to hate my father. Day one of a journey I was forced to undertake, which would stay with me, nagging me, teasing me, luring me by way of its insidious, nearly irresistible legacy, to try and *not* become *Him*. To try to not do as he had done unto me. And I realized also in that moment, although I had not been the one to hit my youngest daughter, I had transgressed in just about every other way possible, in all my stupid and futile quests to be somebody, to override my abysmal anonymity, my absolute insignificance. I realized, in coming full circle as faux judge and sinner and especially now passive observer, I was being made to internalize that everything was in actuality *for* nothing.

What that angel, demon, whatever, did, it may as well have done to any one of us. For we are all dumb and innocent animals, dumb and innocent and yet blindly trusting, which is perhaps the evolutionary vestigial remains of what faith was originally supposed to be. Which makes this all that much more horrific, cold, and bestial. I really am a worm.

Moreover, that angel, *that thing*, that grotesquely and horrifically lovely thing, it is not of heaven but of hell, because *there is no such thing* as heaven.

Or are those two places one and the same thing?

Could it be, that angelic vengeance – however random *it might seem* to a creature as base and lowly as I – is in actually a blessing we are just not capable of grasping? Might there be something *wonderful* at work here that is simply too wonderful for me to grasp?

I realize, this is possible. Especially as I watch the Mary – the newly single mother Mary – turn casually away from where the Joseph stood, to glance at me, to wipe once again my face, my eyes (remember, I am not uttering the first sound of distress or want or need or whatever could be called), to then re-place its blank stare once more upon the majestic wingèd creature which is still standing, serenely, elegantly, in our midst.

The Mary's eyes shift imperceptibly, and our eyes lock momentarily. I try to wipe all thought from my mind. I make not the first sound. I barely blink. Anything, anything to not indicate any desire on my part to be force-fed any more of that rag soaked with whatever it is down there. Anything to not draw any attention on me whatsoever. I remain utterly passive, a baby Jesus doll laying in its manger, in need of nothing, nothing, nothing. I know I can at least control the momentary peace I have in being left alone, even while bearing witness to perversions of reality I could heretofore never have begun to approach in my wildest imaginations, my darkest nightmares.

As this new wisdom grows in leaps and bounds within me, as my perspective keeps shifting in intra-planar fractals, I begin to accept that the more I "get," the less I am as a separate being, and that the less I am, the more actualized, the closer to nirvana, the more fulfilled to my core I am becoming. Becoming. Not a what or a who, but a flux state of being, reliant on nothing. Becoming, as in reducing my arrogant sense of self into a purified abstraction of what was the lowly human, the slug, the straight-jacketed supporting cast member in this, this – what do I call it? This degenerate crèche.

The angel, he, she, it, whatever it was, is, begins to float upwards. I understand this to be an ascension. The angel, it rises slowly, slowly into the air, into the blackened space above us. Its broad wings block our view of the ceiling, the small patch of midnight-blue sky, and the distant stars which pepper that field; also, that pulsating, macrophagic nimbus which, evidently satiated and replete with having given birth and then having been fed, has gone dormant. The angel casts its wingèd shadow over me and the Mary, who meantime, has lowered her head, looks off to the side at nothing in particular, has resumed chewing her cud. Mary's squared-off eyes, her dumb and wordless brown gaze, is affixed into some pointless point in the distance, which I cannot not see. I am still and only gazing upwards from a manger bed that is a grave, a grave that is a manger bed.

The angel's ever-wet gown still drips the watery substance with which it is still, oddly, soaked. These droplets are all the falling tears I will never again shed. They fall like rain, and like a spring shower, have the capacity to clean us up a bit. After all that blood, it is a welcome shift, for all its being yet more unwanted precipitation. I remain warm and dry inside my many layers of swaddling cloth, which so far have repelled the blood, the water, and that stuff in the container, although my neck is chafed and it's has grown quite sore from all the protracted craning, in my repeated attempts to try and see what the hell was going on.

It's just hell, I suppose. Thing is, I no longer care. Much.

It's just heaven, as seen from the backside, upside down and inverted. Iron tines projecting through the ribcage of a gigged lizard Joseph. Shepherd's staff, frog gig – there is no difference.

I am now omniscient in my own pithy context. And I know what I must do. Or rather, what all I must not do.

In my new-found wisdom – which is truly, heart-breakingly infinite, for it is circling me back to absolute zero – I understand how insignificant and small and stupid and worthless I am. Same for Meg, who is no more. Same for the kids, who like all offspring, are just untapped potential – future failure, futility, heartbreak, and betrayal. Same for the congregation, for whom I realize, I never gave a damn. Ditto on those wrapped presents, the beaded crown, that defective ladder, which *I knew* was about to collapse and send me flying. It is *my failings* as human, husband, and father that count, for they have served to justify the erasure of me.

The audacity I possessed, to condemn others when I myself was not ever worthy of even the language employed to denigrate them, leaves me – almost miraculously – with the absolute freedom to cast disregard and discard therefore *everything*. To simply, simplistically exist in *this* here and now. Not in one split second to come, nor in any single hair's-breadth slice of the past. Now. Only now.

And right now, I need to have my bottom cleaned up. I know deeply and profoundly that I am in need of the Mary's primitive equivalent of a diaper change, for me have wet myself. And then, only then, I will be sublimely, joyously happy. And content. I will once again have *everything*. In *that* moment. However, in *this* moment, I do *not* want more of that, that liquid yuck. I not hungry. Just poopy. Feeling another poop about to come. And so, I come to the monumental and brilliant conclusion, I will not yowl like I did before. Forget language. Fuck words. That did not work; those do not work. If anything, they netted me a soaking wet rag rammed into my mouth to the point of gagging, from which I was forced to ingest an inordinate amount of whatever that shit was, which I have already expelled, which, I suppose, I am destined to consume again at some point in the near future. And so, I will mewl a tad more benignly, to simply, sweetly suggest to the Mary that me need sumping. Me gonna need poopoo changey. Me will want kween up. So, me go softer *Boo Hoo* so dis Mama, she not give me yuck. No; she kween me up. Pweeeez.

Den me so, so happy. *So* happy.

* *pertaining to the mythological statue Galatea*

Bell Ringer #1

Clickety clickety click click click. . . tick. . . tick. . .

The coins tumbled only momentarily, being quickly silenced within the depths of the Bell Ringer's red kettle, which must've already been quite full. Surely, I thought, the percussive clang of several coins coming to rest all at once should do the trick, let me pass on by as one of the more generous donors. I made to dash past the VACO volunteer – the Trooper, as they were officially called – for I was, as always and like everyone else this time of year, running late.

"Meeeeerrrrry Christmas to you and thank YOU!" the Trooper exclaimed.

"Meeeeerrrrry Christmas, Milifred!" the Trooper repeated.

I paused. Shoppers rushed past me in the entryway, jostling me in their haste. Had I just heard my name spoken?

"Yes, my dear; I am talking to you!" spoke the Trooper, his tone of voice lowering, taking on the slightest of edges. I immediately sensed in his delivery that he was accosting me, not merely greeting me. I tossed a suspicious glance over my shoulder at him.

He continued, a tad more politely, "How kind it is of you to contribute to VACO's annual holiday campaign, Milifred. But let us reconsider today our giving and be mindful of a biiiiigger picture. What say you about that bottle of nail polish and chewing gum you procured from this very store some years ago? I know you know what I am talking about. . ."

I spun around to face him.

"Don't you think that circumstances, especially given this time of year when all are called to give juuuuust a little bit more, warrant a tad more generosity on *your* part?" His broad grin held not the least bit of warmth.

"Yeeees," the Trooper went on, feigning a business-like air, "I am afraid your donation falls a biiiit short," he inhaled deeply, puffing his chest like a pigeon's, "of what *I* would consider the commensurate payment, considering what you. . . you know. . . did."

There was no way this person should have known my name. And there was no way he – or anyone for that matter – could have known what I had done, wow, a thousand years ago, as a stupid little kid, when just one time I succumbed to a silly impulse and shoplifted a package of gum and a bottle of nail polish.

The detailing of my petty theft – never discovered, never punished or even admitted to by me, instantly rendered me queasy and dizzied. Good grief! Thing is, I hadn't even hung on to those two items. I had thrown them into the neighbor's garbage can that very afternoon, spurred by a wave of shame and guilt that had, back then just like it was now, left me queasy and feeling dizzied.

This most unwelcoming sentry standing guard at the entrance to Krueger's was evidently some new VACO volunteer. VACO stood – stands – for the Virtuous Armies Charitable Organization. They call their volunteers Troopers. One had been stationed at the entrance to Kreuger's for as long as I could remember. This particular VACO Trooper, I had never seen before, at least not since having moved back home. I had recently returned to my hometown with the intention of re-structuring my life, for life in the big city had not proven so great after all. My relocation had so far gone well enough, with a few compromises made alongside just as many practical opportunities having presented themselves in return. My new apartment cost a fraction of the cubby I had rented in the city, and the job I had taken at the call center was going to help open a key door for me, being that my work schedule would now allow me more free time to write, which had always been my dream: to become a published author, and to establish my own small press. This was now my active goal, my plan in action.

Tonight, however, I had rather different plans, albeit directly related to my writing. If truth be told, I was in the process of re-inventing myself for purposes of promoting my literary output. My ordinary but unremarkable presentation of self had so far not served me at all as a writer, an unfortunate reality especially where it came to career-pushing by way of a social media presence. I had become convinced I needed to re-craft my persona into a more direct reflection of the content I was producing. It was my extended plan to undergo a complete identity transformation, including a legal name change. I would then re-launch my writing career as this "new" person, start at a fresh and sassy square one, with a carefully culled first and last name combination to carry me, crafted to enticingly reflect the genres I would both author and publish. I was certain, a more alluring identity would grant me newly freed liberties in myriad ways. In time, I would further establish myself as a curator and editor of a series of anthologies that my small press would publish, to which a loyal cadre of 'signed' indie authors would contribute. And my secret – a terribly fun one, I thought - plan was to have every last one of 'my' authors be of my own making – entirely fictitious. Characters, if you will. They would be me. I would be them. They would, like I, have poetically perfect names, and enigmatic personas, and they would be pretty much impossible to locate. An air of mystery would surround us all – me as their bewitching, proud mother hen, they as my conveniently obscured, privacy-loving brood.

As to my new look, I had thoroughly researched what was 'hot,' what seemed to be garnering the most attention, and had formulated my concept, tip to toe. I had a hair appointment in a few days, the plan being to acquire a set of fake lashes and hair extensions for an ultra-long and thick mane of raven-black tresses. The local resale shops were already proving to be great resources for what I called the twilighting of my overall look – black garments, lace-trimmed this n that, a little purple thrown in for kicks. Today's trip to Kreuger's was to purchase the makeup items I had on my list – a pretty long list, but all of it requisite to the plan. Online tutorials and artful experimentation would help see to the rather complete transformation of my face.

You see, I was already crossing a threshold borne of a slow-simmering undercurrent of deceptive necessity, which I can only ascribe to as fueled by a weird sort of anger, a vehemently determined desire. This whole thing about "looks" had worn thin with me ages ago, and I even held some resentment towards my own self for having quite thoroughly succumbed to its perceived mandates. But I was going to do this no matter what.

My identity crafting would be a multi-tiered metamorphosis per the realities of available time and most especially funds. I was just a regular working single gal on a budget. Perhaps, in time, a nose job might be the thing to do, if and when funds permitted it. Maybe boobs too. Meantime, the absolute *last* thing I needed on this phase one visit to Kreuger's, was to be confronted by a prying little bastard VACO volunteer when all I was doing was going to the store to buy some damn makeup.

I have always considered myself a people reader. A split-second onceover of this nasty little Trooper told me pretty much all I needed to know. I sure as shit had something to dread with this one. This Trooper sported atop his standard issue vest a massive badge, which was affixed over his left breast pocket in lieu of a nametag. The badge looked like the kind of first-place ribbon one might find on a prize pig at the fair. It was ludicrously large, festooned with a gold tassel and trimmed with a sunburst array of prickly-looking, plastic holly leaves. The central medallion bore the insignia "BR #1" in tomato soup red upon a field of emerald green.

BR #1 stood for Bell Ringer Number One. I had seen placards in store windows advertising these accolades since Halloween, leaving me to think, even the stores were hoping to help their shoppers to brace themselves for the annual deployment of insignia-bearing VACO Troopers.

The Trooper stared at me unflinchingly, with a veracity which crossed over into an expression I can only describe as some sort of jolly hostility.

Little fuck. I knew the type:

Bell Ringer Number One is hired to greet and send shoppers off. But Bell Ringer Number One flails that bell-slinging arm of his with abandon, with his god-awful, clangy bell driving everyone nuts. Bell Ringer Number One is oddly irresistible whilst being most certainly off-putting. And he is intensely insistent with his attentions, which bodes wonderfully well for the garnering of funds. Bell Ringer Number One is, in fact, so aggressive with his solicitations and felicitations, that he unintentionally manages to keep the store entrance absolutely clear of loiterers and troublemakers, to the delight of the over-taxed store managers and their recalcitrant security detail, which makes him terribly essential in all their eyes. This incidental guard dog allocation, no doubt, grants Bell Ringer Number One *entirely* too much leeway. . .

Bell Ringer Number One looks for all the world like some combination of a stop-motion Kris Kringle doll and that Vulgarian Child Catcher from that film version of Chitty Chitty Bang Bang. Toss both those characters into a gigantic blender, first set to chop, then to frappé, and voilà, you are left with a nasty concoction of two caricatures, formed into one thick pile of Christmasy. . .

Yep. That'd be this Trooper. A Christmas-clad, elfin piece of shit.

I took in his wizened face. His eyes glittered like rum-soaked raisins squashed into an overhang of frizzled eyebrows. His flushed cheeks were as rounded as a pair of mid-century shiny-bright ornaments. His droll mouth was seated upon the promontory of a wiry and devilishly pointed goatee. And when that Trooper smiled at me as he continued to just stand there, holding his ground, waiting for whatever retort I might try and conjure up from the sick feeling he had instilled in me, those thin lips of his curled up so tight in the corners, I could swear, he must have had a pair of screws affixed to the insides of his gums that he could tighten at will for evil effect.

A Christmas creature from some horror movie, is what he was.

"Now, look here," was all I managed to come up with.

"Yee-ees?" he intoned. Sing-song was evidently a favorite speech style of his.

"Sir," I persisted, gathering steam, "What do you think you are doing, calling me out by name? You don't even know me. . ."

Bell Ringer Number One seemed to shift gears. I assumed this was to respond to me with the civility I was affording him in that moment.

I was wrong.

Bell Ringer Number One raised the tip his nose ever so slightly, so to better look down along its length at me. He hissed this next sentence between clenched teeth.

"*Oh, yessssss, I do, missy.*"

He leaned in towards me.

"If you think five measly nickels are going to obtain my permission and blessing for you to cross *this* post on *this* day in *this* season of giving, you have another thing coming, girl. Do you think twenty-five puny cents is commensurate for your foisting from this very store that package of gum and that bottle of hot pink nail polish that *you know you didn't even really want*, you lil snake, just so you could take it home with you without paying for it, to then, even further, make waste of it by throwing it into the trash?"

I could only sputter, could not formulate the words to protest what had just been thrown *at me*.

What that troll was accusing me of was not only one hundred percent accurate, but a childhood secret of mine which I had *never* disclosed *to anyone*. That no one had stopped me at the store on that afternoon, I had never understood. I could still remember how I had fumbled everything, how scared sick I was, even as I perpetrated my petty theft. I had to have been so clumsy, so obvious. Even back then, I knew what I was feeling as a result of my thievery was not worth the puny gain of those two items. My childish deed had served me my own lesson. After that day, I had stayed away from Kreuger's out of sheer guilt. Since moving back, however, I had presumed myself distanced enough from that incident to be able to simply walk through the store's front doors just as any other, ordinary shopper would, to simply be there as an ordinary, *paying* consumer, like everyone else. Like all petty sinners out there. Them like me. Me like them.

Well, that sure turned out to be one short shopper's honeymoon of blissful ignorance.

"So, what do you have to say for yourself?" Bell Ringer Number One persisted.

"I. . . I don't know what to say," I kept searching my blanked-out brain for some sensible retort. There was nothing I could think of to push back with. I wanted to challenge Bell Ringer Number One. I wanted to punch back with my own accusation. I wanted to punch *him*. But all that came out was:

"How. . . how much do you want?"

"It all depends," said he. "Do you want the one-visit penance payment, or do you wish to purchase a season pass for unlimited ins and outs up through the end of my assignment here?"

Listen to him, the double-O-seven of fucking bell ringers. What the heck?

"You heard me, Milifred, or should I say 'Millie' as you have those gals at the call center call you?"

Bell Ringer Number One was no human VACO volunteer. Hell had frozen over and unleashed its minions to terrorize all of us shoppers into making ransom payments before rushing home with our presents. This was one highly trained Krampian henchman.

No wonder his kettle was nearly filled to the brim. I could see paper bills in there, even paper checks, crumpled, stuffed in with obvious desperation and haste. What poor, old senior citizens had he cornered for those? For what sins had he all demanded penance payments?

But I had neither cash nor check. As most people did these days, I never carried either.

"I have nothing on me." I croaked.

"Well, this *is* the twenty-first century. Don't think we don't come prepared, Millie-girl," Bell Ringer Number One sniffed, whereupon he drew a business card from his vest pocket, which sported – what else? – a QR code. A fucking QR code.

All I could do was look at it, then at him, and then back again at the card. I was dumbfounded.

"Go ahead, Mizz Millie. Flash your camera on that lil mofo," he snorted with a snide, authoritative air.

I took out my phone and opened the camera function. . .

. . . and what to my wondering eyes did appear, but a Ca$hPal website, and a personalized VACO account payment page. There was that same BR #1 emblem, in that same damn font, in tomato soup red, upon a field of green. TITHE NOW TO VACO. OR ELSE. . . it read.

So, was VACO not only in cahoots with the devil, but also employing technology to facilitate its extortions?

"Okay, so how much is it for the season pass?"

I could not believe I was having this conversation. I could not believe I was saying this. That I was even thinking of *complying*.

Shoppers, blissfully unaware – uncaring? – were bustling about, passing by with not so much as a glance our way. For all they knew, I and this VACO Trooper where simply having a friendly, workaday exchange, and I was for all appearances, about to make an online donation.

Lord, help me.

I repeated my question.

"Weeeell," Bell Ringer Number One made a pretense of contemplation, rolling his dark, non-descript eyes skyward as if looking for numbers afloat in the air above him. "With today's prices, that gum and polish would add up to, hmmm, nine dollars and forty-six cents."

"Yes? Okay, then. Fine."

"Weeeell, hold on a moment," Bell Ringer Number One held up a bony finger to shake it in the air at me. "All *you* gotta do is move that lil ole decimal point over to the far right for the season pass price. So, that would make it. . . um. . ."

He made a pretense of focused computing, the little bastard. His droll mouth screwed itself up sideways, way off to one side, so tight as to spiral his thin skin into a stomach-turning, tiny whorl.

"Nine hundred and forty-six dollars?!" I all but yelled. "Nine hundred and forty-six fucking dollars?"

"That'd be about the size of it, Mizz Millieeeee," Bell Ringer Number One intoned with his hateful, multi-note delivery, triumphant.

I did not have that kind of money.

"But I don't have that kind of money!" I cried.

Bell Ringer Number One paused momentarily. For a moment, I could swear he was listening to instructions, as if his replies were being fed to him by way of some sort of device – an implant, or dark magic. I could swear, he seemed to be taking his cues from somewhere, someone else, perhaps because I was so far resisting him, and my resistance was an unusual occurrence which required additional coaching. Hell, I was resisting due to fundamental reality – I *did not have* that kind of money!

"Well, Millie, my girl," he began afresh, "there comes a time when even noble guilt and basic realities cease to work for one such as yourself."

"Fuck you!" I snarled at him. I was cornered on every level. This was fast becoming a waking nightmare.

Bell Ringer Number One paused again, again to heed some kind of directive being filtered through him. He went so far as to glance up and give a small nod.

Bell Ringer Number One drew in his breath, and spoke these words:

"Well, you will. Mark my words, little Missy. It'll take a while, but you will have nine hundred dollars and forty-six cents. You can pay it back in twelve months' time, next Christmas, on the twelfth of December. Twelve months from now, to the day, you are to report back here, to this very spot, and you will give to me five fourteen karat gold – eighteen is fine too – shiny brite golden rings. Yes, as in rings for fingers, with a combined value of nine hundred and forty-six smackaroos! You will. . ."

". . .go to hell!" I burst out. I had had enough.

I put out my hands and placed them on Bell Ringer Number One's chest – and atop that bristling monstrosity of a badge – and I pushed him and his damn badge away from me with all my might.

Bell Ringer Number One, caught surprisingly by surprise – or so he feigned this next bit of drama – stumbled backwards. In trying to regain his footing, he backed into the stand from which his kettle was suspended. And now, entangled in the metal legs, he lost his balance completely and fell riotously to the floor, taking the kettle and its rigging down with him.

"Argh!" Bell Ringer Number One cried. "Look what you have done!"

He sputtered and mumbled as I stood there, frozen in my own shock. Two shoppers stopped to help him up. They glared at me, their faces aghast, their eyes aflame with indignation for having witnessed this assault on a VACO volunteer who was there for the good of Mankind. They looked at me as if I were some enraged, deranged woman.

"Whoa, lady!" one of the shoppers spat my way before turning back to Bell Ringer Number One and continuing with a, "Do you want me to call security? Are you okay?"

Bell Ringer Number One allowed himself to be picked up and dusted off. His chest was heaving in what *I know* was a huge act. He began adjusting his clothes in a spastic show of affronted indignation.

"Oh, ho, Milifred!" Bell Ringer Number One sneered as he held up and out his kettle to receive the dollar bills – fives, tens, twenties – that the two shoppers were now stuffing into it. "Now you have really done it! Just look what you did to my badge!"

I lookedat that damn badge. Its fake holly leaves had been crimped and broken off. What was left looked like a serrated trim of tiny green blades. Well, fuck that badge.

The shoppers departed with Bell Ringer Number One's encouragement and assurances – they were reluctant to leave, seemed quite determined to champion the little bastard. The one kept asking if he could go fetch a manager or a cop, or both.

No sooner were those two shoppers out of sight and the kettle back on its hook, as did Bell Ringer Number One have the fresh audacity to now reach out to physically confront *me*. He stuck that bony finger of his out again, this time straight in my direction, and poked me on the shoulder. Hard. Once, then again; and then a third time.

"Be that as it may," he said in a lowering voice that barely seemed to be coming from his own chest cavity, so deep and different was it from the voice I had heard up until that point, "*you,* Milifred Snodgrass, will pay dearly for your impudence! It will no longer be a simple price of coin to pay, but instead," he lowered that voice down to a menacing whisper, "on a night of HIS choosing, your very soul shall be reclaimed by none other than HE WHO CANNOT BE DENIED!"

The florescent tube lighting overhead flickered. I swear, it flickered on and off in time to his words.

Bell Ringer Number One, continued, "YOU SHALL BE CONSIGNED TO A DEAL WITH HE WHO CANNOT BE DENIED! ON A NIGHT OF HIS CHOOSING, ALL YOU SHALL DO, ALL YOU SHALL ACCOMPLISH, WILL BE GIVEN OVER TO HIM! BE FOREWARNED, THE VERY SOUL THAT RESIDES WITHIN YOU AS OF THIS MOMENT WILL IN DUE TIME NO LONGER BE YOURS, AND WHAT WILL BE LEFT FOR YOU WILL BE NOTHING. AND I MEAN NADA ZIP ZILCH! THAT IS WHAT YOU WILL HAVE TO TAKE WITH YOU INTO ETERNITY!"

Bell Ringer Number One's raisin eyes went bloodshot with the force of his proclamation. They had become the portals to the eternal fires of hell, I swear it. And on top of this, all around us, *everything* had gone absolutely silent. All around us, oblivious humans were moving forward in time, as if the two of us were not even standing there. As if they could move, even, right through us. Shoppers bustled by; a clerk pushed past us with a line of stacked shopping carts. We appeared to have moved without budging one inch from where we stood in the entryway into some different plain, or parallel dimension. It was only Bell Ringer Number One and me inside this terrible, momentary, suffocating place.

There being nothing else to say, or do, I simply yelled as best as I could, "Go to hell!"

Bell Ringer Number One drew himself up in a fresh huff, making ready to yell something commensurate back at me, when all of a sudden, his nose twitched. Yes, it twitched. Visibly. His demonic eyes slid to the left, towards the sliding glass doors. Something, someone had caught his attention.

I glanced at the doors, saw a gentleman dressed as if for a board room meeting, trench coat belted tight, the top edges of a white dress shirt peeking out just above the collar. His was a brisk pace, his eyes quickly shifting, scanning, assessing. In that moment, he caught sight of the Trooper. The man paused but a moment, then made to continue on with the crowd, clearly intent on entering the store without tithing even a single coin to VACO. Bell Ringer Number One leapt to the left like a dancer, right into this fellow's path. His next quarry had been spotted.

". . . and haaaaaaaappy holidays to you, good sir!" Bell Ringer Number One cried out, shaking his bell high over his head. It looked to me as if he could at any moment swing it downwards to strike the man right on the top of his head. Bell Ringer Number One grabbed the kettle from its hook, thrust it out at chest level in front of the fellow.

"Hooooold it right here, pal!" Bell Ringer Number One cried out, that infernal bell still clanging. "It is that time of year, buddy, when all are called to give juuuuust a little bit more, and given your circumstances, doesn't that warrant a tad more generosity on *your* part?"

The man shot me a look of one about to face his executioner. He began to dig frantically in his pants pockets for change, perhaps for bills, his forehead already breaking out with a film of perspiration. And as he was digging in his pockets, and as the cacophony of that damn bell continued alongside the piped in Christmas music, the din of shoppers' voices, and a siren now blaring not far off in the distance, I could hear that demon voice rise above it all like a pestilent, little wall of sound: "Well, well, Douglassssss!"

But then Bell Ringer Number One, having been so quickly distracted by this next shopper, he interrupted himself for a just moment to send a last, scorching look my way. With venomous joviality, he replied back to my lame verbal strike with a menacing and cheery, "So, see you *there,* Milifred Snoooooooodgrass! Now go on, get along with your shopping, little missy!" And tossing a slimy little smile my way, he proclaimed, ere he turned from my sight, ". . . and to you, my new friend, a *very* good night!"

†††

"Son of a bitch," I muttered to myself as I fumbled my way out of the store. I made my way back to my car, weaving like a drunkard, unable to walk a straight line. Despite it being a clear, cold day, I felt as if I wandered in a fog – blinded, blind-sided, dumb founded. My car was parked only a few spaces back, but it seemed like minutes before I finally arrived at its spot. I grabbed the door handle, let myself fall into the driver's seat. I immediately locked the doors.

I sat completely still for a minute or so, working to slow my breathing, trying to steady myself so I could drive home, get there safely, in one piece. I may as well have been three sheets to the wind. Everything swam.

I puzzled and I puzzled.

It occurred to me, perhaps all I would ever have to do, was simply never go back to Kreuger's. Ever again. Yes, that was it. The simplest solution, as they say, is often the best one. Just don't go back.

There was no way I – or anyone for that matter – was obliged to be subjected to harassment by some maniacal VACO Trooper like that, hell bent on extorting innocent shoppers to pay personal *fines* in the name of charitable giving. They, we, were just going about our own, damn business. And all of us were equally cash-strapped, and innocent from within the relative realms of our existences, things simply being what they were for anyone.

For all I know, I had been targeted from way, way back by this son of a bitch. Stalked at some very high level by someone who was willing to wait *this long* to corner me. Fact always exceeding fiction, it could well be, he may have been an employee, or a friend or family member of someone who used to work at Kreuger's, someone who had witnessed me shoplifting the gum and nail polish all those years ago, who had lain in waiting all this time. . .

Yes! That *had* to be it! I *had* been observed after all. But whoever had seen me do it back then, had wisely, benevolently *let me go*. *Of course* there had been *no* reason whatsoever to traumatize a sweet, little girl who didn't know any better! They – this benevolent angel at Kreuger's – had thought it best to let a lesson present itself organically to a child who was as innocent back then as. . . *as she was right now*! Poor, poor me! That fucking asshole Trooper, he had somehow managed to find out about my deed, and that of my angel, and he had stuck his long-ass nose into our business – my angel's and my own, private business – all those years ago, and he had harbored this damning nugget all this time, to dare try and ply it against me now, in the name of a charitable organization. The audacity! Oh, my God, I thought, the lights firing bright and clear now, here was a conniving sleazebag volunteer who had literally researched his way into his lauded Bell Ringer Number One position, who *no doubt* had files of information saved up – thick dossiers chock full of dirty laundry – of sins wrought by ordinary humans, to use it against them – good citizens, loyal patrons of Kreuger's – to siphon off shit tons of dirty money in the name of a reputable charity that would no doubt be *positively aghast*, were it to learn how low this Trooper was willing to go to get it! Oh, my goodness; I realized, *someone* from this endless line of victims needed to be reporting him! To VACO and to Kreuger's! It was all so clear to me now! Yes! Report him and put him away! Strip him of his Bell Ringer Number One status!

But then, I had a sobering thought. I realized, this would mean me divulging my own transgression from my own, sweet and innocent past, which in effect would have me going on record with perfect strangers, as having been a young person of a duplicitous nature, which was *the last* thing I needed at this point in my life, when I was on the very cusp of launching a multi-tier campaign to switch out my entire identity.

Nope. Not for me. So, simplest solutions being what they *also* can be, I changed my mind. I decided to do nothing. Let that damn elf from hell extort his black heart out. I would just stay away.

Soon, Milifred Snodgrass would, in any case, cease to exist. He, that bell ringing bastard, would never be able to find me, no matter what kind of slimy methods, or hocus pocus, he might employ. In fact, once my writing took off and I could afford it, I could move again. Perhaps to the coast. Yes. Somewhere by the ocean. Rich fodder, those historic, sea-side communities. I could write there.

Besides, that conniving bastard wasn't *all* powerful. He clearly didn't know *everything.* He had never breathed the first word, indicated the first shred of knowledge, pertaining to the fact that on the same night I had stolen the chewing gum and nail polish and then thrown it out, that, with my mother about to come after me with the note my teacher had mailed home to my parents about. . .well. . .stuff that should like my silly shoplifting *stay in the past where it belonged*, I had made for a quick dash outdoors *to retrieve* that stupid bottle of polish from the garbage can. And that after wiping the yuck off that bottle of polish, I had given it to my mother as a gift, saying I had bought it for her to surprise her, because the color was so pretty, just like she was, in order to distract her just long enough so I could swipe *that* letter off the kitchen counter *and* switch my mother's gears. So, instead of her trying to corner me with some stupid written accusation about, well, I am not going to even *think it* here, she would actually be hugging me in loving gratitude. *That* other part of my story, the evil minion at Kreuger's had had no clue about. So there.

Fuck that Bell Ringer Number One.

Then and there, in my car in the parking lot of Kreuger's, I took out my phone and looked up the application I would need to download, fill out, and submit for a legal name change, as well as the phone number at the courthouse. I would call them from home, get that ball rolling. As of that very moment, I was taking rock solid steps to cast off the Milifred Snodgrass that VACO Trooper had all but sniped in the name of Mankind. I mean, wow. And on Monday, I would make my request at the call center, which they would have to accept, that I needed to identify with a different name. I would tell them, my well-being – heck, my life – depended on it. It kind of did, really, at least according to that charity minion from hell. But the details of my assault at Kreuger's, my confrontation with Bell Ringer Number One, I would not share with neither Human Resources nor any of my co-workers. As of that moment, the incident was for me done, filed, and closed. And once my name change was official, the rest would be a piece of cake. A big, fat, cherry-studded, brandy-laced, pecan-laden piece of fruitcake. How I would love to have one of those, to stuff into that damn Bell Ringer's mouth until he choked to death. . .

Fuck Bell Ringer Number One, and fuck his invisible boss – how was it he referred to him? He who could not be. . ? I had already forgotten. Either way, henceforth, I would be known to all, and only, as Lilah. Lilah Ravenscraft.

Isn't that a pretty name?

✝✝✝✝✝

The Vulgarian Child Catcher referenced in this story is a character from the musical film adaption of Ian Fleming's *Chitty Chitty Bang Bang*. The Child Catcher and Kris Kringle were both employed only as descriptive devices for the Bell Ringer character, with reverence and gratitude.

Ian Fleming wrote the original story entitled, *The Magic Car*, in 1961 for his son Casper. Fleming died in 1964, and so did not live to see this work in print. Casper was tragically lost to suicide at the age of twenty-three. Roald Dahl, who had adapted Fleming's James Bond *You Only Live Twice*, was recruited to write the screenplay for *Chitty Chitty Bang Bang*. While the Dahl collaborative endeavor was acrimonious and fell quite flat, he is credited with having created the Vulgarian Child Catcher character. Ken Hughes, the film's director, claimed he created the character.

The film's iconic Child Catcher character was portrayed by Sir Robert Helpmann, a ballet dancer who was known to be so kind to the children on set, that it became difficult for them to act frightened by the Child Catcher during filming. Helpmann happened to have false teeth; for optimal effect, he removed them for filming.

†††

Chitty Chitty Bang Bang has been in the public domain since January 1, 2015. The film adaptation release date: December 18, 1968, directed by Ken Hughes, screenplay by Roald Dahl and Ken Hughes, produced by Albert R. Broccoli. The Child Catcher headshot visually referenced is in the public domain.

The visual reference for the folkloric icon Kris Kringle is based on a character in the "animagic" stop-motion picture film *Santa Claus Is Coming To Town*, released December 13, 1970, produced and directed by Arthur Rankin Jr and Jules Bass.

To learn more about Milifred Snodgrass/Lilah Ravenscraft, read "Ravenscrafted" in *Neitherium: Prose & Poetry from the Neither;* see also its follow-up collection, *Göthique: A Ravenscraft Anthology of Horror*, both by K.A. Schultz

A Brief History of Trav'lers
Excerpt: Christmas Morning at the White House

NIMBY-ism, as we all know it and are susceptible to, quickly reverses course when one is struck at home, to the heart, by an event or occurrence which turns the world as one would have known it on its head.

Such was the case of the President of the American Federation, a Non-Traveler (there was never an elected official who was a Traveler), and her first grandchild, the offspring of her own, non-traveling daughter and her son-in-law, an up-and-coming writer who did happen to be a Traveler. The President's pre-born granddaughter spontaneously exited her mother's womb at just under four month's gestation, for what could only have been a matter of seconds, so fleeting would the sensation have been, that proverbial whisper of a maternal warning. It happened, of all days, on a Christmas morning (Yes, the celebration persisted, having been too vital a retail season to homogenize with other holidays, or cancel altogether), at the dawn of a bright, winter's day at the White House, where they also happened to be celebrating the expectant mother's birthday.

To the horror of everyone present in the private library, the pre-born Traveler – a girl – re-materialized from her time-place fold, not back in the safe confines of her mother's womb, but right there, on the carpeted floor, right in front of her own, young mother, who happened to be seated on the floor, in front of the Christmas tree, in the process of opening a gift from her husband. The President's daughter – such a lovely, young lady – had just torn back a section of brightly colored paper, expecting to see nothing else but the antique server she had so wished for. But when she removed the paper, the grisly, heart-breaking sight that met her eyes, what – who – met with the eyes of everyone there in the room with her, catapulted them all into a deepest, horrified grief from which no one ever fully would recover. The loving family just stood there, surrounding the young mother, in a thunder-struck silence as together they beheld the tiny being struggle momentarily, then expire. This imprinting, to witness life so brutally whisked out and away, with the swiftness of a sleight of hand trick, no one else, the President decided then and there, should also ever have to suffer.

There is, sadly, more. That son-in-law of the President, the father of the tragically lost pre-born? A history buff, he had indulgently educated himself in the histories of ancient Egypt and its faith-based practices, but as a spontaneous Traveler, dangerously so. For you see, spontaneous Travelers can only ever fold time-place in random fashion, at tremendous risk to themselves and anyone in their paths, coming or going. His attempts at controlled time-place folds ultimately put him – and others – at great, and most unfortunate risk. More on him in a moment.

You can read "A Brief History of Trav'lers" in its entirety in the 2022 short story & poetry collection, NEITHERIUM

Stille Nacht

(Silent Night)

PREFACE

I am wont, said he, *to stilted inflection.*

It is something I cannot help. Some people, youngsters mostly, have called my turn of phrase odd; some call it quaint.

His parched lips curled, just barely, in what one might construe a half-hearted half-smile. What I could see of his face was in full shadow, and between the broad hat brim and the muffler wound about his neck, difficult to discern. He wore sunglasses despite our being indoors, and it being around seven o'clock in the evening. I could tell, this man was old, and ill.

Antiquated is more like it. Like me, he added after a moment's thought, with a chuckle so hoarse, that no sooner did he attempt it, as did it catch in his throat, causing a fit of coughing to ensue.

I had the sense, here was someone who had never laughed much.

Wet and rattling was that cough of his. Lungs at war with the rest of their companion parts, everything covered in so many layers of clothing, out-moded and frayed-edged. It was quite impossible to see, who exactly was underneath it all.

That I could not see his face was of little consequence to me, being that I too travelled in relative incognito, feeling I had no choice but to do it this way. The residual effects of an accident I had endured some years ago, which had turned me from an ordinary adult woman to an objectified 'marvel,' a 'miracle.' Two words, given what I was left with, that I loathed. But my tragedy had played out in the courts, with a 'win' leaving me in possession of a proverbial king's ransom – although I, from then on the embittered but very 'rich' gal, would have paid ten times that sum, to just have my face back.

This stranger was utterly non-plussed by my appearance, which I appreciated. In fact, the moment our shielded eyes met, he had gestured to me, that I should take the seat opposite him at his table. I was grateful; the *Edelweiss* was packed.

For the life of me, I cannot tell why, but on a blustery Christmas Eve, I accepted a stranger's offer of a seat at his table. I was alone, biding my time on the last leg of a full year abroad, a trip I had forced myself to take to 'reward' myself – a morose way of putting it, I know – with the spoils of my misfortunes. To distract myself. Had it worked thus far? Not really. I had seen so much, read countless books, taken thousands of photos with both my mind and my camera, and I still felt the same.

And therein lies a problem:

†††

I am blessed – or cursed, as it were – with Hyperthymesia. I remember everything. Everything. What I ate for dinner on my fifth birthday, and how I felt about the fact that my mother had had the audacity to serve peas, of which she made me eat precisely three. Three damn peas. What the dentist had said to me on a cold January Monday morning, it was the twenty-seventh, at oh, about eleven-thirty, right before he gave me my first-ever shot of Novocain. He thought himself quite witty, the bastard. I can still taste the flavor of pain and fear which invaded my mouth, my mind. What I wore on my second roller coaster ride, and how my bead bracelet caught on the latch of the safety bar, and the heart-breaking sight of those beads – plastic droplets of pink, blue, and green – tumbling down, down, through the steel fretwork. Oh, how had I cried at the loss.

Countless – no; I *could* count them, but I am not inclined to doing that – mundane and ordinary moments and events, which I could relay to you. In detail. But you would die of boredom and resent the months, even years you would have lost listening to me. Now, my 'condition,' – my way of referring to what others call a gift, or, worse yet, a talent – did get me through school with minimal effort; it expedited my college education as well. Three degrees by the time I was twenty-four, all in esoteric but fundamentally useless areas of study. Upon graduation, I did what most esoterically trained, relatively young academicians do; I took an unglamorous, semi-skilled job which had nothing to do with anything I had studied. It was at an animal rehabilitation facility, my thought being I could perhaps build on random and diverse events and memories, which might better serve my unforgiving mind. Animals might offer me, as is always said, something warm and fuzzy – a fresh, fluffy layer of *nicer* memories. 'Perfect' memory, trust me, is often simply too much baggage for any one individual to drag about with them through life. Hard as rock, and as undigestible. One is left to ruminate over that much more when it is *everything* that gets replayed in one's head, and in exacting detail: incidents, images, settings, conversations, dates and times. Good grief.

I forged a friendship at work with my supervisor, who was a zoologist. Our subsequent times together proved to be the worst links in a newish chain I was trying to forge – this massive, dragging thing with which I was already horrifically weighted. For you see, my boss, my friend, had taken it upon herself to make a pet of one of her rescues, a chimpanzee she had raised from little on, taken in from a lab she had worked hard to shut down. Mr. Bobo.

The rest, as they say, is history.

The rest, specifically for me, resulted in an MA-for-graphic-violence rated mini-series, which, up until now has played itself over and over in my head, whether I wish it or not, ever since 'it' happened – which was ten years, three months and three days ago. And it has been two years, four months, and eight days since I agreed to start taking the meds to curtail them, the traumatic flashbacks having become too much. The stuff somewhat dulls my mind but permits me to quell the insistent playbacks of the attack. They let me sleep, although my dreams are troubled. Vaguely remembered, but troubled, nevertheless. There is a part of me that can tell, some other area of my consciousness has been forced to a chemical quieting; and while I do not like it, I accept it as a necessity. Hopefully a temporary necessity.

Hence this trip abroad. One full year – well, three-hundred and forty-five days so far to be exact, that I have spent here, there, wherever. A new slew of images, incidents, and conversations – superficial and polite, all of them with total strangers, most of them foreigners – to file away, review during quieter hours on the road, in bed when I can't sleep. But while the days, the years, and the experiences accrue, my memories are never wholly pushed back, never bound and tucked neatly away on some imaginary shelf to become a proverbial, more distanced 'past.' I see every volume clear as day; I can read each spine. I know each table of contents and every last damn word on every one of those pages. No; this 'story,' which I cannot yet bring to a close, started on a page with Mr. Bobo clambering up onto my lap and then proceeding to rip my face to shreds.

I still look into a mirror only when with the lights in the room are off, the lighting muted all around. The closest I have managed so far, is a hallway lit with the door left open, so that a sidelong whiff of light illuminates the mirror's reflection just enough, so I can make out only the most basic image. Yes: two eyes, one nose, a mouth with teeth (most of them my own), a neck of sorts, a chin if one can call it that. They are on permanent loan from three different donors, thanks to the 'marvelous' medical 'miracles' performed on me. Experimentation is more like it, if you ask me. But no one asked me, really. Mine is a twenty-first century crazy quilt of a face. It has left me feeling that I am some kind of humanoid alien, forced to wear wigs, masks, and sunglasses when out in public – and often when alone in private – so to not cause undue attention. You would be shocked to hear how often I have been spied through uncurtained windows. Expressions of shock and horror in others' faces have become my nightmare, part two. Children have burst into tears and adults have frozen where they stood when they have seen me full on – many would forget what it was they were in the middle of saying. Too often, strangers' eyes suddenly glisten with empathetic, unshed tears, which have disrupted more brief exchanges than I care to remember. And I remember *all* of them.

I have never once, for the first minute, been able to completely set aside my awareness of the piecemeal, fabricated condition of my look. The physical discomfort, ever-present, is always borne with the *searing* pain I experience, in the unforgiving face of the reactions I elicit in others. Add to that, yes, over and over again, the replays of how it all came to pass.

. . .that moment Mr. Bobo clambered up my legs, and his damp, strong, gripping fingers on his paws – hands, whatever – and how he fell silent as he squatted on his haunches, upon my lap, and how he looked me deep in the eyes with his brown, flecked ones, and then how. . .

Stop. Enough.

I have something else to remember now, to recall, which brings me back to. . .

It was Christmas Eve night, near the close of my Grand Tour, as they used to call it, when I stepped out of the swirling snow and into this charming, half-timbered locale called the *Gasthaus Edelweiss*. Some little voice had suggested to me, this was where I should spend the evening. And when I saw *him*, that same voice whispered, here might be someone with whom I could share – *something*. I had never known that kind of intuitive surge, never heard any 'voice' speak to me with such certainty, borne of absolutely zero past or present reference, all those tedious, accrued factualities which normally drove my decision making. This was, in hindsight, my wholly unknown Yet To Come. It willed me on, into the old bar, and on towards the back of the room. My Yet To Come presented itself in the form of an oddly elegant, but raggedly dressed man, who at a glance may very well have manifested from another time. There was an unmistakable otherworldliness to him. His disposition, made clear to me with his first polite greeting, was quite formal. But it was alluring, in a decidedly singular way.

I was *intrigued.* Truly, I didn't know when I had ever before felt like that. And had that *not* been the case, I would have, naturally, been able to relay the day, the time, the place, what was spoken, done, worn, and so on and so on. . .

But that voice – *my intrigue,* was whispering to me – suggesting, this man and I might have *something* to talk about.

And so, I took my seat on the wide bench opposite him at the *Edelweiss.* And because I am afflicted with perfect memory, I will simply relay to you what he said to me:

PART ONE

I.

Bitte sehr! (You're welcome)

Of course, of course! I am here alone. You may lay claim to the entire bench if you like. You are most welcome to it. I dare say, it would otherwise remain most likely *quite* unoccupied. I have an unfortunate tendency to put people off, whether I wish it or not. . .

Yes. As you please.

Oh, but if you don't mind, I'd prefer if you would *not* light that candle. It actually was lit; I extinguished it. I am not comfortable with much of any direct light, even a small flame such as that. My eyes. It's a long story. I hope that is alright with you. I would not be offended if you wished to sit elsewhere.

But of course. Join me then. I am almost ready for another one of these, and if I may, I would like to invite you to join me as my guest for this next round, in the spirit of the evening.

Good!

Hallo, Herr Schreuter! Ja. . .

(Two beers were ordered up)

Well, true.

Yes. It is quite the hullabaloo here tonight. On the one hand, that would seem ironic, yes? A night when families would most wish to draw close to their home fires to celebrate the holiday. On the other hand, I can imagine, on this night of all nights, all who otherwise customarily – and comfortably – spend their evenings in solitude, would perhaps wish to spend it a little less so.

Indeed! And where better to dispel shades of loneliness than here at the *Edelweiss*, with the rest of the regular crowd, yes?

Aha.

Ich bedanke mich. (To the barkeep: I thank you)

Cheers! And *prost.*

Now, you must excuse this old man. I am wont to stilted inflection, and it surfaces most especially when I have had a few beers. . .

Yes, well, one could call it that. Especially when we are crisscrossing our languages, yes?

You are most kind. It is something I cannot help. Some people, youngsters mostly, have called my turn of phrase odd; some call it quaint.

Indeed. Antiquated is more like it. Like me.

Oh, pardon me. . .

I. . .

Thank you.

No, no; I am alright. . .

Goodness. Please excuse me! My lungs are not in the best of shape. I was never a smoker, neither pipe nor otherwise, but these old bellows of mine have been through the fires. Doubtless, they are as scarred as the prow of a battered pirate ship!

Why yes. And you?

Aha. Yes, of course.

No, not at all. I am not in the least bit nonplussed by your little fabric mask. Keep it on all night if you wish. It is a mite brisk in here, despite the *Gemütlichkeit* which abounds. Why, look at me! I have this thing on, this hand-knit shroud spun about my neck and face from about September on through at least Easter. Especially when I am in higher altitudes, where the air is thinner. But I am always chilled these days. Chilled to the bone. Never used to be. At least, these days, with such a casualness *de rigueur*, I no longer feel obliged to remove all my trappings, which grants me much improved comfort. In my old age, I rather prefer staying bundled up. As such, I too shall permit myself to keep my peculiar costuming in place. You, we, are fine as is.

Yes, the brim does cast a rather long shadow. All the better to peer out from under its protective cover. I can sit here all night and observe unobserved, if you will. It is an agreeable enough pastime. But this beat up Homburg has proven quite the life saver over the years – how many rainstorms, how many miles, have I traveled beneath its diminutive awning! Between it and these sunglasses, my eyes are adequately spared. They tend to an extreme dryness; it is often a task to even blink. I suppose, I have gazed a few times too many upon the sun, having circled both it and this spinning orb as many times as I have. Such is the wear and tear of nomadic beings like me.

Well, thank you. I appreciate the compliment. The lenses are 'polarized.' Whatever that means.

Aha.

Yes, agreed. We have our points of style, no?

Now, let me guess. You are American?

Yes, well, it is a subtle thing, being that there are so very many accents to begin with, on both sides of the Atlantic. I assure you, you fit right in with the rest of this collective of motley imbibers, no question about that, so it is difficult to identify from where exactly the impression comes.

To be sure. I have never been to the United States, but I have always enjoyed reading about it, and it has been interesting to follow the evolution of American television programming, which has been so very popular over here from the get-go. From what I can tell, I do believe I like Americans. There is a casualness about you, a workaday inclination even amongst your more renegade types. Many of your popular figures in both entertainment and history are no doubt reflective of the relative youth of your nation, which fascinates me, as being one born into an old culture and its bygone eras.

Over the years, I have met a few other Americans, but not many. I tend to spend most of my time off the beaten track, places not customarily visited by transcontinental tourists. And despite how small this world has become, there are still countless cities and hamlets where tourism is decidedly rare. As such, the Americans with whom I do cross paths with are of a heartier type, often of the adventuring, hiking sort, which activity has been an, er, hobby of mine since my, eh, youth. Most folk I encounter are rather more than less directly connected to the places I have also wandered, by way of family connection or sometimes for study or research, and as such a tad Europeanized already in their ways. It's funny, but there is a difference. . .

Yes.

Agreed. There are good and welcome aspects, anywhere, really.

For myself? I tended to circulate amongst the more northern climes. They suited me quite well; still do, although now I am forced to really bundle up against the cold. One needs to keep an old carcass good and chilled to preserve it. . .

The farthest north I have been? Would you believe it if I told you that would be the Arctic Circle itself?

Yes. Suffice it to say, those extreme climes are part of what comprise a most difficult set of chapters, if you will, of the book of my younger years. A rough read.

No, really? Well, what an interesting coincidence.

Indeed.

All the way up to the North Pole – yes.

I did. And no, there were not always permanent fixtures up there, at least when I was there. The first time I passed over the region, it was during a storm. There was nothing to see, no marker of any kind as I recall. Had there been something, it would have most likely been swept away by the winds. Fierce and unrelenting winds.

Ah, yes. I remember quite clearly the mysteriously lit, ashy-violet of the ice crystal-filled skies. Minute particles tumbling about crazily, and blindingly so, the frigid winds whipping everything up and about in devilish circles, and keening like an anguished banshee. I remember feeling as if the storms were chasing after me. They pushed hard and cold at my back, urged me ever onward. I still shiver to think back on the absolute, abject desolation which defined so venerable a spot.

No. More thereabouts, in its immediate surrounds.

The Arctic Regions, the Barents Sea. Archipelagos, known over the ages by their Norse names, later on by the names of the northern European explorers and cartographers who dared venture there. A few of them were re-named yet again after the big Wars, of course.

Aye, but those were brutal chunks of rock – iced-over islands clustered about each other, like the crude steppingstones of giants. Those waters and their haggard lands were all quite familiar to me.

No, it has been ages since I have traversed that part of the globe. I dare say, I do not plan on ever going back there.

No.

Yes. What I actually knew as Spitzbergen. That one is central to a network of islands, most of them minuscule outliers, which I came to know intimately, where even I lived for a time. Hostile terrain comprised of ice sheets and rock, lichen and hoarfrost, home only to the most sea-worthy creatures of flight, or those heartiest aquatic travelers of the deep. I am impressed you know about them. You know your geography.

Aha. Yes, well, your field of study would certainly lend itself to some familiarity of these areas.

And where was that?

Indeed. An interesting combination of subjects. Did you teach all of them as well? At university?

Aha. So that was your focus. And these days?

I see.

Yes, you could say that.

So that goes, right?

Aha, indeed.

Ah, yes, the Northern Lights. There is not much in this world to which I would assign the emotion 'love,' but the Aurora Borealis come closest perhaps to anything, that has held a steadfastly warm place in my heart.

No. As a rule, I do not make glib statements to that end. I never have.

Yes, agreed.

I have always wished, I had the ability to paint such a living sky, capture it on canvas as some artists do; but alas, these stiff paws of mine would have difficulty wielding a requisite slender paintbrush. It is sometimes difficult for me to even hold a knife and a fork, and to use them in tandem. The fat-handled, vintage implements they provide us with here at the *Edelweiss* are a godsend for one as clumsy as I.

Indeed! The earth is phenomenally beautiful, and for all the seasons I have seen pass in my day, I have never grown tired of observing every changing of that cyclical guard, least of all the dying off of life when winter sets in, that miraculous stasis before the next turnover to another birth, a reanimated emergence.

The *Polarlichter* – such a symphony of pleasing color! And how they waltz across the heavens. . . I watch for them, especially when the autumn sets in, when the lights are re-ignited as if by fire. It is very nearly enough to justify one's hanging on for yet another year. And I say this as one who has trod over ages and their countless miles, heavily burdened for the most part, where their beauty was, at times, what kept me going. . .

Indeed. I was a troubled man in my younger years. I had the mindset of a child; a thwarted and resentful child, rejected by the one human I thought owed me his unequivocal loyalty. In my torment, I was unable to recognize *his* agony, what so many others in this world were, are, equally mired in. Life is hard. But tragedy can and finally did open the doors – ripped them wide open, and painfully so – for me, which pulled me on a path to personal growth. For me, it was the passing of my creator – er, my Father – which saw to my turning the biggest corner of all.

As such, the Northern Lights will always hold a redemptive beauty for me, for I contemplated the launch of my personal sea change from beneath the veils of their benevolent illumination. Like gently whispered psalms, on those endlessly long nights when I would sit alone and contemplate them, the lights would nigh hypnotize me, and I would fancy they were broadcasting messages to me – measurable, incremental information – lessons I was supposed to learn, to internalize. I would gaze upon them unblinkingly, and I felt I was looking through time, backwards to points of origin which would reveal truths that would help me survive my own self, all the horrific inclinations which had up until that point possessed me. I began to regard the arrays in the skies above me as scriptures – not unlike ancient scrolls being unwound across the heavens – whose gifts were offered without judgement, caveat or conditionality. These experiences built the foundation upon which I could finally set aside a horror-filled past, and with it, all my failings, including the failings *of others* on whom I had depended, from whom I had demanded love, who I had once presumed I was owed something, despite what all I did to destroy the connections I had to them. You see, I was beset with a primal rage, which had fueled my every decision and subsequent action up to that point in my life. It is from that new and most welcome void, with the lights looking down upon me from deepest space, and as I studied their reflections in the deep, dark waters which surrounded me where I had stationed myself, that I was finally able to begin to build on my own *humanity*.

Yes.

Profoundly so.

In Nature's bounty, there are to be found the most accessible – and therefore sustainable – aspects of the divine. This, I came to understand as I grew up, as they say. Older. Wiser. Impetuous, youthful entitlement had stoked me with its toxic energies for. . . oh dear. . . so many years. I had never before understood that it was less to take – and how often I had done *that* by force – than it was to give.

Yes, of course. I see them as far south as here several months out of the year. Especially when I am in the high country.

It all depends.

Seasonal eras of time, long-term shifts in weather patterns paired with the volatile firing of the sun herself. And you? Have you witnessed them yourself?

Aha. What a great memory!

And how young you were, to be able to recall it like that?

Ah – fascinating!

Clearly, that factored into your line of studies. Memory is a bewitching abstract of the infinite realms we tread. Mine has also served me well – too well. Difficult chapters, chronicled and kept just below the waking ken. Books, volumes!

Yes. So that is just as you like to describe it, too? Fascinating.

I have thought this for as long as I can remember. As long as I have had language, the words, to formulate the concepts.

Indeed. Perhaps I share in some of this, er, affliction you speak of.

The current volume I am writing, so to say, I am scripting towards its final chapter. A denouement, if you will. I have been working on this for a *terribly* long time. Many sections concluded, many characters now come and gone, myriad settings dismantled – and, yes, all of it quite ready to be wrapped up.

Oh, no – don't be. One can only live so long.

And so, I shall, as well.

Why, thank you.

No, I am not a writer, but I am enamored of words and their power, their illustrative capabilities.

Yes.

And yes, to that too. You are absolutely correct.

I suppose I ought put it this way, that I am originally from Germany. But I am an itinerant by nature, have been since my youngest years. You could say, I am something of a 'Man without a country' as a couple of your American writers have rather nicely quipped.

No. I have no home, no residence, per se.

You mean, coming here? To the *Edelweiss*? Goodness, let me think. I have patronized this bar for years. . . decades, I suppose. . . if you *really* wish for me to tally the exact count. . .

No, truly. Let me think on this a moment. . .

Oh, no doubt.

This would be year thirty-eight.

Yes, here.

Indeed. Yes, I have seen a few generations come and go. I have, for instance, seen those two over there grow up. A rambunctious pair, they were as children. They know me. They leave me be.

Tonight? Oh, I am awash – positively drenched – in the good cheer this frothy stuff levels upon a thirsting soul. And the beer is not too bad, either.

Yes, well; so that was not said in a manner to convince you? Call mine a dry humor. I am as happy as I ought to be. I suppose.

But of course. Always. And never take me wholly at my word. I am quite practiced in the art of balderdash and dole it out whenever a receptive ear is close enough to receive it.

To be sure. Massive grains of salt!

Well, is that not what endlessly long winter nights in time-forgotten locales like this are for?

Cheers to that!

Generally, yes. My sense of time is quite ridiculously skewed. Quite the lunatic's platform. But we do have ample time to converse, and so you will no doubt hear much that skips about over a rather long stretch of time. I have all night; well, at least until shortly before midnight. Where I am headed later on, I reckon will take me about half an hour, now that I no longer move quite as quickly as I once did. Meantime, I am quite content to stay right here, in this corner booth, and share this space with you, so long as you wish it, too.

Bully for you then. *Prost*! And yes, a Happy Christmas to. . . No, wait, you like to say *Merry* Christmas, do you not? Well then, a *Frohe Weihnachten* and a Merry Christmas to you, to us both!

Cheers. God help us. Everyone.

II.

Oh, yes. This is a good bock beer. Local. It is from the monastery on the other side of the city. Available only this time of year.

Well, I do I have you beat, by a little. I have been here since the bells called their devout to prayer. But who's counting? I am not driving anywhere.

Oh yes, of course. On foot.

No. To be honest, I never have.

No. I have never had a driver's license. Don't believe I ever will, at this point. In all honesty, I have no need for one.

Well, that would require. . . It's complicated. Let's just say, to begin with, I have always had abysmally poor vision to contend with. And to acquire corrective lenses would have been problematic on a number of levels. Just trust me on that.

Yes, that is correct.

Besides, I have fairly good stamina. I can walk for days – and do. And what is called mass transportation these days is ubiquitous. One can hitch rides – er, buy tickets – to anywhere at all, at any given time. I am a stolid creature of habit, so I suppose I shall stand strong on my old-fashioned non-driver status for the simple reason, my mobility as I manage it has always worked exceedingly well for me, including to this very day.

And you? Are you much of a driver back in the States, with your own automobile?

And I suppose, you zip about on those endlessly long superhighways I have seen on the television programs?

Oh, I see.

Yes. I do know about the vast stretches of land that separate your cities, and how your culture has remained quite reliant on your automobiles, and lorries – er, trucks.

It is what it is.

Of course. We have more than our fair share of ridiculous traffic and all its tangential issues here, too. The narrow highways, the hairpin turns. . .

I must admit, I do not envy much those with their cars, or worse yet, their cumbersome trucks. Especially as the places I like best of all, no ordinary vehicle could even begin to make it.

But look at all the people here. There is little no reason to concern oneself with such as cars, or driving, or drivers' licenses tonight. Let us simply toast the fact that for now, we can stay put.

Very well.

Prost, to that. And thank you.

I do fancy myself a bit of a polyglot. It is largely by default, my having spent long spans of time in different countries, and always having been in high observational mode. One must stay keenly alert, now as ever before. One never knows.

What was that?

No. I am something of a recluse. I prefer to listen, for I learned centuries, er, ages ago, there is always much to learn. Endlessly much to learn.

How many? Well, hmmm. I must think on it.

No, not that I know of.

So, there is German, naturally. And English, of course. I am, in fact, enjoying this opportunity to speak English with you. It has been I don't know how many months since I have spoken it.

Alright, let me tally up the languages: I speak French, and Spanish, Dutch, and Danish. My Finnish is passable, my Russian is adequate. I can of course speak Swedish too, but then, the Nordic languages begin to reflect off each other. It has felt quite natural to assimilate these languages, and in some cases their dialects, as I have settled here and there, and as I have then eventually moved on to live somewhere else. I have tried on, if you will, different countries much as one might try on, say, a winter coat. Something that lasts a good, long while, but gets changed up from time to time.

Yes, it is a cumulative process. Your German, by the way is quite good. *Sehr gut*! But I am happy to keep on in English with you. It feels good. My, Father, he preferred the organic elegance of your very fluid and evolutionary mother tongue, of which of yours is in and of itself a highly distinct turn-speak, being that you are from America.

Yes, an older term, I suppose.

My, Father? No, he was of Swiss descent. And Italian, on his mother's side, who was descended from Corsican lineage. My Father was born in Napoli but educated in England and Germany. He traveled most of his life. Was an unsettled but privileged man. His family eventually returned to Switzerland, to their ancestral home in Geneva, where he was to his final days emotionally bound. He forever missed it. In Geneva, there was as well – still is – a family crypt, about as regal a structure as anything built for the living. Such graceful cities of the dead are there, where countless generations lie in repose, allées paved by as many graveyard gardens as cobblestones. The Frank– the family – crypt is deceptively modest; there is a massive subterranean catacomb carved directly into the bedrock below it.

No. There are no living descendants.

Well, yes, of course. I am. I am still, er, alive.

The house? No. It fell into others' hands ages ago. In fact, I believe it was used commercially for decades. A picturesque place, and quite historic.

A hotel, I believe.

Me? No. there was no, eh inheritance. . . The property was handed down to. . .mmm how to say it?

Let me explain it this way: I was not the product of a wedded union. I was not the son of my Father's wife, who, er, died young. Suddenly. Yes, young and terribly unexpectedly. And I was never recognized by my Father's family; but nor would I have ever sought that distinction.

Oh, no; you are not prying. I don't mind.

Yes. Ships passing, as they say.

I have no issue with your questions. It is only that it has been so terribly long since I have given any thought to the details from that, er, era, let alone been made to give voice to them. Conversationally, it is proving to be a daunting task, to relay the particulars so to not frighten off a kind stranger such as yourself.

Fine. A friend. *Prost.*

Suffice it to say, I was never designated as an heir; as such, the business of property holdings, bank accounts, that sort of thing, did not concern me back then, and so their facts were either dismissed or unknown by me.

No, I never lived in the house in Geneva, although I did, er, visit there. . .once, twice. . . But again, that was another time, another world, really.

Now, the family crypt I did visit when I returned from my, er, Arctic expeditions, now over two cent– eh, many, many years ago. It was to bring my Father home. Well, his remains. Home, at long last. My Father spent his life always – how to put it – chasing his own tail. He was never happy as an adult, and he misused the gifts of his intellect alongside those of his station in life, taking in grand educations and using his acumen towards ill-fated means and their inevitably tragic conclusions. The misfortunes of his family, he largely brought on himself, but only insofar as he in his self-centered freedom was permitted to pursue the paths everyone was subsequently forced to travel with him. There was never a new city, or new country house, which could bestow any lasting contentment within him. Eventually, as is often the case with humans who serve only themselves, he took himself to extremes in both situation and place, which is how we both wound up in the Arctic regions. It is there where he fell gravely ill.

Yes. I believe, the loss of his loved ones plagued him until the end, wore him down to nothing.

Yes, that is how it can play out. It is why I was up there, too.

Well, not exactly.

Yes, I have heard of him. Definitely a kindred soul, one who can appreciate such as that.

The mausoleum in Geneva?

Well, do you mind if I rather not say? I mean, I am not trying to. . .

Alright. Thank you.

Yes. That much I don't mind sharing. It is on the grounds of the. . .

Yes, that is it. You have traveled there too then?

No; no longer. Theirs pre-dated the many restrictions which exist today.

Indeed. It is located in a private park, deep in the interior of the cemetery.

Do tell.

Aha. So, you have actually visited there?

You might recall the wrought iron surround. Fine workmanship. Laurel fronds, interwoven. Quite artistically rendered. The crypt is classical in design, much like the others.

Indeed. A rare city house for the dead. Status, rendered in stone.

But there *is* an interesting Latin inscription on the structure, which was commissioned by my Father as a tribute to his father upon his interment there, which I will recite for you: *Hic locus est ubi mors gaudet succurrere. . .*

Yes. *Vitae.*

Loosely translated, it has to do with death serving to help life and the living.

Indeed. Thank you. If you ever find yourself back there again, and you locate the mausoleum, then you can read it, and see and learn the family name for yourself. That is the only way I will concede that knowledge to you. You will think me mad, but I took a vow of sorts, out of respect, actually, following an, er, incident at the crypt, to never speak the name so long as I would live, after. . .

Well, they were a family of academicians. Physicians, scientists.

No. I was never officially adopted. No; no birth mother to speak of. . .

If you don't mind, again, I would rather not say. Forgive me but. . .

Yes. I appreciate your understanding. A few things are still rather painful to recall, and to be perfectly honest, I wish to remain a bit more anonymous. My Father was somewhat notorious in his day, for all his comfortable upbringing.

Sure. Celebrity. Indeed. Notoriety comes in all colors.

As I recall, the men were all schooled in England. Many generations.

The women? Well, er, yes. . . naturally the women too.

I? Oh my, that is a long story. Let us just say, I am largely self-taught.

Be that as it may, Geneva is where his immediate family found their final resting places. There are no living descendants. I have no relatives. My solitude is as a technical matter quite, eh, official.

Goodness. To say I am the last of my line is an understatement. . .

No, not too often.

I have passed through since having delivered my Father's body to the crypt, but I never stay. Big cities intimidate me. People talk of 'stress' these days. That seems to fit the apoplexy which sometimes overtakes me when I am in crowded places – busy, bustling communities are quite disturbing to me. I suppose I would say that big cities give me many, many stresses. I prefer the mountains, the woods. I gladly seek a natural and unforced solitude.

Well, I did spend many summers as a shepherd. . .

Yes, very old school. But one can still find such work in the mountain communities. It is good for the flocks, good for solitary blokes like me.

Not at all.

What to some may have seem a dour and lonesome employment, I enjoyed immensely. Just me and my wards, the robust sheep of the region.

Yes, well, the quest to spare myself from the troubled glances of strangers has skewed many a decision.

Well. . .

Oh, you are too kind. I could tell you were, for whatever reason, somehow more oblivious to my peculiar presentation of self than most anyone I have met in a long, long time. And I cannot tell you how much I appreciate that. It is why I sit alone like this, and with no candle lit, even on busy nights like this.

Tight quarters, indeed.

A function of the small corner of the world in which so terribly many of us have co-existed for so long.

Well, there you go.

Let me be honest with you. I have a, eh, a rather tricky skin condition, among other health issues I contend with, which for the most part, I manage to keep with decent success under wraps. And by that, I do mean literally. Wrapped. See? The ends of the bandages I wrap my arms with show just beneath the cuff of my jacket. And see here? Beneath the gloves, every finger, individually wrapped.

Yes. I have become quite adept at it.

No, no! I am not in the least infectious. You are not under any risk whatsoever.

Well, it does neither hurt to inquire nor to reassure. . .

As it is, I keep my distance, perhaps less so out of any fear of that, and more so because, well, I am acutely aware of my effect on strangers. I know, as with anything, there is a sort of acclimatization that sets in, a desensitization, if you will, provided one is in one place long enough. Here at the *Edelweiss*, it seems, fellow patrons have grown accustomed to me, limited as my exposure is to them. And sure, alcohol has spurred a few odd interactions, but those were quickly squelched by the barkeep, or the owner himself, who is often here as well. They are good people.

Well, there you go!

Thank you. I have been a loyal customer for years, albeit a seasonal one, and I learned long ago, the persuasive capability of generously given *Trinkgeld* – how you call it?

Yes. Tip money. Is a handy device. I leave tips that are as generous as I can make them, from the, er, funds leftover from, er, what my Father left me. I know my generosity ensures this seat in this booth come Christmas time, where for about a week I call this place home. A little television to watch here, a parade of familiar patrons, coming and going, leaving me alone. And this beer, their soups – they are so good. Being more or less on a liquid diet, it is all I require. I am a simple creature, and most assuredly, one of habit. Failing health and issues I have, tip to toe, and so I must heed them.

But honestly, what more could anyone want?

Yes, I see.

Aha.

So, yours is also a permanent skin condition? Then you understand. No. Your fabric mask is cleverly seasonal and, might I add, cheery, with that print. What are those? Little peppermint sticks?

Ah, yes. Candy canes.

No. I don't think it is odd at all. Over the eras, societies have all endured phases of masking. The charade is a familiar one, is it not?

Precisely. And true to history, I might add, hysteria and compliance walk hand in hand. Now as ever before, whether global machinations or isolated incidents as were done before science was even fully separated from the likes of alchemy, quests for dominance lurked at the core of every campaign. I could quite bore you with the roster of epidemics that have given rise to preventative measures manifesting as fashion and style statements over the centuries, in which, I might add, I participated much as anyone ever did. It helped me to fit in, no matter what I actually believed. Truth be told, I am not susceptible to viruses as most humans are. My problem is, er, more of a necrotic nature. I suffer from a very slow but solidly progressive degeneration of the organs, and the residual effects of scarring over much of my arms and legs. As such, I have taken to this covering up of self and run with it. The bandages stay nicely hidden so long as I keep myself under wraps.

Aha. You too, eh?

Well then. . .

True, true. I am quite convinced, we will *never* learn. Mankind is as of yet still repeating His errors, and in ever tighter increments, given how time seems to be compressed by the way everyone does things these days – despite all the knowledge out there.

Yes. . .

Well, here's to that! And to our dastardly disguises! We will no doubt be fashionable once again very soon!

Vive la difference!

Yes. *Prost!*

III.

I do. I administer my own self-care. It is a routine I have lived with for a long time. Happily, as the years have moved forward, so have the products improved. Disposable bandages, for one.

Yes, well. . .

Just trust me on that note. When I call myself an 'old man,' it is an understatement.

Anyway, I go through miles and miles of gauze, but it facilitates my getting out and about. Which does in the end fulfill a rather simple goal. As you can see, it affords me evenings like this at the *Edelweiss*, where I can participate with the rest of modern-day humanity, even if a bit offsides. And meet nice humans like you.

Why, thank you!

The general merriment one generally finds at cozy locales like this is all I ever need for companionship.

Yes, well, alcohol does help dull the pain. . .

I apologize, I may have interrupted you. Do go on.

Oh, I am sorry to hear that. So, you understand that, too.

No?

Aha. . .

Oh dear. . . and you. . .

What? Oh. . .

No, I have not heard about that!

My, my! Well, you have certainly had your share of suffering. Did they have to put it down?

Yes. I imagine so.

You poor. . .

Understood.

But then – forgive me, I am quite in the dark on current, technical 'stuff' as you call it, like this. To be perfectly honest with you, of all the reading I have done, it has only ever been what I was able to procure at zero cost or close to it. Older volumes, defunct editions. Used books. Free books, from library storage rooms, charitable organization warehouses, rubbish bins. . . Reading material scavenged on my travels. My budget is a tight one, so I have had to choose carefully how I spend my money.

Indeed. This, tonight, counts as that. I consider it a good investment.

So, I may as well also confess, I have no technical prowess. I am sorry if I have perhaps not quite tracked everything you are telling me.

You say. . ? Aha, I get it. Well, one hears stories like that, where the purportedly domesticated animal turns on its owner. I have witnessed circus trainers being. . . and their menageries, turning on the crack of a whip into beastly chaos incarnate. Heartbreaking.

Yes? Go on. . .

Oh, dear.

I really am sorry to hear this. So sorry you endured all that.

And so, you are saying the part of your face that I do see above your mask is *partially* yours? And that what is covered by your mask is wholly that of another?

No, not at all.

To the contrary, I am *impressed*. I know something about these, er, sorts of procedures. Am myself intimately acquainted with much earlier versions of that kind of, eh, exploratory science. Experimentation. Fascinating. . .

No, really? So, your eyes as well?

Well, I'll be. Yes, I think I can tell, now that you mention it.

Yes. . . I can see that. Certainly, there is much of artistry in what has been done. Things have surely come a long way. . .

No, you should not worry so much. Your gaze is, eh, I would call it quite steady. And in subdued lighting like this here, it is almost indiscernible.

Indeed. Twin constellations. The twinkle in your eyes – to think, it once belonged to others. Quite poetic, actually. And how well they were was matched to the other.

Oh, I see.

Well, that was not very respectful of them.

Yes, I suppose a certain arrogance comes with the territory.

Agreed. You should have had some say in at least that. . .

Why sure. I am not offended. Neither offended nor put-off. You have no idea from where my perspective all comes. Trust me, mine is a broad platform of acceptance. You can feel right at home. If you would like to fully remove your mask, go right ahead.

I agree. It gets *so* tiresome, to drink beer through a straw. Beer, soup. . .

Yes. Anything.

Yes, well, I use these all the time. My lips, well, they just don't respond as they should, like these old fingers of mine. Hence the difficulty I have forming certain words sometimes – and do not tell me you cannot hear it. On occasion, I try to eat solid foods, but things get a bit too messy, even for me. So, I prefer to use my straws.

Indeed. Let them gawk.

Same. That is why my knapsack is always on hand. I keep a stash with me. If you need a fresh one, just let me know. I have plenty.

There you go.

If you turn yourself a mite, there is a nice patch of shadow that plays perfectly across your face. Subtle but effective, for your sake, but only because you have pointed this out to me. I am completely fine with how you look.

You mean, when you are looking at me?

No. . .

Well, your vision must be far better than mine. I have no idea how mine would be quantified, as you describe it. Twenty-forty does not mean anything to me, but I understand you. So yes; I suppose that is good.

Who knows? I would imagine mine would be rated in the hundreds!

Yes. Hence my idleness when it comes to what once was a favored pastime. I do miss reading books.

Oh, most assuredly. I listen to scraps of conversation of the folk who assemble here. I listen to the television over there. Even when the volume is quite low, and I can still discern most of what is being said. Well, enough so that I can keep up.

Ah, yes. Music. Mankind's gift back to the gods. To God – however one construes it. I do love listening to music. To me, it is the supreme confluence of our abilities. Math, imagery, pattern, and if with words, lyrics. . . illustrative prose paired with melody that can bring untold legions to tears. And the instruments themselves, how they have been crafted over the centuries, how they have evolved alongside all other aspects of society – and now with electricity to power them, of all things.

Well, I must confess, I cannot sing to save my life. I can carry many things, and have; but carry a tune?

I will confess something. You will think me absurd, but I have never sung a song in the presence of another human.

No. Never.

Not exactly. I am self-taught on the *Blockflöte* – how you say that in English?

Aha. Recorder. There is a well-worn one of those in my bag right now.

No. Only the winds and the birds. And my flocks. . .

How about yourself?

Ah, yes.

Of course.

Yes, well those times do come and go.

I do suppose I could get in with an eye doctor. But it's not that simple. . .

Oh no; I am not offended. You are not overstepping any boundaries. I dare say, we seem to share not a few key aspects in our disparate existences. I am guilty as charged in my personal negligence.

Ah, but remember what I told you about taking me at my word. Who is to know?

There you go.

So, I will tell you what. Allow me to get this next round. And if you wish to keep your mask off – and I do think you should feel free to do it, you are in safe company here – then I too shall loosen my scarf, just a bit, just enough to ease it off my own face. I think I might try to take a swig the old-fashioned way. We can together, as a pair of patchworked misfits. . .

No. . . Well now, that is far beyond mere coincidence.

. . . as a pair of misfits, we can enjoy our next beer with our faces freed up. Raise our glasses to our lips the way it's meant to be done, take a good and solid quaff. Yes?

Alright then, it is a deal.

Ja, hallo, Georg. . .

(Another round of beers was ordered)

IV.

Well, let me look. Naturally, between these ancient eyes of mine and the weak lighting here – I can't say that I can make out too much of what you have described.

Yes, I can see that.

Aha. I can see those, too. Remarkable. Victor would have delighted in this.

Vic– Ah, yes. Victor, my father's Christian name. He was, yes, a man of science, but among his myriad peculiarities, he was also er, an, eh, irregular sort of – how should I call it? – inventor. Fascinated by all manner of things, which back then did not have their place in the accepted everyday, but which I dare venture would appear somewhat more commonplace today.

No. At least, I do not think so.

But your work – I mean, the transplant work done for you – is so along the lines of what my Father aspired to. Surgical prowess but a nick or two below that of a Pygmalion, a so-called mad scientist, soon called the artistic genius. These days, it is evidently performed with vast compensation *and* accolades.

Yes. In the demise of another, the demise you suffered is at least somewhat rectified.

Of others. Yes.

Indeed. that 'death serving to help life in the living.' I suppose, my Father *did* make some sense some of the time. . .

You read my tone of voice. Yes, I suppose, I am still trying to convince myself.

Well. . .

I myself do not see what you are calling so horrible. To me, your face bears the signature of someone's skills, like a fine cursive, unique and artistic. I beg of you, do not think me too bold when I simply say, I think you look wonderful.

Oh, and please pardon my frankness. I may be a stranger, but I am no monster. I am just a very old man who has had a few beers on a Christmas Eve night. An old and disheveled sack o' body parts which manages to keep on, still manages to raise a glass. With you.

No. I really mean it. You possess a certain beauty that is hard to dismiss, let alone put into words. Again, I am sorry. . .

Well, then, alright.

Who cares about that? I don't.

Yes. You get it.

And please, do not be spooked by me. I am afraid my enthusiasm is a bit too easily sparked. I live terribly quietly these days, and when I am inspirited, as I am now, I know myself well enough to recognize my pathetic inability to filter my emotions and their resulting expressions. I suppose you could call that a dis-ability of sorts.

Yes, it *is* a nice word. Inspirited. A holdover, I suppose you could say. . .

Oh, it got me into trouble too. I cannot tell you how many predicaments my impetuous self brought about. But these days, I am far too old and lame to be of any trouble to anyone. Why, even the mice approach me for crumbs on the quieter nights, when I sit here late enough, and the place is emptied out.

So please, understand, that if I express myself in such a way, it is because I am quite infected with the merriment of this night.

Well, yes. It is for many a *holy* night. . .

Trust me, your company is a gift.

Now, look at me. Before I undo my scarf, I want to forewarn you, just a trifling cautionary word. I am not a pretty man. I never was. Now, let me get this knitted monstrosity unwound. . . There we go, just a little. . .

Oh.

Are you alright?

Okay. Okay. . .

I must say, it feels quite nice to free my face up. That woolen thing sheds so; it is as ancient as its owner. I am constantly getting fibers stuck on my lips, which, given the condition of my mouth, is more problematic than it ought to be.

Too much information, yes? My apologies. I am afraid the beers are talking.

I am feeling quite. . . Oh, no!

No, nooo. . .

Don't look! Well, damn it!

No. Hold on a moment. I have just lost another tooth. I am so sorry. . .

Yes. A tooth, and it fell into my bloody beer, of all things. Oh, crikey!

No. I don't need anything. I have what I need right here. . .

No, it doesn't.

Oh, I am so sorry!

Hold on. Hold on a moment. Here, I can. . .

No, it is perfectly alright. I am *not* offended!

Here, let me just ease this up again. I have been having some issues with, um. . .

Good heavens, I hope I have not frightened you off!

Well, thank goodness.

Very well. If you insist. Thank you.

Yes.

Okay. . .

It's just that this is. . .

Okay. Thank you. Truly. Here, let me fish out another straw. Are you still okay with yours?

Oh my. We are a pair, aren't we?

Prost!

V.

Listen! The clock strikes the half hour – again already! I cannot believe how the hours have flown.

Yes, testament to what a lovely visit we have had. Are still having.

I will be forever grateful, you saw fit to stay here and keep me company. And I am so sorry, so very sorry about that unmasking thing. I should know better. I am not one to utilize the services of mirrors much; well, ever, and I quite forget how, er, graphic my state of degeneration has become. Living in colder climes helps keep the, eh, disease somewhat at bay, somewhat slowed down. But everyone has an expiration date.

In all honesty, it is my body just reminding me, it is about time to close this book. I have lived longer than most men could ever think to live. I have seen so many changes, that my mind spins with change, and it is time to disembark this crazy carousel. I can hardly keep up, especially now with all this technology, which I have never had the opportunity to test for myself. I am certain I could have learned it, too, but then, these old fingers of mine would not contend well with those tiny buttons and keys I see on the devices everyone is using. In fact, it causes me to wince, when I see the youngsters pounding away, their fingers flying, hitting those small phones like birds' beaks pecking at bugs on the ground. I could never tolerate that; it would be far too painful with these digits of mine. Those devices make me feel my age more than ever before. Older and more passé, even, than when automobiles were. . .

How old am I? In exact years? Oh. . .

No. Well, I do not wish to confuse you. Can we just say, I am twice as old as I was when I was half my age, and that even back then, I was a living fossil?

Aye. The beers. Yes, that's it.

Yes. Well, in about an hour.

What is it? Yes, I should tell you. A midnight mass, which I wish to attend.

No; I do not go regularly; and when I do, I do not participate. Not entirely.

Why I don't? Well. . .

If I were to tell you the rest of my story, where my Father and this place are concerned, I think you would understand a little better. So, keep your mind open as you have, so far, done quite exceptionally well, and I shall tell you a more extreme sort of tale, what many would also classify as a ghost story, if you don't mind that sort of thing. You may wish to take your leave of me at the end, once you have heard it all, and I would not hold it against you. But ultimately, I believe this to be a story of decency; nay, of redemption. I as I sit here now am just another human, being, much as anyone else is, here at the *Edelweiss*. So, take my tall tale for what it's worth, and relegate its details to as much fantasy as suits your capacity to regard me equally as a fictitious beast who in the end was able to fully shed his accursed pelt. If you already suspect me an odd mix and not entirely of this world, you are already well down the peculiar road I offer. . .

PART TWO

I.

This goes back to the years I spent way up north, in the outer reaches of Arctic Circle, following my Father's death on the ship which had in actuality rescued him, where he spent about a month on board, first as passenger, then as patient.

And, I will tell you this story in honesty. I will not gloss over the narrative.

. .

Very well.

'Deal,' as you say.

Once having procured my Father's corpse, I made haste to set off with it under cover of night. . .

Yes. I took it.

Without proper permissions, not that there were many to begin with, given the extreme circumstances everyone contended with on that ship. Formalities were of course in place, as on the high seas there are always protocols. Even so, necessity called the shots. Although my time on board was terribly brief, my interactions with the ship's captain had been civil enough, for all the unfortunate facts of my Father's being there, plus my unexpected presence on top of all that. But I intentionally misled the captain. When I departed the ship, I did so with him thinking, I would be journeying on alone and that I would have nothing to do with the disposal of my Father's remains. Hence, their plans for a burial at sea, once the ship had reached open waters.

I must remind you, I was at this point in my life still steered by decisions made in anger. Anger and regret. Those two drivers – obsessions, really – left me with no room for anything other than reckless ideations. Towards others, towards myself.

At that time, I thought burial at sea for my Father far too dignified a ritual for the pathetic man I saw him as, he who had caused me more pain than all the humans I had ever dealt with, combined. And I had participated in more than my share of hostile encounters with others. To my vengeful mind, his body, his memory, were only deserving of some formally meted out *desecration*. As such, it would fall to me to arrange for a postmortem defilement for this man, so to render onto him what I believed – with all my wicked heart – he had done to me.

Oh yes. Payback of the worst kind.

Always.

It was with this malintent, that I stole my father's withered, wrapped form from its berth in the middle of night, and slung it over my shoulder like a sack of flour – he seemed to weight little more than one. We jumped ship, as they say, and traveled off on a makeshift barge I had laid claim to, one I had found wedged in a crevice of a massive ice cap. I had with me a pair of sturdy oars – and I am sorry to say this – which I had also stolen from the ship. Given the winds and the rough seas, we took off at a brisk pace, and were soon swallowed by the preternaturally eerie and twilit realms of the upper reaches of the Barents Sea. It was as if we were sailing into a deep-space portal. I remember it like it was yesterday.

Yes, I can still see the seas out in front of us. Such an infinite darkness. There was no delineation between ocean and sky. Ice floes dotted the surface like crumbs on a path, glowing, as if with a chemical luminescence. The Northern Lights that time of year were still but a suggestion, little more than soft, acid green brushstrokes pulled across the heavens. The rough seas were as calm as ever they were, which let me tell you, was not saying much. Always such a bitter chop, always such a resistance in those watery regions, as if to keep to human trespassers to a minimum. It is no wonder those harsh stretches had been darkly christened as the 'Devil's dance floor' by the very daredevils who had ventured there.

Now, mind you, being early autumn in this part of the world, it is in effect a season of twilight. The pre-dawn and the dusk, they linger on for hours and hours. I thought it back then as, well, quite lovely. It certainly suited my state of mind. Deep lavenders would barely give way to the inkier purples and pitch black of night, or conversely, they would fade at a slow crawl into the heavy grays of what seemed eternally cloud-bedecked days. The progression of time, of day into night, remained a succession not unlike some purgatorial standstill of time, based on books I have read which have dealt with that sort of subject. It was an ideal climate for anyone bent on a surreptitious business. Needless to say, I was quite acclimated to the unwelcoming elements. And being that there was no other *living* human to torment, it fell to me to set aside for the time being my destructive imaginations. It was a time to bide, to survive.

My father's wasted body was in no time frozen solid. He became, in effect, a passive accessory, a scrawny statue, wrapped for shipment, like some old, plundered talisman I could not leave behind. I still had my plans for him.

We eventually passed into the upper reaches of a massive body of land. I had seen enough maps and could well enough read the stars to know, this was not yet any kind of continental mainland. The land loomed large, however; I could tell from a distance, it was possessed of an eco-sphere all its own, sharply delineated, its shorelines cut off by the backdrop of a mountain range which framed the entire scene before us. We made our way into one of the many fjords. I was certain, this was most likely an area once well-known to whalers, but everything in sight presented itself as a world long abandoned. I steered the barge to a decently accessible stretch of shore, past where the rocky promontories jutted out into the black waters like haggard, unwelcoming fingers. There was indeed a harsh beauty about the place. The sharply spiked mountains, steep and barren, cut the frontage lands off as if they were the protective walls of a cliffside fortress. With this half-lit, barren vista beckoning us ashore, with the ice-cold seas behind us, and with the swirling skies before us a-mix with spectral lights, whether real or imagined, I could hardly resist the welcoming call of the terra firma. This no man's land would serve as our interim destination. By that time, I was near starvation, and had not enough freshwater rations to continue on another day. Looking back, I am certain, I was quite delirious. I remember thinking I had landed near the resting place of some colossal black dragon, against whose spiny back I could rest my own. I was not tempted to venture further inland. I deposited my Father's corpse beneath an outcropping of rock and fell to the ground, and there I fell asleep.

Would you believe me, if I told you I slept for days on end? Well, I did. I had no means to count how many days passed, but I knew from the impending darkness of the day into which I did eventually awake, that I had slept soundly into the autumn season, and that winter would presently set in.

It was in a protected cove near those shores, in an abandoned hovel that had likely once served as a whaler's outpost, that I spent not one, or two, or even five, but a full nineteen years. There I remained in absolute solitude and lived a survivalist's subsistence. There, with my Father's corpse laid in its shallow grave a mere few yards from where I whiled away the time, I slept long, long hours. As if I were hibernating. I would awaken ever so often to venture out in whatever direction

I chose, but I was always restricted as to how far I could make it in on any trip, given the limitations of extreme weather and my own abysmal outfitting, a general unpreparedness consequential of my rash decision-making *non*-skills. I had no tools, no implements for hearth or home, nor for anything suited for excavation, or travel over difficult terrain. I lived as perhaps a Paleolithic Man may have, using only the materials on hand as makeshift tools, by which the bare minimum could be accomplished. But I had my ridiculous stamina, the clothes on my back, and an attenuated hunter's prowess granted me by way of sheer desperation. Starvation lurked insidiously. I killed, but only as absolutely required – a wandering bear, a wayward walrus, a fox that had become too curious; rabbits, assorted vermin. I partook of them in the manner of the ancients of such perma-frosted lands, slicing into their carcasses and consuming the fat, the skin, and the meat raw, on tightly rationed, as-needed bases.

My Father, he spent those years in frozen repose in a makeshift gravesite, which consisted of what little I could cut from the frozen ground, what rubble I could gather at the shore and from the mountain bases, a modicum of protection against the predatorial animals which occasioned by. The grave was more a burial mound than anything anyone here in Europe might fabricate and festoon for ostentatiousness afterlife visitations, but it kept the beasts at bay. My Father's corpse may well have played a role in my own survival, for his scantily wrapped remains, with no malicious forethought on my part, often served as bait.

That first summer, however, I must confess – and it shames me to disclose this but disclose it, I will – I sought to end my own life. It had been my intention from early on, to live only long enough to see my Father perish. And now that he was dead, his psychological pull on me had diminished to a point where I was, in fact, able to stay focused on my own survival. But that first summer, in a fit of deep depression, I thought to accomplish that which I had always planned to do in my more primitive state of mind, which was to build for myself a funeral pyre, onto which I would place myself, and like some Viking, or Indian noble – or his suttee – I would incinerate myself, and thereby join my Father wherever it was that he had descended to. I had long since given up on any notion of salvation, but neither did I think my Father worthy of a lesser circle of hell than I. To me, our destinies were so intertwined, that even in death, I presumed we would be to each other as inescapable as we had been in life. Hell bound or some intermediate station along the way – who was to know?

Be that as it may, I had gathered driftwood over the course of that first year. And not too long before the approximate and assumed anniversary of our arrival upon this quiet and frozen place, which was easily identifiable by that telltale prolonging of the twilight, I resolved to do myself in.

I was in sight of my Father's grave as I shucked my outer garments, as I then seated myself upon my driftwood bier, and then as I gathered up pieces of wood and covered my legs and lap with them. I was in sight of my Father's grave and the rocky shore and beyond that, of the fjord, whose waters glimmered in the moonlight to where they merged with the open seas. Beyond all that, I saw the huge, open sky, littered with stars. Cold, indifferent stars. My flint struck a spark, and I lit the kindling. And as the kindling began to burn and crackle in a horrifically ironic, cheery way, and as the small flames began to seek out and attach themselves to the threads of my chemise, the ragged edges of my fingernails, the hair on my body, my skin, it was then that the lights – yes, those Northern Lights! – struck their own spark.

They all but exploded over my head.

This was the event – the miracle – I alluded to earlier. Now, you will come to know their complete context.

It was as the fires of my funeral pyre began to prey on me, eating away at my skin, singeing my hair, burning into me and sending such searing knives of pain into my body – pain as I had never before felt it – that those damn lights above me began their own dervish.

And the lights danced over me and all around me with such insistence, such glorious insistence, I felt encased by them. They reached down from their infinite plains with scarves of warm rose, of deep purple, and with swaths of spring green as what would bloom upon the Alpine meadows in Springtime, and they reached so low and with such force, that I felt the smoldering hair on my head rise up, up, up in an electrically charged response. And then, I felt this cooling balm wash over me, which was so profound, it overrode the agony that was threatening to overtake my body, my very mind, the last shreds of my sanity. One second longer of that pain, and I know I would have shut down; my sentience would have in that moment given itself over to an unconsciousness from which I would not have returned, as the rest of me would have been consumed by the flames.

It was then with a cry – a cry of anguish and of joy – that I leapt off that burning pile of wood and commenced to roll on the ground, over and over and over again, until I rolled into the waters of the fjord itself. And in that chill rush, I was like some massive human ember reduced to an ashen *and newly born* being. I had just traveled through some supernatural gateway and was being yanked from the demonic maw which would have surely awaited me by way of the magnetic energies which tugged at me with such insistent force, they lifted me right up and out of my abyss. The lights possessed the physical tenacity of a celestial cowherd sent down from Mount Olympus to rope, tackle, and rescue me – the lone and lowly, raging bull – from my own demise.

And I lay there on the shore, letting the frigid waters quell my pain, numbing me, cleansing me, and I sobbed at the sky. Dry, tearless sobs, which wracked my scorched body, against which I was helpless.

I cursed the lights. I gave thanks to the lights. I understood something new, but it was endemic of a language I had yet to grasp, come to terms with, like one who has heard new, foreign words spoken for the very first time.

I realized, I would be at this for some time. I could tell even in that moment, that this was so big, it would take years to decipher, to then transcribe it. And then to assimilate this language, this knowledge, and make it my own.

That, my friend, was the beginning of the rest of my life. A new book, page one. I studied the lights and allowed myself to become wholly absorbed by them. Almost two decades, did I live and learn, there at my whaler's outpost, with my Father close by in his rocky bed.

It was also, to be completely honest, the time I needed for my burns to heal. I am of a peculiar build, and any healing, if it even occurs, takes a terribly long time. It took that stretch of nearly twenty years until my skin had reconstituted itself and was enough intact again, so that I could once more dress myself in all my garments and fasten them properly. It was with my Father's bandages, his sailor's shroud, that I dressed my wounds.

Well, I know that. But my, er, constitution, was always quite extraordinary. I never once did freeze, nor suffer frostbite.

I know. It is hard to explain without getting into the really problematic details, which I with great intention avoid giving voice to. I beg your indulgence.

Good. Thank you. It is hard enough to admit this much to you.

Thank you, my friend.

Alright. Yes.

My Father's body, stripped bare out of dire necessity, was after nearly two decades of unprotected, arctic repose beneath its primitive burial mound reduced to a blackened and shriveled, skeletal rigging, held loosely together by the thin, leathery housing of his mummified skin. He no longer resembled the elegant patrician of his living years. This was now a pitiable and primitive reduction, fragile as a relic. When we departed the island, I was able to fold what was left of my Father into my backpack.

Yes, this one.

In retrospect, I know that it was again in the autumn, and in the year 1818, when I launched my barge from those blessed and brutal shores, to recommence our journey back home. I had resolved afresh to return my Father's body – his paltry remains – to his family. I still harbored resentment, but no longer sought vengeance. It was so simple. The man needed to be laid to rest with his family.

No, not mine. That much never changed. They were never 'my' family. But, I had long been resigned to this.

We were now on our way to Geneva. We endured weeks at sea, at the mercy of the winds, the currents. What nightmarish, wild days, where I barely rested. . . Once having reached the Norwegian Port of Kristiansand, I, er, purchased a replacement vessel, a small but sturdy boat, so we could continue our journey.

Indeed. I set the anchor not far from shore and must have slept again as an animal would hibernate. My rations had lasted, but barely; it was quite some time before I could consume more than a mouthful of food at any given meal. My system had somehow reached a sort of stasis, which I have always chalked up to mind over matter survivalism. It took time to re-adjust.

Oh, you do not want to hear what I ate. Unsavory details, best left unsaid.

So, after I had rested and gathered what supplies I required, we worked our way south along the eastern edges of the North Sea. In Amsterdam, we were able to access the European interior by way of its rich system of waterways – inlets to tributaries, back to rivers, even canals. The boat being small, was perfectly well suited for these waters. And after the atrocious challenges of Barents and North Seas, this kind of water travel was a welcome respite. The cloth-wrapped parcel that contained my Father's folded corpse, I simply kept in my bag, strapped to my back.

I did not mind my passenger. I would even find myself talking over my shoulder to him. . .

Yes, as a matter of fact, I did tend to think of it as the two of us traveling together. Solitude will do that to a person. One takes what company one can.

We crossed through Austria on our way to Switzerland, having charted a circuitous southerly route, due to the conditions of the mountain passes, it now being winter. Given also that there had been considerable flooding due to the unusual amounts of unseasonal rainfall which had plagued the lands that year, I had determined it best, to come in from the south and west, rather than straight down through the mountains, for the waterways were congested with runoff and flowed rapidly, making travel speedy on the torrential rivers and bloated streams. But all this, I could manage with little trouble. These troubled waters were, on top of it all, by and large devoid of traffic, for most humans would not dare navigate such floodwaters. We traveled, therefore, unnoticed.

Yes. Experience can be the most stringent of teachers.

Oh, I have simply been through too much to have viewed it any other way.

It so happens, the flooding was throughout most of Europe. Rivers and streams were dangerously swollen to over-flowing. I saw riverside communities in absolute ruin.

Indeed.

It was late December when I with my, er, cargo came upon the beautiful lands cut by the mighty Salzach, the river here which later came to serve, as you know it now, the German-Austrian border. We were a couple hours – eh, not far – from Salzburg.

Good gracious – I am ridiculously antiquated in my calculations; I will still at times default to older modes of transportation when I envision distances.

Indeed. Guilty as charged, I suppose.

I was quite exhausted and thought it time to take another longer break, both to rest and to replenish supplies before setting out on the final leg of our journey.

Yes.

Generally, at night. I have always traveled in let us call it clandestine fashion. You have endured a fleeting display of my unmasked features, so I dare say you can understand my trepidation over unwarranted exposure, especially amongst strangers.

Oh, I know.

Turns out, it was the twenty-fourth day of December when we made land not far from here. I remember that too, like it was yesterday. It was a Christmas Eve, just as it is tonight.

No. Back then, I had little awareness of or regard for what seemed to be an endless succession of holidays and holy days. I thought this Western culture of ours terribly afflicted with what amounted to little more than excuses to eat and drink too much. I had read extensively on all of them, knew their backstories, what the days were to represent, and was only perplexed by how everything always seemed to de-evolve into displays of consumption. It puzzles me still, although I came to understand the equally pervasive need of humans to fabricate reasons to dispel the gloom of, say, long winter nights, or the requisite solitude independent living brings with it, especially in these modern times, when everyone seems to prefer to live like gypsies, with a bit of *togetherness*. These days, I do see great worth in sitting still a spell and raising a glass with another willing participant.

Yes, indeed. *Prost.*

II.

It was long past sunset when we came upon what I would soon enough learn was Oberndorf, which looked across the river upon another hamlet likewise situated on its banks. In this location, the Salzach was a tempestuously meandering body of water, already with a long history of flooding. With my Father's remains still strapped to my back, as they had been now for some time, I moored the boat at the first quay wall we came upon, an old stone contraption immediately to the west of the community proper. I was able to hide our vessel in the shadows of an unused, conveniently situated holding office on the outskirts of the waterfront. The town appeared to me an agreeable stopover, a genteel community; not too big to cause me anxiety, nor too small as to instantly sound alarms if an ungainly and tall outsider were to be seen walking its footpaths and alleys.

Near the riverbend, I noticed a simple but imposing church, its single belltower fronting an elegant nave, its tall, arched windows aglow. I could see immediately that the waters had breached their banks here too, and with unfortunate consequences, and that it did not look as if this were a unique event. Sandbags lay neatly stacked against the church's foundation walls, which were deeply stained to almost waist high. Damp and rotting debris was piled high at regular intervals, evidence of its having been newly collected. One could tell, those who lived here had been working to save their parish church and her neighboring structures for some time.

The church, its pale walls visibly marred, was of all the buildings I encountered perhaps least of all spared by the waters. Rudimentary replacement entry doors had been nailed into place, leaving only a side entrance, which appeared to be the only utilized point of entry. A lantern glowed bright upon its rickety mounting; a temporary scaffolding erected near the door. I could see the door itself was slightly ajar, as likely for its having been too swollen to more properly close and latch as for its suggesting to passersby, they were welcome to enter in. I knew from my younger years, doors were left intentionally unlocked and windows were adorned with lit candles on one particular night, the night before Christmas. And so, the date was immediately made clear to me. I remembered many a Christmas Eve, and still do, when I would wander cities and villages on my own, in secret, under cover of many a dark and wintry night, to try and peer past the golden frames formed by the candlelight, to see what was going on inside, who was all in there, and what they were doing, together. . .

Yes.

Those moments were some of the saddest and loneliest in my life.

I know. . .

But, that night, I stayed in proximity of that church, having no immediate desire to wander the streets, risk discovery. It was raining, again, but cold; the droplets were already turning to sleet. No one was about. Shielded in the shadows where the light from the windows could not reach, I decided to remain. I just wanted to listen. And through that open door, with its own patch of light splayed upon the ground, nearly reaching over to me where I stood, I could presently discern – barely, just barely – the voices of the humans inside, who had gathered at this late hour inside the church.

At one point, I heard recitations. Words spoken in unison. Next, I heard a chant of sorts, carried upon only a few notes, which repeated themselves over and again. This was delivered by a deep male voice and responded to in similar fashion by the unseen congregants within. At one point, I heard an infant cry, but only for a short while. I also heard some coughing. More chanting, and then I heard someone speak. It sounded as if someone were reading something, by the way their voice was intoned – there was a certain cadence, a monotone. It was of a soothing rhythm. I in my weariness became transfixed and was calmed. My German was as good back then as it ever was, but with the small portal of that side door being the only outlet for the sound from within, whatever it was that was being spoken, remained indiscernible.

Yes. But listen to this. . .

I then heard something else break through a momentary spell of silence. I heard the strumming of a guitar, a soft play of chords, with the occasional picking out of single notes. And then, I heard the voice of another man, who began to sing. He was a tenor, as I would later understand it to be. His delivery was of a clear intonation, and the simple melody upon which his words were carried sailed, as if on wings. Ordinary wings. No grand archangel did I envision as I listened, but rather, some being more of *this* realm – like, say, a young mother, simply holding her child. The construction of this song was of a common construction; almost every note carried with it a vowel, or a word, in the way a child's song, or a lullaby would. The song drifted out of that doorway like a ribbon. It wafted up into the night air, about the churchyard, across the shadows, and it wrapped itself around me as I stood there, stock still, in the dark. At first, I ignorantly thought the melody leaned melancholic; but the longer I listened, the more I realized, that this odd sadness I was perceiving had nothing to do with pain or tragedy, but rather, these were the stirrings of an emotive response founded on a contemplative, quiet sort of *joy*. My heartstrings were being played, and it was as mysterious to me as it was enthralling.

Even the environs paused to receive this incidentally miraculous bit of music. The sleet, which had been sifting through the nearby evergreens stopped, its wet, shushing sound falling eerily silent. The world was standing still with me, to better hear. . .

I remember thinking, I had never heard a song quite like that. So without fanfare, yet so impactful.

The notes and the voice climbed and then descended towards each stanza's resolution, where the timbre permitted an improved clarity of delivery. I was able to discern a few of the words:

Schlaf in himmlischer Ruh! (Sleep in heavenly peace)
Schlaf in himmlischer Ruh!

Now, I have admitted as much to you, it had long ago been my wicked intention to desecrate my Father's remains, the original plan having been to place them into a massive urn than sits atop the portico of family crypt. I was going to simply drop his remains into the open pit of that vessel, to leave them exposed to the elements, and to whatever critters might nose about and crawl between the remaining strips of bandages which held him, piecemeal, together. It was as maggot fodder and nest filler that he, my Father, was to meet up with his final erasure. Can you imagine?

I know.

I shock even myself to think back on how my mind once worked.

But there in the church yard, a flash of more complete understanding presented itself to me. From where it came, I do not know. But when I heard. . .

Sleep in heavenly peace

. . .my spirit was catapulted from one plane to an entirely new and different one.

Much as the Northern Lights saved me from a rancorous death, so did these words gently command me to fulfill this last task of my assignment, but in an entirely different frame of mind. I was somehow assured, what I would *now* be doing was going to be the *one and only* right thing to do.

That night, for the first time so many years, tears fell from my eyes.

Mind you, it was just a few tears. But their cleansing balm was miraculous. My parched eyes had not felt so *normal,* so good, for so long. And because there was a new calmness within me, that the pressure which had plagued my inner self as a residual rage, had painfully pushed against the back of my eyes for so many years, it dissipated. My entire head felt *clearer.* I was able to blink without any discomfort. That tension in my neck – gone. Would that the feeling had lasted, but the gift of my momentary, miraculous state wore off soon enough. My decrepitness could not be denied. By the time we arrived in Geneva a week later, right at the turn of the year, my encrusted eyelids, the acrid orbs of my eyeballs, were back at battle within their sockets. But the throbbing in my head had been permanently stilled. I could verily *hear* silence and thought it nearly quite as lovely as that song.

Oh, but to live in chronic pain, as I now understand you do too, debilitates not only the body, but the soul.

It does. It kills from inside out.

I know. My goodness, how I know it.

My dear. . .

Yes, yes.

You are certain you wish me to ramble on?

Very well.

And so, on that next morning, before the sun had even risen to herald the dawn of Christmas morning, I set off on foot with my father. But I had wings on my feet; it was only a matter of days before we stood at the threshold of the family crypt, I with my fabric wrapped parcel, my Father, cradled in my arms.

The rain and the sleet had meantime turned to only snow, and so I waited once again, as I always tended to do, until cover of night to make my delivery. I fretted about the tracks I would leave on the ground, but presumed mine might be construed as the footfalls of a prayerful relative, paying his respects to his ancestors as the year drew to a close. The brilliance of the snow illuminated my path to the mausoleum. The bare trees, the gravestones, the crypt itself all stood in stark outline, silhouetted as had they been cut out of black paper and laid out upon a background of white parchment.

The lock on the cast iron door was an archaic, forged unit, easily broken. The hinges groaned in protest, but the door eased open by the force of my foot alone, my hands being thusly occupied with their necromanced passenger.

The stairs down to the crypt were littered with debris – dry leaves, acorn splinters, tattered pinecones. My boots echoed on the stone steps. Even the plant matter, when it rustled, it echoed. I had determined to carry the parcel containing my Father's remains down to the subterranean chamber, where I remembered him speaking of it, as being where the body of his own father and that of, er, a young woman had been laid to rest. This woman he had wed. They were married only for a very brief spell. . .

Yes, they had known each other since they were children.

Oh, dear. I would rather not go into that.

Yes. Sad. So very sad.

Indeed.

I felt quite ancient in those days, truth be told, even back then. To even reminisce on what something like that may have felt at one time? I, er, I just don't know. . .

Romantic love? Like many things in my life, that too is part of a shadowy past, which, no, I will confess never found fulfillment. Something that wonderful I relegated to the remnants of nice dreams I may once have dreamt, once upon a time.

And, so, how about you?

Aha.

Indeed.

Well, there you go.

Oh, I agree. It does hurt ever so much, but that is the risk anyone takes. Even casual friendships aside, one of the many reasons, why I have always kept to myself.

As for my Father, he never healed from the loss he experienced when. . .when his bride died so unexpectedly.

Eh, what was that?

Oh, it is nothing. Just a hiccup borne of old memories I haven't tapped in forever.

Yes, of course.

Going back to my mission: I felt it was the least I could do, to rejoin my Father with his bride. There in the crypt.

And so, I did. It was not difficult to locate her casket. Small, slender, carved of a beautiful rosewood, and set upon on a deep shelf, right next to the imposing sarcophagus of my father's father. How easily identified was that one, with its regal fastenings, its gilded trim. On the smaller of the two, I broke open the latches, and into this casket, did I place the remains of my father. The remains at rest therein were petite; so much so, there was ample unused space at the base of the coffin. Dainty velvet slippers, small as doll's shoes, lay at rest upon the silk bedding, splayed outward in opposing directions. Recumbent, loose jointed, not unlike that of my Father's shriveled body parts, but as yet properly dressed; modestly and richly so. I could see just the smallest section of the delicate fretwork that were the greying, skeletal appendages of her legs.

And here is where a decided weirdness set in. . .

In the moment I placed the parcel of my Father's bones onto that coffin bed, I suddenly felt a prickling at the back of my neck, felt the hairs of my head stand on end, arise as if with static pulled straight up. This was, however, not the sensation from some years ago, when the heavenly Lights had practically lifted me up and out of my suicidal inferno. No, there was an iciness to this sensation that was off-putting. It was as if the faintest of breaths had begun to gently assault my skin, even through my many layers of clothing; as if the fingertips of a ghost were deliberately poking at me, goading me, exploring the curvature of my spine, the limits of my stoicism.

I had the distinct feeling, I was no longer alone. I am not wont to receiving paranormal premonitions or signs, having lived far too long amongst the elements to know, the energies of the living world hold enough phenomenal potential to inundate any human with more messages and signs they could ever wish to receive. Mother Nature provides her inhabitants with a symphonic cacophony. But in that moment, I had the unmistakable, uncanny realization, I was disturbing a somnambulant atmosphere in which the catacomb's residents were protectively couched, and that I was tainting it with my bulk, the grime in which I was covered, the din of my heavy footfalls. I was defiling a dark and deathly peace with *who I was*.

Then something else happened. The moment I saw my Father's remains sink into the soft bed of his bride's coffin, the tightly wrapped parcel which contained him unfolded itself. The collection of bones, blackened and unseemingly small – they eased out. I could hear the hollowed *click click click* of the bones as they moved against each other, as if they were settling into their new home. I then saw my Father's skull turn slightly inward; I saw its jawbone fall slack. Then – and I swear this – I saw one of the velvet slippers shift its position. I saw it turn slowly, incrementally, towards the hollowed and blackened skull's face until its toe came to rest upon the cheekbone of the newly arrived occupant.

And if that were not enough, I fancied I heard a sigh. An audible sigh. It could have been the rustle of dried detritus, but to that end would I have to ask, where in the world these shifting breaths of chill air were coming from. The entry door I had pulled shut. Now, it did occur to me, someone may have followed us in, may have been lying in wait, with some sort of malintent directed at me or the crypt's residents, or us all.

A human interloper, I could fend off. I know my strength, especially when righteously fueled. But there was something otherworldly in the energies which spiraled about me. I sensed this to the extent that it stole my own breath away from me, sent a violent shudder through my body, which surprised me, as I had never experienced what I had often heard other humans call a 'cold dread.' I sensed I was not welcome in this place for any additional, spare moment, that the spirits themselves were wishing me gone. And I could not blame them. I felt like a monster and far too beneath their high-born and comely gentility to remain in the same chambers where their well-formed corpses had been put to most elegant, eternal rest. I felt lower than the dirt beneath the pavers.

And so, I did what seemed the only prudent and respectful thing to do. I backed away from the casket, and I prepared to close it. The beloved pair could at long last manifest a union that in life, they never could. I had delivered my Father to his marriage bed. But here is the last of it: as I lowered the hefty frame of the rosewood lid, as the last scrap of light from the lantern I had just, eh, procured disrupted the inky blackness of its interior, I will swear to you to this day, I saw the full folded bridal dress – and the shrunken form within it – turn. It moved ever so slightly to its side, as if making to reach down towards the bundle that lay just off to the side of its slippered foot. Move, that corpse did. As did the skeletal remains of my Father. There was an intimacy to the macabre spectacle, which left me feeling wholly shamefaced.

I still do not know whether to consider this hauntingly sad and romantic incident something magical, or, as some might call it, miraculous, but it was quite unlike the divine intervention of the Northern Lights many years earlier, which brought me my first inkling of joy. No; this incident in the crypt was not that; nor was it even remotely close to the mystical secrecy of that recent Christmas Eve, when I had witnessed like a thief in the shadows that lovely song's performance. I do feel as I did back then, I had indeed breached some other realm, but one far less welcoming. It was a *verboten* realm shared by those who, even in death, were intending to emanate only an ice cold but livid animosity towards me. Against me. They wanted to be left alone. And they wanted me gone. For all the tragic roles I had played in their suffering, they wanted me out of there.

No, I do not exaggerate. Nor do I wish to diminish my guilt.

Yes.

But as a changed man. As I was in that moment, yes. But even so, rejected. And I suppose, rightly so.

The weight of my transgressions – I *still* bear those, and I will do so into eternity.

No. It's alright.

As such, my quick and immediate departure from the crypt was *an imperative*.

Oh, I don't know. . .

Perhaps.

That is very kind of you, to say that.

Oh my; I clambered up the stairs, practically leaping out the door of the crypt! I emerged from that stultifying space into the blessedly invigorating slap of cold reality. By this time, the falling snow had already erased my first set of tracks. I saw no other footprints and felt assured – or even more spooked – that I had been the only living being down there. With the snow falling heavier by the moment, I knew, the evidence of my departure would be likewise erased in a matter of minutes.

No. I will never go back there. And I am at peace with that.

No. I will not be interred there. I would not put it upon my Father nor his family, to endure my presence ever again. My futile tenure as accidental, adjunct member of this now extinct family line was as of that New Year's Eve effectively terminated.

Of course.

Yes, that is how I do feel about it.

Oh, I know.

When my own time comes – and who knows how long that will be – I will seek out my own, completely separate place of final repose. My own means, in my own time. The best thing I can do is to return to my mountain meadows, where I have felt the closest thing to real contentment. I will do it as the wild beasts do, where no humans ever tread, so that my decomposing remains – and oh my, this carcass is getting readier by the day – can sink forthwith into the soil, return from whence it came, as Nature always intended it.

I think of my soul, once and for all rid of this, *this body* to which it has been hitched for so long, and it makes me feel almost, well, happy.

But I wax darkly poetic. Morose men of learning, bookish miscreants like I, we cannot help it. Death lurks, and we know it. The Reaper follows never too many steps behind us. Soon enough, he will catch up with me, and I will welcome him into my company.

Oh, no; can't say that I would.

Well. . .if you were to. . .

My dear, do not try to do the math. Remember what I told you when you first joined me here. That I am a raconteur, and you need not believe me nor seek any logical chronology in any details of what I am sharing with you in the name of our shared and *so terribly lovely* evening of *Gemütlichkeit*. If you are a little confused by the nonsensical timelines I infer, do not worry. *I am speaking only nonsense at this point.*

III.

So, tell me; are you interested in joining me on my midnight excursion? It is just a simple visit to what is these days a chapel, a public venue. Anyone can go.

No, the original church, where I first heard that song, is long gone. The floods took their toll, and at some point, the repeated damage became irreparable.

Oh, no doubt the Wars played a role in all that. I don't know. Certainly manpower, supplies, that sort of thing.

Yes. And not to worry, we can go our separate ways after the service. You have heard the intermittent tolling of the bells. From the sound of it, it appears to be about eleven-thirty. It will be time to go soon. I plan my arrival on the late side and find a spot at the farthest back pew available. My entire goal is to not disrupt anyone, to not be noticed. I participate quite passively. I just sit and listen, a benign, spare congregant in the Lord's house.

Well, either which way, I am going, for it is on this night when that lovely song I told you about is performed. It is an annual pilgrimage of sorts for me, although nothing has ever quite felt as magical as that first time, when I heard it as I lurked just outside the church, like a prowler. One voice, and a guitar. I pay homage to the revelations of that night, and I give thanks for them.

Yes. It is, in fact, built on the same site as the original.

Oh, I know. My legacy is ignoble and best set aside to the distant past, but a simple song like that does seem to be there for anyone who wishes to access it.

Agreed.

Oh, by the way; the people in attendance, quite random collectives these days, they sing along, which is rather interesting, as most of them do not have the best voices. Many do, in fact, falter quite noticeably on the final bars. Still, they sing along, and with enthusiasm. No mandates for skill, not even for hitting the correct notes. I find that fascinating.

This year – and I have contemplated this for some time – I might even try, just a little, to sing along. . .

"It is true, we shall be monsters,
cut off from all the world;
but on that account
we shall be more attached to one another."

FRANKENSTEIN, Mary Shelley

And so, we attended Christmas Eve service. We sat in the back row of the chapel, arriving late and leaving early. I did not know where my new friend was staying at the time, but it didn't matter. I invited him to go back with me that night, to a chalet I had rented a few miles south of Salzburg, an idyllic, isolated hovel nestled into a crook of the sloping mountain lowlands. I drove.

I soon after purchased the place. We have lived there, together, ever since.

I had been suffering from headaches since before my year abroad – the trial had triggered their onset – which only continued to get worse. My love – yes, my love – he told me, I needed to purge my brain of all my memories. He thought it might give me the space, the peace I so desperately wanted. I concluded, this would be the remedy I would seek. He told me, he would dedicate the rest of his life to listening to me, if that is what was needed. My love instructed me to tell him about every single day of my life as I could remember it, sequentially, and in detail. It was the only honest and correct way I could conceive of undertaking this kind of sentience cleansing, for my brain had to date not spared me any single, damn moment, and my head was filled to bursting.

It was then during the purging of my days, page after page as he called it, that we fell into a supremely secreted and private bubble, into which we ensconced ourselves in a most literal sense. My windfall permitted this venture, and our blossoming friendship combined with our joint issues with society demanded a mutual embracing of this peculiar but most wonderous arrangement. We were from that point forward always in solitude. Always. And it was in that solitude, he became nothing less than my David, a statuesque god come to wondrous and living life. And I? I was somehow, inexplicably, transformed into his beauteous and beloved Aphrodite.

And my love listened without fail or falter, with a keen interest and compassion, which elevated him higher and higher in my heart and in my eyes, and ever more so, with every day that I ticked off, every incident I relayed, every scene I described. And so, in the course of six years and forty-two days, my entire life was laid out. Laid flat out, and mapped, and then closed.

We folded that map in ceremonial finality as we – gingerly – laced our limbs over and under and in between each other's. We lay together and we made love. Once. His first time ever. My first time ever. His last time ever, as it was mine. It was brutal, nearly killed us both, he with his failing heart, and me with – how can I put this? – my terribly ordinary capacity to accommodate a being who was *no* ordinary man. Oh, yes; we crafted from our togetherness – in gentleness *and* volatility – something bigger and better than either one of us could ever have dreamt possible.

And with these most recent days having grown long, and my beloved's form having grown weaker and ever less cohesive – he has lost many of his fingers, his teeth are all gone, and he just inadvertently peeled off an ear; he has no hair left anywhere, and his toes have atrophied and curled up into his feet, to the point where he now walks so slowly, so painfully on knotted stumps…

. . .it is time.

Decades ago, he built himself a guillotine up here – yes, a guillotine! – up here, on this fringe of a mountain meadow, to which we have trekked, backpacks loaded, hand in hand, where we now reside in the very same shelter where he had once tended his flocks, way back during the summers of the big Wars. The device is made of dismantled parts of guillotines he scavenged on his travels to France, which were used up until the 1970's. I had no idea. These defunct implements of macabre historical magnitude were stored in government warehouses all over France, easily accessed. He brought parts and pieces back with him from every trip, always keeping track of what he had so far, what else was needed, with the pristine trees up here providing ready timber, trim and true. An odd souvenir to be sure, of both time and place, piecemealed over the course of several years, but the concrete result of a unique mindfulness and persistence, borne of an understanding of what I myself can only see as an inadvertent immortality. He is like a god to me. He is not a monster, a mere creature of folly, the invention of a madman.

But, so far, nothing has been able to kill him. So, he concluded a long time ago, his head, his brain, must be completely severed from his body in order to quite literally shut him down. He has devised it, so that he himself – he alone – will release the blade.

I have a basket in my hands, which I have filled with mountain flowers, so that when his head falls from his neck, it will sink into a similar, ethereal comfort as to what he relayed to me on the night we met, almost twenty years ago. Twenty wonderful years ago. I am so grateful. His dear head shall meet up with a soft bed, fragrant, and full of life.

And I will turn his head just so when it lays there, so that the last thing he sees will be my face, and all the miraculous beauty I can conjure up. And if he musters even the shadow of a half-smile, I will be there to see it, and I will smile back at him.

He knows this not yet, but it is my firm plan to then take this elixir I have brought with me – all of it all at once – so that as I cradle his head, I too shall fall into my eternal slumber. Damn expensive, foolproof this stuff supposedly is, procured by way of an underground contact I sleuthed out online. He doesn't know it, but there is a portion for him too, which will be in his glass when we raise ours, together, in unison, to commemorate the night we did this very same thing, when we met on a snowy Christmas Eve, back at the *Edelweiss*.

I just need to make sure this works, for his sake most especially. . .

So then, as the wild creatures of both day and night make of our stilled corpses a feast – as they should – our spirits will walk down some path, hand in hand, to wherever it is we are destined, and I will sit back and listen to him as I did on that first night, for I will have forgotten everything else. Everything. In a contented and gentle wash of heavenly ignorance, I shall just sit and listen to the voice of my love, and he will be able to tell me any damn thing he wants, and I will think it beautiful, and brilliant, and I will relish it.

K.A. Schultz

Let It Snow

I remember the moment *it* lit.

It. A winged snowflake.

The first one. Of what? A hundred? A thousand? Two thousand? Just how many of those beastly, little bloodsuckers eventually attached themselves to her, fed from her? Where did they come from? Where did they go when they were finished? What purpose did they serve? What purpose do they serve?

And why her?

There are not enough profane words in the universe to describe how I see those, those *things* now.

And to think, how she was drawn in – how she actually let out an involuntary little coo – by those things, when that first one fastened itself to the tip of her finger. She called it adorable. A dandelion seed come to life, reminiscent of a wooly aphid, but somehow more complex, more robust. Still, an insect so innocent looking, you would never have even the first idea, the havoc they could wreak. What seductive capabilities they possessed. Especially when, as in all such attacks, the backup is next called forth to join forces, swarm as a co-joined entity. They are a pestilence. They are legion.

Jesus. She called the damn thing on her finger *her furry little baby bug. . .*

Hers – ours – was more like death by a thousand kisses. Who she was; what we had. Killed off. And it started with just the one, which slowly fell through the palm fronds, parachuting down in a slow motion, tottering with every molecule of shifting air as it descended. And then it landed upon the tip of her outstretched finger. Perched there for a moment until it leaned in, if you will, and sunk its little I don't know what into her skin, just like a mosquito, to drink her blood. Its hairslip body swelled quickly into a small, red berry, against which its frost-patterned wings glimmered in stark contrast. We were both fascinated in that moment. Ignorant, and fascinated.

Looking back, I am not sure what was more revolting; the bug filling up with my wife's blood like some nasty tick, or the way her face changed, very nearly imperceptibly, as she just sat there, transfixed, quietly watching, unflinching and nonplussed.

And now, here I am, looking down upon through shadowy grove, and the gardens just beyond it, as a result of all of this. As a result of them. And what they did to her.

I do believe, I lost her back on that very first morning, there on the terrace, under the canopy of palm trees I used to think offered us some protection from the elements, part of a paradise I presumed I had bought into for the two of us.

Why did I not just take those few steps to snatch that bug off her finger, to smash to smithereens? I still think I could have prevented more of them from seeking her out and then finding her, coming home to roost upon her as they did, her little parasites, had I simply killed off that first one.

Death by a thousand, little kisses.

That first incident changed her. Instantly. Even when that one bug finally flew away, after we watched it lob its swollen self back up into the spotted shadows of the palms, wherein it instantly disappeared, I could tell, something was different. There was a part of her that stayed outside after we went indoors, out there with the experience, from that very morning on, a sort of aural placeholder. Lost already to me as her husband.

And it was to that new energy, that curiosity, that connection, she returned later that very same day. While she thought I was asleep on the davenport in the study. How could I sleep? I lay there with my eyes shut, feeling only a silent trepidation that bordered on panic. Something was afoot. Terribly wrong. It was suspicion and a sense of betrayal I was experiencing, when I rose from my fake nap to surreptitiously make my way to the doors overlooking the gardens.

Sure enough, there she was, on the far end of the terrace where we had had our coffee that morning. But this time, with not the one lacey, little insect perched upon a fingertip, but an entire host of feathery vermin attached to every one of her outstretched fingers, to even the webbing between her thumb and fingers, at the bends of her wrists. There was a veritable *flock* of these creatures which had clearly hearkened to the summons of that first, foraging critter – I don't know what to call them – the scout. *My* harbinger of doom.

And then I saw as twin lines of scarlet began to thread their way down my wife's fingertips. They wended their way along her forearm. I watched as more of the creatures appeared, as if by magic. I watched as they attached themselves to her arm to consume the spillage. I watched, aghast, as my wife's eyelids grew heavy, as she let her mouth fall open, as she sighed. So help me, she was breathing heavily, her breasts heaving, the fabric of her cotton shift moving rhythmically, its snow-white cuffs spotted with bright, red blood. What was this reaction, for God's sake? Pain? Effort? I wasn't ready to go there, to acknowledge what it *really* looked like. And all the while she remained standing, perfectly still. To me, it was obvious, she had no *desire* to disturb or hinder her brood.

It was my breath that caught painfully. My throat that constricted. My ribcage contracted painfully, and my gut heaved. All while out there, outside on the terrace, my wife stood stone still, like a statue, a mothering Galatea adorned with a multitude of beastly, miniscule angels affixed to her fingers, her wrists, her forearms. I felt cast aside, feeling it abysmally perverse, her demeanor, what was going on out there. A molestation is what this was, and she was not resisting, but relishing it. No matter how much I tried to deny what I was reading in her body language, that look on her face. . .

I thought I would become physically sick over what I was witnessing, what was being implied by my wife's dream-like state, this wanton reverie of hers, chin tipped up and back, her slender neck exposed to the heavens. . . I could no longer remain motionless. I bent over at the waist, grabbed hard at my midriff to contain my guts. The sudden movement gave away my presence. I became, all of a sudden, the lurid one, the leering Peeping Tom. For she startled, her face turning quickly in my direction, and it was then when my first flush of ill-feeling blew up, for it registered with me that her angry expression, aimed wholly on me, was of shocked infuriation. Hers was a piercing gaze, laden with rejection and disdain. My wife's affront at my unwelcome invasion could not have been broadcast more painfully. *I* was the one who should have been the insulted one! *I* was the one who should have been shaken up! My wife looked at me as if *she* had caught *me* in bed with a cadre of lovers! The fleeting image of a praying mantis flashed through my mind, and I was the lowly male, and I was being rejected, by my queen. *I* was the unwelcome parasite.

The creatures lifted from her, a cloud off flittering white, like a puff of smoke from a clean, chemical explosion when it surges into the air. My wife inhaled deeply when as one the mass detached itself and thrust itself skyward. Airborne, picturesquely afloat, the winged beasts rose up and veered to the left, navigating with intent. They were gone in an instant.

She looked again at me. I could have sworn, a sneer lurked in her expression. But I had done nothing.

My wife spoke not a word to me for the rest of that day.

Over time, she spoke less and less to me. She eventually ceased making eye contact with me. When my wife wasn't gazing out a window, looking up into the heavens – for what; the next batch to show up? – she busied herself with solitary activities: gardening, the housekeeping, reading, and writing. She scribbled furiously in notebooks which she kept hidden, whose whereabouts remain unknown to me, even to this day. She did anything, it seemed, to avoid me. *I* became the uninvited nuisance, the pest.

As things were with my job, I could not be home much of the time. I blame her solitude – the solitude to which I effectively consigned her – as instrumental in this separation, her eventual metamorphosis. I worked in harsh, remote locations in developing lands, by necessity staying away for long stretches at a time. Our relocation to the tropics had been with full intent to keep us more accessible to each other – well, me more accessible to her at home – there being no children, nor pets, nor living extended family to anchor either one of us elsewhere. I presumed – such ignorant arrogance in retrospect – that the beauty of the tropical oceanside community, the climate, would foster a fresh contentment within her, which had for years diminished, little by little. I see clearly now, we had both been stoically putting on a good show for quite some time. Where we now lived, it was almost unheard of, that a woman would work outside the home at the level of society we defaulted to by way of my income and our background. But I had given my wife my blessing, for her to explore work opportunities outside the home purely for the sake of her own well-being – provided it was a safe and flexible enough employment, that we could be together during my sojourns at home between projects. So far, nothing had come of this, so my wife was at that time still whiling away her days in what superficially could, should, have passed for supreme comfort. Looking back, I know it had come to represent for her a jewel-lined prison cell. One can sense involuntary emanations of resentment, whether one wishes it or not.

I learned only towards the end of summer, that my wife had let our housekeeper go on the very first day after I had departed on my next assignment, and that she had spent all those months at the house entirely alone. This was right after she'd been first bitten – infected – by those nefarious critters. I had no idea. When I returned home, the house had appeared impeccably clean as always, and our evening meals continued to be served up on the buffet as if by magic, just as our housekeeper had always done it. I had, have, no idea, how my wife managed this extra, quite sizable realm of additional duties, most especially her slightly deceptive presentation of dinner service, which she somehow conjured and kept up remarkably well. But then, even when home, I was always busy, always preoccupied. Ensconced in my office, keeping up my correspondences, researching, and drafting. So preoccupied was I, looking back, that I never even noticed the myriad, small signs. In hindsight, I suspect mine was a willful blindness to the many layered situations we were dealing with, together and separately. As such, generally completely alone, did my wife spend her, our, last summer. Same for the autumn months, and then throughout the onset of the winter, which was ever as hot, sunny and of course snowless as had been all the other days and seasons preceding it. Nothing where we displaced northerners now lived spoke to either one of us as being of wintery good cheer, or of Christmas, or the encroaching new year. Languid heat, sunshine, and a palette of intense, tropical colors surrounded us both, filled our sensibilities to the brim, day after day.

No doubt, given the onset of this oddly seductive, new component in her life, this was how my wife wanted things. With no one to watch over her, there were no witnesses. No one to watch as she came to a point where she was heading out nearly every morning to situate herself in the palm grove, where she would recline on her chaise to await the tiny beasts. She would lie there, so still, so motherly and observant, as the creatures would loft in from who knows where to settle like drifting snow upon her, to bite and suckle from her until nearly bursting, when they would eventually detach themselves and flitter up and away, leaving her alone again with the ocean breezes to caress her bare, bleeding skin as the minuscule wounds began their preternaturally quick healing process, as time and again she languished after the fact, their visitation having been brought her to otherworldly states of some kind of prolonged ecstasy.

Looking back, it was so obvious she was also hiding her physical self from me. The long robes she would always wear, morning, afternoon, and evening, under the pretext of whatever – a spate of illness, a touch of chill, a little too much sun. What my wife was doing, was hiding all the little scars of those bite marks. With only candles to burn at night, at her insistence, and the few oil lamps in my study I refused to have removed, it was often too dark in the house to see much of anything, at least in any great detail, which would have clued me in as to how she truly looked, how she was really doing, had I caught her in any state of undress. To see her with any clarity would likely betray just how she was occupying herself during the day, and so the extreme modesty I grudgingly accepted was lamentably as much my own, deliberate avoidance maneuvering as it was her success at a cloying sidetracking. My wife deceived us both with the quiet industriousness and stiff propriety of a most proper lady of the house.

Had I the wherewithal, I would have noted the pallor of her face, the lavender shadows underscoring her weary eyes, her slightly hollowed out, depleted cheeks. I would have seen how the tendons of her neck had become a delicate brace of tendons nigh too frail to hold aright any such wonderfully formed face. And with all that hair – tangles of ringlets which cascaded down her slender back, which fell unruly, coquettishly across her brow – which in the end simply hid, as did the dim lights, the diminishment of her body, the dulling of her prismatic eyes. Those windows to her soul had captivated me into believing when I first fell for her, that what we shared as a couple would hold out long past those fevered, first months of romance, which would grow deep and sure and sustain us until the end of our days. Those windows tricked me.

But all that was back when I had only human competition to contend with. Who would have thought, it would not be any swarthy, masculine predator, nor any lithe seductress to come for my wife, attach itself to her like some angelic parasite.

No.

It was a bug. A stupid bug. A god-forsaken emissary of some kind of primitive composition. Tiny, beautiful to behold, but with the lurid thirst of a jungle mosquito, the miniscule maw of a vampire.

And nor was it one, or two, or ten, or a hundred to come for her. In time, it was an Old Testament-level pestilence that infected my wife, claimed her as host. For some untold reason, they had selected her. Sought her out, to attach themselves to her, feed off of her, month after month after month, until towards the end of the year, I came to a point where I decided I needed to sleuth this out for myself.

I feigned my final departure to the canal zone. I did not leave home that day.

I drove off as I normally did, but then made my way around to the back end of our property via a vastly circuitous, off-road route. It took well over an hour, being that our lands comprised several acres, and the only other way to access the property was through a secondary gate located at a far corner of our walled gardens, which hardly anyone knew of, being that the area was completely overgrown with massive, flowering vines. It was late morning by the time I finally came up upon the low, stone wall that bordered an open field which looked out over the ocean. I still remember how beautiful the sky was. Deeply clear, the darkest blue. The day had already grown warm; it was silent but for the hush of the winds and their interplay with the long grasses and wildflowers.

It had been almost a week since I had last spoken with my wife. She had taken to sleeping in one of the guest rooms. Because of the hysterics of my most recent confrontation with her over her self-imposed isolation, during which she had torn her dress from her thin shoulders, pulled hair out from her head in bony, clenched fists, I had seen fit, cowardly as it may have been, to give her complete space. No interference, no challenge, at least until I could figure out how else to approach her and our situation. Perhaps get her to a doctor. Get her back to the States.

What a mistake that turned out to be, for I was in the end punished over having both trusted my wife and the anomaly – those vampiric bugs – as not having been the dangers they really were, and the evil covenant they had made with each other. This incremental invasion cannot have been anything other than something she had instantly found herself welcoming in, wanting more of. Otherwise, I have to believe she would have said something to me. She would have come to me for help. She would have joined forces with me to rid ourselves of this nuisance. Perhaps this would have involved letting others into our isolated sphere. Strangers called to investigate what in the world these things were. And to exterminate them.

Instead, my wife's connection with these things resulted in her having been sucked nearly dry – and her having willed it on, with no regard as to what it was doing to her, what it was doing to us.

By the end of December, she was skeletal, but she was radiant. Gaunt, but glowing with an inner light that frightened me, revolted me.

And me – here is the pathetic point I came to: I ceased going outdoors when home out of *fear* I would be forced once again to witness these perversions being meted out on my wife's person. Once, twice, it had been bad enough to see ever increasing numbers of "her" feathery swarm seeking her out to feed off of her. So help me, the last and final time I witnessed her in the thralls of bloodied connectivity with those creatures, that is what did it. It was as if I had walked in on a lovers' tryst, as if Eros himself were consuming the woman I had once thought was mine.

I can still hardly bring myself to recall the sight of her levitating over the grassy field, with those things affixed to her, holding her aloft as they suckled on her. Hundreds of them. And her clothes in a heap on the ground. For Christ's sake, she had to have removed them in anticipation of their descent. Their white feathery wings fluttered madly as their unseen – too small to make out – mouths were attached to her skin. Her bared breasts were clearly heaving in that breathless, sexual way, as when something deep inside is being breached and crested. I felt betrayed, and repulsed, yet I could not take my eyes off her, so extreme was this rapturous apparition, its mystically perverted elegance. And when she began to cry out into the void which held her aloft, and her wordless calls played over the lush fields, cutting through me like a slutty, seismic wave, there beneath the benign clouds and indifferent, cradling blue sky, I could no longer look. Oh, I heard her, and so help me, I felt an echoing response heating, building in my own loins, but I felt reduced to the role of a leering pilgrim, relegated to lurking offsides as a goddess, my goddess for God's sake – was pairing up with a universe in which I had no part.

She may as well have been receiving the stigmata. Are you familiar with that altarpiece by Gian Lorenzo Bernini, the Ecstasy of Saint Teresa? Where a winged seraph – grinning like some blood-lusting minx – hovers over a beautiful, albeit heavily garbed woman, arm raised, arrow poised, ready to strike? And where Teresa, reclining against the ledge of a cloud, a cliff, her head thrown back, eyes closed, has readied herself for sublime *penetration*? Yep, that's the one. A lush, grandiose, monstrance that proclaims in marble and gold for all the world to see, that yes, carnality need not require the mundane gymnastics of one human doing onto another that which they might perhaps want for themselves. St. Teresa in ecstasy – that was my wife on that afternoon, albeit whilst held in the myriad arms of a pestilent thrall.

We endured a quiet Christmas Day that was barely acknowledged. My wife was not interested in going to church. She asked me if we could make a donation to the local hospital's charity fund in lieu of gifts to each other, which request I could not refuse. It was one of the loneliest days of my life, that last Christmas Day with her, alone, at home. I took not one but two long, meandering walks. When I returned home from my second walk, my wife was gone. Again. I could only wonder, where she had disappeared to, all the while trying with all my might to *not* envision a sordid picture of her, again *with them*. We had a simple supper that night; my wife, despite her depleted condition, ate ravenously. That's the thing – she was always starving. Naturally. To me, disgustingly obvious as to why. And these days, my wife was so thin as to be almost, somehow, translucent. Her pale skin glimmered. I swear I could see the lacework of her circulatory system, faintly visible, veins and arteries diminishing to rose and lavender threads which ran wild just beneath their gossamer exo-housing. Even the light, it began to emanate *through* her. When she stood against the sun, I swear, I could see the ever so slightly darkened scaffolding of her very own bones – slender, opaque shadows centered along each forearm, along the lengths of her fingers, down along her calves to where they diminished to almost nothing.

New Year's Eve promised to be an equally melancholy holiday. My wife did, however, to my surprise, to my fear-washed glimmer of hope, ask me to join her on the hills overlooking the bay at midnight to watch the fireworks. We walked hand in hand, in silence, to the crest of the hill, but once arrived stood an arm's length apart from each other on that same, damned field of grasses where I knew she had so often, too often, spent time alone. Tonight, we would watch the fireworks as they were launched from the wharf. Together. The explosions of red, pink, orange, and white looked like the very flowers that forever bloomed in our gardens.

For lack of anything better to say, or to propose, I set out to broach the subject with my wife, that perhaps we ought rethink our move to the tropics, that we perhaps should move back to New England, maybe to some new town along the coast.

My wife listened with a thoughtfulness that led me to believe, this was something she was willing to consider. When she broke her silence, though, it was to simply say how much she missed the snow. I stupidly thought this was her way of saying, she was missing home, too.

My darling, I had replied back to her, *if only I could magically make it snow for you right here, right now!*

My reply seemed to trip something in her. She turned to me and grabbed my arms with her wispy hands. There was a surprising strength to them. I reveled in her touch. It had been months since she had touched me. So long. Too long.

Darling! Yes! Snow! she cried, with the happiness of a child whose wish had suddenly been granted.

I could see her eyes fill with tears. Tears of joy? None of this made sense to me.

Oh, let it snow, let it snow! She called out to me, to the skies.

Let it snow, let it snow! She repeated.

And all while the fireworks continued far below, miles distant from us, sparkling flowers no bigger than my fist falling and fading from sight, all while the dark heavens over us stretched into a black infinity, and the Milky Way glowered over us, a translucent swath of reaching from one corner of the sky to the other, my wife scanned the horizon with such an air of anticipation, I was left bottomed out, my foolish assumptions quickly quashed, rendering me sick with an all-too familiar, dread-filled anticipation of what I immediately suspected, she was now somehow calling forth into my presence. Again.

And there they were. A luminous cloud that rose up like its own sort of ghostly firework, over the crest of the hill. No sound, no commonplace insect-like buzz. Just a billowing form that emerged into our line of sight, moving smoothly, undulating as a single entity as it quickly made its way towards us. My wife watched with the smallest of smiles on her face, perversely aglow with no uncertain measure of happiness – and a sort of satisfaction.

I quickly realized, whatever was about to happen, *would this time include me.* And this filled me with joy. Foolish, illogical joy.

My wife kept her hands on my arms, so that while we were still facing each other, we were each craning our necks to watch the approach of these winged creatures. The snowy cloud wavered, quivered over our heads. The mass was breathing in and out, I swear it.

And then, the cloud burst over us, and the feathery creatures began to drift slowly towards the earth, over us both.

It was the most beautiful thing I had ever seen. My wife's face was lit like a child's on Christmas morning, an angel's at the gates of heaven. I had never seen her so beautiful.

The feathered beings fell all around us, the gentlest of flurries. They swirled softly, spiraling all around us. They landed on my shoulders, on my nose, my arms and on the tops of my feet. Where they landed, they stayed. I was soon covered in these crystalline entities.

And then I realized, none had lit on my wife. It was only me they were adhering to.

I was, for once, this time included! I could not bring myself to resist. What was there to fight for? To fight off? I had already lost the woman I had ages ago thought would be mine until death did us part. But a part of her had already died, and with it, whatever it was we had thought we had. Here, now, appeared to me some kind of chance to be rejoined with her, an opportunity to perhaps, maybe, get her back. To at least exist on some same page with her, even if for just a little while.

I expected the creatures to bite into me with their miniscule mouths. I awaited some unfurling of a multitude of proboscises, so sharp as to pierce me, as if with needles. Everywhere. But nothing came of this expectation, even while they continued to accumulate, covering every inch of me, growing thick in the process. Every horizontally oriented surface of me was soon piled high with these snowflake-like beasts.

All at once, something shifted and every one of them that had come to rest on me whirred into action. No, there was not the first twinge of a piercing. I realized – belatedly, so entranced was I, so sidetracked was I in my desire to be in some kind of communion with my wife as this event was evolving – that these winged bugs, this swarm, had set about with the spinning of a massive web, into which I was in the space of less than a minute, completely bound. I could not move, but nor could I even let myself fall over, do anything to disrupt what was happening to me, for these beasts were simultaneously holding me aloft as they spun their web. They encased me in a trap as strong as a strait jacket, soft as a cashmere shawl.

When I opened my mouth to call for help, to try and scream into the night despite my knowing no one would hear me, a small swarm of those feathering monsters kamikazed en masse into my mouth to stuff it. They wriggled spasmodically as they perished, but they filled my mouth with such force, it became impossible even to close it. I was gagging, gape-jawed, my mouth painfully split apart. Bitter tears leaked from my panic-stricken eyes.

And my wife, she just watched, a sprinkling of her miniscule minions having come to rest in her hair, a few on her shoulders. She watched, cruelly dispassionate, but now with a look of such obvious satisfaction that instantly were severed the few, remaining, frail filaments of our marriage, that which had connected us as two *humans* to each other. Hers was a menacing expression. She was not one of them, but someone, something, *far more dangerous*.

Completely encased, trapped in a webbing and held rigidly at attention, the beasts drew me backwards so that my body was soon laid flat upon the ground.

My wife. My wife, oh my God, she fell to her hands and knees and crawled over me. She climbed atop my midriff, and straddled me. With her face inches from mine, she opened her mouth ever so slightly. I had the absurd ideation, it was with the intention to kiss me. Instead, a glistening, pink pipette unfurled itself, commenced to flick about my face, striking my cheeks, my forehead, tracing my eyelids, the tracks of my tears. Tasting, testing. It felt like a warm, wet snake frenetically mapping my features.

I could not help myself – I felt my cock grow hard. Rock hard. I was otherwise paralyzed with fear and the entrapment of a webbing that held me as had I been wrapped in nylon roping. And yet, my cock stood on ribald end, with such a roiling pressure, such an agonized carnal desire, as I had never before experienced it. I was wracked with lust. My wife then raised her skirt, and I saw through transparent veils of darkness what could only be described as two long, twig-like appendages where once her luminous legs had been, and a torso so wasted away as to be nothing but a body fully reduced to that of a humanoid wasp, with a waist so pinched, breasts like buttons, and hips angled out with such a geometric harshness, as to be the exoskeletal form of a female insect predator. This was no longer my wife, even though there she still was – sort of – her familiar, beautiful face mere inches from mine.

But when she mounted me as this thing she had become, and in one purpose-filled, slow lunge lowered herself onto me, taking me deep into her I don't know what, I exploded within her caustic depths. And this preying, monstrous thing hovering over me was more woman to me in that moment than any woman had ever been before.

I came; oh, how I came. I died a thousand little deaths. I succumbed to her one, big kiss with such violent finality, I passed out cold.

†††

I am awake now, and my view of the gardens, and what I can all see from here, is so beautiful, it pains me to think, this phase cannot possibly be long enough for this world for anyone to enjoy, least of all me. Too soon, I will be deprived of the beauty that exists here, below me, in the gardens nearby, out there on that grassy field, and beyond that, the ocean, and that infernally deep blue sky.

I am still confined within the webbing into which I was knitted. Untold numbers of my wife's insectile army did their work exceedingly well. I cannot move an inch. This thing is not really a cocoon, for I feel, well, nothing *different* inside. There is *nothing* going on inside of me. I am just me as I was, but somehow unnaturally, weirdly so. I am exceedingly comfortable – softly cool during the day; warm, blanketed by night. I am aware of my torso, and my legs beneath it, pressed gently against each other down to my crossed ankles, my feet. My arms rest snugly, folded over each other upon my chest, my thumbs touching, fingertips hooked over my clavicles. And I feel no urge to move. None. I do not sleep, but I am not tired. I have not eaten in days, but nor do I feel any hunger. I am in some waking stasis. Were I not so obviously on the cusp of an imminent demise, I would be fascinated by this overwhelming sense of contentment which carries my consciousness as if borne on the gentlest of wings. I am replete. I sense a completeness of a horrifically unnatural – or is it supremely natural? – kind.

At about the level of my abdomen, however, I can see there is something that cannot be anything else than an egg sack, interwoven to my silken confines, my soft shroud. It has the rounded shape of a pillow, fabricated of countless layers of webbing. It has grown visibly, as I have gazed down upon it over these last few days. I study it idly, observe it with a passive fixation. The egg sack pulsates, the slightest erratic twitching. Life is growing in there. I feel a ridiculous sense of pride. Miniscule life is churning within, eminently hearty in its own context. And I know what life it is that exists inside this downy white uterus. They are the offspring I somehow sired in the depths of my wife. Well, whatever it was, that had become of my wife. I have not seen her since New Year's Eve, not since we consummated a sex act that was so sublime in its finality, it hit that irretrievable point where pleasure crossed over into absolute pain. What is left of me is content to die, and to do it whilst in the act of nourishing my offspring. However many of those vampiric spiderlings it will be, which will no doubt very soon emerge from that thing she fabricated as I lay spent and unconscious in an orgasmic oblivion no ordinary human is intended to survive, I have no way of knowing; but I reckon, it will be legions of them. I died a thousand little deaths, and I will die again, one last and final time, by way of the thousands of little kisses of my children, when they affix themselves to me. May they freely drain what has been left for them.

Just below the egg sack, I can see the outside edges of what appears to be a blood-soaked patch of webbing. Blackened now, it suggests there was heavy bleeding, which went on for some time. I do not know what happened, do not want to consider what may have happened, given the mantis-invoking possibility which is now mine to bear in my forced solitude. I refuse to consider that my bloodied housing has anything to do with this peculiar and utter passivity which I am feeling – or not, as it were – in this here and now. I am suspended, and yes, for now still animated, but just barely so.

Clearly, I have been consigned to some life order that pre-existed me, us, all of us, a species as innocuously dainty as it is beautiful, as unique as every snowflake that has ever crystalized and fallen, come to rest upon an eyelash, a shoulder, an outstretched hand, and when amassed into an arctic infinity, as primordially lethal as any weapon ever was. I am no more mere husband; I am Father. I am Prey.

Beware of the Uhrkind

Beware of the *Uhrkind*
Who stands motionless at the edge of the garden
Waiting, silent and patient, for whichever unattended little one
Might dare look past the frosted panes and into the blizzarding depths
Right there, the Uhrkind stands, peering back from a point where the kinder grass
is consumed by the needles and teeth of an ever-encroaching *Uhrwald*
Oh, but when flurries strike with such fury
By their crystalline shards the scene is so beautifully lit
Its components snow-feathered, ice-fractiled
'tis by design, this wint'ry distraction!

Look out for the *Uhrkind*
A child as old – no – *older* than Time
Jaded and starved as would be any tormented beastling
For this child, you see, has been set aside
As a default participant, almost since the beginning
It is in want of a crust, it is parched and thirsts for a drop,
But it is likewise deathly desirous of that fresh-rendered soul
You merely *think* you have kept well-hidden beneath your thick coat

Beware of the Uhrkind
Once lost to a frigidly bitter turn, taken so very long ago
Left to fend for itself on a crumb-scattered path
Which led to nowhere – just nowhere. It led nowhere at all
So, when on a midwinter's night, such as this
For a scrap of attention, the lamb plaintively cries
Into the far, frigid corners of the northernmost skies
Foolish child, this one was, to wander off in the cold like that!
So broken, it simply did as it had been told. . .

Go, you; get away from me! Go! said she.

All it sought was a sidling glance, one idled and approving nod
From a mother whose heart had been thrown from her own, ignorant breast
To be flung by some malintent o'er the crest of the glacial-clad Alps
What a painterly sunset did it bleed!
But what a harsh night for the rest did it breed. . .
From ages immemorial
Some of them, best forgotten. . .
The rejected ones still swear, despite all, their fealty
They have no choice, for they know no better
As do all the others, who have paid oh, so dearly
Whether they wished it
Or not

For you see, pain paid forward like this is the autograph of an underworld god
Who hath dug deep and long into the bowels of the Earth
Because there is always a cost to love given *in fraud*
The *Uhrkind,* knowing only this, takes what scraps it is handed
Even if those dregs are as afterthoughts pithily granted

Beware the Uhrkind!
Depleted, it will in due time only take
To carry away in its violet-tipped grasp
Whatever ignorant heart of the next one comes along
For it will have obeyed right down to the last
And done onto others as was done to it, too
Until at last, 'neath the pines at the shadowed perimeter
You inhale one fractured and finishing gasp
As from within, you are crystalized
So to join the recumbent others, who lie there, sidelined
Forgotten in their deep-frozen rest
They are who blanket the fields
Their souls cut plum clean from their sad, little chests
Cold as hell are those spirits, whence the pattern is repeated
Clear as glass for the flaying
Their limb, now stripped bare, are wholly depleted

From, "A Killing Repose," published in GÖTHIQUE 2023, now also in this volume. Here, the "childlike apparition" is first referenced.
I have named it the Uhrkind

The Grandmother and those who yet call the *Uhrwald* home had lost loved ones in the last, such storm. A taxed heart had given out as one tried to shovel a path to the well; a hunter, returning home with his catch, had instead become lost, then found the next day, mere meters distanced from his front door, buried in a drift at the base of a towering but unsheltering and indifferent tree. And the twins, a boy, and a girl who had been, it was whispered, lured outdoors to play in the snow by some childlike apparition, known to appear when the storms were at their worst, to entice the youngest and guilelessly unafraid away from the safe harbour of their homes. The children had disappeared without a trace, their footprints instantly erased by the blizzarding gales. . .

Uhr – clock, time (German)
When placed in front of a noun, *Uhr* changes from noun to modifier
Uhrwald – ancient forest
Uhrkind – ancient child, child out of time, from another time

Precious Inkwells

I.
Is it morbid
To think you have never looked so beautiful?
For the wells that once held your eyes
Are far lovelier now, blood-filled to their brims
Where once they glinted, a-smiling, over a warm cup o' mulled wine
There now lie cooled stilled twin pools
This dark poet's preferred elixir
Congealed and coagulated just so

Let me then fill this elegantly hollow'd and feather'd quill
With what is left of you
So that I may craft
Khrystmass sonnets & Yuletide carols
Wint'ry odes and whispered pleadings
To honor you, my wond'rous love
Less, yes, to who you once were
More now, to this *thing* you have become

II.
Redolent, acidic repose
Prayerbook pressed against my breast
Brittle, incrementally withering
My jaw loosens and shifts
Laughter's fleeting talisman. . .
Ah yes, I remember. . .

My hands relax
Fingers splay wider upon winged clavicles
Which ease out, and spread
My weighted pelvis
Sinks languidly
Into a quick-sanded and straw-lined bed
As my legs
Disconnect and turn themselves outward
Less for motility inclined
More for corruption primed
My velvet gown fades as the mistletoe wilts
Whilst I keep a silent night's watch
From above, below – whatever –
to observe, unfeeling, as the rest of me fails
But I dare not blink
Lest the scarlet were to spill
From these, your two most precious inkwells
Onto my hollowed and withering cheeks

Sibling Revelry

No; no, there is no contest
Can't say there ever was
Those long, hard years so filled with strife
Just part of our troubled life
Absolved, from all you once conspired
My headless dolls, I took in stride
Forgotten, sure, your countless lies
Though none may've been what I'd have done
'twas envy's hold, which spurred you on
(I s'ppose, you could not help it. . .)
And now? Your invitation's brought me here
The truce you offered – words so dear!
This sumpt'ous wine, those twinkling lights,
Will make for a most blessèd night!

But, Sister, where are all the other guests?
When was this party to commence?
No, wait! Please stop!
What hold you fast in your gloved hand?
And why look you 'pon me like that?

Oh, dear Sister reconsider
All I could have been before
I'll be for you, and so much more!
I know we can be best of friends – the truest sisters 'til the end!

There, there, dear Sister
It's all alright

Khrystmass

I promise, we will ne'er more fight
You have my solemn, sibling's vow
So, come up here, sit with me now
The view's so broad, the sill so wide. . .

Lean farther here; the better, dear. . .
To gaze upon this midnight clear. . .

(And now, with just one trifling push. . .)

Oh, sibling's foolish paradigms
Splayed o'er the pavers, now's come *your* time
You fell onto your rightful place
That bloodied mask suits best your face
I know you'd thought 'twas *mine* to die
But here *I* stand, the sovereign child

Belsnickel's Feast

My love, my love,
What a fetching creature!
How could one resist?
Her gaze, inviting
Her arms, wide open
Her legs, eagerly splayed in receptive accommodation
And that small chamber, reached only by way of yon rose-red, beribboned threshold
Wherein pearlescent sentries stand guard, ready for attack
To make of the infiltrator mince fit for a Khrystmass Eve's banquet
(Or, better yet, satiated and replete, a carnivorous Belsnickelian beast) . . .
My love, my love
How delectable
How warm, how wet
How thoroughly scrumptious!
What ripe catch should dare escape?

And so, I wrap
Deftly, tightly
And I bind
And then I cut
And slice
And pull, and pull, and pull, and pull
So, inch by reluctant inch
(Screaming 'til her voice breaks)
She relinquishes
Her pliant and pinkened, personal sheathing
Marzipan wreaking
Blood christened, soft a-glistening, sweet trickling

It gives way, gives way
Until at long and arduous last
She is draped, newly incarnate, across my quivering and triumphant arms
A flesh-edged swaddling intended for only the most obsessed of fiends
Who dare steal, knife-wielding, into bedchambers under cover of darkest midnight
To take what they truly most want:
A new, much prettier suit
For *me* now to don
So *I* can at long last become
As fetching and inviting
As my love, my love, my delicious love
Once was

Snow's Rescue

Yet another ling'ring midnight crawls slowly overhead, heavy, stagnant, and thick
I lie in my crystalline sarcophagus, frost bitten, rigid, stiffened
I am waiting, waiting, and waiting. . .

Even the stalwart ones saw long fit to best stay home, ensconced
Warmer, safer, 'midst familiar company surrounded
Whilst I, the innocent born, must bear alone an envy, so wickedly manifested
In the end, left in an enforced solitude; silenced, unaccounted for
An incorruptible postulate, by now, by most forgotten
In poisons' tenacles enwrapped, here I am held, spellbound and fast
My stasis insidious, lethargic, and never-ending

Why, oh why, must I exist only to have suffered another's scornful machinations?

The wan moon, so I imagine, slinks amongst the fracturing cloud breaks
Its glow is that of an inconsequential candle, set against cold and indifferent
constellations
This woodland tomb, this valley, are but a ocean's bed graveyard for cast-off gods
and deviant angels
A nave by haggard evergreens buttressed, in snowy whorls ice christened
Spired sentinels of oak and ash, they stand, swaying yet unmoved
Whilst I recline, keenly, agonizingly aware
Of the unfeeling universe which surrounds me

. . .my frozen limbs
. . .this matted hair
. . .the stiffened fabric of my gown, threadbare
Blood spent and by frost rendered to that of a carved carnelian plinth

Bereft of voice, my breath lies stilled, and held within
In desp'rate hope I pray, I pray

For a Princely redeemer, as was foretold
For him to breach this brambled keep, to set his one, true love at long last free. . .

And lo! What's this?

The crunch of stirruped boots disrupts the silence. . .
A broad-shouldered shadow breaks the monochrome plain. . .

He comes! He has arrived!

The glass coffin lid he casts roughly aside
Brittle shards burst and scatter
Leather gloved hands lift me up, I am gathered
Into broadsword arms, jewel-clad
My body floats up as were it by a blessed cloud bedded
Here I am, your Galatea!

I await like a fairy tale's inanimate puppet his life-gifting kiss. . .

But no. . .
'tis not to be. . .

For this Prince, he has been infected and grown foul
He is now by hell driven
And though he seeks no more a beloved bride
By an immoral and insidious appetition he has, even so, come for me. . .

He leans in, his fetid breath reeking of a defiled death
And bites off the tip of my delicate nose
He swallows it whole
And licking his lips, decides it best to consume the rest of me
So, into the flesh of my tender, young neck
He sinks his sharp teeth and drinks long and deep
Down to the dregs my immaculate soul
He drinks down the last drops of my ambrosial soul

Coarse Vespers

Torn scalps, my dear, do tend to bleed
Spilled secrets flow 'midst slurried creeds
As ghosts, once roused, return with mem'ries best forgotten...
Dragged to the surface, rent from the core
Invoked are sordid tales of yore
You *could* call it a different kind of beautiful. . .

'tis there for those who dare drink deep enough
Of the unrelenting, ice-cold falls
Born from the loins of tattooed canyon walls
Thrashing, thrusting, violence homed
Resurrected now as lurid tomes

Genesis' antithesis – is there any difference?

In the end, indiff'rent waters
Apportion their opposing calls
They meet then with a dead and cooling calm
What a still oh so still mirroring pool remains
Into which, compelled to look, we see *ourselves*
Peering back through toxic depths, a poison-laced baptismal font
The primordial elixir

Into this, yes, dip your hand
So you can write about it
Freshly penned; with luck, in time ennobled
Coarse vespers, these words, in brilliant scarlet, clotted

Peer Here

Peer here
Into this portal
This small window, gold framed
A breastplate implanted
To permit one and all a more permanent view
Of the massive heart which now beats therein
For you see
My md
Had grown up
Cut his teeth
On perhaps one too many
Seussian solutions
And by far too many Jonesian contraptions
So, when he saw fit to install this four-chambered apparatus
Into the dark depths of my surgically cloven chest
This Frankenstein incarnate dared to see fit
To keep the interior of my torso most brightly lit
By way of this small window, gold framed

So, go ahead and peer
Into this small portal
Wherein you will see
A new heart intended to beat endlessly
As of course, yes, it should
But, if indeed, it happens to be three times too big
Whether that might be out of generosity or disease
Who can tell?
Who cares?
Peer here
Peer here!

Innocence

Your words trickle down the nape of my neck
Droplets let fall from a spectral fingertip
These are nothing more than whispered hints
Suggestions, or dark promises?
I feel your cold breath, though when I look back
I see nothing but that which I've passed
But I know you are there, somewhere
Understand, I am *so* sorry
It was an accident – I promise!
But, materialized in the shadowed corner of what was once our shared room
Do you now stand there as guardian on my behalf
Or do you wait for some small crack
In the glass of the frame into which I alone can still look?
My stoic façade resists
My innocence insists
It is all that keeps you from breaching that thin, silvered plain which exists, for
now, to separate us
Do tell me, my love,
If crossed,
Will you force me to do to myself what *I swear* I did not do to you?

He's Here!

Mama! Mama! He's here! He's here!
Who is, honey?
Santa!
Oh, sweetie, I know it can be difficult. It's not so easy, sometimes, growing up. . .
But, Mama, you don't understand! He's here and he has a. . .
What? Now, come on! If you want to stay up. . .
No, Mama! He said he was going to. . .
Sweetie! Enough!
Mama, let me finish! He said he was coming for YOU, and he had a . . .

ENOUGH! I am a VERY patient person. But you have now taken this too . . .

Mama?
Mama?

100-word horror

Marie

At rest upon ice-cold sand and leafy debris, I look beyond the stage. Hundreds of fists shaking, mouths howling soundlessly. Palpable hate, fathomless glee, aimed at me.

The sand warms, dampens; Boschian faces melt and merge into a quivering mass of matted hair, close-set eyes, rotting teeth.

My focus dims. I see now only my children, their flower faces, corn silk hair.

Laughter. Yes! I can hear it! Echoes, heart-cradled, alive like ocean waves within the flawless spiral corridor of a seashell.

From inside this palace, my husband commands wordlessly:

Be brave, my love – we shall be together in a...

100-word horror

Snow Day

I woke up
And with no more school
I decided
To go outside to play
Because that is what kids do
And I played in the snow
Despite all that cold
Despite all that bitter bitter cold
Because that, you know, is what kids did
And we rumbled and we tumbled
And we played this game we called 'war'
Because that, you know, is what kids do
(It was, back then, all we knew)
And I laughed, somehow
As I rolled about and around on that frozen rock-hard tundral ground
And I realized only after, had the soldier's teeth been crowned in gold
They would have long since been extracted
Because that, you know, is what was done
But as it were
The soldier's teeth were still all there, in his mouth
So, when I fell
My hand I cut
On the small tines of his perma smile, which was left jutting out
Of the frozen and the snow packed and icy ground

As experienced by my father as a child in Kharkov, Ukraine, in the mid-1930's

Earlier versions of the following were published elsewhere:

"A Killing Repose"
*Crow's Quill zine, SNOWED IN, Quill & Crow Publishing, 2022
and GÖTHIQUE, 2023*

"Santa Domnia" *NEITHERIUM*, 2022

"Santa Domnia II, Hellscape Wrought" *GÖTHIQUE*, 2023

JACOB A DENOUEMENT IN ONE ACT:
Introduction & Stave I, opening scene are from the novella of the same name,
published as a hardback collector's edition in 2019 & in 2021 for all formats

"A Brief History of Trav'lers" *NEITHERIUM*, 2022, excerpt

*Featured in PSYTHUR 3 by Ravens Quoth Press (2025):
"Precious Inkwells" and "Mermaid's Tale"*

All books are available via Amazon and Ingram